WARRIOR MINE

Michele James

PRAISE FOR THE DESTINED SERIES

The Lion & The Swan

"What an amazing book! Well developed characters, complex and entertaining plot, beautifully described details and settings. Very difficult to put down. It cries for a sequel! Book two, hurry! ~ conniecutie

"The purity of love between Assad and Oona is undeniable and beautiful. I adore Oona's strength and dedication to her sister. Assad was the perfect alpha, sensitive, strong, and passionate. Great, and moving tale." ~ Andrea

The Stallion & The Tigress

"Love these books! Fun, witty, sensual and adventurous!!! Should be made into movies!!" ~Laura L. Sockey

"The strong woman (and the way her chief rival woos her) is wonderful. Especially because the leading lady is every bit as strong as her suitors! She chooses! I love the horses and the races and the way historical places and people are shown. This book stands alone, but it's also so cool that when you read Book 1 The Lion and the Swan, you get some of the backstory of this romance. Can't wait for Book 3 in this Destined Series. ~Kathleen Canney Lopez

"In this myth, the heroine, as her nickname suggests, is as powerful if not more so than any man. The men melt at the sight of her, but only one man will do, no matter the obstacles and there are many. The races by themselves are beautifully rendered. Kudos to the author for this romantic masterpiece. The book although number 2 of 3 is complete and stands alone." ~Plume Sobriquet

The Eagle & The Lynx

"Compelling read featuring a strong, righteous female lead. Intriguing romance and well-developed plot complete with subversion, betrayal and redemption. Looking forward to the next generation in the saga of The Destined!" ~jwrvt

"Book three of the Destined series brings the romance, adventure, and steamy love scenes of the first two books." ~MCB

The Stag & The Owl

"This final book in the series doesn't disappoint. Alina feels her true love has betrayed her but things change and Roark falls for his prisoner. Their many adventures and misadventures as they try to get Alina to safety are so well written and described. Almost hate to see this series end but what a wonderful way to end!" ~secret1

"Following the history of how all the women are linked by blood and love. To find love only to lose it due to someone's lies and deceit. Time and patience wins the heart of the man she loves. Great reading!!" ~dkinghorn

www.**BOROUGHSPUBLISHINGGROUP**.com

WARRIOR MINE

ISBN: 978-1-957295-16-9

For all my family and friends who told me this would be published someday.

ACKNOWLEDGMENTS

Though *Warrior Mine* is my fifth book to be published, it is the first book I ever wrote. It stayed in its *box under the bed while* I wrote my Destined series, and I brought it out, dusted it off, and rewrote it, applying all the lessons learned over the years of writing and being published by Boroughs Publishing Group.

While the story remains basically the same, I think I've smoothed out the rough edges and learned to "kill my darlings."

Thanks to Boroughs Publishing Group and its excellent editors. To the SoCal Romance Writers group for all the support and networking, and to all those who encouraged me along the way.

WARRIOR MINE

CHAPTER 1

The Dream

Summer 778 - Gaul, on the Pyrenees border

Lara

Lara woke with a start as the faceless warrior grabbed for her hair, her heart pounding as hard and fast in her chest as the hoofbeat of his black charger echoed in her ears. She sat up on her bedroll and focused her gaze on the surrounding meadow, slowing her breathing and lifting her sweat-dampened hair from the back of her neck.

A wet tongue licked her chin.

"Wolf?" She blew out a shaky breath at the soft whine he gave and buried her fingers into the ruff of his thick russet fur. "Just a dream, boy," she murmured. "Just a dream."

A dream she'd had every night for the past thirteen nights straight. A dream she'd hoped wouldn't find her here in the high meadow, a place of peace and solitude where she brought her small herd of milk goats to every summer solstice. A dream that had turned out to be as impossible to outrun as the man in it: a warrior whose face remained hidden behind his helmet, but for the cold, steel gray of his eyes as he chased her down.

She stood on shaky legs and gazed up to a sky as clear and blue as a robin's egg, without a cloud in sight. The soft morning sun would be glaring hot by noon. "We'll be taking the river path home," she told Wolf, her constant companion since she'd found him four years ago as a half-dead, newborn pup alone in the woods. He'd fit into the palm of her hand then. Now he was as big as the goats she signaled him to round up.

After plaiting her unruly curls into a long braid, she piled it high atop her head and pinned it in place. She bundled up her bedroll and few cooking utensils, threw the pack over her shoulder, and carried the two sacks full of yarrow, sorrel, and mustard seed she'd gathered over the past two days to the goats and slung them over Nana's back.

Glancing around the meadow, she strolled over to the little pool formed by a natural outcropping of rocks and pulled her waist knife to cut a blood-red rose from a vine heavy with blooms. It felt like velvet and smelled of pure attar. She stripped the stem of its thorns and wove it into her braid, then she pulled her skirts up between her legs and tucked the hems into her waist belt. She'd learned the freedom of movement this gave her years ago, and had never fully given up the habit, despite her Aunt Sophie's repeated warnings about being caught in such a state.

Which had happened only once, when Ranulf, the Count of Oloron's snake of a son, had spied on her and followed her into the wilderness five summers ago.

Lara tightened her waist belt, checked the strap to the small dagger she wore tied around her thigh since her run-in with Ranulf, who wore her mark on his chin to this day, and smiled grimly.

Birdsong filled the dry mountain air as Lara, Wolf, and the goats made their way down the mountain's side, playing hide-and-seek with the sun as it dappled the canopy of oak wood or reflected bright and metallic off the rippling river.

Yet as warm and sun-filled as the day was, Lara couldn't shake the shadows of her dream, causing her to look over her shoulder at every rustle of leaves or snap of a twig.

By noon, the cool morning had given way to the heat of day, and after stopping to share the last of her jerky with Wolf, she waded knee-deep into the river to rinse her hands and splash cold water onto the back of her neck.

Shivering as icy cold rivulets soaked into her tunic and pooled at her belt, she pulled an errant strand of hair from her neck and stuffed it back into her braid. She turned for the shoreline, but then stopped. Wolf stood erect at her side, his ears cocking back and forward, his nose thrust high in the air, sniffing furiously.

"What is it, boy?" she whispered. His ridge of fur standing on end from neck to tail, he fixed his gaze on a grove of oak along the river's bank and growled low. Lara pulled her knife and dagger, then set her feet as a shadow the size of a large beast moved in the tree line. "Heel, Wolf." She turned to run for the opposite shore, then stilled as the shadows there moved too.

Lara swallowed hard and gripped her blades tighter.

"Do not fear, lady," a man called, his voice low pitched and deep timbred.

Despite his assurances, every nerve in her body screamed at her to flee as the biggest, blackest horse she'd ever seen emerged from the shadows, its head and chest covered in lacquered plates. The warrior astride the charger wore a helmet that covered his face to his nose, and a vest of iron rings set over a sleeveless tunic of leather a shade darker than the tanned bronze of his thickly muscled arms.

There was a short sword sheathed at his waist, a longsword at his saddle, and leather gauntlets tucked into his waist belt. At sight of the gauntlets, Lara's throat constricted. She lifted her gaze and squinted to see what she could of the man's face. The man curled one corner of his lip, then the other, displaying strong, straight teeth grinning down at her through the dark stubble of his short beard.

"Truly, Lady." The man pulled his horse up at the water's edge. "We mean you no harm."

We? Lara whirled around as another armed warrior emerged from the opposite tree line on a gray steed. She shuffled sideways, giving her a clear view of both. The warrior on the black giant doffed his helmet, sat it down on the pommel of his saddle, and ran a hand through thick black hair worn short in the northern fashion.

As the black-haired warrior dismounted, Wolf growled low. "Stay," she commanded softly.

She gripped her knives even tighter and glanced at the warrior on the gray, who made no motion to dismount, then turned her attention back to the black's rider, who was wading into the water, toward her.

Though Lara was tall enough to stand eye to eye with most men, this man was taller than her by a full head. He had a high, wide forehead and thick black brows. An old scar slashed across his right eyebrow and down his cheek, and his nose looked to have been broken more than once and was as crooked as his smile. Neither of which softened the hard line of his jaw one whit. He stopped no more than two paces from her, and his eyes were the color of honed steel.

"Have we met before?" His deep, resounding voice resonated throughout her body.

Had they met before? Only every night for the last thirteen nights. Lara shook her head. "No."

He cocked his head and offered a slow, lopsided grin. "Let me introduce myself, then. I am Captain Talon Guiscard, king's soldier, newly garrisoned at Crossroads Keep."

He offered her his hand, large, tan and corded: a warrior's hand, well used to wielding the short sword at his side and the longsword sheathed at his saddle.

Lara wasn't about to lower her knives. She'd been running from that hand too long and too hard.

"What is your purpose here, Captain Guiscard?"

"Here? Today?" His half-smile widened fully. "A leisurely survey of the river's course." He let his gaze take a *leisurely* survey of her damp tunic and bare legs. "And all the wondrous sights it offers."

With her tall frame and auburn hair, Lara was used to being stared at by men. From villagers she'd known her entire life to the hundreds of soldiers garrisoned at the Keep over the years.

Yet no man's gaze had ever unnerved her quite the way this man's did. And she didn't think it was entirely due to her dreams.

Lengthening her spine, she lifted her chin and met his gaze head on. "Have you had your fill yet, Captain?"

"Nay, Lady," he answered, his grin cocksure. "There are some sights a man will never have his fill of."

"Nor of their own charms, apparently." Lara dripped her voice with honey. "Meager and oafish though they be."

"Oho, better watch yourself, Talon." His mounted companion doffed his helmet, and a head full of golden curls spilled down. "That red hair of hers is no lie, and her tongue is as sharp as those knives she still grasps."

"Aye." The captain glanced down as Lara laid a hand on Wolf's scruff, holding him at bay, then he grinned up at her as he took a step closer and plucked the rose from her hair. "She is a thorny beauty she." He twirled the rose in his blunt-tipped fingers.

Lara glared from the rose to his grin. "And you, sir," she hissed, "are an arrogant ass."

He burst out laughing, a rich, hearty laugh that caught Lara unawares. Then she remembered how he'd chased her in her dreams, merciless and unrelenting. Not about to let him catch her now, she leapt to the side of him. He grabbed for her, and she lashed out with her dagger and felt it bite flesh.

"Bloody hell, woman." The woods echoed with his curse.

She scrambled up the riverbank and ran fast and hard with Wolf at her heels, then turned onto a game path, listening for the sounds of boot fall or hoofbeat behind her.

Nothing but her own rapid panting filled her senses, and she turned onto a smaller game path for another hundred paces, then hid in a thick bramble where she worked on slowing her breathing. Mostly she waited to see if the men followed her, and hoped her goats wouldn't run off. Telling herself they knew the way home if they did, she prayed the soldiers wouldn't take their anger at her out on her goats.

***

"What ails you, child?" Sophie eyed Lara closely as they approached the gates to Crossroads Keep, the king's holding in the province and garrison to the latest posting of soldiers. "Are you ill?"

"Nay, Tante." Lara patted Gaea's neck and shifted on the mare's saddle for the hundredth time in the short ride from their home to the keep, Wolf loping alongside them.

Sophie the Sixth. The healer lived up to her title today. Her gift of a sixth sense had always come with an uncanny ability to read people and foresee the future. She'd picked up the title of prophetess as well as a baby when Lara had been abandoned in a basket on the healer's doorstep. Sophie had raised Lara as her own, and Lara usually told Sophie everything, but hadn't spoken a word to her of the steel-eyed warrior chasing her down in her dreams, or of her encounter with him and his companion at the river yesterday. Why she hadn't, she couldn't have said, though she was fairly certain she'd be trying to explain it to Sophie soon enough. "I'm overtired, is all."

"Well, you won't be getting any rest anytime soon." Sophie sat back in her saddle as the palisade gates to Crossroads Keep creaked open. "By Berta's count, there's twenty horse soldiers returned from the Moorish wars. All of them battle tested and all of them needing a patch-up of one sort or another."

Lara gave a wan smile. Though she'd been helping Sophie tend the ills and injuries of troops garrisoned here for as long as she could remember, there had never been a Captain Talon Guiscard to deal with before. She gave a deep breath. What lay ahead was as intimidating as the sheer size of the opened gates. "They always do."

They followed Denys, the stable boy sent to fetch them, through the bustling courtyard, greeting the villagers who stopped with their baskets of wares and foodstuffs to give nods of recognition in return. But they pointedly ignored the newly garrisoned soldiers, who stopped midstride at their first sight of the two women riding with a wolf-dog at their sides. Outside the stables, a lone soldier lounged askew on a bench, his eyes as puffy and red as his cheeks as he watched them approach. Wolf growled low, and Lara gave the man her back as she dismounted and handed Gaea's reins to Denys.

"Over here, Sophie dear," Berta called out over the din, waving her fleshy arm at them from the outdoor ovens.

Sophie and Lara untied their sacks of medicines from their saddles and made their way through the maze of tables laden with baskets of grains, greens, and new summer apples, to where Berta, her daughter, Enid, and granddaughter, Marta, greeted them with floury hugs.

"Smells good." Sophie took a deep breath as Enid pulled three loaves of rye from an oven. "How does this garrison like your cooking?"

As generous of body as she was of spirit and plate, Berta smiled with satisfaction. "This garrison likes my cooking just fine. In fact, the captain and his second have made sure to compliment me on it each meal."

Sophie nodded. It was well known Berta was the best cook in the province. "What manner of man do you find this captain to be, other than sensible enough to compliment your cooking?"

"A sensible man in general." Berta wiped her doughy hands on her apron. "He says please and thank you, and most of his men mind their manners and keep their hands to themselves. All the chambermaids keep talking of it."

"And not all of them are happy about it." Enid, her mother's daughter in looks and mien, arched her brows as she sorted apples. "A few are quite disappointed, for there are more handsome men in this troop than not, and not all of them young." She looked pointedly at Berta, who blushed and giggled like a girl still in side-braids. "Mother has caught herself a handsome graybeard with her cooking."

Sophie peered at Berta, who had been widowed ten years ago and never looked twice at a man since as far as Lara knew, and there wasn't much among the women they didn't all know. Berta and Sophie had been friends for the past thirty years, both of them young brides when they'd first met and both of them gray-haired widows now. Berta's middle daughter, Patience, was Lara's best friend, and had been since they were old enough to toddle around together.

"Well now." Berta planted her hands firmly on her hips. "The pots of water are boiling and there's a basket of clean linen strips beside them that need tending."

"Let's get on with it, then." Sophie hitched her sack up. "There's twenty men need tending too, and I'm curious to meet this new captain."

Lara clutched her sack to her chest and nodded dumbly. Maybe it would be best to confess to Sophie about the captain now.

"You'll have to wait to meet the captain." Berta tossed another lump of dough onto the table. "He rode up into the mountains this morning. Anglbert says he's looking for something very particular."

Lara choked and coughed and toed the ground at her sandaled feet.

Sophie gave Lara a sideways glance. "Anglbert?" she said to Berta.

"Mother's graybeard," Enid told her, and Berta flapped at her like an angry hen.

"He's not my graybeard." She clucked.

Enid laughed. "One more roast pig, and he will be."

CHAPTER 2

The Chase

Talon

"Four apples, no more." Talon handed the stallion's reins over to Denys. "He's had two already this morning, no matter what he tells you."

The stable boy grinned. "Aye, Captain, I won't let him fool me this time. And, Sir, the healers are here."

"Good." Talon flexed his bandaged left hand. He'd washed the cut given to him by the flame-haired, hazel-eyed wildcat he'd come across in the mountains yesterday, but the wound could have used a good healing balm. The thorny beauty had left her mark.

Not that he blamed her. He grinned. The first sight of her knee deep in the river as she stood off two armed warriors with nothing more than two puny knives and one large canine that looked more wolf than dog was something to savor. Her legs had been bare up to her sleekly muscled thighs, her wet skirt and tunic plastered to her womanly curves, and her auburn curls had fallen free from their pins. He'd stood no more than a few feet from her as she'd studied him with her changeling eyes of green and gold and burnt umber rimmed with rings as black as her thick lashes, mesmerizing him with her voice of smoked honey and her blinding smile—right up until she'd called him an arrogant ass and sliced his palm. He chuckled and ran his good hand back through his hair. He'd asked for it, and she'd given it to him.

His troop had ridden with King Charles into Spain last spring, taking city after city from the ruling Moors in the name of Gaul and Christendom. After razing the city of Pamplona, which still left a bad taste in Talon's mouth, the army had laid siege to Zaragoza, setting up camp on the Erbo River. Talon was a man of plans and action, and his company of horsemen formed to be fast moving and hard fighting, not to sit on their backsides waiting for sickness and starvation to win the day. He'd hated the sweltering plains of Spain and hated the thought of innocent women and children dying slow deaths behind the walls of the besieged city even more, so when Charles had asked for a troop to return to the border valley of Oloron to man the garrison and guard against raiding Basques, he'd been the first to volunteer. They'd arrived three days ago, and he'd been glad to find the villagers well used to supplying goods and workers for the garrison. Leaving Anglbert in charge yesterday, he and Phillipe, his second-in-command, had scouted the valley's western border, following the river up the mountainside, where they'd come upon the wildcat and her wolf.

Today they'd scouted the valley's northern borders, where they'd found no signs of Basques or wildcats. Disappointed as he was about the latter, Talon figured he was bound to run into her again at some point during his stay at Crossroads Keep. She'd been heading downriver yesterday with her goats, and Oloron was the closest settlement of toths and villages to the border wilds. He'd just have to keep looking.

Heading for the hall, a two-story stronghold of wood and stone built to house troops twice the number of his, he noticed a distinct lack of his men at their tasks in the courtyard. He found them inside the hall, gathered around one of the long dining tables. One by one they lifted their heads as he approached, strange grins spreading across their faces as they stepped back from the table, revealing a slim figure with a thick auburn braid hanging down to the middle of her back, bending over Anglbert's knee.

Phillipe had regaled the entire troop with the tale of their captain and the red-haired, long-limbed goat herder at supper last night. They all watched Talon as Anglbert looked up with the same strange grin plastered on his face.

"Captain," Anglbert said, and the auburn-haired goat-herder instantly stiffened. "May I introduce the valley's healers: the ladies Sophie—" He nodded toward a wizened, white-haired woman with a shrewd gaze. "—and Lara."

"Ladies." Talon gave the snowcapped healer a quick nod before turning to the younger woman. He gave her the briefest of grins as she lifted her gaze, her eyes as big and mesmerizing as he remembered them, eyes that grew even bigger as he held his bandaged hand up. "I'm glad you've come, for I've a recent wound that needs tending."

Her cheeks flushed a becoming rosy pink and she dropped her gaze back down to Anglbert's knee.

"Sit here." The old healer called Sophie indicated the bench beside her, across the table from Lara, who steadfastly refused to look his way as he set his longsword down on the bench and took the proffered seat. He held his hand out to Sophie, who peeled away the bandage and inspected the cut that ran from the edge of his little finger to the base of his thumb. "'Tis fresh, kept clean," she said, prodding the wound's edges with her fingertip. She looked up from his palm, her pale, blue-gray eyes holding his. "How did you come by this nasty slice, Captain?"

Talon glanced from Sophie's probing gaze to Lara, who slid a sidelong glance at him, the apples of her cheeks flushing even pinker. She hadn't told the old healer of their meeting in the river yesterday; he'd wager coin on it. "I foolishly attempted to pluck a wild rose," he told Sophie. "Barehanded."

"Foolish is right." She tsked as she dropped his hand. "For only a fool would try to pluck a rose barehanded."

"Or an arrogant ass." Talon grinned as Lara's head shot up, her wide eyes meeting his, then narrowing. "But then it was a particularly beautiful, thorny, rose."

Lara dropped her gaze and her long, slender fingers shook as she laid a linen strip across Anglbert's knee. She wore a brown work apron over a sleeveless gown of mossy green, and Talon took in the sleekly muscled lines of her arms up to her neck, where loose tendrils of auburn curled at her nape. He followed the graceful bow of her neck down the length of her back to her sandaled feet, admiring the high arch of them, and met the baleful stare of the hound that had growled him off at the river yesterday.

The beast had to weigh ten stone at least and looked to be solid muscle beneath his thick coat of reddish-brown, and his upright ears were at full alert as he watched not only Talon but every other man in the room with his unwavering stare. The beast shifted and yawned, showing off a rack of teeth made for tearing and ripping flesh from bone, then seemed to grin at Talon, his tongue lolling between his large fangs.

"The dog," he said as Sophie took his hand and began to gently scrub the wound with a soapy rag.

"You mean Wolf?" she asked, though there were no other dogs in the hall.

Talon nodded. He'd seen a few wolves in the wild before, but always from a distance. "Is he a full-blooded wolf?"

Sophie's keen gaze sized Talon up. "No," she said after a moment. "He has the white teeth of a dog, not yellow like a wolf. Lara found him in the wilds when he was a pup. Likely his mother abandoned him because he's a half-breed and she recognized him as being different."

Talon and the wolf-dog eyed each other. "He guards his mistress well."

Sophie wiped the soap from his hand. "He does. Even I, who have raised them both, would never dare raise a hand to her in Wolf's presence."

"No sane man would, I should think." Talon had been sane enough yesterday when he'd first come across them, but the sight of her red hair curling around the oval of her face and the challenging tilt of her chin had been too much for him. He'd been too long without a woman, and she was a woman to tempt any man. She'd tempted him to the point that he'd braved her beast of a dog and her sharp points, then paid with his flesh for his brazenness. He'd admired her spirit as much as he'd cursed his own foolishness, which was why he hadn't chased her down yesterday, and why he wouldn't give her away now. "You say you raised them both. Are you the girl's grandmother?"

"In a manner of speaking." Sophie's gaze 'arrowed on Talon's, then she dipped her fingers into a tub and smeared a soothing balm that smelled of rosemary on his palm. "You take a great interest in a girl you've just met and spoken nary a word with, Captain."

Talon flexed his hand, impressed at how the tight edges of his wound were already easing, then glanced at Lara, who was diligently wrapping Anglbert's knee. "I take a great interest in many things, Madam."

***

Lara

Lara tied the last strip of linen around the knee of Berta's kindly graybeard, then peered down at the captain's boot, letting her gaze travel up the length of his leather leggings over the swell of his calves and well-muscled thighs. Why hadn't he chased her down with those legs after she'd sliced his palm yesterday? Or told Sophie it was she who had cut him today? Peering up at him from beneath lowered lashes, she found no answers, only his unnerving gaze.

"Leave the poultice on until tomorrow morn." She spoke down to Anglbert's knee, her cheeks too hot to look him in the face, then reached into her bag for a tub of easing liniment and set it on the table. "After you remove the poultice, rub a handful of this into your knee three times a day for the next seven days, then as needed. If you run out, Berta can bring you more."

"Not you?"

Lara looked up into smiling brown eyes. "There's no need for me to bring it, unless of course your knee worsens."

"What of the captain?" The lines around Anglbert's eyes deepened as he grinned. "His cut is deep and his poor mind near to festering."

Lara glanced at the captain, whose brow looked more angry than feverish as he glared at Anglbert. "Sophie will take care of his wound better than I."

"Perhaps." Anglbert tugged at his beard. "But what about the poor man's mind? He's been suffering a sickness of it since yesterday."

"Since yesterday?" Lara suddenly felt a little feverish herself.

"Aye, lady." Anglbert nodded somberly. "He seems to have picked up a cursed bad ailment from splashing around in the river."

Sophie's touch was already on the captain's forehead, and then she ran her fingers down his neck and kneaded below his ears. Eyes of honed steel stared straight into Lara's over Sophie's head, and she was halfway up and out of her seat before she realized that not only Sophie but several soldiers were watching her. She sat back down.

"As I said," she told Anglbert, "Sophie will take care of him better than I. She's a very learned healer."

Sophie cleared her throat, her drawn brows telling Lara she may not have known what, exactly, was going on here, but she knew something was. And she would be expecting answers from Lara the next time they were alone. Lara looked around the hall. The soldiers who'd needed tending had been seen to. So while Sophie and the captain were discussing his lack of symptoms for the strange fever Anglbert claimed he suffered from, she took the opportunity to pack her bag and slip away from the table and out the kitchen door..

Walking quickly past Berta and Enid, Lara didn't call Wolf to heel when he stopped to beg treats from them. He'd be along shortly. Once inside the stable, she spied Gaea and Honey, Sophie's little dun mare, together in a stall past the soldier's horses and headed over.

"Hey, boy." Distracted, she stopped at the stall housing the captain's black steed and held her palm out. The stallion sniffed and blew at her hand and looked almost as large and imposing standing in its stall, munching hay, as it had in full armor at the river yesterday. She rubbed his velvet muzzle and stared into big, intelligent eyes almost as black as his coat. A smile chased her lips as his master's piercing gaze stole her thoughts. The hard line of his jaw … big, strong hands plucking the rose from her hair… "You're a handsome beast," she told the horse. "Much like your master. Maybe you can tell me why you both chase me night after night."

The stallion pricked his ears, and the hairs on the back of Lara's neck stood on end as she slowly turned around to find a squat man with a turnip nose and rheumy eyes swaying on his feet behind her with an ugly, lascivious leer on his fleshy face. The same man that had been lounging outside of the stables when they'd ridden in.

"I ken tell ye." Even his sweat reeked of stale spirits. "I ken tell ya why mens would chase ye, mishy."

Lara looked toward the open door to the stables. The drunkard's beefy body blocked her way out. Instinctively, she glanced around for Wolf, but he wasn't there. She met the man's beady, bloodshot gaze, her back up against the gate to the stallion's stall. "Please, sir." She tried to keep her voice calm. "I've no wish for trouble."

"Trouble?" The man swayed closer to her. "Ish not trouble I'll be givin ye, mishy."

Lara smiled as sweetly as she could manage, then pushed off the gate to run by the man, but his arm caught her around the waist. She let out one shrill whistle as the man fell, taking her with him and knocking the breath from her as she hit the ground. A ham-fisted hand clamped over her mouth, and she bit down, hard. The man jerked his hand away with a string of oaths as foul as his breath. Lara scrambled up, then turned to run for the door as he grabbed a fistful of her skirt and yanked her back, causing her to stumble and step with the full weight of her body on his knee, which gave way beneath her sandaled foot with a sickening snap of bone. Bellowing in pain, the man let go of her skirt and grabbed above his knee, then his scream turned high-pitched and wordless as a snarling Wolf came bounding straight for him.

***

Talon

Talon grabbed his longsword at the first scream and bolted halfway out the hall by the second, a primal wail that sent shivers up his spine, which was nothing to the sudden quiet after. He was out the kitchens' door when a shrill voice called from the stables amidst the frenzied whinnies of horses, followed by Lara running out of them with Wolf at her heels. She glanced Talon's way, then raced across the courtyard for the back gate as if a horde of bloodthirsty Saracens were after her.

Talon ran over to the open door of the stables and found a man writhing on the floor in front of the Black's gate while the stallion stomped and snorted at him from his stall. Fulrad.

"In the stables," Talon yelled to the men pouring out of the hall. He looked toward the back gate, which was only large enough for one person to pass through and unguarded, in time to see Lara throw it open, so he doubled his pace.

The girl could run on those long legs of hers, he'd give her that. She'd made it the hundred feet to the river by the time he'd made it through the gate, holding her skirts high and wading across the knee-deep water to disappear beyond the tree line as he made his first splash. Matching his stride to his breath, Talon concentrated on the trail she was leading him on. He'd grown up hunting and tracking game in the wilds of Neustria with his father and older brother, and he'd tracked men as a scout for the army. Tracking a woman with a dog shouldn't prove too difficult.

The snapping of twigs and crackling of leaves ahead told him she wasn't gaining any ground on him, though she wasn't losing any either. He thought again of her long, lean, well-muscled legs as she'd stood him off in the river yesterday, and he was hard-pressed between admiring and cursing them. Hell, he was hard-pressed between admiring and cursing *her*, as she had him. And she had admired him. He'd seen the look in enough women's eyes to know it when he saw it. Yet she was the only woman who'd ever looked at him like that and then run away from him. Twice now.

She led him through a maze of thick brambles that grabbed and bit at his bare arms, leaving trails of blood trickling down them. Beyond the brambles it opened onto a meadow, and on the other side of the meadow an even thicker wood. He pushed on, ignoring the biting brambles, for he had a gut feeling that if he didn't catch Lara before she made the woods, he never would. She was halfway across the meadow when Talon burst out of the brambles. Wolf slowed to turn and look at him, and Talon sucked in a big gulp of air, then yelled, "*Hold.*"

The dog turned in a slow arc and headed for him at an easy lope.

"No, Wolf," Lara called over her shoulder. "Come."

Wolf slowed, hesitating, and Talon let out a loud snarl. The wolf-dog crouched low and then sprang into a full run as Talon set his feet and held his longsword high.

"*Wolf. Noooo.*"

Lara's scream rang in Talon's ears as Wolf leapt and Talon jumped aside, slamming the flat of his sword across the beast's shoulder and sending it sprawling to the ground. The hound scrambled to get its feet up under it, and Talon kicked its head. He didn't want to kill the beast, but he didn't want it coming back after him either. Wolf lay breathing but motionless as Lara ran toward them and stopped ten paces away, leaning toward Wolf one moment, the woods the next.

"He'll live," Talon said with more effort than he cared to show. If she bolted again, he wasn't sure he'd be able to catch her. "Lara." He called her by her name, getting her full attention, her expression wild with fear. "Wolf lives."

He stepped back from the dog's prone form, and Lara approached, step by slow step, watching Talon until she stood on the opposite side of Wolf, out of Talon's immediate reach. He held his empty hand up, palm out, and Lara dropped her gaze to Wolf and let her breath out in a rush when his chest rose and fell. She stood there watching the dog breathe while Talon worked on slowing his own breath and trying his damnedest to not so much as twitch in her direction.

After what seemed like an eternity, she looked back up at Talon. "What of the man in the stables?"

Talon held her gaze, glad to see some of the wildness gone. "He was alive when I saw him," he told her. She sucked a quick breath in and blew it out. "What happened?" he asked, though he could have guessed. Fulrad was the only drunkard among his men, and a mean one at that.

"He was drunk." Her voice quaked, yet she kept her gaze even with his. "He made a lewd suggestion. I told him I didn't want any trouble." Talon quirked his brows and held up his bandaged hand. "Well, I did," she said, raising her chin a notch. She pressed her full lips tight and shook her head. "He wouldn't listen. He grabbed me, we struggled, I, I stepped on his knee, trying to get away, and then Wolf—"

She dropped to her knees, cradling the unconscious dog's head in her lap as she ran her hands over his head, neck, and shoulders.

"Why did you run away when you saw us?" Talon asked as she moved her fingers over the hound's ribs. "We wouldn't have let anything else happen to you."

She raised her brows, her distrust obvious. "He's a king's soldier. I thought Wolf killed him."

Talon ran his bandaged hand back through his hair, wet and slick with sweat. "Well, lady, you and Wolf do defend yourselves ably, if not wisely."

She stared at his bandaged hand and her chin trembled. "What now?"

"What now?" he repeated, forcing himself to be Captain, whose man lay injured, possibly dying, back at the Keep, and not Talon, who wanted nothing more than to cup her quivering chin and tell her everything would be all right. "Now I take you back to the keep, where we'll see to the extent of the man's injuries and get his side of the affair."

"He may not be able to tell his side." Her voice of smoked honey cracked as she stroked the dog's neck. "Wolf had him by the throat before I called him off."

"Bloody hell." Talon tensed his jaw and shook his head. "The man's name is Fulrad and he's not just a soldier: he's the king's cousin." Which was the only reason the drunken lout was a part of Talon's troop. As a favor to Charles himself. "Cousin or not," Talon told Lara, "the king's laws do allow for defending your person."

Her gaze held his, wide and pleading. "Do you always follow the king's laws to the letter?"

She was asking him to turn around and let her run away, to escape into the woods as he had yesterday. But yesterday it'd only been about Talon and Lara. Today it was about a king's subject injuring a king's soldier. "I'm a captain in the king's army, lieged directly to Charles himself. It is my sworn duty to uphold the king's laws. And the king's law decrees that you be brought before the valley's count next Mallus."

Her face went white.

"Until then, you're my prisoner." He held his hand out. "Give me both of your knives, hilts first."

CHAPTER 3

Prisoner

Lara

The captain picked up the still-unconscious Wolf and carried him back to the keep, which was no easy feat: Wolf weighed ten stone at least. While holding Wolf hostage was one way to keep Lara from bolting, it was also a kindness she didn't expect. It threw her because it made it harder to be angry at him. She really wanted to be angry at him, at least as angry as she was at herself for getting into this mess. She had injured, and possibly killed, a king's soldier. And not just any soldier, but the king's cousin. The enormity of what she'd done and what could be done to her for her actions sank in. Soldiers ran ahead of them to open the door to the main hall. Her feet were heavy and sodden as they passed through, her chest felt as if it were being crushed.

"Lara."

She looked up and met the captain's steady gaze.

"Breathe." He took a slow breath in and blew it out, nodding as she did the same. "That's it. Breathe."

The captain handed Wolf over to a brown-haired, short-bearded giant of a man called Tree, who followed them as the captain took Lara by the arm and led her up the stairs. At the top, she glanced down into the common room, where Sophie sat on a chair next to the injured man laid out on a cot, his throat and leg bandaged, red spots of blood seeping through the one around his throat. She met Sophie's worried gaze before the captain pulled her along the hallway, open on one side to the hall below, and through the last door on the other side into a large bedchamber, where Tree laid Wolf down next to the cold hearth.

"You and Wolf stay here," the captain told her. "Do not attempt to leave this chamber."

He and Tree left, closing the door behind them, and the outside bolt slid across with a loud thud. Lara knelt by Wolf, who lay unconscious to the world around him but was breathing steadily, then grabbed two large pelts off the bed and laid one down on the floor next to Wolf's back. After taking hold of his legs, she rolled him over so that he was lying on the pelt and then covered him with the other, a little concerned when he still didn't make a sound as she rolled him. She lifted his lip and checked his gums, which were pale, but not dangerously so. The best thing for Wolf right now was to let his body rest and hopefully recover.

Lara wandered about the chamber, which was as large as the entire ground floor of her and Sophie's house. The four-poster bed had red drapes that were pulled back and was situated against the outside wall next to an open window facing the courtyard. She glanced out the window. While she might be able to make the two-story drop, she had no way of getting Wolf out safely or unseen. She turned from the window and opened the two chests at the foot of the bed. One held men's clothing, neatly folded and freshly laundered, as well as an otter cloak and a fur throw. The other held a pair of men's boots and sandals, two bars of soap, a book of maps, a dried rose folded into a square of embroidered linen, a set of carving knives, and a wood figurine of a woman with an oval face and long hair curling down her back. She ran her fingers down the flowing lines of the figurine, then shut the chests and went to a table where a square board sanded smooth and covered in small, alternating squares of black and natural wood sat. Figurines were positioned on the squares, half of them carved out of what looked to be some kind of bone as white as alabaster and the others out of black stone.

Each side had eight pieces with wide bases that tapered up to round tops, along with two in the shapes of turrets, two horse's heads, two tall, robed figures topped with crosses, and two intricately robed figures with crowns: one with a beard on its featureless face and the other with long hair down to its waist. Nothing else gave her any clue as to whose chamber she was in, though she had a good idea. She checked the door, even though she knew it was locked from the outside, and then lay down alongside Wolf, closing her eyes and taking some solace in the steady rise and fall of his chest beneath her hand and the absence of any wheezing or crackling, while trying hard not to think of all the stories she'd heard of the punishments meted out to women for protecting themselves against men, much less the king's cousin.

When she opened her eyes again, her fingers stuffed into the familiar thickness of Wolf's fur, it took her a moment to realize she was lying on the floor with a light blanket over her and to remember where she was and why. And that she hadn't had a blanket over her when she'd lain down beside Wolf, whose body was warm to her touch and whose chest rose and fell in a steady rhythm.

The chamber was dark but for the low glow of a candle on the table where the board and figurines sat. Lara pushed herself up to a sitting position, every muscle from her neck to her toes pulling tight. She tried to gently rouse Wolf, but he was still out to the world. She rearranged the pelt over him and went to the open window. A half-moon shone brightly in the night sky, illuminating the soldier sitting on a bedroll directly below the window, his back propped against the manor wall.

"Damn," she whispered to the night. "He doesn't trust me one whit."

Stretching her sore, tight back, Lara turned from the window and took in the chamber as her eyes adjusted to the dark. The hearth fire was still unlit and the bed empty, but there was a pile of pelts at the foot of the door.

And lying sprawled out in the middle of the pile, the captain slept soundly.

"Not one whit," she muttered.

The captain's eyes were closed, and his breathing was slow and steady. The only clothes he wore was a linen breechcloth, and she stood staring at the impressive breadth of his chest, lightly furred with dark, curly hair, and how it tapered down to a flat belly ridged with muscles. He had one leg propped against the pelts, and his bandaged hand rested on his knee. She skimmed over the manly bulge filling his breechcloth. A telltale white of a scar ran up his inner thigh from his knee to a hand's width below his groin.

Lara sucked in her breath and let it out slowly as she retraced the scar's snaking path. Not more than one man in twenty would be able to survive such a wound, even fewer would come out of it walking without a limp, much less running and fighting.

Shifting her stance, she saw his short sword on the pelts at his left hip, the hilt where he could grab it instantly. His longsword was tucked behind his back, its hilt to his right side, its blade poking out to his left.

"*Iesus Christus*," she swore softly in the cleric's Latin. "Who does he think he's guarding, the devil himself?"

His eyes opened, shards of silver pointed directly at Lara, and she jumped back.

"Don't even think about it," he growled low, his hand on the hilt of his short sword.

"Think about what?"

"Using my sword against me."

"I wasn't."

"What were you staring at, then?"

"Your leg." She glared down at his scar. "I was hoping it gave you great pain."

He chuckled and held up his bandaged hand. "Not nearly so much as a certain troublesome wench has given me."

Lara gnashed her teeth. "You think me troublesome? For defending myself against a drunken soldier who thought it his right to take whatever he wanted from me? Against possible rape? Should I have simply lain down in the straw and taken it? Do you truly believe it fair that I'm held prisoner here," she waved her arm, "in your chamber, until the count deems to hold Mallus?"

"This is tsafest," he said with maddening calm. "For you and everyone else."

"You must think me very dangerous."

He held up his bandaged hand and gave a lopsided grin. "Now why would I think that?"

Lara glanced around the chamber for something to throw at him.

"I'll send a man to the count tomorrow to find out when Mallus will be held next."

Lara snorted. As if finding out when she was to be tried by Count Nithard would make her feel any better.

"Until then," he continued, "the bed is yours, if you so choose."

"Let us have a right understanding, Captain." Lara strode over to Wolf and plopped down beside him. "I may be your prisoner, but I will not be your whore. I will never share your bed."

"Aye, well, as much as the idea intrigues me," he said, giving a low chuckle, "it wasn't what I meant. Besides—" He rubbed his hands up and down the nicks and scrapes on his bare arms and grinned at her from across the chamber, his teeth showing white against the black of his short beard. "—I don't think I could spare that much blood."

***

Warmth and light played around the edges of Lara's lids as she stretched her sore, stiff body. A wet nose stuffed into her ear, and she let out a sigh of relief to see Wolf's big, brown eyes staring into hers, full of life and awareness. "Morning, boy." She kissed his nose and ruffled his fur.

"Noon's more like it."

Lara sat up and followed Sophie's voice to the table where she sat, along with a platter of bread and fruit and cheese.

"How fared you the night, child?"

Child. Lara pushed herself up off the floor with a groan. She was twenty-two years old, an old maid by most people's estimations, but to Sophie she would always be a child.

"I passed the night safely and comfortably enough," she said as she took a seat at the table and tore off a chunk of bread.

Sophie's gaze went to the unruffled bed, and Lara nodded toward the pelts piled neatly to the side of the door, her cheeks flushing hot as she recalled how unchildlike her reaction to the captain had been.

"I slept on the floor with Wolf, as you found me," she told Sophie. "The captain slept on the pelts by the door." The furrow between Sophie's brow lessened, but the shadows beneath her eyes remained. "Were you up all night with the wounded soldier?"

Sophie shook her head. "Not all night. Berta took a turn watching over him, as did the captain."

"The captain?"

Sophie nodded. "Early this morn."

"Why would…?" The door opened, and Lara went quiet as the captain walked in, nodding to her and Sophie as he strolled over to the chests at the foot of the bed. She lowered her voice. "Why would he do that?"

"He said he wanted to be there when the man came to."

Lara glanced over at the captain, who was rummaging through the chest that held his clothes. "No doubt to get the man's account of what he will say happened first."

"What did happen, Lara?"

"I went to the stables to wait for you. The soldier, Fulrad, must have already been there, sleeping his drunk off in an empty stall, because I never saw or heard him until he was right behind me."

Sophie's brows knitted together. "What were you so distracted by that you let a drunkard sneak up on you and catch you unawares?"

Lara shrugged for an answer.

"Where was Wolf?"

"Outside, begging treats from Berta."

Sophie pressed her lips together and shook her head, her way of chastising Lara for not waiting for Wolf, for walking into the stables alone when there were twenty strange men about. For doing exactly what Sophie had taught her not to do her whole life. "Couldn't you have called out for help?"

"I asked him to leave me be." Lara leaned in close. "But he wouldn't heed me. He was drunk and determined to have his way. I tried to get around him, to get away, but he grabbed me and pulled me down into the straw. I fought him and managed to get back up, and I stepped on his knee." A shiver ran down her spine at the crunch of knee giving way beneath her foot, the snap of bone breaking. "He screamed, and Wolf came running in and took him by the throat. I was afraid Wolf had killed him, and I panicked. I ran." She glanced at the captain, who had pulled a pair of leather breeches from the chest and was inspecting them. "The captain chased us down and brought us back here."

She sat back, expecting to get an earful from Sophie on how she had once again acted rashly and gotten herself into a mess for it. Sophie let out a long, slow sigh.

"I saw this soldier, this Fulrad, lying drunk on a bench outside the stables when we rode in," she said. "I saw him ogling you then and didn't say anything. I should've warned you to keep an eye out for him. I'm getting old." She pursed her lips and shook her head. "My sixth sense is slipping."

"Your eyes are still hawk sharp, Tante. I too saw him outside the stables when we rode in, but not inside the stables, not until he was on me."

Sophie nodded and patted Lara's hand on the table, then she narrowed her eyes at the captain sitting on the edge of the bed, lacing the breeches he'd pulled from the chest. "What does the captain plan to do about it?"

"He's determined to be a good soldier and follow the king's law to the letter, which means he intends to take me before the count, next Mallus."

"Before Nithard?" Sophie hissed.

"Yes."

"We must get you free of this place," Sophie whispered in the cleric's Latin, the language they used when they didn't wish to be understood by others. A language Sophie had been taught by nuns, and Lara had learned from Sophie. "Get you to the Hollow until this troop packs up and leaves." She took in Lara's torn, dirt-stained gown. "Perhaps Ber—the cook could offer to escort you to the bathing house. There's a window to the river's side if I remember right."

"You remember right," Lara answered in kind.

Sophie squeezed Lara's hand. "I'll speak with the cook on my way out. You ask the captain for a bath."

Lara took her first full breath in almost a day, smelling fresh air and freedom. The captain folded the breeches and put them back in the chest, seemingly oblivious to their whispers.

"He's neat," Sophie said.

Lara nodded.

"And handsome."

Lara shrugged.

"And spellbound by a goat herder with the longest, tannest legs a man ever laid eyes on, I'm told, who sliced his hand with her dagger in the river the day before yesterday."

Lara swallowed, hard.

"By all the saints, of which I should be one—" Sophie's look scolded. "—you've met the man twice in two days and have left him bleeding both times, and you wounded and likely crippled one of his men."

"I only protected myself against his drunkard of a man, whose injuries are a result of his own actions," Lara said in her defense.

"And though I did slice his hand the first time, it was the brambles that made the captain bleed the second time."

"Aye, while chasing you down." Sophie looked long and hard at the captain, who was now rummaging through the other chest. "You be careful, Lara. There's more to him than meets the eye."

Lara scoffed. "He's a man like any other," she said, knowing she was lying as she said it. He was a man like no other she'd ever met, handsome without being vain, neat without being prissy, a warrior who could've easily killed Wolf, yet chose to only lay him out, then carried him half a league back to the keep. A jailer who could've forced himself on her, yet had slept on the floor and offered her the bed. "I can take care of him as well as any other man."

"As well as you took care of the count's son?" Sophie challenged.

"I thought I took care of him quite well."

A loud slam made Lara jump in her seat, and she turned to see the captain scowling at them from his closed chest. He strode over to the table.

"I have business to attend elsewhere," he told them. "And I'm tired of your whisperings. So…." He addressed Sophie. "Your visit is over, madam." He looked to Lara. "If you have any requests, ask them now."

"Let me go?" Lara gave him her most ingenuous smile, and it was hard to tell which was louder: his snort or Sophie's tsk.

"I meant personal belongings," he said. "Clothes, necessities, that sort of thing."

"Wolf could use an outing, he isn't trained to a chamber pot as well as I," she said, and the corners of the captain's full mouth twitched up and then clamped back down. She smoothed her dirty hands down her tattered skirt. "I could use a bath."

He stared hard at her with those steel gray eyes of his, then dipped his head. "I'll make arrangements."

***

Lara stopped her pacing at the sound of voices beyond the door. The outside bolt was thrown open and she stood back as Wolf came bounding in, looking none the worse for yesterday, followed by the captain and two men carrying a wooden bathing tub. The captain directed the men to set the tub in an empty corner of the chamber, then proceeded to pull the draperies down from around the bed while two more men, each lugging a heavy wooden post nailed into a base, set them at an angle and tied a rope from one post to the other. The captain hung the drapes across the rope as Berta bustled in with Lara's blanket from home and set it down on the bed. Berta waved her over as she unfolded the blanket to reveal Lara's nightshift, a clean tunic and skirt, her best gown of dusty blue linen, her brush and comb, and a bar of her favorite rose-scented soap.

Lara ruffled Wolf's ears. "So that's what took you so long." Sophie must've gone home and packed up her belongings.

"The captain," Berta whispered to Lara. "He told Sophie you weren't leaving this chamber until Mallus. And then only under armed guard."

"Hmmph." Lara glared at the captain's broad back as he opened and closed the newly hung drapes. "We'll simply have to think of something else."

Berta said nothing, though her pursed lips spoke plenty.

"What?" Lara snapped. "You don't think I can outsmart an oafish soldier?"

Again, Berta said nothing, and Lara swept up her blanket and belongings and strode over to the hearth and plopped down on Wolf's pelts, where she watched as house servants carried buckets of steaming water and poured them into the tub. The two men who'd carried the posts in came back with a cot piled with bed linens they set against the far wall by the newly made bath chamber as the house servants returned with more buckets of steaming water for the tub. At a look from the captain, Berta shooed everyone out. He stood before Lara, who sat back on the pelts and glared at him.

"God's blood," he muttered. "It's akin to treeing a…" He stopped and held her angry gaze for a moment before clearing his throat. "A hot bath and soft bed are luxuries I've come to appreciate after years on the march. Enjoy yours while you're here."

CHAPTER 4
Inquisitions
Talon

Carrying a pitcher of wine and two cups in one hand, Talon tried the door to his chamber with the other, not at all surprised to find the inside bolt shut. "Open the door, Lara."

He heard the bolt slide and then the door creaked open. He stepped into the chamber, and his senses were instantly assailed by the sweet yet spicy fragrance emanating from Lara's freshly washed hair, its long, loose tendrils starting to dry and curl. She wore a clean tunic of yellow linen and a skirt of ocher, her waist belt, minus its knife, cinched around her slim waist, her feet bare. He coughed and turned and slid the inside bolt shut. "So we won't be disturbed," he told her, hiding his grin as her hazel eyes sparked amber.

He set the pitcher and cups down on the table and pulled a chair out, indicating that Lara should sit, admiring the sway of her skirts as she approached. Her eyes weren't the only thing catlike about her. Even as stiff and sore as she must have been after yesterday, she moved with an ease and a grace that the practiced women of Charles's court strove for and seldom attained.

She took her seat, and he sat across from her and filled both cups with wine. "We will sit and talk awhile." He pushed a cup over to her.

She picked the cup up left-handed, sniffed the wine, and took a sip. "What are we to talk about?"

He took a long swallow of his wine. "You."

"A jailer's curiosity about his prisoner?"

"Precisely."

She took another, longer drink of her wine, set her cup down, and folded her hands together on top of the table. "Let the inquisition begin."

Talon grinned despite himself. He'd determined to be very captain-like, though it wasn't easy when his mind kept straying to the fullness of her pink lips and the stubborn tilt of her patrician chin. "You're lefthanded," he said.

"I am."

"In the Saracen lands to the east, they would call you sinister-handed."

Her eyes challenged him. "Here they call me witch for it, among other things."

Talon took a drink of his wine. Being a witch wasn't a crime, though he'd never had a woman claim to be one so blatantly. She was testing him, trying to find out if she could gain any advantage over him, but he was neither a particularly religious or superstitious man. He tended to believe in things he could see and hear and touch. "Are you?"

She gave a little half smile and shrugged.

Talon gave a dismissive laugh. "How old are you?"

"I will be twenty-three this autumn. How old are you?"

"I turned thirty last month. I thought we were to talk about you?"

"We are, are we not? Is it against the king's law for us to talk about you as well?"

"No." Apparently, she wasn't going to let Talon's professed fealty to the king's laws go, and he didn't want to keep hearing about it for the next twelve days, which was when the next Mallus would be held. A special hearing to decide her case. That was the answer sent by Nithard Midered, Count of Oloron and magistrate to the province, in answer to the message Talon sent him this morning. The same count whose name had made Lara pale and the old healer break into the clerics' Latin and make plans to help Lara escape and send her into hiding at a place called the Hollow.

The second son of a landed nobleman, Talon had been meant for the church and had studied under the monks from the age of twelve to sixteen, when he'd run away from the monastery, stole his father's favorite horse, and spent the next two years making his way competing in riding tournaments. It was at a tournament in Tours that he'd caught the king's attention, and when Charles found out Talon knew how to speak, read, and write not only in the Frank language, but in Latin as well, he'd made him a royal courier. The youngest ever.

He'd heard and understood every word spoken between Sophie and Lara and had only acted ignorant and uninterested. Even if he hadn't known what they were saying, he wouldn't have let Lara go to the bathing house. He'd bathed there daily since being garrisoned here. He knew of the westward window facing the river, as he knew she would shimmy out of it before getting so much as a toe wet. Still, he was impressed that she'd seriously considered it. The high ladies of court would've simply sat on his bed and cried, trying to win his sympathies. Or tried to get him into bed and then demand his favor for theirs. Not Lara. She was as different from the ladies at court as a wildcat to a house kitten, and he was curious as to her breeding.

"What is Sophie to you?"

"She's raised me since I was a swaddling babe abandoned at the gate of the Abbey St. Marie."

"You're an orphan?" And likely a bastard.

"I am."

"How did Sophie come to raise you?"

"The Abbot Rogert asked her to."

Talon clamped down on his grin. "I meant why Sophie and not a childless couple or a family with children?"

"You would have to ask the abbot."

This time Talon didn't try to hide his grin. In truth, he was glad she had wit as well as beauty. Yet as much as he was enjoying their game, there were questions he wanted answered.

"I sent word to Count Nithard today," he told her. "He sent word back that he'll hold a special Mallus in twelve days to rule on your and Fulrad's case."

She sat still, all but for her eyes, which flashed gold, then narrowed. "The count is all obliging politeness."

"So it would seem."

She crossed her arms and glared at Talon. "How is Fulrad?" she finally asked. "I haven't heard since this morning."

"He lives and seems to be resting easier."

She nodded and let out a ragged sigh. "What, exactly, are his injuries? I forgot to ask Sophie earlier, and she didn't tell me."

Because they were too busy discussing Talon and the count and how to get her free of here. "His knee is gone, the bone shattered, his shoulder out of joint, and the four holes from Wolf's fangs in his throat are still seeping."

She pressed her lips together and looked ready to cry, whether for Fulrad or herself, Talon couldn't tell.

"Sophie says he'll likely speak again," he offered.

"And you will be there to hear him."

"I will."

She blinked, her hazel eyes glistening. Even distraught and on the verge of tears, she sat stiff and proud: cursed beautiful. Which brought him to his next question.

"Should I be expecting any challengers at my gate?"

She shook her head, sending a waft of spicy sweet fragrance his way. "There will be no challengers coming to fight for me."

"Are all the men in this valley blind fools, then?" he blurted out, confounded by the perfumed air he breathed in. "Or do your thorns keep them from trying for the prize?"

"Perhaps they have enough sense to fear being shredded for their uninvited attempts." Her voice was as arched as her brows.

"Or no stones enough to try." Talon eyed his bandaged hand. His prize for thinking with his stones instead of his brain.

"I never said none had ever tried." Her voice dripped honey, as it had at the river right before she'd called him an arrogant ass. "Nor that none had ever claimed the prize."

Talon sat back, her words stinging as smartly as the slice across his palm had yesterday. Her smile turned smug, and it occurred to him that she'd intended to get a rise out of him, and it had worked. Too well. He pushed his chair back, stood, then gave her a stiff dip of his head before he turned and strode from the chamber, throwing the outside bolt shut. He should've stayed and pretended it didn't matter to him that she'd been plucked before. Yet it did, though he couldn't have said why. Which pretty much explained everything the red-headed, hazel-eyed witchy wildcat made him feel.

***

The last of the candles sputtered out in the common room before Talon stepped over snoring soldiers to climb the stairs to his chamber. Lara lay in her cot, pretending to sleep, Wolf on his pelts on the floor beside her. Talon knew she was pretending because she'd laid her hand on Wolf's head to quiet him when he growled at Talon entering the chamber. He stripped down to his breechcloth, washed up, and, ignoring the big, soft, empty bed, threw the pelts he'd slept on last night against the door, then settled into them for the night, grinning as he heard the sound of her fist hitting her pillow and her loud harumph as she flopped over on the cot.

He woke up several times to her pacing back and forth across the chamber, keeping away from him and the door, and he was up at dawn and out of the hall by daybreak. He stayed away from his chamber all day, though it seemed every time he looked up at the open window while about the day's business, which was every time he passed by it, she was either pacing back and forth across it or sitting and staring out of it. After the evening meal, he sat with his men in the common room drinking and telling stories they'd all heard and told a hundred times before, along with a few new ones, most of which had to do with the captain's current bewitchment. He let them jape away, only because Sophie and the house servants all left for their own homes after supper and weren't there to hear, and Fulrad was heavily sedated and floating in and out of awareness.

Talon only drank one cup of ale himself. He didn't dare guard the door to his chamber drunk, sure the caged wildcat would run right over him, claws out and at the ready if he was impaired in any way. When he entered his bedchamber a little before midnight, Lara was in her cot, pretending to be asleep again, but was back to pacing not long after he settled onto the pelts.

Seven days passed this way, seven days of watching her pace past the window all day, and seven nights of having his sleep interrupted by listening to her footsteps in the dark. Seven days of not a word spoken between them, when Talon could take it no longer.

He returned to his chamber after a light noon repast and leaned against the open door as she whirled around midstride. "Will you give me your word that you'll swear not to run, ride, swim, or fly away if I let you out walk outside?"

"Yes," she said without hesitation. "I swear."

"Come on, then." He held the door wide. "All you had to do was ask, you know."

"I didn't want to be any trouble." She strode out the door, and Talon swallowed his grin.

He led her and Wolf out the hall of watching servants and into the courtyard, where even more curious eyes followed them as they crossed the courtyard and passed through the guarded back gate and out onto the open field. When they reached the river, Talon sat down on the grassy bank, and Wolf lay down beside him, offering his belly for a rub.

Talon chuckled at the surprised look on Lara's face. "We've become friends," he told her. He'd been taking Wolf out each morning and evening to relieve himself, and though he'd asked the dog a hundred questions about his mistress over the past days, Wolf had only ever told him where he liked to be scratched or where he liked to sniff.

Lara gave the dog an accusing glare, then lifted her skirts and waded into the river, grinning as Talon sat up straighter, ready to jump up and chase her if she bolted. Still grinning, she tucked her skirt hems into her waist belt and dipped her hands into the water, splashing handfuls onto her face and the back of her neck, sighing as rivulets ran down her arms and chest and looking much as she had the first time he'd come across her and Wolf. She wandered around in the water, her face to the sun, and Talon relaxed, enjoying the sight of her. After a while, she sat down on the riverbank and leaned back on her arms, letting her head hang back, her loose hair falling to the ground in a pool of silken, auburn curls.

Talon watched the play of sunlight on her creamy skin, the rhythmic rise and fall of her full breasts beneath her damp tunic. He breathed in the heady, spicy sweet scent of her, and let himself imagine what it would feel like to run his hands up and down her sun-warmed skin, to bury his nose into her fiery mane, his cock stones deep into her womanly flesh. He started to reach for her and jerked his hand back, having no wish to bleed today. Standing abruptly, he offered her his hand. "Let's walk some more. Then perhaps we can both get some sleep tonight."

They followed the river's course in companionable silence, unlike the cold silence of their shared chamber. Yet as much as Talon was enjoying the brief respite, there were questions he wanted to ask her. He'd ridden out with Phillipe into the valley of toths and villages several times over the last few days, to survey the land and meet the people, to ask them about Sophie and Lara and Count Nithard and his son, Ranulf, whom the two women had mentioned the first morning of Lara's confinement in Talon's chamber, thinking him ignorant of Latin. The people had offered little about the count and his son, other than the fact that Nithard had ruled the province for over twenty years, that they figured he was no better or worse than most counts, and that he had a daughter named Ravenna.

When it came to Sophie and Lara, the people told him they were the valley's healers, that Sophie had raised Lara since she was a babe and taught her the healing arts, as well as the arts of prophecy, which they spoke of without fear or rancor. They told him if Sophie the Sixth made a prediction, it always came to pass one way or another, that it was best to stay on her good side, and that Lara, while good-hearted, had a temper to match her fiery red hair. They also told him of the many times the two healers had saved them or a family member from sickness or death, and that most babes born in the province with their help had lived, along with the mothers. A claim that brought up old memories for Talon. Memories that he'd kept buried deep and had only ever told Phillipe about when deep in his cups.

He glanced up at the afternoon sun, loathe to disturb the fragile peace between himself and Lara, but it was time. "What form of Latin were you and Sophie speaking to each other the other morning?"

"The cleric's Latin. Sophie taught me it, as the nuns taught her."

"Sophie was at a nunnery?"

Lara nodded. "Until she ran away to elope with her first husband, Leopold."

"Go on."

Lara measured him with her gaze, obviously deciding exactly how much, or little, she was willing to tell him. "They'd been childhood sweethearts, whom she'd cried over when her father sent her away."

"The nunnery wasn't her choice, then?"

"No. Leopold was. He went after her two years later, when he'd saved enough coin to strike out on their own together. They journeyed as far west as they could and still remain in Gaul, which is how they came to settle in Oloron."

"I see." Like Talon, Sophie had left a life in the church chosen for her by others. He felt a thread of kinship with the old healer, and admiration. "You said this Leopold was her first husband," he said. "What happened to him?"

"He only lived to plow the land they bought here for two springs before he died of the pox. It was after his death that Sophie took up the study of medicines and healing."

"Who was her second husband?"

Again, she eyed him for a long moment before answering. "He was Orlando, captain of the count's guard."

"Count Nithard?"

Lara shook her head. "Count Reginald, Nithard's brother."

"Nithard inherited from his brother, then?"

"In a manner of speaking."

"What do you mean?"

"Count Reginald and his wife both died of a violent sickness within a day of each other. Their only child, a daughter named Isabeau, disappeared soon after."

"Disappeared?"

"They say she walked up into the mountains one day never to be seen again, that she had gone mad after losing her parents." Lara lowered her voice, though there were none to hear her except him. "They say Nithard was madly in love with Isabeau, his own niece, but she would have none of him because he was not only her uncle and married, but she was secretly in love with another. After Isabeau disappeared, Nithard claimed his brother's lands and title and has ruled as count since."

"What of Nithard's wife?" None of the villagers had mentioned a countess to Talon.

"She died giving birth to Ravenna."

The sound of his mother's screams, the dark red of her unstaunched blood, all rose from the depths of Talon's exhumed memories. "Sophie couldn't save her?"

Lara's keen gaze held Talon's as if she could see the turmoil his old memories had dug up. "Nithard would never deign ask help from Sophie the Sixth."

"Even for his dying wife?"

"Especially for his dying wife." Lara gave a soft snort of disgust. "She'd already given him a male heir and a daughter to marry off. She'd served her purpose."

Talon had seen enough of arranged marriages among the titled to know how most of them worked, but the cold, calculating cruelty Lara's tale told of Nithard was a thing he couldn't fathom. His father had at least loved his mother and had grieved her death for years. He shook his head. "To be raised by such a father."

"To be judged by such a man." Lara's pointed gaze held Talon's before she turned and headed back toward the keep.

CHAPTER 5

Mallus

Lara

Lara rode between the brown-haired giant called Tree and a young soldier with dark hair and serious eyes named Dardinel. Captain Guiscard rode ahead of her, and his second, the blond-haired man from the river named Phillipe, rode behind her as they made their way east, meeting up with Sophie on the road in front of her and Lara's home, a home Lara had been away from for too long now. A growing crowd of villagers trailed them along the way, until it seemed half the province followed them through the gates of Oloron Manor, home of Count Nithard Midered.

After dismounting, Lara stood between her guards, plastering a brave smile on as she thanked all the people who stepped up to wish her well, truly grateful to look on their familiar faces and hear their concern for her. A few of them even dared step up to the captain to vouch for her. Imposing in his vest of mail ringlets, arm bands, and leather gauntlets, with his short sword strapped to one side of his hips and his longsword to the other, the captain was unfailingly attentive and polite, assuring them he knew no ill of her, all the while flexing his scarred, bandage-free left hand.

Too soon, the captain nodded to Tree and Dardinel, who took their places to each side of Lara and Wolf. Sophie stepped up behind them and Phillipe took rear guard. Like the captain, his men wore arm bands of lacquered leather and their soldier's jerkins and breeches rather than the Roman robes of court, each of them armed with waist knives, short-bladed *spathas*, and longswords, though Phillipe was the only other one to wear a vest of mail. After smoothing her best gown of dusky blue linen with a matching undershift, Lara adjusted her waist belt with the knife in its beaded sheath the captain had returned to her that morning, though not the dagger she usually wore at her thigh, and walked head high toward the manor house.

Both sides of the wooden door opened, and she glanced back over her shoulder at Sophie, who hadn't been inside the manor house for over twenty years now. Lara had never even been through the manor gate before. They entered the main hall, a cavernous maw dank with heavy tapestries and dark, ornate walls and furniture that seemed to swallow Lara whole. Her heart beat in her ears and her breath quickened as she gathered her skirts in her hands, ready to make a run for open air and freedom, but Sophie was shaking her head, and a low voice sounded in her ear as a firm yet gentle hand gripped her upper arm.

"Lara?"

She looked into the captain's steady gaze.

"Breathe." He took a slow, deep breath in, and she did the same, the two of them blowing their breath out even slower. They took another slow breath in and out together, and another. "Are you ready now?"

She shook her head no. "Yes."

He held on to her arm until they were standing before a long table where the count's stewards were already seated, with two seats left empty in the middle. Lara began to shake as a steward rose and announced the count, and her teeth chattered as Count Nithard walked in, followed by his son, Ranulf, the two men who hated her most in this world. Four men-at-arms took their positions standing behind them as they took their seats. Lothair, the biggest and burliest, and captain of the guard, stood directly behind the count. Wolf nosed her fingers, and she laid her hand on his head.

Lara hadn't been this close to Nithard since she was a young girl. His dark hair hung in loose ringlets down to his shoulders in the Frank style, dyed black with kohl, along with his beard. He wore a burgundy robe with silken hems embroidered with the black and gold of the house of Midered over his slight frame, and rings of gold set with onyx and rubies on his slender fingers. His eyes were so dark in his thin face that they too looked black, abetted by the kohl lining his lids. Ranulf, a younger version of his father, wore a robe of the same colors, though its hems weren't silken, and his fingers adorned with only one ring of gold and onyx. The count's gaze skimmed over Lara and then fixed on Sophie behind her for a long moment before returning to Lara. He smiled, quick and fleeting and so chilling that she would have bolted right then but for the captain's firm grip on her arm.

Acknowledging the captain with a stiff nod of his head, Nithard tugged at his hems and spoke low to the steward Roumel at his left. Sitting at his father's right, Ranulf caught Lara's gaze and smiled, sure and smug. Lara grit her teeth and narrowed her gaze. Nithard, she feared. Ranulf, she despised. Both men's gazes were drawn beyond her, and Lara turned to see the crowd of villagers filing into the hall. She gave a little smile of her own, knowing how it must have aggravated the count to have so many common people in his house.

The count raised his hand, and the hall went silent. "Captain Guiscard, as count and magistrate to the province of Oloron, I bid you welcome."

"Sir Count." The captain dipped his head and gave Lara's arm a gentle squeeze. "I present to you the Lady Lara."

"Lady," Ranulf scoffed, and the captain's grip tightened on Lara's arm.

"She is the accused?" the count asked, though he knew she was.

"She is," the captain answered.

"And your man?" Nithard glanced around. "The injured soldier?"

"Is not yet able to travel. I will speak for him." The captain pulled Fulrad's written statement from his jerkin pocket and laid it on the table in front of the count, who tapped it with the tapered nail of his index finger.

"His injuries must be severe indeed," he said, "if he is still unable to travel so short a distance."

"They will keep him abed awhile longer," the captain said.

"What, exactly, were his injuries?"

The captain cleared his throat. "His knee is broken, his shoulder out of joint, and his throat pierced."

"His throat was pierced?" The count pretended to be shocked, though he and every other person there had known the extent of Fulrad's injuries since almost the day he'd acquired them. "How was his throat pierced?"

"By the dog, Wolf." The captain glanced down at Wolf, standing at Lara's knee, alert and at the ready.

The count made a show of looking Wolf up and down before picking up Fulrad's written statement, reading it silently, and then out loud. "It says, my name is Fulrad Demonte, king's soldier and cousin." He paused as gasps filled the hall, and Lara realized that the captain and his men had kept that fact a secret until now. "Who," Nithard continued dramatically, "having been lured into the stables by the witch whore called Lara with promises of her favors, was partaking of them when I caught her trying to cut my purse." He paused again with great effect. "When I tried to stop her, she and her wolf attacked me with murderous intent, leaving me crippled and useless to my king and country." He laid the parchment back down with a flourish and beaded his black gaze on Lara. "What do you, the accused, have to say?"

"The soldier, Fulrad, was drunk when he came upon me in the stables," Lara answered, her voice as shaky as her legs. "I asked him to leave me be, but he would not. He—" She stressed the word, her voice stronger, her legs steadier. "—attacked me. I only defended myself and the hound his mistress."

Nithard arched his black brows. "He was drunk you say?"

"Aye, his breath smelled as strongly of wine as his judgment was affected by it."

"You were close enough to smell his breath and tarried long enough to know his mind?"

"One only had to be downwind to smell him. And it took but a moment to know his mind, for he was most specific in his threats before he grabbed me and threw me down into the straw."

Muffled laughter crept in behind her, but before her the count didn't look amused.

"Were there any witnesses?" he questioned.

"No," Lara admitted. "There were none."

"What of witnesses to his character?"

Captain Guiscard stepped forward. "Fulrad is well known by me and his fellow soldiers to be a drunkard and a bully, and his purse, still attached to his belt, was empty of coin. None of which was found on the lady's person."

"If that is true, I wonder that you keep him in your company, Captain," Nithard said. "I had been led to believe you do not normally tolerate drunken behavior in your men."

"We all have our duties, Count."

"And yours is to play nursemaid to the king's cousin," Nithard said with a thinly veiled sneer. "Is it not?"

The captain gave a slight dip of his head, and a muscle ticked at the side of his clenched jaw as whispers rose and fell behind them.

"You have given us an account of this Fulrad's character as you see it," the count said to the captain. "What of the... lady's? Has she given you any reason to doubt her word or virtue?"

Lara closed her eyes and pressed her lips tight. Why had she gone and told the captain that her prize had been claimed? That she was a witch? She opened her eyes to a loud snicker and Ranulf practically squirming in his seat. She glanced sideways at the captain, the muscle in his jaw ticking double time as he flexed his scarred hand.

"The lady has given me no reason to doubt the truth of what she says happened with Fulrad," he told the count, and Lara released the breath she hadn't realized she'd been holding. Sophie was right about him. He played this game with much more skill than she. He'd defended her honor most ably, if not her virtue. Which was her own damned fault.

Count Nithard sat back, a small smile playing at the corners of his thin lips as he addressed the hall. "Do any here know of any instance in which the accused has acted other than right and virtuous?"

Ranulf stood and smirked at Lara, whose blood went cold. She swayed on her feet and was steadied by the captain's big, warm hand cupping her elbow.

"The floor is Ranulf Midered's," his father, the count, said.

Ranulf strolled around the table, stopped in front of Lara and the captain, then turned his back to them as he presented himself to the stewards. "As you have all known me my entire life, you know that I haven't always had this scar." He twisted his head from side to side as the stewards made a show of inspecting his whiskerless chin, then he turned to face Lara and the captain, whose grip on her elbow tightened. "It was the accused, the witch Lara, who marked me with her knife."

He stepped closer, his chin high for the captain's perusal, and Wolf growled. Lara laid her hand on the dog's head. "Down, Wolf." He stopped growling, but still stood at the ready, his intent gaze following Ranulf as he smartly backed away.

"Captain," Count Nithard said. "If you would put the dog at a safe distance. We wouldn't want the beast to bite through my son's throat now, would we?"

Lara chuffed, and the captain gave her a warning glare before he glanced over his shoulder and nodded to Sophie, who stepped up and took Wolf by his collar. Sophie leveled her gaze on the count until he gulped and ran a shaky finger along the neckline of his robe as if it had suddenly become too tight, then she stepped back and stood behind Lara and the captain with Wolf firmly in her grasp.

"Ahem." Count Nithard cleared his throat and tugged on his robe's hems. "You may continue," he told Ranulf.

"It was the summer of my seventeenth year." Ranulf swaggered back and forth in front of the assembly. "I was on my way to study with the Abbot Rogert, a birthday present from my esteemed father."

Lara snorted as Ranulf stopped and bowed low to the count. It was common knowledge that Ranulf had never studied anything except women and swordplay. He bragged about it often enough.

"I came upon the accused, the witch, Lara, alone and standing stark naked in the river." He paused as gasps and whispers filled the hall. The captain tightened the hold of his scarred hand on Lara's elbow. "Lured by the sight and promise of her flesh, as any young man would be, I went to her, and she kissed me. I fell into a strange, hazy dream, from which I awoke to find her cutting at my purse string. I pushed her away and she lashed out with her knife at my throat." He paused again, his gaze sweeping over the assembly. "It was only by the grace of God that I escaped with my purse and my life."

"And the proof?" the captain demanded.

"The proof is this witch's mark I now carry." Ranulf flicked his fingers at the scar that ran across his chin, marring his pretty face. "It reminds me daily of her treachery."

"A man earns many scars, boy," the captain growled, the scar on his cheek gone white. "That piddling scratch proves nothing."

Ranulf stood speechless, his hand on the jeweled hilt of the knife at his waist. The count coughed once, twice, and Ranulf looked to his father, then lifted his hand from his knife and his lips into a semblance of a smile. "The witch will show her own proof against her," he said with a smug sneer. "For her skin was the tanned bronze of a pagan's used to traipsing naked in the woods, not pale and untouched by the sun as a good, pure, Christian maid's should be."

He moved toward Lara, and the captain pulled her behind him, standing between her and Ranulf, as solid and stalwart as a stone wall.

"No need to get your hackles up, Guiscard," Ranulf said. "I've only to show her legs to prove my words."

"You will show nothing of her, Midered." The captain's voice was low, and his big, corded hand was on the hilt of his longsword. "I have seen her legs," he said loud enough for all to hear. "And I say they are lily white. Perhaps you truly were dreaming and fell down and cut your chin?"

Lara couldn't move, couldn't breathe. If Ranulf challenged the captain's assertion and the count demanded she show her legs, she was as good as hung. She instinctively stepped in closer to the captain, her nose no more than a handsbreadth from his broad back, and he stood even taller and squared his formidable shoulders.

"Perhaps I was dreaming," Ranulf ceded with a shrug of his much slenderer shoulders. "Perhaps not. Yet who can blame me, for a dish once tasted…"

Lara sucked her breath in, and the captain's entire body tensed and stilled.

"It is, of course, the magistrate's decision," Ranulf finished with a bow to his father.

Lara peeked over the captain's shoulder at Nithard, whose gaze was fixed on something or someone behind her. She turned around and gave a feral grin. The count was staring at Sophie, who stared right back at him with her sure, Sophie the Sixth half-smile.

"We will accept Captain Guiscard's word on the witch's legs," Nithard announced. "And whatever other parts of her body he's had the opportunity to see unclothed." A grassfire of whispers swept through the hall, and Lara's cheeks burned. "The accused will come forward."

Lara stepped out from behind the captain, her shoulder just touching his arm.

"Was it you who scarred Ranulf's chin with your knife?"

Lara lengthened her spine and lifted her chin. "It was," she said. "I cut him when he accosted me in the river."

Nithard pressed his lips together and narrowed his beady gaze on her. "Do you truly expect this court to believe that twice—" He held up two fingers and waved them in the air. "—twice now, you have been accosted by men of good standing, without provocation, and that both times you have walked away without so much as a scratch whilst leaving one man, a seasoned soldier, with grave injuries, and the other, a young nobleman schooled by sword masters, with a witch's mark? That you, a mere woman, a healer schooled in the old arts, did so without trickery or evil intent?"

"If I had gone after yon nobleman with evil intent," Lara spat toward Ranulf, "he would not be here spewing lies. And you and he both know it."

Nithard smiled as smug as a cat about to spring on a mouse, and Lara bit her lower lip. She'd meant to stay calm and keep her temper, as Sophie had warned her to do. Not to let herself be goaded into a display of anger such as she'd just shown. She glanced at the captain, who stood rigid, the muscle on the side of his clamped jaw ticking triple time.

Nithard cleared his throat and held a hand up. The assembly went quiet. "Though the accused claims she did but defend herself in the case of her attack on Fulrad Demonte, she has failed to prove it to this court. Therefore, we pronounce her guilty. Guilty of excessive force against a king's soldier and kinsman, which caused him grievous, and possibly lifelong, injury."

Lara went numb, the count's words buzzing in her ears as if from a distance. She could neither move or speak and barely remembered to breathe as Sophie stepped up to stand beside her on the opposite side of the captain, Wolf in hand. The count held Sophie's gaze for a long moment, then coughed and tugged on his robes.

"Therefore," he announced, "this court declares her *lidi* to the king's garrison and its captain until such time as the soldier Fulrad can once again take the field for his king, or the full wergeld of three hundred gold solidi is paid."

The assembly sucked its collective breath in as Lara released hers. The count could have ordered her to be hung by the neck until she was dead, and would have, she was certain, were it not for Sophie the Sixth standing beside her. As it was, he'd made her *lidi*, an indentured servant to the captain and his company.

Nithard held his hand up and the assemblage went quiet. "As for the dog, Wolf, we declare him vicious and a danger to all men and sentence him to immediate death."

"Wolf vicious?" Lara grasped the captain's arm with both hands. "Please. He did nothing but protect me. You know this. You know Wolf."

Steel-gray eyes held hers, eyes she found impossible to read. The captain pulled his arm from her grasp and addressed the count, his voice as tight as his jaw. "Sir Count, I will take responsibility for the dog and see to its punishment personally."

It was a request in wording only; even in her frantic state, Lara could tell that much. As, apparently, could the count.

"So be it," Nithard said. With a wave of his hand, Mallus concluded.

CHAPTER 6

Protection

Lara

"Three hundred gold solidi," Lara cried as soon as she was inside the captain's tent staked out in the courtyard of Oloron Manor. "It will take a lifetime to earn that amount."

"As Nithard well knows." Sophie closed the tent flap behind her. "As he knows that Fulrad will never take the field for Charles again. He has done what he could and made a slave of you."

"He has tried." Lara slipped into Latin as she heard the captain speaking to one of his men outside the tent.

"What do you intend to do?" Sophie spoke in Latin as well.

"I intend to make my way to the Hollow. To stay there until this garrison has left Oloron."

"Then what? You'll never be able to return to Oloron as long as Nithard is count and Ranulf his successor."

Lara gnashed her teeth. Sophie was right about Nithard and Ranulf. They'd been given their shot at her and taken it. They'd made her *lidi* and would never willingly give her back her free status. "What do you suggest I do?" she asked Sophie, who could see farther ahead than most.

Sophie laid her hand on Lara's shoulder and looked her straight in the eyes. "I suggest you stay and be *lidi* to the captain. Serve out your sentence, for now."

Lara shook Sophie's hand off. "What? No."

"Just hear me out," Sophie insisted. "Captain Guiscard has proven himself an honorable man, has he not?" Sophie arched her brows at Lara, who stood untouched and intact despite her time living in the captain's quarters, surrounded by a troop of soldiers. Sophie indicated Wolf, still alive and standing at Lara's side despite Nithard's ruling that he be put to death. "Has he not?"

"Aye," Lara admitted grudgingly. "He has."

"A *lidi* has her master's protection."

"A *lidi* has a master."

"True enough. Yet I see certain advantages for you with the captain's protection."

"*Protection*? If I stay here, he will be the one I need protecting from."

Sophie's wizened gaze narrowed on Lara's. "How so, child?"

Lara opened her mouth to say, what? That her reaction to seeing the captain in his breechcloth every night was anything but childlike? That she dreamed of his low, resonant voice and piercing eyes when she did sleep? That she found herself dwelling on his masculine good looks and raw maleness when she was pacing the chamber they shared because she couldn't sleep? She clamped her mouth shut.

"For me then," Sophie said. "Do this for me."

"But Tante." Lara was suddenly, ridiculously, close to tears. "*Lidi*? I cannot. Not to him."

"Better to him than others."

Lara shook her head. Adamant. She may have been an orphan and likely a bastard, but she was freeborn. "Better to none."

"I can't argue that," Sophie admitted, making sense at last. "Yet you've given Nithard his chance at you, and he won't let it go. I can only protect you so much from him in this." She laid her gnarled hand on Lara's arm. The hand that had raised, comforted, and chastised her but had never pointed her wrong. "What I propose is this. Stay. Stay and be *lidi* to the captain, a good, hardworking *lidi* who does not trouble her master."

Lara chuffed. "Your plan has already failed. He thinks me troublesome to the core."

"Tell him to talk with me, then," Sophie said. "He's only had fourteen days of you, I've had nigh on twenty-three years of your troublesome ways."

A man went into a coughing fit outside the tent, and Sophie's grip on Lara's arm tightened.

"God and nature did not make you so strong-limbed and hardheaded for naught. Work hard, be obedient, earn your master's respect, and I will be making love potions galore to sell to the valley's women intent on catching themselves a strapping soldier."

"Love potions?" Their love potion was the only false tincture they knowingly sold. "A summer's worth of good coin, to be sure, but three hundred solidi worth?"

"We'll figure it out as we go. Until the captain proves other than right and honorable, I want you to swear you will stay under his protection. He dislikes these Midereds and makes little effort to hide it. As long as you don't anger him too much, he'll stand between you and them as he did today."

The instinctive sense of safety Lara had felt when he'd done so couldn't be forgotten. How he'd stopped Ranulf from showing her legs. How he'd gone against the count and saved Wolf's life. "You're right enough about the captain not liking those lying snake Midereds." She took a deep, slow breath in and let it out. If Sophie wanted her to do this, there was a reason. This much she'd learned living with Sophie the Sixth. "All right. I'll stay and be *lidi* to Captain Guiscard and try not to anger him too much."

"Good." Sophie patted her arm. "'Tis good. Much depends on this, you know. On you."

"No, I don't know." Lara rubbed her temples, which had begun to throb. "Always you tell me much, but never what. You speak in your seer's riddles, and my head is near to splitting so that I can't think straight."

"There will come a time when you'll know what." Sophie took Lara by the hand and sat her down on a bedroll. "Until then, you need to rest. The captain will be supping with the count, and you should try to get some sleep."

"You'll stay with me?" Lara was bone tired and weary.

Sophie sat down beside her. "I'll stay with you, child."

Laying her head on Sophie's lap, Lara closed her eyes with a sigh, content to be Sophie's child for a while longer.

***

Talon

Talon gave Lara as much time to rest and himself to think as he could without offending Count Nithard by arriving late to sup with his household. He considered not having her attend with him, but the day's events and her conversation with Sophie in the tent, of which he'd heard every word, had raised more questions than they'd answered. Talon didn't like unanswered questions, especially ones he found himself in the middle of.

It'd been obvious almost as soon as the count and his son had taken their seats at Mallus that Nithard had it out for Lara. And almost as obvious that he feared Sophie the Sixth, whose calm stares and half smiles had visibly unnerved him. In fact, if it hadn't been for Sophie and Talon standing beside Lara, he'd have wagered coin on Nithard sentencing her to death along with Wolf. He didn't know the cause of the enmity between the healers and the count, but he was determined to find it out. Lara had been right when she'd called Ranulf a snake, and his father was as clever and sneaky as a weasel. The best way Talon knew how to draw either out of their holes was with bait, and Lara was the best bait he had.

He entered his tent, where she lay with her head on Sophie's lap, awake and watching him with her wary cat eyes, Wolf curled up beside her.

"You will sup with me and my men at the count's table, Lara," he told her. "Ready yourself." He looked to Sophie. "You're welcome to join us."

"No." The old healer shook her head. "I would be anything but welcome at the count's table. I'll return home and take Wolf with me."

Talon nodded. "That'd probably be best."

He waited outside the tent as Lara made her preparations, then as she stepped out with her hair freshly combed and braided, her gown of dusty blue skimming the womanly curves of her body, she caught him off guard. He tried not to envision her strong, sleekly muscled and tanned legs, legs Ranulf had apparently seen as well, the knowledge of which left a bitter taste in his mouth. He clenched his scarred hand, all too aware of the similarities between Ranulf's story of meeting her in the river and his own. Even so, Talon was man enough to admit he'd deserved his slice, and he'd wager coin Ranulf had deserved his as well. "Come on," he said brusquely. "We don't want to insult Count Nithard by arriving late."

They entered the dining hall as the company was being called to table, and Talon accepted the seat offered him beside the count's daughter, a pretty, petite, dark-haired, dark-eyed young woman who sat to her father's left and Ranulf to his father's right. Talon indicated that Lara should take the seat to his left, and Tree to hers. Phillipe and Dardinel mixed in with the stewards and their families, whose daughters were instantly batting lashes and flashing quick, flirty smiles at them. Talon recalled Sophie's plans for her love potions and smiled to himself. Perhaps his purse would be filled with three hundred gold solidi after all, and his tight-lipped, stone-faced *lidi* would be free of him, and him of her, a thought that turned his smile dour.

"Where is the witch's hound, Guiscard?"

By the insolent tone of voice and the fact that no one else here dared call him Guiscard without the proper address of Captain, he knew it was Ranulf who spoke. "Wolf is safely tucked away,

Midered." Talon leaned forward so that he could meet Ranulf's sneering gaze. "Do not fear."

"I fear no man," Ranulf insisted.

Talon smiled. "No. Only women and dogs."

Ranulf fumed as a dark troll of a man standing guard at Nithard's back bristled. The other three men-at-arms looked to him for their lead, and it was to him that the count looked and slowly shook his head. The troll stepped back half a step, though he still huffed and bristled. At a look from his father, Ranulf slouched back in his seat.

Talon glanced at Lara, who sat still and silent beside him as the servants carried out platters of roast meat, summer vegetables, and freshly baked loaves of rye. Despite what the count had declared and everything that had happened, he'd been considering how to overturn her sentence when he'd overheard her and Sophie speaking inside the tent. It was true what Sophie had told Lara. The count had done what he could to ruin her, making her *lidi* to him, whore to a troop of soldiers in the eyes of the valley's people, whether true in fact or not. He'd half expected Sophie to agree to help her escape to this Hollow they'd mentioned twice now and had been as surprised as Lara when Sophie told her to stay instead. To stay and be *lidi* to him, under his protection.

Sophie had been right about another thing as well: Talon didn't like the count or his son one whit. Which was one of many reasons why he'd sworn his silent oath to protect Lara from them without any greater understanding of Sophie's reasons than Lara apparently had.

Lara remained silent throughout the meal, pushing more food around on her trencher than she ate. Ravenna, on the other hand, talked nonstop into Talon's ear, asking him about the march into Spain and the horrible, bloodthirsty Saracens, barely stopping long enough for him to answer before she was on to some tidbit of local gossip or fashion.

The main course finished, bowls of fresh fruit were brought out, and Ravenna popped a strawberry into her mouth and licked her lips.

"How was the king when you last saw him, Captain?" she asked, smiling prettily, her lips stained red from the berry's juice.

"Hot," Talon said, and his men chuffed and nodded, each as glad as the other to be gone from the sunbaked Spanish plains. "Cursed hot."

"I wonder he does not return soon, then." She popped another berry into her mouth. "It is said the queen is about to make him a father again."

"Is it?" Talon knew he was hearing the news long before Charles would. It was a strange thing, the life of a soldier, always on the move, away from home and family for months to years at a time. Not a good thing for a husband or father, which was one of many reasons Talon never intended to become either. Of course, soldier and king were two different men, and Talon didn't envy Charles the politics he had to play as king, but he could be happy for his friend, who loved his wife and children. He held up his goblet of finely detailed pewter and offered a toast. "To Charles and Hildegard. May their lives be full with children and long in years."

"To Charles and Hildegard," Phillipe seconded.

Tree lifted his goblet. "To the king and queen."

Dardinel lifted his. "To a long and fruitful reign."

Ravenna sipped her wine and batted her lashes at Talon, ignoring Dardinel, who was closer to her in age and sitting directly across from her with his handsome face, brown curls, and big brown eyes that left most young women swoony. Yet the more Talon ignored Ravenna, the harder she pushed for his attention. He leaned back in his seat and caught Ranulf leering at Lara, which he'd been doing throughout the meal, despite her refusal to even acknowledge his presence. Perhaps that was the secret to this family: they only wanted what they couldn't have, which wasn't much by the richness of their dress and manor house.

Determined to make sure Ranulf got nothing more of Lara than he'd already had, Talon leaned farther back in his seat, blocking the whelp's view of her and scowling at the thought that kept eating at him. He was fairly certain Ranulf was the lucky son of a bitch who'd claimed her as his prize at some point in their history together. Across from him, Dardinel took in his scowl and crossed arms and sat up straighter, as did Phillipe and Tree.

"Why so serious, Captain?" Ravenna asked with a pretty pout.

"I was wondering what it is that causes your brother to stare so intently at my lidi."

"If I know my brother, 'tis the toss of her skirts, a toss he's partaken of before and no doubt wishes to partake of again." She laid a dainty hand on Talon's forearm and turned to Ranulf. "Brother," she said loudly, drawing the entire tables attention. "Captain Guiscard would know of your interest in his new *lidi*."

"Why, my interests in his *lidi* are many and varied." Ranulf addressed Talon. "Some old and some new. All enough for me to inquire of the captain if he would be willing to sell her to me? At a profit, of course."

Talon gritted his teeth to keep from calling the whelp out then and there. He looked to Dardinel and Phillipe, who sat alert and at the ready. Tree shifted closer to Lara. Unlocking his jaw, Talon glanced down at Lara's hand on her waist knife. "*Mihi crede.*" He spoke low and in Latin. *Trust me.*

She sucked her breath in and narrowed fierce, feral eyes at him.

"Why would you want to buy this *lidi* from me for over three hundred gold solidi?" he asked Ranulf. "When you can see for yourself how troublesome she is?"

"For you perhaps, Guiscard." Ranulf offered a self-satisfied smile. "For me she will be no trouble at all."

Lara gave a very unladylike snort, and Talon made a point of looking her up and down. Her face was pale but for the flushed apples of her cheeks, her body taut and ready to fly, her hand now gripping the hilt of her knife. He reached down and pried her fingers from the hilt and raised them to his chest.

"Three hundred gold solidi plus." He made a show of playing with her long, sinuous fingers. "'Tis a generous sum." He lifted her hand and touched his lips to the backs of her fingers, her knuckles white from the tight grip she had on his. "But then she does have more than generous charms, on this, at least, you and I agree."

"Four hundred gold solidi," Ranulf offered.

Talon's hand froze with Lara's in it. "God's blood, woman," he swore low. "What exactly did you do for him?" He caught her other hand right before it reached his cheek and wrestled them both back onto her lap.

"Well, Guiscard," Ranulf crowed, sure now that Talon would sell the troublesome wench. And maybe he should. Better the whelp wake up with her knife in his back some night than Talon. "What say you, man, do we have a deal or not?"

Talon stared hard at Lara, daring her to give him a reason to sell her. She glared right back at him, the amber in her eyes flaring into smoldering embers, then she took a deep breath in and flattened her fisted hands beneath his in her lap. Letting her breath out, she dipped her head to him, everything in her mien and manner showing her to be the good, obedient *lidi* Sophie bade her be but for her heated gaze.

He turned back to Ranulf, whose tongue was practically hanging out of his mouth. "The thing is, my purse is full enough for my simple needs. And I have my own ideas on how she will best serve me and my men."

Those men choked and sputtered, and Talon stood, tired of the day's games. His men stood too, and even Lara rose from her seat without being asked.

"Thank you for supper, Count Nithard." They'd brought supplies enough with them to spend the night camped out in the manor's courtyard, but after today Talon didn't intend to spend another moment in the Midereds' company more than was necessary. "We'll be returning to the keep tonight as there's business I must tend to early tomorrow."

He took a silent, seething Lara by the arm and led her out of the manor house. She strode straight into his tent, kicking first one bedroll and then the other until their ties came undone and they lay unfurled and rumpled on the floor of the tent.

"Feel better now?" Talon asked.

"No," Lara snarled.

Talon chuckled. "Would another bedroll help? Perhaps a tunic of mine? My shin?"

"You think this funny? Do you truly think kicking anything else will make up for what I've been through? I was attacked by your drunkard of a soldier and kept prisoner in your chamber. I've had to listen to lies being spewed about me and made *lidi* to you for defending myself against the drunkard and then Sophie..." She stopped, the realization that he knew perfectly well what Sophie had asked her to do clear on her face. That he'd understood every word they'd spoken to each other in Latin in front of him, thinking him ignorant. She jabbed her finger in the air toward his chest. "And you, you made it known to the world that I'd be serving you and your men as whore." She glared daggers at him. "I am telling you here and now, Captain, I will not."

"Be at ease, Lara." He was insulted she didn't know him better by now. "I've no intention of forcing my or my men's attentions on you. If I'd wanted you badly enough, you'd have been heels up by now. That little show was for the count and his son."

She jerked her head back as if he'd slapped her. "You thought it necessary to humiliate me in front of the count and his son for entertainment?"

"You'll survive the humiliation," he said. "Better that than Ranulf's loving hand." Her eyes went wide. "Is he who Sophie wanted me to protect you from? What prize is the whelp so eager to reclaim?" Her eyes grew even bigger and her mouth opened, but she said nothing. "Why do I even ask you anything when you and your Sophie the Sixth only speak in riddles and half-truths?"

"At least I do not lie," she hissed.

Talon stood at his full height. "When have I lied to you?"

"You feigned ignorance," she said in Latin. "To spy on me and Sophie."

"As any soldier would a prisoner's dealings," he answered in kind. "Besides, I didn't lie. I never claimed ignorance. You assumed it."

"Aye, from your foolish grins and oafish manners."

"Oafish manners?" he roared. "Did not my oafish manners save your pretty little neck and Wolf's today?"

Her eyes blazed, then cooled. "They did," she admitted grudgingly. "You did." She glanced around the tent, looking anywhere but at him before finally meeting his gaze again. "Thank you. For myself and Wolf."

Talon grinned. "There now. That wasn't so hard, was it?"

"No," she said through gritted teeth. "Of course not."

CHAPTER 7

Lidi

Lara

As *lidi*, Lara woke each morning at dawn and helped Berta, Enid, and Marta prepare and serve breakfast to the company of soldiers. After breakfast, she would tend to various soldiers' aches and ailments, then she would tend to Fulrad. Though he couldn't speak yet, he managed to say plenty with his sneers and leers and rude, guttural grunts as she cleansed and bandaged his neck wounds and rubbed a healing balm of comfrey, chamomile, and yarrow on his knee. Every morning, she would have to cajole and threaten him anew to drink the tisane of white willow bark for his pain and swelling, his grimace each time he swallowed a mouthful of the bitter brew small recompence for dealing with him.

Once Fulrad was dealt with, she was free to spend her days as she always had, tending to her animals and gardens, drying herbs and flowers, mixing tisanes and tinctures, and riding into the villages and toths to tend the people and animals of the valley. She saw little of the captain during the day, and then only in passing as he rode his black steed patrolling the valley's borders, having left the daily running of the keep to Anglbert, though he was always back at the keep when she returned in the late afternoon to help cook and serve the evening meal. Then she would tend to Fulrad again, repeating the morning's ritual with the addition of a glass of wine, the one thing he took from her without complaint.

Several days into this new life, Lara picked wild blackberries from the vines bordering her property and strawberries from her garden and baked three pies with them in the keep's ovens, which the company made short work of after having eaten their fill of roast goat, summer squash, and oat bread.

"My compliments on the pies, Berta." The captain leaned back in his seat as Lara helped clear the empty platters from the table. "I can't remember when I've tasted one so delicious."

"Why thank you, Captain, but they weren't made by me." Berta beamed at Lara.

"So, you can cook," he said with a teasing grin that Lara was learning to recognize. "Or at least bake."

Lara dipped her head. "As I told you, m'lord."

He furrowed his brows at the title he hated, which was why she used it. "I tell you what, Lara the pie baker. I'll pay you a copper for a pie all my own."

"How many pies can you eat in a day?" Lara quickly calculated how many coppers equaled a gold solidus.

He laughed, low, deep, and more pleasing to her ear than she cared to admit. "One at a time will suffice. My favorite is berry, any kind."

"Mine is peach." Phillipe jangled his purse.

"And mine is plum," Tree added.

Before she finished clearing the table, she had orders for five pies from five soldiers, making five coppers toward her wergeld, which she pocketed before heading up to the captain's chamber that she still shared each night. Shutting the door behind her, she glanced around. One of her new duties was to keep the captain's chamber orderly, but there was nothing for her to tidy up. The captain was as neat and careful of his belongings as he was of his person, bathing each afternoon before supper in the tub in the antechamber.

"You're welcome to bathe before I do," he'd offered the first night she'd returned to the keep as lidi. "Or after. No sense in wasting a tub of hot water."

She'd thanked him and told him she bathed at her house, and then he'd ordered three bars of sandalwood soap and one of rose from her, grinning sheepishly as he'd asked for the bar of rose soap.

"A gift for a woman?" she'd asked, pocketing his coin.

He'd shrugged for an answer, and the image of Ravenna, who'd sent a servant to buy a vial of love potion from Sophie that afternoon, had come to Lara unbidden. She'd imagined him grinning at Ravenna the way he sometimes grinned at her, slow and sure and teasing, and she'd almost told him she was out of the rose soap and would have if not for the coin.

He still came up to the chamber late, spending the evenings in the common hall with his men, and now that he wasn't guarding the door against Lara, he slept in the big, four-poster bed while she slept in the cot, Wolf on his pelts beside her. They were seven nights into this new dance when the door to their chamber pushed open shortly after Lara had retired, and the captain walked in carrying the strawberry pie he'd bought from her that afternoon. Phillipe followed him in, carrying a pitcher of wine and three cups. Lara was sitting on her cot, counting her growing hoard of coin, a copper between her fingers as the captain set the pie on the table and Phillipe set the pitcher and cups down alongside it.

"How much?" The captain nodded at the ornately carved wooden box that Lara kept her coin in. It was the first time he'd asked about her earnings.

She dropped the copper into the box and shut the lid. "Fifteen coppers, three silver pieces, and one gold solidus."

"How much of it is from Sophie's love potions?" He elbowed Phillipe in the gut. "Amelia, the steward Braun's daughter, gave Phillipe a sweet libation this very noon."

Phillipe made a show of feeling his head, his chest, his gut. "Is there anything in particular I should be noticing?" he asked Lara, his blue eyes laughing.

"Aye," she told him. "A brunette named Amelia."

"She is rather pleasant in a rather bland fashion." He winked.

"She pays with good coin," Lara told him. "As have half the women in this valley." Phillipe grinned, and the captain snorted. "Be careful who you take a sweet drink from, Captain," she warned him. "Half of those women intend their potion for you."

"It will do them no good," Phillipe said, shaking his blond curls.

Lara gave the captain a sly smile. "Over two score of marriages in the province have been initiated with a vial of Sophie's love potion."

"If it's marriage they seek, they're poisoning the wrong men," the captain vowed with a savage certainty that gave Lara pause.

"But if it's a night of pleasure only." Phillipe wagged his blond brows. "Then I'm their man."

Lara laughed, the captain scowled, and Phillipe poured the wine into the three cups as the captain set up the figurines on the game board, all black on one side, all white on the other. He motioned for Lara to sit at the table with them.

"The game is called Shah, or King," the captain told her as Phillipe moved one of the domed white pieces a square forward. "It was a gift from the Emperor of Byzantium, who taught me how to play my second time there as courier to Charles."

"How many times have you been to Byzantium?" Lara asked, impressed. A courier was someone educated, someone the king trusted with secretive information, but then the captain did read, write, and speak Latin, and was lieged directly to Charles.

The captain moved a black piece forward. "Three. I traveled my second with Phillipe as my guard, which was how we met."

"Ten years ago this past spring." Phillipe moved another white piece.

Lara took a sip of her wine. "How long have you been soldiers?"

"Eight years," Phillipe said as the captain studied the board. "When Charles realized what a strategist Talon was, not to mention good on a horse and handy with a sword, he talked him into becoming captain of a company of horsemen, a special troop that could ride hard and fast when needed. Then they talked me into joining, promising me travel and adventure, women and glory."

He was grinning at Lara as he said it, his blue eyes twinkling, and she found herself grinning back at his easy charm. Charm and good looks that had no doubt gotten him many of those promised women. Taking another sip of wine, she glanced at the captain, whose gray gaze had turned somber and brooding. Phillipe chuckled, and the captain flashed him a withering glare before picking up another black piece and moving it.

"What are the figurines made of?" she asked.

"The black are onyx," the captain said. "The white are ivory."

"Ivory?"

"The tusk of an elephant."

"Elephant?"

"A massive creature the size of three oxen with legs as thick as an oak trunk," the captain told her. "And a head as big as a boulder with big, floppy ears the size of trenchers and a long, rope-like nose called a trunk that can wrap around a full-grown man and pick him up and carry him."

"Truly?" Lara was amazed at the captain's description of such a fantastical creature.

"Truly." First one side of the captain's mouth crooked up and then the other, giving the hard planes of his features a boyish cast, and Lara understood all too well why half the valley's women wanted him to drink their love potions.

"Talon." Phillipe was grinning as he looked from Lara to the captain. "You should carve an elephant for Lara." He turned back to Lara. "He carved one for the emperor of Byzantium that sits on the mantel at his summer palace."

"Did you carve the figurine of the woman in your chest?" Lara could have bitten her tongue as soon as she asked it. She'd just admitted to going through his belongings. "I'm sorry, Captain. I didn't mean to pry. Well, I mean, I meant to when I saw her, but it was my first night in my ca— your chamber."

"Don't worry about it," he told her with a shrug of his broad shoulders. "I would have done the same."

"Who is she? The woman you carved?"

Phillipe coughed and sputtered on his wine as the captain's smiling gaze grew somber once more. He stared hard at Lara for a long moment, and she tilted her head and stared right back, trying to figure out what had happened. To figure him out.

He stood. "Don't touch my bloody pie," he growled at Phillipe, who sat grinning as the captain strode out the door and slammed it shut.

"What was that about?" she asked Phillipe, who chuckled. "What did I say? I apologized for going through his things and he accepted. Was it the woman I found in his chest?"

"Aye," Phillipe said, sobering. "It's the woman."

He said is, not was, and he watched Lara as he said it.

"Who is she?" she asked again.

"Who is she?" Phillipe pulled at the short curly blond whiskers of his beard as if weighing his words. "She is a dream."

***

Talon

Talon resumed his habit of staying late in the common room after supper, prolonging his self-imposed torture with a pitcher of wine and a game of Shah with whomever he could get to play. More often than not, it was Phillipe who would play him, Phillipe who would say at least once a game, "Just tell her. Tell her who the woman is."

But Talon had no intention of telling Lara the carving was of her. That after coming across her in the river that day, he'd stayed up most of the night cutting, carving and smoothing her womanly curves and flowing lines. That he'd dreamed about her day and night since. He wasn't about to make things between them more complicated than they already were.

If he was lucky and Lara was sleeping when he finally made his chamber, he would pad over to her cot, pet Wolf, and watch her sleep until she stirred, which was longer and longer as she grew more used to his presence. If he wasn't lucky, and she was still awake and sewing or reading the book on herbs the abbot had brought her, there would be an awkward silence between them as they each sought their beds.

That the Abbot Rogert of the Abbey St. Marie had come himself to Crossroads Keep expressly to visit with Lara, to check on her welfare and loan her a priceless tome, said much of her standing in the valley. A standing many others felt it necessary to point out to Talon. Daily he would meet some villager as he rode his rounds who would tell him how Lara had saved them or some member of their family from death or disease, or some mother would hold her round-cheeked babe up and say, "My child wouldn't have made it into this world alive and whole if not for the healer, Lara."

There were others, though far fewer in number, who would sneer and whisper behind their palms as he rode by, and though they wouldn't say it to his face, he heard from others what they said behind his and Lara's backs. They called Lara whore, not lady, witch, not healer.

She may have cured half the valley of their illnesses, but she had infected him with a sickness the cure for which he would've had to make her what those people called her, his whore. And that he wouldn't do.

Nor would she let him.

Not without a fight.

He already bore her mark that said to the world he'd tried to touch her without her say-so. As did Ranulf, whose story had spread far and wide since Mallus, and who'd added to it since, declaring that he'd touched all of her by her say-so many times before that day, before they'd had a falling-out.

Lara hadn't spoken one word of it to Talon or anybody else he knew of. Of course, that left out Sophie and the entire gaggle of women who lived along the road that ran west from the town's marketplace to Crossroads Keep, all of whom seemed to be related to Berta. There was her daughter and granddaughter, Enid and Marta, who worked at the keep, as well as another daughter, a pretty brunette named Patience with freckles as big and brown as her eyes. Patience was married to a leather worker named Willem, whom Talon had gone to with an idea for a saddle with stirrups, a thing he'd seen horsemen in the east use to great advantage. As he'd explained to Willem, a rider could stuff their boots into these straps with wooden toe holds, allowing them to stand up and over their saddle and turn and twist about without becoming unseated.

They were drawing designs for the stirrups in the dirt floor of Willem's workshop when Wolf came loping in and came straight to Talon for pets.

"Berta said Wolf had become fond of you." Willem raised his brows. "You should consider it an honor. The dog doesn't take to many men."

Talon gave Wolf's hind end a good sound pat, and then the dog sidled over to Willem for an ear rub. "He seems to have taken to you as well."

"Aye, well, it took a while," Willem admitted.

Talon glanced out into the empty yard. Lara must've been in the house, for wherever she was, so was Wolf. "You know his mistress well?" he asked Willem.

"My wife is Lara's closest friend." Willem's steady gaze held Talon's. "If it wasn't for the fact that I know from Lara herself that you treat her well and fair, we wouldn't be doing business this or any other day."

Talon had to give the tradesman credit, standing him off for the sake of his wife's friend. He nodded and offered Willem his hand. "Fair enough."

Willem shook his hand and pulled a newly tanned cowhide out to spread on his worktable. They were making their measurements when Wolf pricked his ears forward, then loped back outside to where Lara and Patience and a tow-headed lad of three or four years walked out into the yard. Lara spied his black horse tied to the post by the shop and stopped in her tracks.

"Ladies," Talon called out from the open door. "Good afternoon."

"Good afternoon, Captain." Patience waved over. A gentle breeze pinned her apron to her belly, full and round as a small melon. Following Talon's gaze, she pulled her apron away with a shy grin as Lara strode past him toward the road. He smiled and dipped his head to her, and she gave him her backside, a not altogether unpleasant view. He turned back to Willem and Patience watching him with interest and rubbed the back of his neck, vowing to himself not to be so obvious in his admiration for Lara's twitching skirts in the future.

***

His vow lasted through supper but was broken by breakfast the next morning when Talon caught the sway of Lara's skirts as she cleared away the bowls from the table and disappeared through the kitchen door. He stood and noted several of his men watching him with foolish grins on their faces. At least they were watching him and not Lara, else he'd have to knock a few heads.

"Let's go," he commanded. "Our mounts won't run drills by themselves."

He made it as far as the stables when he realized he'd forgotten his riding gauntlets in his chamber. "Damn it. Phillipe, I need to go back for my gauntlets. Get the men started."

"Yes, Captain."

Talon scowled at his grinning dolt of a lieutenant, who'd been riding him hard over his undeniable infatuation with Lara, then he turned on his heels and strode back to the house, grumbling about being cursed and damned by a twitchy skirt and changeling eyes. The doors to the hall were open for the summer air. When he entered, Lara was tending to Fulrad at his cot by the hearth fire.

Fulrad could speak again, but his mood hadn't improved apace with his ability to talk and be understood. Nor had he even attempted to walk yet, wasting his days and nights camped out on his cot, ignoring the crutches under it, belly aching about anything and everything, but especially about Lara walking around freely while he lay broken and sober. Talon shook his head and set his jaw. Fulrad's neck wounds were healing over without any sign of infection, and his knee, while still a swollen mass of crepitus, was no longer bruised and mottled. The longer he stayed prone, the more his muscles would atrophy, and the less likely it was he'd ever walk again. King's cousin or not, it was time the lazy bastard started helping with his own recovery.

Talon veered from the staircase toward Fulrad and Lara, and he saw her spine and shoulders stiffen. He came to a stop behind her, where Fulrad couldn't see him.

"Where will you go then, eh, bitch?" Fulrad rasped as Lara rubbed a stringent balm on his knee. "Where'll you go when the captain's done with you? After he and his men've had their fill of you? No man'll have you then, a used-up, put-out whore."

The only sign of response from Lara was her stillness before she wiped her hands with a rag and turned to toss it onto the pile of dirty washrags next to the washbasin. She saw Talon, and her cheeks flushed and her chin lifted as she glared daggers at him as if he'd been the one abusing her.

Talon stepped into Fulrad's view and glowered down at him. "If you *ever* dare speak to her like that again, I will personally finish what Wolf started." He laid his hand on the hilt of his short sword as Fulrad shrank into his pelts. "Do we have an understanding?"

Fulrad put a hand to his throat. "Aye, Captain."

"See you keep to it."

Talon turned to Lara and held his hand out. She slapped it away.

"I can take care of myself." She got to her feet and strode out of the hall, up the stairs, and slammed shut the door to the chamber she shared with him. The chamber where he'd left his riding gauntlets sitting on top of his chest.

He gave Fulrad one last, hard glare, then stalked out of the hall and to the stables, where Denys held the Black at the ready. Jumping onto his saddle, Talon sent the stallion into an easy canter and headed for the open field where his troop were riding drills.

"Where are your gauntlets?" Phillipe called out as Talon rode past him to where jumps were set up. "The pair you went back for?"

"In my chamber," Talon snarled over his shoulder. "Caged with a spitting-mad wildcat." He glanced up at the window to his chamber where Lara paced back and forth behind it as Phillipe's laughter drifted over. Talon urged the Black into a slow gallop and circled the stallion around the half dozen jumps, warming the horse up and trying to cool himself down. After the third circle, he looked back up at the chamber window, where Lara was now sitting on the sill, facing the field. He leaned over the Black's withers, and the horse broke into a run and jumped the first and lowest pile of logs without slowing. He reined the Black toward the second, higher jump. If he couldn't reason Lara out of his head, maybe he could ride her out.

Trouble was, the harder he rode, the deeper the stallion's hooves pounded Fulrad's vile words and Lara's flushed cheeks and flashing eyes into his brain. Talon couldn't wait to send the damned drunkard packing. His only qualm would be setting him upon his poor horse. The rangy bay was a foul-tempered beast, but Talon had always put that on Fulrad, for he'd seldom seen a horse go mean for lack of reason.

Lack of reason was certainly what he was suffering from, keeping that thorny beauty in his bedchamber night after night. Despite what he'd told her in the tent the night of Mallus, he did want her, badly. He'd hoped the more he was around her, the more he'd get used to her and the less he'd want her, but the opposite had happened. Every time he so much as looked at her or thought about her, which was about a thousand times a day, he wanted her. It was driving him mad. She was driving him mad.

He sent the Black straight at a jump he could make in his sleep, yet even in his sleep he dreamt of Lara. He looked up to where she sat on the windowsill, the creamy oval of her face framed by her wild mane of auburn curls. Curls that smelled of rose that he itched to bury his nose in and run his fingers through. The Black pushed off his powerful haunches, and Talon leaned over his withers as the stallion took the jump. Midjump, Talon glanced up at the window. Next thing he knew, the Black shied right, and he was sailing over the stallion's head, tumbling head over ass as he hit the ground and cracking his forehead on something hard. He lay there as the world spun around him until he could see one cloud in the sky where there'd been three and then two, then he pushed himself up to sitting, holding his head with both hands as the world resumed its spinning. Something warm and sticky coated his left hand and he lowered it. Blood smeared his palm. His blood. He considered standing, then decided to sit a while longer.

"Captain?" He tried to lift his head and squinted to see who it was that called him, then closed his eyes against the too-bright glare of the sun. "Talon, lad, you all right?"

Only Anglbert called Talon lad. He raised a hand in answer, knowing the pain his own voice would cause him.

"He's alive, at least," another voice, Phillipe's, said. But it was a woman's sandaled foot that stopped toe to toe with his boot.

"Captain?" Lara loomed over him, blocking the sun so he was able to look up at her. She leaned down and gently touched a fingertip to his forehead. "You've got a nasty gash on your head. Which happens when you butt heads with a rock."

"Good thing it was my head, then, eh?" Talon managed to croak out, and she laughed and didn't disagree as a pounding pulsed from his forehead to his crown and down his neck. She pressed a cloth to his wound, and he noticed her bag of medicines at her feet. "How did you come to bring your bag?"

"I saw you fall."

"Oh. Indeed."

Wolf sniffed his boot where his blood had dripped onto the toe, and Talon reached out to pet his head and missed. He heard men's laughter as Anglbert and Phillipe reached down and grabbed him underarm.

"Slowly, slowly," Lara told them as they lifted Talon to his feet. Concerned hazel eyes stared into his, and Talon was glad to see there were only two of them. "Can you stand on your own?" she asked him.

He shifted his feet into a wide stance, braced his legs, and shook off Anglbert and Phillipe. "I can stand." He took a step, then another. "And walk." He wobbled over to the Black, who was holding his right front leg up. Talon started to bend over to take a closer look but had to stop as the pounding in his head turned into the loud rushing of blood. Bracing himself against the stallion's shoulder, he slowly straightened and surveyed the distance back to the stables.

"You know, friend," Anglbert said loudly enough to make Talon wince, "Talon really should be wearing his helmet and gloves if he's going to go around falling off that mule of his."

"That he should, friend." Phillipe smirked. "But then that is the very devil of it, for I've never known him to fall off anything with four legs before, even with a horde of bloodthirsty Saracens trying to knock him off."

"Nor I." Anglbert eyed Talon. "'Tis the curse. He worsens daily with it."

"Aye," Phillipe said solemnly. "It's the curse, poor bastard."

"What curse?" Lara glanced amongst the three of them, innocent of their game. But Talon wasn't. He knew exactly what Phillipe and Anglbert were playing at.

"It's the curse of two braying asses forever at my ears," he growled. He took the Black's reins and stumbled toward the stables.

"Take care, lady," Phillipe called out as Lara followed him and the Black. "He can be a cursed grump."

"Cursed is right," Talon grumbled as he led the limping stallion away. Cursed and damned by the sway of those very skirts following him.

CHAPTER 8

Scars

Lara

"Sit." Lara pointed the captain toward the stool outside of the Black's stall as Denys stabled the stallion. Wolf came sniffing in behind them.

A groan escaped the captain's pressed lips as he sat and leaned his head back against the wall, eyes closed. His sun-bronzed cheeks were paler than usual, with bright pink spots in the middle, and a fine sheen of sweat glistened on his nose and forehead. Wolf lay down at his feet as Lara let the captain rest for the time it took Denys to finish setting the Black up in his stall and another stable boy to bring the two buckets of water she'd asked for, one of which she set down beside the captain and the other in the stall with the Black. She pulled a stool over to sit facing the captain and dug into her bag for a washing cloth and tubs of cleansing and knitting balms.

"Captain?" He opened an eye and peered up at her. "I'm going to wash the blood from your wound." She dipped the cloth into the bucket of water. He gave her the slightest of nods and closed his eye. "I'll try to be gentle."

He sighed. "I'm sure you will."

Lara wasn't quite sure if he was teasing her or not but decided to let it go. She wiped the drying blood from a gash over his left eyebrow that was an inch in length but shallow enough it wouldn't need stitches, then rinsed the cloth and dipped a corner of it into the cleansing balm and gently washed the skin around the wound. She wiped the soapy balm away and then sat back, letting the wound air dry. "Well. You'll soon have another scar for your collection."

Both eyes now open, he peered up at her, though the flesh around his left eye was already starting to swell. "My collection?" He offered a more lopsided grin than his usual. They both knew he'd caught her watching him strip down to his breechcloth before bed a dozen times at least. "What collection would that be?"

"I am a healer." She felt the sudden need to wipe her own heated face and neck down with a cool rag. "I do notice such things."

He flexed his scarred hand. "As well as give them," he said with a teasing grin.

"You're never going to forgive me for that, are you?" she half teased back. "You know as well as I do you deserved it for your brazenness."

"And had my hand served back to me bloody for my transgression. And rightly so." He held her gaze for a moment, then lifted his marked palm up to her. "Peace, lady?"

Lara took his hand in hers, the feel of his warm skin and calloused palm causing her cooling skin to flush once more. She lowered it to his lap. "Peace, Captain."

He nodded and leaned back against the wall, closing his eyes with a heavy sigh as Lara wrung the washcloth out and hung it over the stall's gate. She put the tub of cleansing balm back in her bag and sat forward, taking in the captain up close. He wasn't a pretty man like Ranulf or the young soldier Dardinel; he had too many scars and his features were too rough-hewn, too hard. But he was a handsome man, ruggedly so, his maleness palpable. He opened his eyes, staring straight into hers.

"So," she said, sitting back and putting a little distance between them, "what is this curse that bedevils you?"

"Curse?"

"The curse that Phillipe and Anglbert spoke of, that causes you to fall from your horse?"

"Ah, that curse." He clamped his lips together and slowly shook his head. He wasn't going to tell her.

"Well then, what must you do to break this curse?"

He snorted and rubbed his jaw. "Nothing much. Just tame a wildcat barehanded without bleeding to death."

"A wildcat? Barehanded?"

He looked down at his scarred palm. "Apparently."

"Then you will be free of this curse?"

He cocked his head at her and shrugged. "Who knows." He laid his head back and closed his eyes with a groan.

It would do no good to press him further, this much Lara knew about the captain. She also knew that curses weren't always so straightforward. Did he really need to tame an actual wildcat, or did the wildcat represent something or someone else? Was it a woman, as wildcats were usually portrayed? The carving she'd found in his chest came to mind, and how Phillipe had described her as a dream. A dream of what, or who? It wasn't her. The captain had declared he didn't want her in no uncertain terms the night of Mallus. As far as Lara knew, he hadn't shown a special interest in any of the women in the valley, though plenty had shown interest in him, especially Ravenna. She'd bought half a dozen vials of love potion from Sophie since the captain had been garrisoned here and had let Sophie know they were all intended for him. That kind of attention could turn any man's head. Lara wrinkled her nose at the thought of the captain burying his nose into Ravenna's hair and breathing in the scent of her rose soap, then admonished herself. Why should she care whose hair he chose to sniff?

She got back to the business of tending to her patient and pulled a long strip of bandage from her bag and set it by the tub of knitting balm, then pressed another dry cloth to his wound to soak up the bloody seepage. He didn't wince or even twitch.

"Captain," she said softly, then louder when he didn't respond. He opened his eyes, and it took him a moment to focus on her. She held a finger up in front of him. "Can you follow my finger without moving your head?" She moved her hand back and forth, and he tracked and followed.

"I know what you're doing." He sat up straighter and took a deep breath in and blew it out. "I've done it a few times myself to men with head wounds."

"Then you know what I'm going to ask you next?"

He took another breath in and exhaled. "Yes, I only see one of you. No, I don't feel dizzy or sick. And yes, my head hurts like hell."

"Good. That's good." Even so, she didn't want him nodding off again. "What sort of short sword is it you carry? It's not what the men of Gaul usually carry. Not a spatha."

He squinted through his good eye at her. "It's called a falcata. The soldiers of Rome use them. They're lighter made than a spatha, but the blade is as strong."

"Was your falcata made in Rome?"

"It was, by the swordsmith Reynaldo."

"The horse head hilt," Lara said. "It fits you."

He cocked his head at her, then winced and cupped the back of his neck.

"You should soak a towel in hot water and lay it across your neck and shoulders," she told him. "It will ease some of the tightness." He grunted, and she scooped some of the knitting balm onto her fingertip. "This is a balm of yarrow and comfrey." She smeared it over his wound then wiped the excess on a rag as he touched a tentative fingertip to his eyebrow. "You're lucky." She unraveled the length of bandage. "It won't need stitching and should heal well with only a bandage for several days."

"Good. I've been pricked by a healer's needle before. It wasn't a pleasant experience."

"Your leg?"

"It took fifteen stitches."

Lara winced involuntarily, her body remembering.

"You've been sewn up too?"

She pushed her left sleeve up and pointed to a faint white line that ran up the inside of her upper arm. "When I was ten, I dove off the old oak into the river and got sliced open by a stick. Sophie closed it with six stitches."

"No fun, is it?"

She shook her head. "None at all." She held the bandage up, and he sat forward. She wrapped it around his head and breathed in the unexpectedly heady scent of man, horse, and leather. "Wash the wound in your bath each night. I'll bandage it again after. Otherwise keep it dry and clean and no more headlong dives into the dirt."

The captain snorted. "Tell it to that brute there." He waved a hand toward the Black. "A stallion who charges into battle but shies away from flies."

The horse snorted right back, and Lara laughed softly as she tied the bandage off. She closed the tub of knitting balm, then put it back in her bag before grabbing an apple from the bottom of it and stepping up to the gate of the Black's stall.

"He'll not let you near him," the captain warned her. "Not when he has his ire up like this."

"We'll see about that," she said in a singsong voice. "Shan't we, Black?" The stallion pricked his ears forward and the captain sat erect on his stool. "You remember me, don't you Black? We first met at the river and then several times since." She held the apple out on her open palm, grinning as the stallion gently plucked it from her hand. "I've been bribing him with apples for a while now."

"Traitor," he growled good-naturedly at the stallion, who munched his apple, unconcerned. The captain stood with a slight groan as she picked up her bag, then followed her into the stall. He took hold of the stallion's bridle and patted his neck as Lara ran a hand over his withers and down his injured foreleg.

"There's a swelling on his fetlock. No cuts or scrapes." She squeezed the joint, gently at first, then applying more and more pressure until the Black tried to pull his leg away, then she slowly bent his hoof forward and backward, noting the stallion's reaction.

She lifted his hoof, taking a good long look at the underside. "His hoof looks fine." She set it back down on the ground and watched as he shifted so the leg didn't bear any weight. Standing upright, Lara ran a hand down the stallion's powerfully muscled back and haunches. "I think he twisted it. Bad enough that he'll need to be kept off it until he can walk without limping." The captain nodded and swayed on his feet. "You should sit and rest as well."

"No, I'm—"

She pointed at the stool on the other side of the gate. "Sit. Now."

"Yes, mistress."

Lara waited until the captain was safely on the stool, then she pulled out the same tub of ointment she used on Fulrad's knee, scooped up a handful, and rubbed it into the stallion's fetlock, grinning as the horse nickered and blew into her hair.

"You should be quite flattered," the captain said as she scooped another handful of ointment from the tub. "He's never let anyone but me tend his wounds before. He can be a contrary beast at times."

Lara grinned. "Much like his master."

"Ouch." He clapped a hand over his heart. "Yet another scar to add to my growing collection."

"One you'll recover quickly enough from, I'm sure." He cocked his head and said nothing, and Lara couldn't read the expression on his face, what with his left eye swollen almost shut and the bandage covering his forehead and brows. "What breed of horse is the Black?" she asked, rubbing the salve into his leg. "I've never seen one so big and black that wasn't a plow horse."

"He's a Friesian," the captain said as Wolf ambled over and laid his head on the captain's lap. "From Friesland, a land far north and east of here." He rubbed Wolf's ear. "Do you know of it?"

"I've heard the name, but that's all I know."

"I went there as an emissary for Charles, ten, no, nine years ago now, and came back with this black brute as an unbroken yearling. There are whole herds there as big and black as him."

Lara stood and wiped her hands on the rag hanging over the gate. "A horse from Friesland, a sword from Rome, a board game from Byzantium. Do you always take something from the places you've been?"

"I suppose I do," he said. "When I choose a place to stay, my land from Charles, I plan on going back to Friesland and buying a dozen good broodmares for this brute to cover and raise sleek black foals for the king's army."

"So." Lara gave the captain a sideways glance. "You do intend to stop your wanderings someday?"

"My wanderings?" He chuffed. "I've been tending to the king's business and fighting his wars."

"And seeing much of the world in the bargain." She recalled the few stories he and Phillipe had told her of their travels, how the captain's eyes would light up with the memories. "You would miss it, I think, traveling the world."

"The travels, yes." He shifted on the stool with a low groan. "But not the traveling. There comes a point in a soldier's life where your body remembers every freezing wet or sweltering hot sky and hard-packed piece of earth you laid your bedroll, where a comfortable bed under a sturdy roof in a dry room sounds better and better."

Lara nodded. "I can understand that. Still, the places you've been, the things you've seen…"

"You would like to see more of this world, I think. To not always stay in this valley."

Lara's heart sank. "Why do you say that? Do you mean to take me from here when you leave?" As his *lidi*, she wouldn't have any say in the matter if he did.

He stared hard at her for a moment, his jaw clamped tight. "Not if you fulfill your obligations to the king before then."

"As I have every intention of doing," she snapped.

He rubbed the back of his neck, then his jaw. "I just meant, the way you listened to Phillipe's and my stories."

"I've swum in the Mediterranean Sea," she told him, surprising herself as well as him. She had determined to tell him as little about herself as possible, to keep as much of her life to herself as she could, yet it felt more right than wrong to be telling him this. Why, she couldn't have said, only that it did. "I've stood in your Neustria Sea as well. We journeyed there the summer I was eight, Sophie, Jumper, and me."

"Jumper?"

"Sophie's rat terrier."

"You and Sophie traveled as far as the Neustria Sea with nothing more than an ankle-biting terrier? And back?"

"We did."

"Why?"

Lara shrugged. "Sophie said we must go and so we went. We left here early spring and returned late autumn."

"Do you always do what Sophie says?"

"Mostly."

He chuffed. "Why do you do what she says, when you don't do anything anybody else says?"

She thought of giving him some smart answer, then decided on the truth. She'd already told him that she and Sophie were witches, as much to make him wary of them both as anything else. Whether he believed it or not was up to him. "Because Sophie has the knowing of things. Things past, present, and future. A sixth sense."

"Sophie the Sixth. I've heard her called this. Nithard called her this. He fears her." He held Lara's gaze. "Why?"

Lara flashed him a feral grin. "She foretold his death. She told him when the first silver showed in his hair, he would die choking on Frank silver." Her grin turned conspiratorial. "They say that's why he dyes his hair and beard black, hoping to cheat death."

The captain barked out a laugh and then hung his head between his hands with a long, drawn-out groan.

"Does your head hurt badly?"

He lifted his gaze to hers. "Not half as much as looking at you does."

Lara stared into eyes as gray and brooding as the sky before a summer storm. Eyes that poured a soft, wet heat into hers. A heat that stirred and simmered deep in her core. A horse whinnied, and startled, she seized the tub of balm and thrust it into the captain's hand. "Rub this into the Black's leg four times a day until the swelling is down. And don't ride him for several days after, for his sake. For your own." She picked up her bag. "I'd advise staying off any horse for at least a day, maybe three. I'll send Denys for you and tell Berta you're to stay in the cool of the hall and do nothing more strenuous than eat pie."

CHAPTER 9

Witches Brew

Talon

Talon turned the roan, an easygoing gelding he used as a secondary saddle and pack horse, off the road onto the path that led past the windbreak of chestnut trees bordering Lara's and Sophie's property. He'd passed the property daily on his rides around the valley but had never ridden onto it. Lara was generally private about her personal life, and he'd respected those boundaries until now. There were questions he wanted answers to and figured Sophie could answer them. Whether she would, he was about to find out.

He pulled the roan up at the end of the path, where a raven cawed loudly as it swooped over and past him. Talon leaned back and shaded his eyes as the bird landed on the roof of the house. Swaying in his saddle, he gripped the pommel and grit his teeth until his blurring vision cleared and he was able to take in the property. The two-story house, though small, was built of stone and wood with a thatched roof and faced west into the open yard and river beyond rather than east toward the road. Vining roses heavy with blooms of red, pink, yellow, and white covered the southern facing, and he breathed in their heady perfume that also seemed to carry Lara's spicy sweet fragrance.

A large bed of purple-flowered rosemary and lavender bushes ran along the southern border of the yard with various herbs growing around and between them. West of the herb garden, sunflowers stood as tall as a man with squash vines climbing their stalks, the yellow and gold flowers buzzing with bees. A small orchard ripe with peaches and plums and summer apples bordered the river, where a wooden deck had been built into the bank, a well-worn path leading from it to the house. To the north side of the orchard, a small barn with a fenced paddock homed Lara's leggy chestnut mare and Sophie's sturdy little dun, both of whom grazed contentedly amongst a small herd of goats as a flock of chickens scratched and pecked the ground around their hooves. The mares lifted their heads and Talon followed the direction of their gazes to the house, where Sophie stood in the open doorway, a ginger tabby rubbing against her skirts.

"Welcome, Captain," she called out.

Talon inclined his head to her. Welcome was a good start. He dismounted and tied the roan off to a post when Wolf came lumbering out of the barn. Talon slapped his thigh, and the wolf-dog went to him, his tongue lolling as Talon patted his head and rubbed his ears.

"You've tamed the wolf, I see," Sophie said, "if not the wildcat."

Talon snapped his head up and grimaced as he swayed back on his heels. His head stopped spinning, if not aching, as Sophie waved him toward the house and then disappeared through the open door. Wolf loped back toward the barn, where Talon assumed Lara was, as the dog was never far from her side.

"Come in." She beckoned from inside the house as he stood in the doorway, then took in his bandaged head and swollen eye and lifted her chin at a table and four chairs. "Sit." She pushed sprigs of cut lavender and rosemary to one side of the table. Talon took the seat facing the open door. "I'll get us both a cup of cool cider."

Talon looked around the tidy house, every corner of which was put to use for one thing or another. A rocking chair sat by the hearth, a pot hanging on the frame over the firepit, unlit in the heat of the day. A spinning wheel and several baskets full of spun wool took up the corner between the hearth and the west-facing window for light, and shelves stacked with tubs of liniments, vials of tinctures, and baskets full of dried herbs and bandages lined the east-facing wall. The rafters were hung with bunches of drying herbs and flowers, and the south wall had a worktable pushed up against it, a bowl of knives and ladles on top, and pots and pans hanging from hooks over it. A ladder led to an upstairs loft, which he assumed was the women's bedchamber.

"I can give you something for your head." Sophie set a cup of cider down in front of him. "Your neck and eye as well."

"Thank you. I'd appreciate that." Talon took a long drink of the cider, letting it slake his parched throat as Sophie took a seat opposite. The fact that she hadn't asked him how he injured his head meant Lara had already told her. Lara, whom he hadn't seen hide nor hair of since he'd ridden up, and who he'd wager coin was hiding from him in the barn. Which was perfect for his purposes. "It was one of your potions I came to inquire about," he told Sophie. "Your love potion. My men have been offered these potions from the women in the valley almost from the day we arrived. I want to know what it is. What it's made of."

"The women in this valley have been giving men this same sweet libation for a score of years, Captain. Your men will suffer no ill effects."

"While that's good to know, it's not what I asked." He sat back and crossed his arms, waiting for her answer. He was a captain of battle-hardened soldiers, a courier who had traveled much of the known world and conversed with kings. He was used to asking a direct question and getting a straight answer. He wasn't going to let Sophie get away with her vague seer's riddles, as Lara had called them.

Sophie held his gaze with her own for a long moment, and then crinkled her eyes as she chuckled. "It's rose hips for vigor, lavender for verve, honey for sweetness and energy, a dash of wild mustard seed for fire, and a drop of peppermint oil for soothing calm."

"That's all?"

"As I said, your men should suffer no ill effects from it." Her gaze narrowed on his. "I do expect you to keep this knowledge to yourself. You are one of only a few who know."

"Why is that?"

"Few ask. And I answer even fewer."

"What about a wildcat?"

Sophie tilted her head at him with a puzzled expression. "Of course, she knows."

"No, what I meant was would she drink this potion?"

Sophie tilted her head in the opposite direction. "It would take a neat trick to get it past her nose. She's been lapping it up since she was a kitten."

Talon nodded and glanced down at his scarred palm. "The trick for me would be to get it anywhere near her nose without being shredded."

Sophie chuckled. "Patience," she advised. "Patience and perseverance, they will get you closest to the wildcat without further bloodshed."

Talon was listening, but he wasn't convinced, which must have shown.

"I've known her since her first mewling hiss," Sophie said. "If she's got her fur up, back away, give her space, let her come to you."

Sophie's advice made sense. It was how Talon would approach an unbroken horse he was trying to tame. Though truth be told, he wasn't sure he wanted to tame Lara. Her sharp points were part of what made her so intriguing, although he could do without her thorns constantly pricking him.

"Taming a wildcat has repercussions for both the man brave enough to try as well as for the wildcat," Sophie said as if reading his thoughts. "In truth, if you weren't a king's soldier, always away at war or court, I might encourage it." She paused and looked deep into his eyes, into his soul. "However, you are what you are, and she is what and where she is, and I would not have her left alone with a belly full of bastard kittens."

Talon sat back, chastened by her cold, hard honesty. "Nor would I."

Sophie pressed her lips together and nodded. "I believe you. Which is why it's better to leave her untamed."

Talon chuffed. "And so I remain cursed on sight and damned by oath."

"The curse I know of. I've seen it on you since day one. But the oath?"

Talon held Sophie's piercing gaze that told him she expected him to be as honest with her as she'd been with him. "It's the oath I pledged outside my tent the night of Mallus while listening to you two talking inside. My oath to give her the protection you made her swear to stay under."

"Ah, I see."

"I'm glad you do." Talon tapped a finger on his cup of cider. "Because I don't. I understand you wanting her under her master's protection while she's a *lidi*, but what's the advantage you see in my protection specifically?"

Sophie sat back and pursed her lips. "Count Nithard fears me. But his son, Ranulf, does not. Despite his foolish bragging, he does fear you, the strength of your sword. That is the advantage I see in your protection."

"What's the cause of the trouble between Lara and Ranulf?" He dreaded the answer. "Was it a love affair gone wrong?"

"Love?" Sophie barked. "Ranulf doesn't know how to love anything or anybody but himself, just like his father."

She stood and rummaged through her baskets, leaving him as unsatisfied with her answer as he was with his own imaginings over what Lara and Ranulf's relationship had been. He drained his cider, and Sophie set a vial of love potion on the table along with several packets of dried herbs.

"Measure out a spoonful of herbs for each cup of boiling water, then stew it until it cools enough to drink." She pushed the packets over. "Most men I would tell to drink a cup before retiring, but you,

you should drink two. And soak in a hot bath each night, as hot as you can stand it."

Talon picked up a packet and sniffed it. "What's in it?"

Sophie laughed. "Do you never imbibe anything you don't know the contents of?"

"Not if I can help it."

"It's feverfew for the ache in your head and neck, nettle and dandelion to reduce the swelling, spearmint for the palate, and valerian and calendula to invite slumber."

Talon pocketed the herbs and eyed the vial of love potion as if it were poison. He stood, and Wolf trotted back into the house and looked up at Talon, his tongue lolling. But still no Lara. Why wouldn't she even come out to greet him, a guest in her house?

"Wolf," he asked the hound, "where's Lara?"

The dog walked over to the cellar door, which creaked and then squeaked as he stood next to it, tail wagging. Talon gave Sophie an accusing glare and then picked up the vial of potion and stuffed it into his pocket. "Madam," he said with a stiff bow of his head. "I do thank you."

***

Talon's head pounded and his neck seized every time he turned his head. He had no stomach for his supper, which had Berta flapping over him like a wet hen. She tsked at his half-eaten bowl of stew and said something in Anglbert's ear that caused the graybeard to pull on it as he peered at Talon. Phillipe spoke into Anglbert's other ear, the two of them grinning and whispering and chuckling until Talon pushed his bowl aside and stood.

"Madam." He ignored the braying asses across the table. "I'm retiring to my chamber. Have the maidservants fill my tub, hot as a man can stand it, and leave a pot of steaming water on the table."

"Of course, Captain." She bobbed her head. "I'll see to it at once."

"Good." He glared at his so-called friends. "Then you can talk of me all you want." *And maybe my* lidi *will come out of hiding.* He glanced over at the kitchen door, through which Lara hadn't walked once this evening, though it was part of her duties to help serve supper. He considered that he was her master and could have commanded her to do so, then he touched his hand to his aching head. He'd bled enough today.

The maidservants filled the tub, eyeing him and giggling every time they walked past with their buckets of steaming water as he sat at the table, letting his tea brew. Once they were gone, he drank one full cup of a brew that was bitter at first taste and then sweet by the first swallow, the easing warmth sliding down his throat and into his belly and leaving a minty taste on his tongue. Drink by drink, swallow by swallow, the knots in his gut and neck began to loosen. He sat back and closed his eyes to a pair of big, hazel cat eyes fringed with thick, dark lashes smiling at him.

"Damned." He straightened, poured his second cup of tea, and downed it as quickly as possible without burning his tongue or throat. Then he stood and stripped and stepped into the tub, lowering his tight, aching body into the welcoming heat of the water. "Cursed and damned."

Grabbing a drying cloth, he rolled it up and set it on the tub's edge and laid the back of his head on it. He closed his eyes and tried to relax and enjoy the enveloping heat, but still those smiling cat eyes danced around his mind along with the constant question of how much Lara had heard of his conversation with Sophie, and how much she'd understood. He soaked and mooned a while longer, but still had no answers, so he sat up and then slowly peeled the bandage from his head and dunked under the hot water, wincing as his cut stung. He soaped, rinsed, and soaked until the worst of the soreness had left his back and shoulders and his head had stopped pounding and merely ached, then he stood and dried himself and put on a clean under tunic and pair of linen breeches. He was sitting at the table, wondering whether to drink a third cup of the tea Sophie had told him to only drink two of, when a soft knock came on the door.

"Enter."

Lara carried a kettle in one hand and a basket in the other. She set the basket full of clean linen bandages down on the table, then poured steaming water from the kettle into the washbasin before setting it down on the table. She pulled a chair out and sat on it so she was almost knee to knee with Talon, eyeing the cut above his brow while Talon studied her, the arch of her brows, the high cut of her cheekbones, the fineness of her pores, and the fullness of her lips. Sophie's tea must have been working, because he was content to sit and stare, to watch her strangely shy smile and concerned gaze as she dipped a cloth in the washbasin, wrung it out, folded it up, and gently pressed it to his wound.

"How does your head feel?" she asked.

"Like the Black sat on it."

"He just about did." She gave a quick grin, making Talon think he should have drunk that third cup after all.

She removed the wet compress, then gently probed the area around his cut with her fingertip, her tantalizing fragrance of rose soap and earthy woman teasing his senses. She lowered her hand, and Talon sucked in a breath of cleansing air as she left the table to rummage through her bag and pull a tub out. She returned to the table with the tub of liniment she'd smeared on his cut in the stables and opened it.

"Willem told me you and Patience have been friends since you were very young." He tried to distract himself from her nearness.

"Aye." She smeared a fingerful of ointment over his wound. "Since the day we met at one year of age."

"She's Berta's daughter?"

"She is."

"Can she cook as well as her mother?"

"Nobody cooks as well as Berta." Lara wiped her hand on the washrag. "But Patience is a good cook, when she gets good food to cook."

"When doesn't she?" he asked as she closed the tub. "The valley is rich in field and the woods in game, and Willem is a skilled leatherworker."

"Aye, he is, when he can get good work."

Talon didn't understand. The valley was full of people, from field workers to farmers to tradesmen, all of whom would need the talents of a leatherworker at one point or another. "When can't he?"

"Whenever it's the count's work," she said, arranging the bandages in the basket. "He refuses to become the count's man, so Nithard won't send work Willem's way. Nor will others who are afraid of the count or covet his trade. So, Willem and Patience keep their free status and their bit of land, and Patience drinks mead and eats squirrel and chicken when she needs red wine, beef, and venison."

"There are difficulties with her pregnancy?"

Lara shrugged. "Maybe. I'm not really sure. It's only…" She held his gaze and measured it, and he must have been the right distance. "I feel anxious about this pregnancy."

"What does Sophie say?"

"That everything's fine."

Talon laid his hand over Lara's on the table, and she didn't pull away. "Yet you're still worried."

Her eyes grew mossy green, and she dropped her gaze to their hands and nodded.

"Well, I'm not," he said, and she lifted her gaze. "Do you know why?" She shook her head. "Because she has the best of healers watching over her."

Lara slipped her hand out from under his and stood. "Is that a compliment, Captain?"

Talon glanced from her hand at her side to her teasing smile, wondering what his name would sound like on her lips. Wondering if things would be different between them had they met under other circumstances. But they hadn't, and things were how they were. "Aye." He answered her with a purposely cocky grin. "A compliment truly meant from an arrogant ass with meager charms."

"I see I pricked your pride that day as well as your hand." She gave the faintest twitch of her full, lush lips.

Talon clutched his hand over his heart. "Some wounds go deeper than others," he said so mournfully that Lara laughed out loud, soft, sweet, and melodious. He reached for her hand, and she skittered away, pulling a bandage from the basket. She stood behind him and started to wrap the bandage around his head. Talon closed his eyes and gave himself up to her gentle but firm touch, her smell, the rhythmic sound of her breathing. Then she stopped and he felt the void as she stepped back from him. He opened his eyes. She was standing in front of him, arms akimbo, surveying her work. Talon reached his hand up and tested the bandage. "You would be a good healer on a battlefield."

"While I thank you for the compliment, Captain," she said as she gathered the used washrag and bandages up, "I have no interest in going to war."

"It was never my intention either."

"Then why did you become a soldier?"

"Why?" He stretched his arms up and back, wincing a little as his shoulders strained and his neck pulled. Still, he wouldn't have left his seat for gold as Lara sat back down across from him. "Why was more *how*."

"How, then?" she pressed, and Talon chuckled.

"Sophie isn't the only one to ferret out information in your house, I see."

She gave him a saucy grin that made him grit his teeth to stop from groaning. "It's we west-end women. It's said a man can't keep a secret from us."

"Is that because you're all witches? Or because you all listen at cellar doors to private conversations?"

Her eyes widened and her cheeks flushed, then she lengthened her spine. "How is that any different from listening to conversations in a language you feigned ignorance of?"

"Other than being in plain sight?" Talon said, and her chin lifted. "Nothing," he admitted. She dipped her chin to him, and they sat silent for a long, uneasy moment, though he could see she clearly had something more to say. "What is it?" She pressed her lips together and shook her head. "Whatever it is, Lara, just say it."

Hazel eyes held his, as hesitant as he had never seen them. "Who, ah, who is the wildcat that has cursed and damned you?"

Talon didn't speak. He couldn't. Neither his mind nor his mouth could form a single coherent response.

"I, ah, I heard you mention her," she added, "when you were speaking with Sophie today."

Talon's first impulse was to tell her. Tell her it was the vision of her standing in the river that had cursed him on sight, his oath outside of his tent that had damned him to protect her not only from Nithard and Ranulf but from himself, from the fate that Sophie had warned him of. For Sophie was right. He was a soldier in the king's army. He would leave here, he would leave her, sooner more likely than later. He had no intention of leaving her with his bastard in her belly. "Then it's Sophie you should ask," he said at last. "Or any other west end woman, for I will not tell you, and you cannot witch it out of me."

***

Lara

The captain pushed himself up from his chair, gimped over to the bed with a cricked neck and crooked spine, and lay down flat on his back with a stifled groan. Lara set the used water basin and rags outside the chamber door and then wandered around, picking up and refolding clothes already folded and stacked on the captain's chest.

She set another log to the hearth fire, though it was plenty big and warm enough, and moved one of the white Shah knights to block a black bishop. She glanced at the captain, his eyes closed, his breathing slow and rhythmic.

"Sweet Mary, Mother of Jesus," she cursed softly, used to having the chamber to herself well into the night. "How am I going to sleep with him here early tonight?" Wolf ambled over and nosed the closed drapes to the little bathing antechamber and then looked up at Lara, wagging his tail. Lara pushed the drapes back and swirled a hand through the still-warm tub water. Between treating the captain in the stables and his showing up at her and Sophie's house that afternoon, she hadn't bathed in the river today. A warm bath sounded enticing. "Good idea, Wolf."

She gathered her nightshift, closed the drapes, and sat on the edge of the tub, untying her braid and drumming up enough courage to get naked with the captain in the chamber, even if he was sound asleep and she was enclosed, out of sight. After stripping quickly, she stepped into the tub and lowered herself chin deep into the water, which smelled of sandalwood soap. Of the captain.

Sophie had been right about him figuring out Lara had been listening to their conversation, her ear pressed up against the cellar door. She hadn't been able to hear or understand most of what was said between them, but she'd heard him mention his wildcat, and she'd understood the melancholy timbre of his voice when he'd called himself cursed and damned. Again, Ravenna's pretty, pouty face came to her unbidden, and the hairs on the back of her neck stood straight up. Ravenna had bought three more vials of love potion from Sophie only a few days ago and had let it be known that all three were meant for the captain. Was that why he'd asked Sophie about the potion's ingredients? Had he drunk Ravenna's offerings? Knowingly? Willingly?

Lara took several deep breaths in and out, in and out, trying to clear her mind of Ravenna and potions and the captain and his curse, but her mind kept returning to a pair of brooding gray eyes, one bruised and swollen, staring at her and telling her it hurt more.

"More." She sighed, letting the look in his eyes wash over her. Why would it hurt him to look at her? Did he blame her for his falling off the Black? All she'd done was sit in the window and watch him on the stallion, admiring the way horse and rider moved as one, churning up earth and sailing over logs with a power and grace she hadn't witnessed since watching another horse and rider win a tournament in Neustria fourteen summers ago. The same summer she'd told the captain about in the stables, where he'd looked at her so that her breath caught and her insides stirred just thinking about it now, about more. "Arrgghh."

Lara kicked the tub and slapped the water. She didn't understand it, any of it, any of him. She sat up, slapped the water again with a wordless curse, then splashed down and submerged her entire body under the water. Maybe she could drown the man from her mind.

She'd only released one bubble from her nose when she was yanked up to her knees and then her feet, gasping for air and spitting mad. She tried to push away, but the captain's arms were like iron bands holding her tight, her bare breasts pressed against his chest.

"You bastard." She swung her head up, slamming into the captain's jaw. He let out a grunt of pain but didn't loosen his hold on her.

"I thought you were drowning." His ragged voice sounded as if he'd swum a league through a storm-tossed sea to get to her. He ran a hand through her wet hair and pulled her head back until her gaze met his. "God's blood, Lara, I thought you were drowning."

She was drowning. She was standing in a tub of water drowning in the wet heat she felt everywhere her bare skin touched him, from her breasts plastered to his soaked tunic to her belly, which met his with every gasping breath. His body was hard against hers, giving off a heat that Lara's craved. She leaned into it, into him, and the shock of it shot through her and stood him straight up. He dropped his hold and stepped back, away from her. He set his jaw, and the scar on his cheek blazed white as he raked her from head to toe with his steely gaze.

Lara covered herself with her hands. "You're bleeding." Her voice was a hoarse whisper as she shivered.

He touched a finger to his bloodied lip and glared at it, at her. "Don't I always?" He turned on his heel and was gone.

Gone from the bath chamber where Lara stood dripping wet and naked, not knowing whether to laugh or cry or curse or scream. Gone from the bedchamber by the thud of the door slamming shut and a loud shouting of men's voices from the hall below.

Her mind numb, her senses scattered, she forced herself to think, to move, to dry herself and don her nightshift before stepping out into the empty bedchamber. The captain's tunic was wadded up on his bed, the entire front of it soaked from where her wet, naked body had pressed up against it. Lara picked it up and held it to her nose, breathing in the damp scent of sandalwood and man, of him. She threw it back down on the bed.

"Don't be a fool, Lara," she chastised herself. "You were a naked woman in a man's arms, was all." *A big, strong, upright man.* "Don't make more of it than it was. Don't end up as Sophie warned, with a belly full of his child. Leave that to his wildcat."

***

Warmth swamped Lara's arms and legs, and she leaned into it, seeking a hardness her body craved, sighing with disappointment as she sunk into softness instead. She burrowed her nose deeper into the softness, catching soap, leather, and musky male scents. Talon. Rolling onto her back, she opened her eyes to a drape-less bedframe.

She shot up. What was she doing in Talon's bed, with his tunic in her hand and the sun's rays shining in on her through the open window? And when had he become Talon instead of Captain? Wolf lay beside her, thumping his tail, and she buried a hand into his fur, into something familiar as she glanced around the chamber, empty but for them. The open drapes to the bathing chamber caught her eye, and it all came back. She remembered Talon yanking her up out of the tub water, soaking wet and naked. She remembered the hard breadth of his chest pressed against hers, the rawness of his voice in her ear, the feel of his hand in her hair. She remembered the searing heat of his gaze, his loins. She remembered when he'd become Talon.

She threw his tunic down onto the pillow where she could still see the dent from her head and jumped from the bed as if singed.

"Sweet Mary, Mother of Jesus." The way she'd leaned in to him…. The way he'd stiffened and stepped away from her…. "What have I done? He thinks me a wanton woman. A woman he doesn't want."

She started to pace, trying to calm herself, to keep from bursting into tears of confusion and frustration. Why had she leaned in to him? Why did she want to do it again? To feel his hardness against her and drown in eyes that filled her with her own strange heat? Why, if he didn't want her, was want all she felt when he looked at her the way he had last night? The way he'd looked at her in the stables and told her it hurt him more. More than what? She stopped pacing and stood at the open window, staring out into the sky as if it could give her answers. The only answer it gave her was that she'd slept late into the morning.

"Come on, boy," she told Wolf as he pushed his nose into her hand. "We'd better get moving. Berta will be furious with me for missing breakfast."

Yet when Lara walked into the kitchen where Berta was kneading and flouring loaves of rye, the cook only gave her a cheery smile.

"Did you have a good sleep, dearie?"

Lara nodded sheepishly and poured herself a cup of cider from the pitcher.

"Good, good," Berta said. "The captain'll be pleased to hear it when he returns."

"Returns?"

"Oh, aye, he's gone hunting. Anglbert's to be in charge while he's away, and we were to let you sleep in. That's what the captain told us when he came down this morning."

"This morning?" That meant he'd gone back up to his chamber at some point, that he'd seen her sleeping in his bed with his tunic pressed to her nose.

Berta handed Lara a slice of bread. "Came down at the break of dawn, ate a bowl of porridge, and had me pack him three days' worth of food."

Lara let out the breath she'd been holding, grateful for the time and the distance and more than a little worried he'd left so disgusted with her. "I'm off, then, Berta." She took the bread with her to eat on the way home, where she would have to try to hide her flustered thoughts from Sophie.

"Let Phillipe know."

"Phillipe? Why?"

"Captain said to."

CHAPTER 10
Orders

Lara

Phillipe waited on the bench outside the stables, his dappled gray saddled and ready to go. "Shall I keep a discreet distance?" he asked as Lara stopped by him. "Or would you like a ride?"

"I'll walk, thank you. But you needn't keep your distance. Your company would be welcome."

"I'm glad somebody thinks so." He led his horse alongside her. "Talon was in no mood for it this morning."

Lara gave Phillipe a sideways glance as they walked through the gate and onto the road. "Was Tal… the captain angry when he left this morning?" she asked, dreading his answer, yet needing to know.

"The man was in about as foul a temper as I've ever seen him."

Lara's heart sank. The expression on her face must have as well, because Phillipe reached out and laid a brotherly hand on her shoulder.

"Maybe if you told me what happened?"

A vision of her naked body pressed up against the captain caused Lara's cheeks to flush and Phillipe to stare at her with raised brows. She shook her head as if she could shake the shameful vision out and tried to remember what had passed between them before. "I, ah, I asked him about the wildcat that has cursed him."

Phillipe raised his brow. "What did he say?"

"That I should ask one of my west-end witch cronies." She eyed Phillipe. "What if I asked you?"

He pressed his lips together and shook his head. "I cannot. I've been sworn to silence upon pain of death or dismemberment."

Lara chuffed. She and Phillipe both knew the threat would never be carried out. He was the captain's oldest and closest friend. "So which witch should I ask?"

"Ask any one of them, I would imagine they all know."

Lara didn't understand. Why was the identity of this wildcat a secret only to her? Did the captain not trust her to keep her tongue if asked? Hadn't she been keeping her tongue all this time the people of the valley had been calling her his whore? She glanced at Phillipe, whom the captain had ordered to keep watch over her while he was gone because he didn't trust her not to run away, which meant he didn't trust her to keep her word. She kicked a pebble with the toe of her sandal and sent it skidding across the road.

"I wouldn't worry over much about Talon," Phillipe said. "Whatever happened between you, he'll come around. The man is a great horseman and captain of men, but he knows nothing of women."

Lara let out an unladylike snort. "I find that hard to believe." She'd seen the way Ravenna and other women in the valley looked at the captain. The way they looked talking about him as they paid her good coin for vials of love potion. All he had to do was drink one of their offerings, and he'd be offered anything he wanted from any one of them.

"I'm not saying he hasn't known his share of women," Phillipe continued, and her cheeks flushed hotter. "Only that he doesn't really *know* women."

Lara swiped at her cheeks and eyed Phillipe. "But you do." It was more statement than question.

"I am the middle child of seven," he told her. "With a brother and two sisters born before and after me, and a mother, God rest her sainted soul, who ruled us all, including my father, with a velvet fist." He smiled, a little sad and wistful. "Aye, lady, I know women better than most men."

"And the captain?"

"Is the second of five brothers, who watched his mother die in childbirth when he was a stripling lad of eight years. And who, at the age of twelve, was sent by his still-grieving father to the church to become a priest."

Lara felt keenly for the boy the captain had been. She may never have known her mother, but she had Sophie. "Does he remember his mother well?"

"He keeps the memory of her close. Yet when he speaks of her, he speaks of her smile. Like the sun beaming down on him. He says no other woman has ever smiled at him like that, only a young girl in side braids with a sprinkle of freckles across her nose."

"He doesn't speak of her often, then?"

"His mother? Or the girl?"

Lara gave Phillipe a look from beneath leveled brows, which made him laugh.

"My sister, Evangeline, could give that very same look," he said. "And no, the captain doesn't speak of the girl or his mother often, rarely, in fact."

"I never knew my mother," Lara told him. "I think it would be much harder to have known her and then to lose her at such a tender age."

"My mother passed three years ago." Phillipe turned to a more somber tone. "When I was a man fully grown and out of my family home over twelve years, and it near did me in. Talon was a good friend to me through those dark days."

"I'm sure he was." If Lara had learned anything about the captain, it was how solid and steadfast he was, stubbornly, maddeningly so at times. She'd also learned more about the captain's past in the last quarter league than she had in the last thirty days, so as long as Phillipe answered her questions, she would keep asking them. "How long was the captain in the monastery?"

"Four years," Phillipe said, and Lara's jaw dropped. "I know." Phillipe laughed. "Can you think of a least likely match between church and man?"

"Actually, I was thinking he likely spoke Latin better than I." She recalled the things she and Sophie had spoken of in Latin in front of him, of their plan for her escape from the bathing chamber. And then her thoughts went to last night, how she'd pressed her naked body against his when she should have pulled away. As he did.

Phillipe gave her shoulder a brotherly squeeze. "I don't know what happened between you two last night, but I do know a smile of welcome from you when Talon returns, and he'll forgive you anything."

Lara shook her head. "He was angry when he left."

"He'll have three days to cool off." Phillipe wanted to make her feel better, she was sure, yet his choice of words caused her body to flush from head to toes at the tactile memory of the captain's hard heat against her skin. She almost tripped over nothing, and Phillipe grinned at her in a way that wasn't helping her recover her step or her composure, though he did have the good graces to remain silent until she could meet his gaze again. "I was thinking," he said when she did. "Since I'm to be your guardian shadow these next few days, how would you like to learn to play Shah?"

"I'd like it very much." The game had interested her greatly the night he and the captain had played in their chamber.

"Tonight then, after supper. But for today, where am I to shadow you from?"

"You really don't have to, you know. I won't tell if you don't."

"You wouldn't, would you?" Phillipe wagged a finger at her. "But I would know. And if anything happened to you, the captain would have my boll... head."

It was useless to argue. The captain, who obviously thought her too troublesome to behave herself, had given his orders. "Since it's well into the afternoon already, you may shadow me at my home. At what was once my private home."

"I do apologize."

Lara laughed. She'd always liked Phillipe, as little as she knew him, and the more she knew him, the more she liked him. She eyed him with mock severity. "We'll see if Sophie even lets you in the door."

Sophie not only let Phillipe in, but after an afternoon of showing him around their property, she sent him back to the keep with half a peach pie.

"Sustenance for Lara's Shah lesson tonight." She grinned, and it earned a wink of his blue eyes and a kiss on her weathered cheek.

The lesson went long into the night as the game was complicated, but Phillipe was a good teacher and, he said, Lara a quick learner. By the time the pie was eaten and Phillipe said his good nights, the moon was high in the midnight sky. Yawning, Lara gazed longingly at the captain's bed, which was so much larger and softer than her little cot. She circled it like an unsprung trap, edging closer each pass until she picked up his pillow and held it to her nose, breathing in the mingled scents of sandalwood and rose, then tossed it onto the bed and plopped down on her cot.

She dreamed of black and white knights carved of stone and bone, chasing a woman of wood across a checkered board. Then Lara was the woman, a woman of flesh and blood, standing naked in the middle of a river with a knife in each hand as a huge, black warhorse with ivory-boned tusks charged her. A gloved hand grabbed her by the arm, jerking her off her feet and pressing her to the hard breadth of a man's armored chest, the metal so cold it burned her skin.

She woke with a start, her heart beating through her ribs. The first gray steaks of dawn lit the sky through the open window, and Lara rose from her cot. She'd never get back to sleep.

Phillipe waited for her outside the stables after breakfast, and they walked to her house with Phillipe leading his horse as they had yesterday. Sophie took advantage of his presence and set them to thatching holes in the barn's roof. It was hard, hot, dusty work, but with Phillipe's help and company, the time passed quickly. And it kept Lara from constantly worrying about the captain and all that had happened between them the night before he'd left on his hunting trip.

After supper at the keep, Phillipe walked Lara up to her and the captain's chamber. They drank wine and played Shah, and she managed to capture one of his black knights before he took her white queen and king.

"Tomorrow night, then?" Phillipe asked now they were done and he prepared to leave. "I'll give you a chance to capture both my knights."

"The captain will be back," Lara reminded him.

"He can play winner next time." Phillipe threw her a wink and a grin.

Lara grinned back, looking forward to it. Shah was a game of strategy and constant planning; she could see why the captain liked it. If she'd learned anything about him, it was that he seldom did anything without a plan. "I'll bake pies," she told Phillipe. "Strawberry for the captain and peach for you."

She may not have known what she was going to say to the captain when he returned, but she could bake him his favorite pie. Sweeten his ear.

***

Lara marked the measuring string around Patience's belly and studied her friend's face, noting the deepening hollows of her freckled cheeks and the dark circles under her eyes. "The babe is growing bigger whilst you are growing thinner."

"I did the same with Wyatt."

"No, you weren't this thin with Wyatt. Nor this tired."

"I didn't have a three-year-old to chase after then." Patience smiled indulgently as her son burst into the house from his father's workshop. Willem and Phillipe had gone there to discuss Phillipe's order for a saddle with stirrups like the one Willem was making for the captain.

"Papa said... Papa said bwing him and Phiwip dwink, pease." Each freckle on the lad's cheeks mirrored his mother's, only somehow more chaotic as he jumped in place. Lara beamed down at her godson.

"Tell Papa we'll be right out with their drinks, thank you," Patience told Wyatt, who turned a full circle and ran back out of the house.

Wolf looked up at Lara, tongue lolling and tail wagging.

"Go." She waved him off, and the hound loped after Wyatt. Patience started to push herself up off her stool. "You sit," Lara ordered. "I'll get the mead." She filled two cups from the pitcher on the kitchen table and set them down on the small table beside Patience. "There's something I want to ask you."

"Ask." Patience offered a quizzical brow. In all the years they'd known each other, they'd rarely couched their questions. But that was part of Lara's problem: she wasn't sure she wanted to know the answer. "Lara?"

"Do, ah, do you know who the captain's wildcat is?"

Patience's brows arched. "Aye."

"Is it... It isn't Ravenna, is it?"

"Ravenna?" Patience said with a laugh. "No, it isn't."

"Oh." Lara let her breath out in a rush. "Good."

"What made you think it's Ravenna?"

"She bought three vials of love potion from Sophie and made sure to tell her all three were meant for the captain."

Patience flicked her hand dismissively. "From what I know of the captain, he'd rather drink the Black's piss than a love potion from Ravenna."

Lara dropped her jaw. "I can't believe you said that."

Patience shrugged. "It's the truth."

She eyed Lara and laughed again, making Lara feel like a fool. She was acting like one too, not just up and asking Patience who the wildcat was. Yet she was suddenly skittish of hearing the answer. Maybe she was better off not knowing. Besides, it really wasn't her business. The captain and his troop would be leaving the valley sooner or later, and she would be staying here, unless she hadn't paid off her debt and he took her with him, in which case she should've been happy to sell Ravenna a dozen vials of love potion, triple strength.

"Mama, Mama, Mama." Wyatt ran back in waving his arms in wild circles. "Capin's here, Capin's here, an he bring Papa a buck wif big aners an Granmama peasants to cook."

"Peasants?" Patience looked from Wyatt to Lara, who peered out the window to see the captain's two geldings tied to the post, one packing a buck and a brace of birds.

"Pheasants," she told Patience, who shook her head with a giggle.

The captain stood with his back to the house as Willem and Phillipe hoisted the buck from his horse and laid it on the ground. He wore a vest of sleeveless leather over his bare, tanned arms, and breeches that hugged his well-muscled thighs, the length of which Lara could still feel pressed against hers. Wyatt ran out of the house with Wolf on his heels, and the captain turned and grinned at the lad and the hound, his teeth white against the black of his beard. He looked wild and untamed: a true hunter. He glanced over at the window Lara watched from, and she sucked her belly in as he had his when she'd leaned in to him and felt his hard heat against her nakedness.

CHAPTER 11

Names

Talon

Talon thumped his chest and braced himself as Wolf planted his front paws on his shoulders. "Hello, old man." He rubbed Wolf's ears. "How've you and your mistress fared while I've been away?"

Wolf gave him a big slurp on his chin, then dropped down and ran over to Lara as she came out of the house with Patience. Talon had planned on having until after supper before seeing Lara and speaking to her about what had happened between them the other night, but his plans seemed to mean nothing when it came to her.

"Come, Patience," Willem said as the women walked over. "See what Captain Guiscard has brought us."

"Wyatt said he brought us a buck." She looked to Talon as she stopped by Willem. "Not that I'm ungrateful, far from it, Captain, but why?"

"I wanted the antlers for carving," Talon told Patience. "And a bit of the hide for my saddle, the rest is yours."

"You have twenty men to feed," she said. "Surely they would enjoy fresh venison?"

Talon shrugged. "They eat more than enough venison on the march, hunting as we go." That wasn't a complete lie. They did eat venison on the march, whenever they were lucky enough to get it. He glanced meaningfully at Phillipe, whose eyes widened with understanding.

"We would all prefer your mother's roast pig any day," Phillipe added. Which was also true. The men would prefer anything Berta cooked to camp food.

Patience eyed Talon and Phillipe, clearly hesitant to believe them. Willem laid a hand on her belly and whispered something in her ear.

"Thank you, Captain," she said. "It's very generous of you."

"You're most welcome." Talon allowed himself a small smile of satisfaction. At least this plan of his had worked. Patience would have the red meat Lara said she and the babe needed and Willem would have an extra hide to work and sell. He chanced a glance at Lara, who smiled at him as bright and warm as the summer sun. "Come on," he said to Phillipe before his renewed resolve to keep his honor and hers melted into a pitiable puddle at his feet. "Let's get this buck gutted and skinned. I've a hankering for a bath and roast pheasant for supper."

"Willem and I can dress the buck." Phillipe offered a grin that meant he was up to no good. "You go, get these birds to Berta and take your bath. Take Lara with you. She has a couple of pies to bake." He turned his grin on Lara. "Peach for me and strawberry for you, free of charge as I recollect."

"A free pie?" Talon eyed Lara as his belly rumbled loudly. "From our mercenary friend here?"

Lara bristled, Phillipe laughed, and Willem and Patience shook their heads at each other as Talon swung up onto the roan's saddle and gathered the sorrel's reins.

"In that case." He offered Lara his arm. "Can I give you a ride?"

"I can walk."

"Yes, but riding will get you there faster. I promise I won't bite."

She looked at him as if he'd devour her whole. "I'll walk." She turned to Patience. "I'll be back to check on you in a few days. Be sure to eat as much venison as you can stomach."

"She will." Willem gave Lara a nod, then another to Talon. "Thank you."

Talon turned the roan toward the road as Lara took off running. It was over a league back to the keep, but when she took her skirts in hand, he knew she meant to run the entire way. He kept the horses to her pace and sat back in his saddle, admiring the flash of her shapely calves, slim ankles, and the sway of her skirts. Remembering how he'd chased those skirts through the woods and brambles a moon ago now.

The guard at the watchtower called out their return, and Anglbert was at the gate, waiting with a parchment in hand.

"A missive from the king," he said as Talon dismounted. "It came this morn."

Talon unrolled the parchment. "We're to meet Charles and the returning army." He looked up at the gathering crowd of soldiers and villagers and saw Lara had stayed to hear as well. "We leave in three days' time." Her eyes grew wide as he held her gaze for a moment before turning to Anglbert. "Send a man to Count Nithard. He's to collect the valley's war tithe in fresh supplies, which we're to take to Charles."

"Aye, Captain. I'll send Oswald and Dardinel."

Talon spied Denys and waved him over. "Take the pheasants to Berta." He handed the lad the roan's and sorrel's reins. "Tell her the count, and however many men he travels with, will be supping with us this evening. She'll know his numbers better than I."

"Aye, Captain."

The crowd dispersed as Anglbert gave out more orders in preparation for the evening and the march, leaving Talon standing there with Lara.

"Lady?"

"I, ah, I wanted to thank you," she said. "For the buck. For Patience and her babe."

He grinned, remembering how hard it'd been for her to thank him for saving Wolf's life, for anything. "You're welcome."

She grinned back, quick and fleeting, before dropping her gaze from his with a pretty blush to her cheeks. Talon thought it a good time to beat a hasty retreat and started for the hall.

"Captain?" Lara stepped a little closer.

He stopped. "Yes?"

"I want to go with you."

"With me?"

"On the march. To meet the returning army."

"What? Why?"

"I can serve as your healer. It would fulfill a season of military service, which would pay off my wergeld."

"No."

"Why not?"

"Because war is no place for a woman. You yourself said you'd never willingly go to war."

"But this wouldn't be war," she argued with a stubborn set of her chin. "You're just meeting up with the king and the army. Bringing them fresh supplies and escorting them back to Gaul."

"Back through mountains crawling with Basques."

She lifted her chin another notch. "I deserve the chance to work off my wergeld."

"No."

"But—"

"God's blood, Lara. These same Basques lost their city of Pamplona to the army of Gaul. We burned their city, their homes, their—" The cries of women and screaming children assaulted Talon's ears, the stench of burning flesh his nose. "No. Don't mention it again."

***

Lara

Lara considered putting extra salt in the captain's strawberry pie, and would have, but for the fat buck he left with Willem and Patience. Kneading and rolling the dough for the crust with a ferocity that raised Berta's brows, Lara felt the cook's proprietary eye on every berry she pared and every peach she pitted until the pies were safely in the ovens.

"Here." Berta handed her a bowl of risen bread dough. "Pound on this awhile, then if you still feel the need to pummel something, there are pheasant to pluck."

Lara handed the dough over to Enid and grabbed the pheasants, which she not only plucked but spit and roasted too, preferring the solitude of the roasting pit where she could watch the comings and goings of the soldiers and workers in the courtyard to the noisy, crowded bustle of the kitchens. She saw the captain once, bathed and dressed in his good forest green jerkin, leaning over the cooling pies Berta had pulled from the ovens before she chased him off. He'd glanced around the grounds until he spied Lara, then stood there staring at her for a moment before turning and striding back into the hall.

The sun was touching the peaks of the western hills when the watch called out the count's arrival. Lara kept to her seat at the roasting pit, well hidden from the front entrance to the hall where the count and his company would enter. She glanced at the door to the indoor kitchens where she, a lidi, would enter through to serve the company. The captain stepped out of it, looked straight at her, then turned around and went back in.

"The captain," she said to Wolf, who had his nose as close to the roasting pheasant as possible without singing his whiskers, "sometimes he does the oddest things."

Soon enough, Berta waved at her from the same door as two kitchen maids headed toward the roasting pit with platters for the pheasants.

"Come, Wolf." The hound would stay inside the indoor kitchens while she helped serve the meal. "Time's up."

She ran her fingers through her hair and plaited it into one long braid as she walked to the kitchens, then removed her work apron and smoothed her skirt and stood for Berta's inspection.

"Take the platters of bread and cheeses first," Berta ordered as the kitchen maids carried the roasted pheasants in. "Then the squash and green beans and the cold ham while I carve the pheasant."

Lara picked up a platter of fresh baked rye breads and herbed cheeses, squared her shoulders, and stepped into the dining hall. Count Nithard and his son and daughter sat to the captain's right, and the count's men-at-arms mingled in amongst the garrisoned soldiers. She carried the platter over and stepped between Phillipe and Tree. They sat across from the captain, and she set the platter down before dipping her head to the captain, the ranking host of the meal, and bit down on a grin at the wary expression on his face. He looked worried about what she might do or say in front of the count and his company. Pressing her lips tight, Lara meekly dropped her gaze to her hands, stepped away from the table, and turned for the kitchens.

"I see you tamed your vixen *lidi*, Guiscard," Ranulf said loudly, though only his father sat between him and the captain. "Well done."

"I see your manners haven't improved one bit, Midered," the captain answered as Lara made the kitchen door and pushed through it.

"The snake," she hissed as the door shut behind her. Then it opened again as Enid blew in.

"That wasn't a very good start to the meal." Enid shook her head.

Berta paused her carving knife and fork over the pheasant. "What happened?"

"The captain and Ranulf were at each other over Lara from almost the moment she walked in," Enid told her mother, who tsked at Lara.

"Excuse me." Lara set her hands on her hips. "But wasn't I the one bowing and scraping? Wasn't I the one insulted by Ranulf?"

"And wasn't it the captain who took Ranulf to task for it?" Enid challenged.

"It isn't my fault the captain despises Ranulf," Lara said. "In fact, it shows his good sense."

Berta set down her knife and fork and put her palm to Lara's forehead. "Are you feeling all right? Because I'm fairly certain you just said something nice about the captain."

Lara playfully slapped Berta's hand away. "I could stay here in the kitchens with you, Tante," she pled, her grin dripping honey.

"No." Berta picked up the fork and knife. "Now they've seen you, they'll be looking for you and wondering why you stopped serving."

"You're right." Lara huffed. "I should've slit Ranulf's throat that day instead of his chin. I could've buried him in the woods, and nobody would've ever known."

"You would have." Berta pointed the knife tip at Lara.

"Aye, well." Lara hoisted a platter of cold ham. "I still say it would've been worth it."

Apparently, Nithard had taken control of his son, because Ranulf kept quiet and only insulted Lara with his sulking scowl as she set the platter of ham down. Both the count and his son wore the full Roman robes they'd worn at Mallus and looked rather foppish compared to the captain and his men in their leggings and jerkins. Lara had never seen the captain in a robe, but assumed he owned one, for he'd been at court with kings, a thing she had to admit intrigued her about him.

That he intrigued Ravenna, who wore a body-skimming gown of red silk with a low-cut bodice, was as obvious as the woman's preening smiles as she leaned forward to face him and afford him a better view of her charms. That he steadfastly ignored her smiles and her charms gave truth to Patience's assertion that Ravenna wasn't his wildcat, which somehow made Ranulf's leers easier for Lara to stomach.

The main course done, the captain and the count started making their plans for the march to meet Charles and the returning army.

Serving the honeyed berries, Lara heard them discussing a cook's wagon. The captain's company didn't travel with one, so the count would have to provide one.

"There is a retired soldier the next province over who I've heard will hire himself and his wagon out," Nithard told the captain.

"One cook for our twenty and your fifteen?" The captain speared a berry. "He'll need a helper."

"Begging your pardon, Captain." Lara formed a plan as she spoke. "I know of a lad who would hire out as a cook's helper to serve out his season of military duty."

"Go on," the captain said.

Lara glanced down at the platter of meat scraps. "His name is Hamm. He's the only son of a widowed mother who taught him how to cook."

"Does he cook as well as you?" Phillipe asked, and Lara froze, fearing he'd seen right through her crazy plan. Then she remembered how he'd eaten her cooking at her house the past few days.

"Almost," she said.

"Then I say aye," Phillipe told the captain. "Hire the lad and ease his widowed mother's worries."

"You would," a harsh, hoarse voice rasped. All eyes, all ears, turned to Fulrad, who sat at table to sup with the company for the first time since his injuries. "You would know," he rasped louder. "You were up in the captain's chamber with her every night he was gone, tasting her cooking." He jerked his head toward a horrified Lara. "I seen you. Hell, everyone here seen you following her around by day and going up to her chamber by night, they're just too afraid to tell the captain."

The hall was silent but for the scraping of Phillipe's chair as he stood.

"It was by the captain's orders that I stayed by Lara's side during the day." He spoke slowly, clearly, to the room at large, then he turned to the captain, whose jaw was set as hard and unyielding as stone. "After supper, we played Shah in your chamber before I came back down each and every night."

The captain nodded wordlessly at Phillipe before glancing at Lara, his expression inscrutable.

"You, Fulrad." The captain kept his voice as steady as his glare. "You have slandered my good friend and comrade, as well as my lidi, who has done nothing but serve me and my men well. You are no longer welcome at this table. Leave it. Now."

"I am the king's cousin." Fulrad puffed his chest out. "You cannot ban me."

"Try me," the captain said, and for the first time since Lara had known Fulrad, he made the smart choice and said nothing. "Now go," the captain told him. "Go find your corner to squat in and remain there until I return with your cousin the king. Then he may deal with you."

Lara shook as Fulrad pushed himself up onto his crutches and hobbled over to his pallet, muttering curses under his wheezing breath. When she looked back to the table, the captain was watching her, the telltale scar on his cheek gone white. With a quick bob of her head and a dip of her still-shaking knee, she turned and walked as fast as she could without actually running to the kitchens.

With Wolf at her side, she pushed open the kitchen door to the outside and then she did run, straight for the roasting pit. Sitting on the bench, she poked at the fire's embers and Fulrad's vile accusations, at the captain's expression before he heard Phillipe's explanation, and how the captain had believed Phillipe without hesitation. Worried he wouldn't have believed her so readily, not after she'd practically thrown her naked self at him. Which she tried desperately not to think about.

Instead, she thought about how she'd set herself up to pose as a lad, a cook's helper, who would be marching with the captain's and the count's company of men to meet the king's army. How once the march was completed, she would have fulfilled a season of military duty in lieu of Fulrad, and how the king himself would have to declare her wergeld paid and her freedom earned.

The slow thump, thump, thump of Wolf's tail interrupted her musings. Looking up from the embers, she saw the captain walking toward them and hoped he couldn't see her face in the dark. If she looked as guilty as she felt, she'd be a dead giveaway.

"Here you are." He didn't sound angry, but Lara thought it good to apologize nonetheless.

"I'm sorry, Captain," she said. "I know I shouldn't have left the hall without asking your permission."

"Don't worry about it. It was probably the smart thing to do."

"May I quote you on that for Sophie when she hears about it?" And she would.

"You may." The captain offered a slow smile in the fading embers of the fire, and she smiled back at him, relieved. The whites of his teeth disappeared, and he coughed once. "Will you return to our chamber with me? I've a hankering to play a game of Shah, and Phillipe says you're a quick learner. I'll even share my pie."

***

Talon

Talon sat across the game board from Lara, his castle in eminent danger from her knight. Phillipe was right, she was a quick learner and a smart player, if a bit impetuous. Charles always said you could tell much about a person by the way they played, and Lara played like quicksilver, quick thinking and mercurial, and cursed beautiful leaning over the board with loose tendrils of auburn framing her face, her brow furrowed in concentration.

She took his castle, and he allowed her a moment of gloating before taking her white knight with his black.

"Oh." She sat back with a huff. "You, you—"

"Truce, lady." Talon chuckled and held up his hands. "No name calling, in any language, no bedroll kicking, no bloodletting for the next three days until I leave. Deal?"

She made a show of thinking on it and then gave him a solemn nod. "Deal."

She went back to studying the game board for her next move, and Talon studied her, memorized her. She truly was the most intriguing woman he'd ever met. As intelligent as she was beautiful, as kind and gentle with any creature that needed her ministrations, including him, as she was fierce and fearless when fighting for that same friend or creature. She'd shown true grace handling being made *lidi* to him, along with enough spit and fire to make it interesting.

"Lara?"

"Hmm?"

"Speaking of name calling."

She looked up from the game board and fixed impossibly big, hazel green cat eyes on him. "Captain?"

"Talon," he said. "My name is Talon. I would ask you to call me by it, at least here in the privacy of our chamber whilst we play. And maybe you can play at not hating me so much?"

She studied him much as she'd studied the board. "I don't hate you, Talon," she said at last, her words, his name on her lips, his absolution. "I hate what you are."

"The king's soldier?"

"My jailer."

Talon sat back in his chair. He couldn't blame her for hating her jailer. He would hate anyone who was his, or hers.

"Well then." He raised his cup to her. "You are soon to have a month free of the me you hate."

She raised her cup to his jaundiced toast. "To freedom." She took a sip, then set her cup down to take his knight with her queen before grinning from ear to ear.

"Boldly done." Talon chuckled, then moved his black queen, positioning her to take the white queen in another move before *he* sat back and sipped his wine, mesmerized by the play of changing expressions on her face as she tried to figure out what he was doing.

A knock at the door broke their concentration.

"Enter," Talon said, irritated by the interruption.

Ravenna stepped in, dressed in a thin, gauzy nightshift that showed more than it hid as she sauntered across the chamber and stood before the back light of the hearth fire, her dark eyes raking Lara from head to toe.

"Ravenna." Talon barely looked her way. "Is there something I can do for you?"

"You can send your *lidi* elsewhere for the night. Perhaps to your second's bed," Ravenna said, her voice low and suggestive. She ran her hands down the waist of her sheer shift and swayed her hips. "You'll have no need of her tonight, Talon."

He heard the sharp intake of Lara's breath and saw the glint in her narrowed eyes. If looks could kill, Ravenna would have bled out then and there.

"Do you play Shah?" he asked Ravenna.

"Do I play what?"

"Shah." He indicated the game board. "Do you play?"

She pursed her red, stained lips. "No."

"My *lidi* does. And all I've need of tonight is a game of Shah."

"But, Talon." She thrust a puny hip out. "I'm offering you an entirely different game."

"You may call me Captain." He stood and escorted her to the door. "And you have nothing to offer me that I care to play with or for." He opened the door and gently eased her out into the hallway. "Give your father my compliments on what a fine, virtuous daughter he has raised should he awaken on your return to your guestchamber."

He shut the door behind her, threw the inside bolt, and resumed his seat across from Lara, whose mouth twitched up at the corners.

"She bought three vials of love potion, all for you," she told him.

"There's not enough love potion in the world," Talon vowed, and Lara gave up the fight and broke into a grin.

"Patience said you'd rather drink the Black's piss than drink a potion from Ravenna."

Talon laughed, short and quick. "Patience is right." Then he asked, "When did she say this?"

"Today, when I asked her if Ravenna was your wildcat."

Talon held Lara's gaze a moment. "You thought it Ravenna? You thought me smitten with her?" The insult came with how she would ever think him infatuated with a spoilt brat like the count's daughter.

"Only because she was so smitten with you and determined to get you," she said, soothing his ruffled pride a little. "And Ravenna is very used to getting what she wants."

"Not from me."

A slow smile spread across Lara's face.

"Did, ah, did Patience say who she thought my wildcat was?" he asked her.

"No."

"You didn't ask?"

Lara shook her head. "I didn't think it my business after all."

"Good," he said more gruffly than he'd intended. It wasn't like Talon hadn't considered telling her that she was his wildcat about a hundred times a day, but what purpose would that serve now? He was leaving in three days to march across Basque territory into Moorish Spain. He could be killed or maimed. The last thing he wanted to do was make Lara grieve him, or worse, tend to a cripple the rest of his life.

"It's not."

He took her queen and then her king, and then he bade her good night and sought his bed, if not sleep.

CHAPTER 12

The March

Talon

Talon sat on Lara's cot as she slept and brushed an auburn curl from her cheek. "Lara."

"Hmmm?"

"I don't want to wake you, but I wanted to say good-bye."

"You're leaving?"

"I am." She wouldn't remember this conversation when she woke. She never remembered the conversations they had when she talked in her sleep. Talon remembered them all. Some were short, strange, and cryptic, making little to no sense, while others were full and coherent, like the one they were having now.

"Where you going?"

"To meet Charles and the returning army. You'll be free of me for the month I'm gone." He ran his fingers through her unruly mane, wishing he could gaze into her changeling eyes one more time before he left. To see if they would be a soft, mossy green or bright with burning embers. Wondering for about the thousandth time if she would leave before he returned. "Will you be here when I get back?"

"Be a good *lidi*. Stay under captain protection," she mumbled, then buried her face into her pillow.

Talon knew from experience she wouldn't talk again, at least not for a while, and he'd run out of time. He gave his knee a pat, and

Wolf laid his head on it, tail wagging in anticipation of their morning outing. "Not this time, old man. You must be a faithful hound to your mistress and be her protector once more." Wolf gave Talon's hand a slurp and he ruffled his ears. "I'll be keeping an eye on Ranulf, whilst you, my friend, will have the biggest rat of all to watch in the count and his mad little vixen of a daughter, who's very jealous of our wildcat." Talon gazed down at Lara, at the curve of her back, the swell of her hips, and the long, lean, well-muscled length of her legs. "My coin's on our wildcat. Though knowing a wolf and a wizened old witch are on watch makes me feel better about leaving my auburn-haired, hazel-eyed beauty."

Lara coughed and buried her face deeper into her pillow, and Talon stood, then picked up his pack as he gave the chamber one last look. He had everything he needed, but not what he wanted.

He shrugged and slung the pack over his shoulder. A soldier's life never took into account what he wanted.

"Fare well, Lara." He rested his hand on the door. "See you in a month."

"Godspeed, Talon."

***

Lara

Talon's step faltered and then the door shut behind him. He'd thought she'd been talking in her sleep again, something she'd done her whole life according to Sophie. But Lara had been awake since Talon had first stirred from his bed. She'd heard everything he'd said to her and Wolf.

She was his wildcat. It was she who'd cursed him on sight and damned him with his oath to protect her. She who he wanted but wouldn't let himself have. He was protecting her not only from Ranulf and Nithard but also from himself. That was why he'd left so abruptly the night she'd leaned in to him, naked…why looking at her hurt more.

All things she would have plenty of time to think about and brood over for the next month. Right now, she needed to get moving.

After getting dressed, she snuck down the stairs and out the hall's front entrance while the troop were breaking their fasts with a feast Lara should've been awakened to help cook and serve. Since she hadn't been, either as a kindness of the captain's or a way to avoid saying good-bye to her awake, she took advantage of the extra time and ran out the main gate, waving her farewell to the watchtower as she headed for home. A home she could stay at, free to live her own life and sleep in her own bed again for a month at least if she gave up her plan. Yet if her plan succeeded, in a month's time, she'd be home free for the rest of her life.

Sophie waited for her, clothes and scissors at the ready. "Are you sure you want to do this?" She'd been against Lara's plan at first but had agreed to it on second thought. Which gave Lara hope and courage that it would work.

"I'm sure."

Sophie grabbed the hank of Lara's braid almost before her backside hit the chair. Lara concentrated on petting Wolf and telling him how he would need to stay and be a good dog for Sophie while she was gone and trying to ignore the shearing sound of the scissors and the gentle tugging at her hair. Then it stopped and Sophie held Lara's braid in her hand.

"Well." Lara gulped and ran both hands through her shorn hair, marveling at how light it felt between her fingers.

"Well." Sophie tied the loose end of the braid with twine and handed it to Lara.

Refusing to cry over something as unimportant as hair, Lara gulped back tears and climbed the ladder to their bedchamber. She opened the chest that held her personal treasures and laid the braid beside a crown of dried flowers, a keepsake from her and Sophie's journey to Neustria, given to her by the young god who'd won the riding tourney on a blood bay stallion. A god who'd never removed his helmet and who'd ridden under the name of *Vagus*. Wanderer.

Touching the crown, Lara sent out a silent prayer that the journey she was about to embark on would go as well as that journey had, then shut the chest, squared her shoulders, and stripped out of her gown and shift. She pulled on a breechcloth and a pair of worn linen breeches she'd bought off Willem and cinched in her waist belt to keep them from falling off. At least they were long enough to cover her ankles, and she was able to wear her own boots. After grabbing the threadbare under tunic and faded brown woolen jerkin she'd also bought from Willem, she descended the ladder and stood bare-chested before Sophie. Taking a deep breath in, she held her arms out.

"I don't envy you this." Sophie bound Lara's bosom and pulled the knot tight under her breasts. "Especially since it'll be rare you'll be free of it. Won't it?"

"Only when I sleep, I promise."

"Your kerchief too." Sophie tied it loosely around Lara's neck. "You must sleep with it on, else some keen-eyed soldier realizes you don't have an Adam's apple."

"It will never leave my neck. I swear."

Lara slid the threadbare under tunic on and the jerkin over it as Sophie opened a tub of olive oil mixed with brown acorn dye. Lara poured a small amount into her palm and rubbed it in her hair and over her face and neck and arms, repeating the process until her exposed skin was a nut brown.

"Is my hair dark enough?" she asked Sophie, who nodded and then pursed her lips.

"Well now. I never saw this."

They both burst out laughing.

"I'm going to miss you." Lara gave Sophie a heartfelt hug, then kissed Wolf on the nose. "You too, boy." Slinging her pack over her shoulder, she gave Wolf the hand signal to stay before she opened the door. "See you two in a month."

***

Talon

Talon grabbed his empty bowl and headed for the cook's wagon. Seven days into the march, and he was already bored, saddle sore, and hungry. At least the food on this march was a cut or three above the usual camp food, which also meant there was always a line of men as worn out and hungry as he at the wagon.

"Chicken stew tonight." Tree raised his steaming bowl up as he walked by Talon.

"Chicken stew," Talon echoed, close enough now to smell the savory aroma. His belly growling, he leaned in to inhale more of the teasing scent and caught sight of the cook's helper, the widow's son Lara had recommended, a scrawny, gangly lad with dirty brown hair peeking out from under his cap whose direct gaze Talon had yet to meet. Though Hamm was his name, he seemed to answer most to "hey, boy." He was an odd lad who kept to himself and the cook, Plutarch, but he knew his way around a cooking fire. Lara had been right about that.

Hamm would jump off the moving cook's wagon daily to gather wild greens and herbs from the roadside that would show up in the stew that night, giving it a completely different taste from the previous night's stew even if the meat was the same old chicken, rabbit, or squirrel. A rare treat for soldiers on the march, used to stuffing tasteless gruel down their throats just to fill their empty bellies with something warm. Now Hamm ladled two servings of stew into each man's bowl, his head down, his gaze never wavering from his task.

"A man could starve in this bloody line," Talon grumbled loud enough for one of the count's men, who was trying to badger the lad into serving him a third ladle full, to hear. "Let the rest of us have our firsts before you start demanding seconds," he said much louder and clearer.

His little speech got nods all around and a few "hear, hears," then the brute demanding more stew turned around with a snarl on his hirsute face.

"Ah, bloody hell."

It was Lothair, Ranulf's second, who was snarling at Talon one moment and yelling and flinging hot stew around the next.

"My hand," he screamed at the hapless Hamm, who stood holding an empty ladle. "You burned my hand."

"I-I'm sorry, sir. You turned as I poured." Eyes cast down and gripping the empty ladle in his left fist, the lad backstepped until his backside hit the wagon.

Talon set his bowl down on the plank of wood used as a serving table. One thing you never did was back away from a bully. It was akin to turning yourself into a bloody lump of raw meat in front of a starving cur.

"Sorry, you say?" Lothair waved his hand around. "You scald my flesh and you're sorry?"

"I can put a salve on it," the boy offered, never looking up.

"Here." The old cook offered Lothair another bowl of stew. "Sit and eat your stew and I'll be right over to fix your hand up."

"It's your boy's gonna need fixing up." Lothair shoved the cook aside and lunged for Hamm, who sidestepped his charge so quickly, Lothair plunged headfirst into the side of the wagon and knocked himself out right before Ranulf and three others pushed their way into the snickering crowd.

"What's this?" Ranulf stared down at Lothair as he began to moan and stir. "What happened here?"

"Lothair tripped over his own beard and fell," someone called out, followed by loud guffaws.

"You think this funny?" Ranulf scoured the crowd of soldiers. "My man out cold is funny?" The count's men all managed to wipe the smiles from their faces, but Talon and his didn't even try. "You, boy." Ranulf pointed at the cook's lad, who peered up at him from beneath his cap. "What happened here?"

The lad kept his head low and his voice lower. "I was serving him. He turned away as I poured, then his hand was where his bowl had been. I said I was sorry, but he came after me and hit his head on the wagon."

"Lothair hit his head hard enough to knock himself out?" Ranulf's black eyes bored into the top of the lad's cap. "Without a trip or a push from anybody else?"

"Nobody touched Lothair." Talon stepped up and stood in Ranulf's face. "And this goes no further."

"Ah, the good Captain Guiscard," Ranulf sneered. "The defender of whores and hounds and fey lads."

The lad's breath sucked in and let out again in a slow hiss, and his fist still clenched the ladle's handle. The mouse might have teeth after all.

"That's me." Talon kept his voice flat and unconcerned over the insult given him. "Talon Guiscard, patron saint of strays."

He heard the shuffling of feet as men around them positioned themselves for the possible fight to come. Tree set his bowl of half-eaten stew down and stood between Hamm and a groaning Lothair as Phillipe and Anglbert came strolling up, longswords drawn and laid across their shoulders.

"Are we having a party?" Phillipe stopped to one side of Talon and Anglbert the other. He glanced down at Lothair, who struggled to sit up. "Has Lothair started the party without us?"

"Get him up," Ranulf snapped at his men. He pointed at Hamm. "You, boy, you'd better stay clear of him and me."

Talon watched them haul Lothair up and walk him toward their section of camp, not turning his back on the pack of curs until they were out of sight. Left in peace, he and his men then got back into line for their supper, rehashing the lad's encounter with Lothair and congratulating David on his victory over Goliath.

"Nice dodge, lad." Talon dropped a hand on his shoulder.

"I'm sorry I missed it." Phillipe grinned over at him. "Did your widowed mother teach you it?"

"No, sirs," the lad spoke into his chest. "Only how to cook."

"Well done there as well." Talon held his bowl out, inhaling the savory steam rising over it. "Your mother, does she have a sister named Berta?"

"They are, uh, cousins, sir."

Talon clapped a hand on the lad's shoulder again, not as bony as much as small-boned. "That explains a lot. Cooking must be in your blood. If you can stand the road, you'd make a decent living at it."

"Don't let Charles get hold of him." Tree retrieved his bowl of stew. "He'll never give him back."

Talon swore he saw the corners of the lad's mouth twitch up before his head bent even lower over the pot.

"He'll have to fight me for him first." Plutarch brandished his ladle, which gave all the men there a good laugh and turned the lad's cheeks a very unmanly pink under his tan.

CHAPTER 13

The Unveiling

Lara

"Sweet Mary, mother of Jesus, that was close." Lara hunched over the pot she was scrubbing in the river, her heart still racing. "Too blessed close." She looked over her shoulder, half expecting to see Sophie there ready to skin her alive for the scrape she'd just gotten out of. But of course, Sophie wasn't there, only the glow of campfires through the trees.

She rinsed the pot and held up the ladle, turning it this way and that as she admired Hamm's weapon of choice. She dropped the ladle into the pot and started walking back to camp, her free hand on the hilt of Sophie's old knife in its plain leather sheath, Lara's weapon of choice. Plutarch, the cook whose wagon she shared, kept a short-bladed scramasax sheathed at his waist and a longsword in the wagon. He'd been a soldier in King Pepin's army who was now too old to fight and too used to the road to quit it, so he'd become a cook for hire, and wasn't bad at it.

He was a kindhearted man of late middle years who liked telling her, telling Hamm, tales of his travels as both soldier and cook. Lara enjoyed his tales and his company, company she should be seeking before the night got any darker. She made her way to the tree line when the hairs on the back of her neck stood on end. She pursed her lips, ready to whistle for Wolf, but Wolf wasn't there; he was at home with Sophie seventy leagues away. Lara pulled at the bindings around her chest and gritted her teeth, looking forward to being able to loosen them before bedding down, her nightly release from the chaffing and the constant strain of being Hamm. Though she'd considered trying to sneak away and make her way home too many times to count, it was too late to turn back now. If she tried to leave the march, they'd hunt her down as a deserter. All she could do was stay as Hamm and complete the march while staying out of Lothair's way and the captain's notice.

She stepped deeper into the trees, but a twig snapped up ahead of her.

Tightening her grip on the pot, she slid her knife from its plain leather sheath at her waist belt. "Who's there?" She kept her voice low and guttural. "Show yourself."

A man stepped out from behind a tree not ten paces from her, and Lara sucked her breath in as the captain stood in the dusky light.

"The mouse has ears." He nodded at the knife and pot she clutched. "As well as claws." He closed the distance between them in several long strides as Lara lowered her chin. "It's good to see you're on your guard, Hamm. Though I wouldn't be stepping away alone at night anymore, if I were you. A bully always strikes when the odds are in his favor, and curs always attack in packs."

Lara relaxed her grip on the pot and sheathed her knife. "Thank you, Captain." She tugged her cap down lower. "I'll keep it in mind."

"Good," he said. "Do."

Lara started to nod, then grunted her assent instead. She walked away from the captain, leading with her shoulders rather than her hips and glanced back when she hit the open ground of the camp. The captain followed her and continued to until she made the safety of the wagon, when he strolled off in the direction of his men's tents and bedrolls.

She set the pot and ladle in their place and was double-checking that everything else was put away for the night when Phillipe and Anglbert, then Dardinel, Tree, and the captain, all armed to the teeth and carrying their bedrolls, spread them out by the fire next to the wagon.

"You've found yourself a protector." Plutarch lay down on his bedroll with a tired groan.

"Saint Talon of the Strays." Lara shook her bedroll out and laid it next to Plutarch's, then sat cross-legged on it and peered over at the captain and his men on the other side of the fire. They spoke low or stared out into the night. In the captain's case, he whittled on a piece of wood.

"Be glad of them," Plutarch told her. "I know Ranulf's father of old. If he's anything like Nithard, he's not to be trusted."

Lara chuffed. "Ranulf is just like his father. You say you know the count of old?"

"Aye, before he was count. I was a man-at-arms for his brother, Count Reginald. I served at Oloron Manor when the Lady Eileen and her daughter, Isabeau, still reigned." He took in a deep breath, and Lara knew a tale was about to be told. "Ahh, Hamm, me boy," he said. "You're too young to've been blessed with a sight of the fair lady Isabeau. In grace and heart and beauty she ruled over every man in the whole of the valley but loved only one. Harald."

"Harald?" Lara scooted closer to Plutarch. She'd heard the tale of the lady Isabeau since childhood, everyone in the valley had, but she'd never heard the name of the man Isabeau had loved and scorned Nithard for.

"Harald was a man-at-arms of her father's as well," Plutarch said. "He was a good friend and a good man to have at your back in a battle. They were secretly married, Harald and Isabeau, right before we went off to war. Only the abbot, myself, our captain, and his lady knew of their marriage."

Lara scratched at her bindings. "Why was their marriage kept secret?"

"They were to announce their marriage when we returned from the war, but when we came back bearing the sad news of our captain's death in battle, it was to find them all gone. My captain's lady to visit family somewhere in the east, the count and his wife dead and buried, and Lady Isabeau vanished. They said in her grief at losing her parents, she walked off into the woods, never to be seen again in this world." He gave a heavy sigh and stared beyond Lara into the past. "They were an uncommonly handsome couple, her so slim and graceful with soft blonde curls and eyes like a cat's, and him a man built straight up and down with hair the color of fire."

"What did Harald do when he found his lady gone?"

"He searched for her for a year straight." Plutarch sounded tired and worn out from the day, from the years past. "Then he went and got himself killed in battle." He gave a sad smile and pulled his blanket over his shoulders, though it was warm as day. "I was there. I held him as he took his last breath speaking her name."

***

Talon

They made camp on the Spanish side of Roncesvalles Pass as the sun began to set. The call came as dusk turned to dark: "Riders in."

Brys and Oswald, the men Talon had sent ahead to scout for the returning army, rode into camp with two other riders wearing the king's colors.

As he dismounted, Oswald said, "Charles is two days' ride from here, three at most." He eyed Talon's empty bowl.

"Did he give you a message for me?" Talon asked.

Oswald nodded and rubbed his backside as the others dismounted. "He said to tell you you were wrong, and he expects a cow to be roasting when you meet up."

Talon chuffed. "He'll eat half the cow while feeding me a whole lot of I told you so." He greeted the king's men with a handshake. "Bertrand, Guy, your timing is perfect. I was on my way to the cook's wagon."

Bertrand grinned with every mouthful of savory rabbit stew, returning to the wagon for seconds and thirds, and Talon worried that Tree would turn out to be right, that once Charles learned of Hamm's talent at cooking, he would steal the lad for himself. Of course, it would be a great opportunity for the lad if he became a king's cook. Talon would simply have to work supper invites from Charles on future marches.

After they'd eaten, Plutarch tapped a cask of ale as the men settled themselves between the fire and the wagon, their post for the past three nights.

"What's that you're whittling, Captain?" Anglbert eyed the piece of antler Talon carved.

"It's meant to be an elephant."

"Is it meant for anyone in particular?" Anglbert nudged Phillipe with his elbow. "A gift for a beautiful wildcat perhaps? A bribe to help soothe her anger at being left out?"

"Left out of getting herself killed or worse," Talon grumbled, in no mood for their humor. He didn't need a reminder of what he'd left behind. He knew damn well what he'd rode away from and was fairly certain she finally knew as well. He'd thought her sleeping when he'd called her his wildcat, among other things, but now he wasn't so sure. She'd never woken again after talking to him in her sleep before, which made him think she hadn't really been asleep. Her last words to him, "Godspeed, Talon," were seared into his memory, along with the sight of her thin nightshift draped over her womanly curves and the feel of her naked body pressed against his.

Hairs raised on the back of his neck, and he turned to find Hamm listening to their conversation, the lad's gaze dropping to his feet as soon as he was caught looking. Hamm quickly melted back into the pots and pans as Ranulf, Lothair, and three of the count's men made their way over.

"What news, Guiscard?" Ranulf addressed Talon, though he sized up the newcomers. "I was told riders have come in."

"Bertrand, Guy." Talon nodded to the king's men and then to Ranulf. "Ranulf Midered."

"Son of Nithard Midered, Count of Oloron," Ranulf told the two unimpressed riders. "I am his man on this march." Bertrand nodded acknowledgment, saying nothing, and Guy did the same. "Well, man," Ranulf demanded of Bertrand. "What news from the king?"

Bertrand took one long look at Ranulf and shook his head. Talon had fought side by side with the man in three campaigns and as many brawls, and though he could've guessed the gist of what Bertrand's answer would be, he still grinned as Bertrand gave it.

"The king's news was for Captain Guiscard. Seeing as how I've told him already, my job's done. You want the king's news, you get it from the captain."

"Well, Guiscard?" Ranulf huffed. "What news?"

Talon should've simply told Ranulf the king's message and let the cur slink off, but ten days' marching hadn't improved his temper, and he'd had it with the whelp. He stood, placing no hint of emotion in his manner or voice. "Say please."

Every man within hearing distance fell silent. Talon was certain they looked like two dogs circling, hackles up, but he didn't care, and was almost disappointed when Ranulf stepped back.

"Why not?" Ranulf sneered slyly. "The word got me under your *lidi*'s skirts. It should work for a bit of information from you."

He said it loud enough for all to hear, playing to his audience as he had at Mallus, but this wasn't Mallus, and they weren't in his father's hall. Talon was done talking with the braggart. He cut the steps between them when a flash of elbows and cloth flew at Ranulf, someone shrieking like a fury and smashing a lead pitcher up the side of his head.

Ranulf crumpled to the ground, and every man there stood speechless, staring at Hamm, whose fist still clenched the pitcher, then at Ranulf, who lay unmoving and groaning.

"He had no right," Hamm spat down at Ranulf. "No right to be saying those things about her."

The lad's chin came up and so did his gaze. Disbelief turned to certainty, then to anger as Talon stared into hazel eyes sparking bright with amber and fringed with dark, sooty lashes.

"You cut your hair," he said, and Hamm raised a slim hand to his greasy mop. "You go too far, Lara."

***

Lara

The captain scowled at Lara, his glare daring her to defend herself, the scar on his cheek blazing white. All around them the names Hamm and Lara were being spoken over and over again, the voices changing in tone from surprised mumblings to grumbling mad.

The captain jerked his head at Phillipe. "No one is to go near the river until I return."

"Aye, Captain."

He grabbed Lara by the arm. "You, with me."

"Where?" She almost tripped as the captain pulled her away from the crowd of angry men, and she glanced over her shoulder to the wagon where Plutarch stood with a ladle in one hand and his short sword in the other, a dazed expression on his face. "What are you going to do?"

"Drown me a wildcat."

Lara dug her heels in, but it did no good. The captain only pulled harder, half dragging her over to his bedroll and saddle. He dug into his saddlebag and palmed something wrapped in linen and a clean tunic, then he pulled her to the river, stopping at the shoreline and stuffing the small package in her hand.

"In you go." He nudged her toward the water.

Lara eyed the freezing cold water. "Now?"

The captain's steely glare took her in from boots to cap. "Now. Be sure to wash your hair. I'm not smelling that greasy mop all night."

Lara didn't ask what he meant. She didn't dare. She stepped into the river, trying not to gasp as she waded waist deep into the bone-chilling water. She spied a small pool formed by a breakwater of large rocks upriver and made her way to it. The package he'd given her was the bar of rose soap he'd bought from her, which she'd assumed he'd intended for some other woman.

She set the soap down on a rock and eyed the pool. Shivering, she considered inching her torso down into the water, but that would only prolong the inevitable. She took a deep breath and dropped until her backside hit the river bottom, her head completely submerged. Pushing up to her feet, she shook the water from herself as she spit and cursed. "Jesus, Mary, and Joseph it's freezing."

"Then quit your caterwauling and start scrubbing."

Teeth chattering, Lara glanced around the pool as the captain gathered wood at the shore. She could wash herself fully clothed and sit by the fire he was building to dry, but that would take all night, and neither she nor the captain had that kind of patience. Besides, if she was already going to be soaking wet, she might as well get her body and her clothes as clean as possible, and her clothes would dry much faster off her. Plus, she could finally be free of her tortuous bindings.

She peeled her jerkin off her goose-pimpled body and then her under-tunic, breeches, and breechcloth and laid them on the rocks, then glanced at the shore, where the captain was tending his kindling fire. She attempted to untie the knot to her bindings, but her fingers were too cold. Biting her lower lip, she looked over at the captain as he stood watching her.

"What?" he barked.

Lara shook her head and worked harder at the knot. The splash of water caught her attention and she looked up. The captain strode through the river toward her, the water darkening his leather breeches to the tops of his thighs.

"Here." He stopped in front of her, so close she could have reached out and touched the stubborn set of his jaw. "Let me." He took the knot by each end, and Lara glanced down quickly, grateful that the water came up to her waist, hiding her nakedness below. "Don't worry," he said. "You've got nothing I haven't seen before."

She didn't know if he was speaking of her in particular or women in general. Either way it brought hot blood to her cheeks and chest as he deftly untied the soggy knot. He held the loose ends out to her sides, and she took them in hand and turned her back to him, waiting for him to leave the pool, knowing better than to demand he return to the shore when he didn't move. Not with the mood he was in. Her fingers shaking from more than the cold, she peeled the sweat-stained bindings away.

"I hope you brought some healing salve with you," the captain said, his voice rough and close. "You've got a few raw spots from the bindings."

She dunked underwater, relishing the numbing cold on her sores and an inner ache that had started somewhere deep in her belly and moved lower. Coming back up, she reached for the soap on the rock, only to find it gone. She looked over her shoulder to where the captain stood no more than two paces behind her, brandishing the soap with a determined set to his jaw.

"Your back could use a washing."

Lara reached back to pull her hair up but found only air and wet skin. She dropped her hands to her sides, and the captain muttered something about manes to mops as she stood waiting for the scrubbing that Sophie would've given her. She almost jumped out of her skin at the first touch of his hands, which were surprisingly gentle as he massaged the soap around her sores, expertly working his thumbs into the muscle and sinew up and down her spine. She swayed forward as he found a tender spot below her shoulders and dug her feet into the sandy bottom to keep from stumbling. He kneaded his strong fingers up her back and around the base of her neck where he pressed his thumbs into the point where her spine met her shoulders, and Lara groaned and stood three inches taller at least.

He continued to knead his way up her neck and into her hair, rubbing delicious circles into her scalp.

"There." He stopped, and Lara almost swayed back into him. "I've wanted to get soap and water on that mop for days."

His breath tickled Lara's ear before he lifted his head from hers, and Lara craned her neck to get a glimpse of his face. He loomed over her shoulders, his gaze fixed on her breasts, which swelled under his rapt attention, her nipples growing instantly hard and pushing up to the heat in his eyes like seedlings to the sun. Lara's breath came hard, but it was Talon's she felt as he stepped closer, the entire length of him pressing against her backside. He laid a hand on her bare hip, then traced it up her side until he cupped her soapy breast. Her legs turned to wet sea grass as he drew circles with the pad of his thumb around her nipple. Lara could barely think, much less see straight.

"Ahem, ah, Captain."

He stopped his play and growled low in Lara's ear. "Christ, if it isn't your hound interrupting us, it's mine." He stepped away from her, standing between her nakedness and the shoreline. Phillipe stood with his back to them. "What?" the captain snarled as Lara dunked and rinsed.

"Sorry, Captain," Phillipe said over his shoulder. "But Ranulf's pitching a fit, demanding the right to whip our girl Hamm here. Thought you'd like to know."

"What I'd like to know," he muttered to Lara, "is a woman less troublesome, which would be any woman other than you." He pulled his rolled-up tunic from the back of his waistband and held it out to her, his gaze raking her bare breasts. Lara hastily donned the tunic. "Come on." He took her by one hand as she pulled the tunic down to her knees with the other. "Let's get this over with."

They made the shore as Ranulf, Lothair, and two more of the count's men came down the path. Phillipe stood to one side of the group with both his short and longswords drawn as Talon strode right up to Ranulf, still holding Lara's hand.

"What do you want, boy?" he growled.

"Your bitch *lidi*." Ranulf stared at Lara. "I owe her a knock upside the head."

"You touch my *lidi*…" Talon dropped his hold of Lara's hand and pulled his falcata from its sheath and pressed the point to the soft underside of Ranulf's chin. "You won't have a head."

Ranulf's face contorted as Lothair made for his sword.

"I wouldn't." Phillipe shook his head at Lothair, who looked from their four men to the captain's and Phillipe's two with a smug snort. Phillipe closed the distance between them and pressed the tip of his longsword against the brute's belly before Lothair could draw his. "Numbers don't count for everything," Phillipe said. "Were I you, I'd go right back up the way you came with your belly intact and your young master's head still on his shoulders."

The captain twisted his sword under Ranulf's chin enough to draw a bead of blood on its point, and Lara didn't move, let alone breathe, not until Ranulf gave a snort and stepped back, both hands palm up.

"Just keep a short leash on your bitch," he spat when he was out of the captain's reach.

"Just keep your distance." The captain didn't lower his sword. "You and your father's men."

"She has got you whipped, Guiscard."

The captain said nothing, but the scar on his cheek was white and his jaw set as Ranulf headed back up the path, making whipping sounds and laughing with Lothair.

"That was an amusing night's entertainment." Phillipe gave an exaggerated waggle of his blond brows before swiping sweat away from them. "I must say, Lara, you've livened up a boring march a bit. And we haven't even met up with the rest of the army yet."

"Now you see why I told you no?" the captain said through gritted teeth as he sheathed his falcata. "You couldn't keep out of trouble with only forty men, what do you think will happen with four thousand?"

"I was doing well enough as Hamm."

The captain laughed, short and harsh. "You had Lothair intent on strangling you as Hamm and another of Ranulf's men bragging on how he was going to give it to Hamm up the ass first time he got the lad alone."

Lara dropped her chin, embarrassed beyond speech.

"Phillipe," the captain ordered. "Set up my tent, two guards each shift, three shifts a night."

"Aye, Captain."

"And you." He pierced Lara with his gaze of honed steel, taking in his tunic on her, which only covered her legs to her knees and was soaked up to her belly. "Go dry yourself and your clothes by the fire. I can't have you walking through camp like that, or I'll be fighting my own men off."

CHAPTER 14

Roncesvalles Pass

Talon

Talon stepped through the flap to his tent. "Prepare yourself." He told Lara. "The king awaits."

She stood smoothing her tunic, then hitched up her breeches, tightened her waist belt, and pulled her cap down over the mop of brown curls that brought a scowl to Talon every time he looked at her.

"Come on." He led her out of his tent, a space so small he'd lain only an arm's length from her the past two sleepless nights, staring at the curves of her backside and silently cursing himself and her.

Phillipe and Dardinel took their positions to each side of Lara, with Tree behind her. As Talon led the way through the three rings of tents between their camp and the king's, scores of men stopped to stare at the cook's boy that was a girl, fooling an entire company of soldiers for a hundred leagues. After staring down one mouth-breathing, hirsute group of Bretons, Talon looked over his shoulder at Lara, her eyes wide and her expression wary as she glanced wildly from one man's lascivious leer to another.

He slowed and took her hand. "Keep your eyes forward."

She grasped his hand, and some of the wildness left her eyes, though none of the wariness. Any other time, he would've been mush at her holding on to him, but he was still furious with her. They arrived at the king's large, comfortably appointed tent hand in hand, and he had to pull his fingers from hers to present her to the king.

"My liege." He dipped his head to Charles, who sat facing them across his table as two menservants discreetly melted into the tent's shadows.

Charles looked Lara over from cap to boots, his expression giving nothing of what he thought away. Talon clamped down on a grin. If Lara thought Sophie's scoldings were an ordeal, he couldn't wait until the king was finished with her.

"So." Charles eyed her sternly. "You are the infamous Lara, who crippled my cousin, became captive and made *lidi* to Captain Guiscard here, who, when told by your master, my captain, that you were not to come on this march, disguised yourself as a lad, a cook's helper, and came despite what you were ordered." He paused, warming to his lecture. "You have also almost gotten yourself beaten, or worse, twice now, causing my captain no end of trouble from having to assign two of his men to guard you day and night when they should be guarding me, to causing him to pitch his tent, when he greatly prefers his bedroll out under the stars on these hot August nights." He turned to Talon. "Is that about it?"

Talon shook his head. "Not even by half."

Charles's eyes lit with amusement, but Talon didn't think it was funny. Any of it. Nor would Charles if it'd been him who'd been made her jailer, driven to distraction by her day and night.

"So," Charles said to Lara. "What have you to say for yourself? Do you truly expect me to call your wergeld paid, your service to the crown rendered in full for disobeying the captain's, your master's, direct orders and causing him no end, and that is a direct quote, of trouble?"

Lara stood silent as Charles steepled his fingers and tapped his fingertips, a thing he'd once admitted to Talon he did to avoid smiling when he didn't wish to be seen doing so.

"No, Sire," she answered Charles at last. "I do not expect to be rewarded for my disobedience."

"Smart answer." Charles unsteepled his fingers. "But then Talon did say you were an intelligent woman." Lara slid a sideways glance at Talon, who coughed and shifted on his feet as Charles sat back, still eyeing Lara. "Now the question is, what do I do with you?"

"I could cook for you, my king," she answered quickly. "Then I would be no more trouble for Captain Guiscard."

"Yes, well." Charles stared at Talon's cheek, so Talon reached up and rubbed it, feeling nothing but his old scar there. "You could cook for me; however, I am assured by my captain's second that I would have immediate trouble in the form of forty soldiers protesting the loss of their cook. Therefore, I think it best you stay with Captain Guiscard's troop and cook for them as you have been." He glanced between them, finally resting on Lara. "And because I trust my captain's decision on this matter, he will decide, when this march is over, how much of your wergeld has been paid by your service to his company."

Lara dropped her chin to her chest. "Yes, my king."

Charles indicated that they should sit. "Talon told me you play Shah," he said as Talon pulled a chair out for Lara. "I've not played since he deserted me outside of Zaragoza to go galloping back across Spain and take up the post at Oloron. A post he seemed unusually eager to take up." Charles winked at Lara. "Now I see why."

Lara's cheeks turned a pretty shade of rose beneath her dyed tan as Talon took his seat.

"I was eager to get out of a boring siege and leave the cursed heat of the Spanish plains," he grumbled.

Charles chuckled, then looked to Lara. "White or black?"

"White," Lara answered.

Charles turned the board so that the black pieces faced him. "Now watch and learn, Talon." He reached for a black pawn. "Watch and learn."

"Watch and learn?" Talon snorted. "It was I who taught you how to play."

Charles flashed Talon a quick grin. "I wasn't speaking of the board game, man."

The king beat Lara handily their first game, when she was still glancing wide-eyed around his tent as much or more than she was concentrating on the game. She played the second game with her more usual attentiveness, keeping her eyes on his every move and taking her time to make hers as Charles and Talon spoke of the failed campaign behind them and the march still ahead of them.

"You still think the Basques will retaliate?" Charles asked.

"Wouldn't you?" Talon held Charles's gaze. "If it were your city burned, your women and children dead?"

Lara's head shot up, her attention off the game and on them.

Charles let out a heavy sigh and sat back in his chair. "I know the razing of Pamplona did not sit well with you—"

"The great army of Gaul slaughtered innocent women and children," Talon ground out. "To say it didn't sit well with me is beyond an understatement."

"I understand and even commiserate with your feelings on this," Charles told him. "However, unfortunate as it is, the lives of innocents are often, too often, I agree, a casualty of war."

"Unfortunate?"

The king held up his hand. "Your point is made, Captain, which is why I wanted you here. Your company will be my second guard from here to Oloron." He glanced at Lara. "This way you'll be able to watch over the both of us." He leaned across the table toward Lara as if sharing a secret. "Our Captain Guiscard here is a mother hen at heart, with rather large, sharp talons I would not wish to feel sunk into any part of my anatomy."

"A veritable patron saint of strays." She eyed Talon as if he'd actually grown feathers and talons.

Charles burst out laughing. "She knows you better than you let on."

Talon motioned for Lara to move her queen, and she set her white queen before the black king. Charles widened his eyes as his mouth gaped.

Talon grinned. "Checkmate."

***

Talon woke to a cry piercing his ears and heart. He rolled off his bedroll and laid his hand on Lara's shoulder as a keening moan escaped her lips.

"Lara, wake up. Wake up, my rose."

Her eyes fluttered open and focused on his. He helped her sit up, glad she was coming back to him, gladder still she'd been so far away when he'd called her his rose. She started shivering, and Talon held her, his nose in her shorn curls as she buried her head into his shoulder. He sat there holding her close as the gray of dawn broke, sharing his warmth and slowly rocking back and forth, murmuring soft shushing sounds into her hair until her shivering subsided, until she lifted her head and pushed away from him, though not far. Her palms still pressing against his chest, she took a deep breath in, then let it out slowly.

"Stay close by the king when we ride." Her voice was barely above a whisper.

Talon cupped her chin and tilted it so he could meet her gaze and found his old friend the wary wildcat staring back at him. "Why do you say that?"

"I dreamed I was coming to a place of high rocks," she said, her voice as shaky as her breath. "The rocks formed a tunnel. When I came out the other side, I was standing on a ledge, looking out over a field...a field covered with the bodies of men and horses." She clapped a hand over her mouth, stifling a sob. "They were...everywhere. There was blood...everywhere."

Talon pulled Lara close and held her tight. "It was just a bad dream."

"No." Lara grabbed his tunic with both hands, her eyes wild. "I don't just have bad dreams. My bad dreams come true."

"Are you saying you have foretelling dreams?"

She held his gaze. "Yes. That is what I'm telling you."

Whether true or not, whether Talon believed her or not, it was obvious she believed it. She had no reason to lie. In truth, Talon had never known her to lie, other than by omission. And whether her dream came true or not, time would tell. Either way, it would do no harm to act as if it were true.

"I tell you what," he whispered fiercely in her ear as the sounds of men moving about outside infiltrated their tent. "I'll stay close by the king today and you stay close by me. Deal?"

"Deal."

Lara's quick agreement to Talon's deal worried him almost as much as her dream did, and he made sure they both kept to it by insisting she ride between the king and himself as the army prepared to march east for the mountain pass.

They made Roncesvalles Pass by high noon, and the bulk of the army were on their way down the eastern slope of the mountain when the blare of a horn blasted through the oppressing heat, sending a chill down Talon's spine. A second blast rent the air, then a third, then silence.

"That's Roland's horn," Charles said. "He rides rear guard behind the baggage train. Go," he told Talon as his personal guard closed ranks around him. "Go."

Talon swung the Black's head west, and his men lined their warhorses up behind him and double checked their weapons. Lara slid the roan in alongside Tree's bay gelding.

"Stay with the king," Talon told her.

"But the cook's wagon is back there. Plutarch is there."

"What of your dream?" A shiver ran down his spine.

"If it comes to pass, there will be many in need of a healer."

***

Lara

They weren't the first to reach the pass. As they sat their horses and stared out at the field littered with the bodies of men and horses felled by Basque arrows, it was impossible to distinguish the cries and moans of the dying from those who found them. The horrible tableau of Lara's nightmare spread out before her, and she fixed her gaze on the overturned cook's wagon. She sent the roan flying down the hill, dodging the bodies of soldiers and horses and camp followers bristling with the arrows that had killed them. They'd been ambushed, and the rest of the army had been too far ahead and too late to help them. Talon had been right. The Basques had claimed their revenge.

She pulled the roan up at the cook's wagon and leapt out of the saddle, kneeling down beside Plutarch, who clung to his rapidly fading life with an arrow sticking into his chest and another in his belly. His face was ashen, his lips already turning blue as she cradled his head in her lap.

"Hamm, me boy." He fought for breath. "Salt the stew, will you?"

"I will, sir." Tears streamed down Lara's cheeks. "Just a pinch, just like you taught me."

"Ahh," he gurgled. "You're a good lad." His body gripped and his face contorted, and he went into a coughing fit and heaved up bloody spittle. All Lara could do was hold him and watch his life drain away. He reached a shaking hand to her wet cheek. "Why do you cry, my lady Isabeau?" he whispered, then his hand dropped, and he was gone.

Lara swaddled Plutarch's body with his longsword at his right hand and his ladle at his left, then slid his short sword into her waist belt. She kissed his cold, weathered cheek, pulled his death shroud over his head, and walked away as others picked him up and carried him to the mound of dead. Numb and mute, she made her way to the line of wounded, where she was unable to do anything more than comfort them as they rattled their last breaths.

When the last of the wounded had passed and the king's soldiers were preparing the funeral pyres, the captain appeared at Lara's side. Neither of them speaking, he took her by the hand and led her to their horses, where he lifted her up onto the Black's saddle and swung up behind her, gathered the roan's reins, and turned the horse's heads east. Lara considered protesting his coddling, but his chest was so warm and comforting against her back and his arms so strong and capable around her that she had neither the will nor the desire to do anything but lean back into him, her head tucked safely under his chin.

They made camp at dusk, but instead of helping her dismount, he told her to stay astride the Black, gave orders for his tent to be pitched, and pulled a blanket out of the sorrel's pack. After slinging the bundled blanket up to Lara, he swung back up onto the Black, and they rode downriver for half a league, stopping when they came upon a small pool formed by rocks and protected by head-high bushes along the shore.

Once she'd slid down off the Black, Lara dropped the blanket on the grassy shore and walked straight into the pool until she stood hip deep in the water, oblivious to the cold. She looked down at her hands, stained with the blood of the dead and the dying, and plunged them into the water, scrubbing at them, one against the other. Another larger, calloused pair of hands covered hers and stilled them, then lifted them out of the water and placed a bar of soap into her palms.

Lara turned into the big, solid chest she knew would be there. What she didn't know was that it'd be bare, or so warm, or that the smell of a man's sweat could be so enticing. Nuzzling a light furring of black chest hair, she breathed in the scent of leather and sandalwood, of Talon. She pressed her lips to his skin and tasted the salty sweetness. His hands stroked her hair, pulling her head back until her gaze met his, shining silver in the moonlight, then his mouth was on hers, slaking and demanding.

She thrilled to his kiss, the feel of his muscled back beneath her fingers, his skin warm, responsive, alive. He plundered her mouth with his lips, his tongue, and Lara surrendered to him, to his touch drifting up and down her back, pressing her so close her heart beat against his ribs. She broke away for air, for sanity. The heat of his gaze mesmerized her, drawing her back to him like a healer to nature's cures. She sighed, letting out the breath she'd been holding her entire life, and he kissed her again, his lips stealing her breath and giving his heat until the ache between her legs began to grow and throb. Talon growled low in his throat, and it rumbled down to her core. He scooped her up into his arms, and she buried her nose into his nape, breathing him in as he carried her to the blanket on the shore.

Lara eased down until they stood breath to breath, chest to chest. Her heart hammered against his, and her breathing grew ragged as he trailed kisses from her jaw to her throat, one big, strong hand running up and down the length of her back as his other cupped her backside and pressed her belly to the growing bulge in his breeches.

Panting, Lara almost fell into him as he stepped back, leaving a chasm between them that Lara's body instinctively leaned in to close. He cocked a slow smile, then grabbed her tunic by the hems and lifted the tunic off her before tossing it onto the blanket. Then he pulled her in to his chest, and Lara half sighed, half moaned at the warm, living, tactile feel of his bare skin on hers. He rumbled low and deep and kissed her mouth, her jaw, her throat, her shoulder, a visceral groan escaping Lara's throat as he cupped her breast in his hand. He took her nipple in his mouth, and Lara gasped and moaned as he suckled first one, then the other, his tongue drawing tantalizing circles around her nipples.

She arched her back to give him more, to give him all, and mewled like an orphaned kitten when he pulled his mouth from her breast, then purred as he deftly untied the stays to her breeches and breechcloth. They dropped to the ground, leaving her naked and exposed to the night air, to him. She shivered, though the heat of his gaze warmed her from the inside out, then he shucked his own breeches and breechcloth and Lara forgot to breathe.

As a healer, she'd seen naked men before—she'd even seen him stripped down to his breechcloth many times, an impressive sight to be sure—but she'd never seen him naked and fully aroused. Her breath left her in a rush, and she sucked in another at the raw masculine beauty of a man carved from bone, muscle, and sinew.

His grin was all male as he took her hand and pulled her down onto the blanket beside him. They were on their knees, chest to chest, his erect cock pressed against her belly, his breath as ragged as hers as his hands roamed over every inch of her, his tongue tasting and teasing her until she slid her tongue into his mouth, shy, tentative. His groan resounded from her mouth to her toes. Emboldened, Lara kissed him, explored his mouth with her tongue as she ran her hands over the breadth of his shoulders and down the muscled length of his back to his buttocks, marveling at their taut roundness. He took her hand and laid it over his cock, which stood proud and hard and pulsing with a heat Lara felt throbbing deep inside her. All she knew, all she wanted, was that living heat.

He moved his touch over the thick thatch of curls between her legs and cupped her mound. Lara moaned and pressed harder into his hand, then gasped as he pushed a finger through her curls, gently rubbing and slowly stroking her flesh until she was moving in his hand.

"Are you ready for me?"

Talon's low rumble broke through Lara's haze, and she licked her lips and focused her gaze on his. "Hmmm?"

He grinned, slow, sure, and so damned male that Lara melted in his hand. He pressed against her shoulder with his other hand until she lay back on the blanket, then he covered her body with his, keeping his weight on his elbows, his thick erection nestled in her bed of curls.

"Open for me, my beautiful rose," he rasped.

Lara spread her legs to the warm, blunt tip of Talon's probing cock and moaned as his flesh touched hers. He kissed her eyes, her mouth, her neck as he began to move against her, slowly pushing his cock just inside her and then out, tentatively repeating and testing her will to take him fully, then pushing a little deeper, a little harder each time, until she was moving with him, desperate for the feel of him, all of him. She grasped his buttocks, and he thrust himself inside her. Lara gave a little yelp at the quick, sharp tear of pain, and Talon stopped moving.

His gray eyes pierced hers. "Did I hurt you? Do you want me to stop?"

"No." She clung to him, craving him, craving more. "Don't you dare stop now."

She moved beneath him, and he moved with her, sheathing himself deeper inside, filling her with a need she never knew she had until him. She gave herself to his pace until all she knew, all she felt was him: his hands, his mouth, his taste, his scent—the friction of his skin against hers, his hard heat plunging and pulsing deep inside her, all feeling and sensation pooling at her core until she cried out with a bone-melting release.

***

Talon

Talon sat gazing down at Lara as she slept with her head in his naked lap, her slightly parted lips red and swollen from his bruising kisses, her warm breath tickling his sated cock. He pushed a damp curl from her forehead and kissed her brow, inhaling her musky sweet scent. She shivered, and he pulled the corner of the blanket up over her shoulders, sorry to cover her glorious nakedness. And she *was* glorious, from her lush lips and sensuous mouth to her firm, full breasts, slim waist, and curvy hips, to her long, lean, shapely legs. Yet it wasn't just her physical beauty that drew him to her, for she was as intelligent as she was beautiful, as rash as she was intelligent, as kindhearted as she was stubborn, and full of surprises.

The way she'd made love to him—fiercely, passionately, holding nothing back—hadn't surprised him in the least. It was who she was, how she lived her life. What did surprise him was that she'd turned to him in the river, that she'd let him kiss her, let him make love to her, *with* her. What surprised him even more was the thought of what they'd done *as* making love. He'd wanted many women in his life, and he'd had most of those he'd wanted. He'd lain with those women, had enjoyed carnal pleasures with those women, many of them women of rank in one royal court or another, and all of them experienced sexually. But he'd never considered it making love until… Lara.

She nestled her nose into his thigh, and Talon tucked the blanket around her legs, his cock tightening as he remembered the length of them wrapped around his hips. She slid her hand up his thigh, and Talon sat there in sweet agony, torn between wanting to let her sleep and aching to stir her and move her once more. He told himself it didn't even matter that Ranulf had her first. That whelp wouldn't know how to make love to a woman. Hell, he wouldn't know how to make love to anybody or anything other than himself. What mattered to Talon was Lara had come to him tonight of her own free will, had made love to *him*.

She'd turned to him to feel the living warmth of another being after watching so many others succumb to death, as he'd turned to her. He was a battle-hardened soldier, and the bloody aftermath of the ambush had unsettled him. It was only one of many such horrific scenes that would live forever in his memory. He still remembered his first battle as if it were yesterday, and today's slaughter would haunt Lara for the rest of her days. It was why he'd forbidden her to march with them, to keep her from witnessing the horrors of war, or worse, to be killed herself. Yet she'd been determined to come and had fooled him and forty other men until she'd given herself away in a fit of anger. His fierce wildcat.

She twitched, and Talon tucked the blanket tighter around her as it slid from her thighs. Dampness crept under his touch, and he drew away. A small stain on the blanket left a dark stain on his fingertips, and it carried the scent of copper.

Virgin's blood?

That explained her little yelp when he'd first entered her, but not why she'd lied about Ranulf or being a virgin. Talon racked his brain trying to remember exactly what she'd said to him that day, and realized she hadn't actually told him that Ranulf, or any other man, had been her lover. He'd assumed it, and she'd let him, never challenging his assumption until the night Hamm had cracked Ranulf across the head with the pitcher. "He had no right," she'd said as Hamm. "No right to be saying such things about her."

Bloody hell.

Talon sat there cradling Lara, trying to make sense of it, to comprehend what she'd given him this night.

"Nooo." Lara cried out, her whole body jerking. "Oh God please. *No.*"

Startled, he held her tight as she thrashed from side to side. Her eyes flew open full of pure, primal terror.

"Lara, what is it?" He fought to keep his voice level. To keep from squeezing her too tight. More than a little worried after her dream last night and the massacre today. "What did you see? Tell me."

Her eyes focused on his, and every single thing he'd felt making love to her was reflected back in their depths. Then tears pooled her eyes.

"I can't." She shook her head, sniffing back her tears, then pushed away and sat so they weren't touching.

What Talon wanted to do was pull her back, to hold her and kiss away her nightmare. To make love to her until nothing else mattered. What he did was take a deep breath and follow Sophie's advice. Lara had come to him this night of dreams, flesh, and coursing passion, and it had been more than worth the wait. He could wait until she came to him again.

"Come on." He stood and held a hand down to her. "We'd better get back to camp."

***

Lara

Lara sat forward in the saddle, refusing to lean back into the comfort of Talon's chest as she relived her dream over and over again. Talon had fallen. In her dream, he'd slumped over the Black's neck and slid off his saddle, boneless as a sack of grain onto an open field, where he lay in a pool of blood, his eyes dulled and unseeing. After lying with him, having him so deep inside her that she could still feel him there, he had died.

Her body still flushed hot every time she remembered the feel of his hands, the taste of his mouth, his skin, the hard heat of him pulsing inside her, and her mind reeled every time she realized anew what she'd done. What they'd done. Oddly enough, she felt no shame, no regret, no sense of wrong. Rather, she was in awe of how right it had felt, how he'd known her body better than she, how she'd responded to his. To him. For the first time, she truly understood how it could be between a man and a woman, and what she would lose when he left. She could only pray he left her of his own volition, not as he had in her dream.

She knew he'd died a little today, that it'd cost him to look on the dead faces of so many of his fellow soldiers, that it was this cold, dread ache they'd both felt, the emptiness they'd both needed to fill that had caused them to turn to each other for comfort, to warm their souls with the living heat of the other. She knew this as she knew she couldn't lie with him again, couldn't make love with him again, and survive losing him completely.

Just as she knew she could never tell him of her dream, of seeing him fall lifeless into a pool of his blood. She'd told him her dream of the slaughter at Roncesvalles Pass, and it had come to fruition. All her dreams did, one way or another.

When they returned to camp, Phillipe was waiting outside their tent. "King Charles wants to meet with you, Captain. Yesterday."

Talon dismounted, and Lara ignored the hand he held out to help her down from the Black. "Stay here until I get back," he told her, then called for Tree and Dardinel to stand guard as she entered the tent.

Unable to sleep, Lara paced the confines of the small tent, going over and over everything that had happened that day, until at last she heard Talon speaking with the men outside. She plopped down on her bedroll and feigned sleep as he entered the tent, peeking up at him from beneath lowered lashes as he stripped down to his breechcloth, flushing warm at the sight of his well-muscled torso and the trail of dark fur that led down to his breechcloth, and the memory of what lay not so hidden in the manly bulge beneath it.

"Sleep well, my lady wildcat."

He fell asleep in ten breaths. Lara knew because she counted them, envious of his ability to sleep anywhere, anytime, and to wake up alert and at the ready no matter how long or short a time he'd slept. She didn't sleep the rest of the night. Not with the chance of dreaming again. She lay stiff and cold despite the warm summer air, fighting the near constant urge to curl up against Talon's big warm body, and was up before dawn broke. She snuck out the back of the tent and was sharing her day-old flat bread with the roan when Talon found her.

"You shouldn't be wandering around the camp alone." He came to her side. "Tree and Dardinel are beside themselves looking for you."

Lara shrugged and wouldn't meet his eyes. She couldn't.

He cupped her chin and raised it until her gaze finally met his. "Lara, what happened between us last night—"

"Can never happen again—"

CHAPTER 15

Birth

Lara

They rode through the gates of Crossroads Keep at dusk, and a feast of cold meats, cheeses, summer greens, and fruits greeted them from Berta and the kitchen servants. After supper, Talon and Charles escorted Fulrad, on crutches, to the king's pavilion, which had been set up in the middle of the courtyard, and Lara retired to the chamber she shared with Talon to find the tub full of hot water and her soap and clean clothes laid out on her cot. Never had a bath felt so good.

She soaked in it until the water started to cool and her fingers pruned, then she donned her soft, clean nightshift and passed out on her cot. She woke up screaming Patience's name at some point in the night, then woke up in Talon's bed the next morning, alone. She'd woken from her dreams every night since her dream of Roncesvalles Pass, calling out the names of those she saw die in them: Talon, Sophie, Wolf, and now Patience. And every night, Talon would comfort her, whispering soothing words into her ears and holding her safe in his arms until she fell back to sleep.

As tempted as she was to roll over and sleep the day through, she threw the covers off and stood at the open window. The courtyard buzzed with soldiers and villagers going about the day's business, hustling and bustling around the king's pavilion of blue and gold as tents of every color along with small campfires and lines of horses covered the fields. After splashing water on her face, Lara dressed for the day in a clean tunic and skirt, then went downstairs.

She looked for Fulrad out of habit, but he wasn't at his cot. A few stragglers ate breakfast at the long table, but otherwise the hall was empty of soldiers. Lara grabbed a slice of bread and a plum from the kitchens, then continued out to the ovens, where she found Berta, who put her to work making pies.

She'd finished paring the fruit and was starting to mix the dough when a sharp bark caught her attention. She braced herself as Wolf came bounding toward her, scattering soldiers as they jumped out of his way with various curses and exclamations.

"Hey, boy." She laughed as he turned circles around her, tongue lolling and tail wagging. She ruffled his ears and thumped his sides. "How've you been, eh?"

The crowd of curious soldiers parted as Sophie walked past, and Lara threw her arms around her and gave her a big hug.

"Let go of me, child," Sophie chided, "before you break my old bones."

Lara stepped back, eyeing Sophie as closely as Sophie eyed her.

"You look well, Tante."

"Well enough."

"How'd Wolf do?"

"He waited for you by the door the first two days and nights, then went missing the third day. I'm pretty sure he went looking for you up at the Hollow, because he was gone for four days. When he came back, I dosed him with belladonna for the next five days until he finally gave up trying to nose you out and instead lay around moping and looking miserable."

"Aww, Wolf." Lara eased down to hug the hound and kiss his nose. "I'm sorry, boy. It was a cruel thing to do to you."

"Was it worth it?" Sophie asked.

Memories of it all hit her, and she focused on Sophie's question. "King Charles has left my fate up to Tal... the captain. Who hasn't told me of his decision yet."

"Perhaps he's waiting until after the king has left."

"Most likely."

Sophie ruffled Lara's cropped hair, her natural auburn growing out at the roots. Then she glanced at Lara's flour-covered arms, where the darker skin dye had faded, and at the balls of dough ready to be rolled out. Giving a sigh, Sophie rolled up her sleeves. "Well now, there's a supper to prepare and a king to prepare it for. Marta." She called out to the girl carrying a pot of pitted plums. "Go find your grandmother, child, tell her I have news of Patience and the babe."

"Is everything well with them?" The memory of last night's dream filled Lara with dread.

"The babe has dropped," Sophie said. "It'll be coming soon, but yes, Patience and the babe are doing well. The buck the captain left them and the cask of red wine he sent made a marked difference."

Lara hadn't known about the wine, yet it didn't surprise her that he'd sent it, or that he'd never mentioned it to her. She glanced at the king's pavilion at the same time Talon walked out of it and headed straight toward them.

"Ladies." He bowed from his waist up. "I've come with an invitation from the king to sup with him at table tonight."

"We'd be honored." Sophie eyed him as closely as she had Lara.

"The Midereds have been invited as well," he told them. "I assume they'll be on their best behavior with the king here."

"We shall see," Sophie said.

"Yes." He gave a tick of his jaw. "We shall." He met Lara's doubtful gaze and his jaw ticked again. "Madam," he said to Sophie. "If I could speak with you, in private."

"Of course, Captain." Sophie gave a quick glance Lara's way before following him inside the hall.

Lara had two pie crusts rolled out before they came back out, neither giving anything away by their expressions as they walked back toward her. Shouting broke out, and soldiers jumped aside as a cart pulled up. Willem jumped down and ran to where Talon and Sophie joined Lara.

"Patience is in labor." Willem panted as hard as his cart horse. "Where's Berta?"

"Inside the kitchens," Sophie said.

Lara was already untying her work apron as Willem ran into the kitchens, running back out with Berta on his heels a moment later.

"What can I do?" Berta asked Sophie.

"Stay here and feed the king. Lara and I will be with her." Sophie turned to Talon as Willem loaded her bag onto the cart. "Please give our thanks and regrets to the king for his kind invitation to supper tonight, Captain. Unfortunately, babies come in their own sweet time."

"I will." Talon took Lara by the wrist. "Take the roan. You'll get there faster, and if you need anything or anybody from here, you can send Willem back on him."

Lara nodded. "I need to get my bag from upstairs."

When she came back out, Talon was waiting for her with the roan saddled and ready.

"Remember," he said, giving her a leg up onto the saddle. "If you need anything, just send Willem."

"I will." Lara fought the urge to reach out and smooth his furrowed brow. "Try not to worry so much, Captain Talon Guiscard, patron saint of strays and fey lads, this is Patience's second babe, and Sophie says she's been doing well."

He nodded and folded his hand over hers as she took the reins. "What of your latest dream?"

Lara swallowed the terror she'd felt when she couldn't staunch the flow of Patience's blood in her dream, the horror of watching the life drain from her friend's face. "Giving birth is a bloody business. I've had the same dream before every babe I've helped birth into this world," she lied.

Talon said nothing, but his expression told her he wasn't sure he believed her. He gave her hand a squeeze, and Lara rode off, trying not to dwell on the fact that Patience's babe was early, or that it was birthing her fifth child that had killed Talon's mother. A fact he was no doubt worrying over as well.

***

Sophie leaned back in her chair at Willem and Patience's kitchen table and stretched her neck and shoulders, letting out a long, weary, happy sigh.

"What time do you think it is?" she asked Lara.

Lara stifled a yawn. "Close to midnight at least."

A lusty wail filled the little house from the bed loft above them, and Sophie and Lara sat grinning at each other like two fat tabbies with bellies full of milk.

"Patience is going to have her hands full with that one," Sophie said. "Strong-willed and demanding he is, coming when he wanted as he did." Another wail pealed out, and then soft grunts and rootings followed by the proud cooing of the new parents. "He knows what he wants and when he wants it, this Wilric does. Much like the captain, who told me you've been waking from your dreams, calling out not only his name, but mine and Wolf's and Patience's every night since you dreamed of the massacre at Roncesvalles Pass."

Lara winced as each name hit her like a physical blow.

"What happens in your dreams?"

Lara shook her head.

"Sometimes sharing a fear can lessen it greatly." Sophie eyed her up carefully.

A rush of blood pounded through Lara's head, and she licked at sudden dry lips. "What if it would only increase the fear, person by person?"

Sophie's face paled and she looked as tired as Lara felt. Then she quirked her brows. "What did you dream of Patience?"

Lara looked down at her hands, washed and clean of the leavings of childbirth. "There was blood. Too much blood. I couldn't staunch it. Patience—"

"Giving birth is a bloody business." Sophie repeated Lara's own words that she'd used to allay Talon's worry. "Patience and the babe are both doing well."

Lara let out a relieved breath. "True."

"What did you dream about me?"

The blood that had been pounding in Lara's head drained to her toes.

"You can tell me."

Lara clasped her fingers together in her lap and met Sophie's gaze. "I, ah, I wrapped your death shroud over your face."

"As you will, someday." Sophie was too quick and too offhanded in her reply. "As it should be. I'm glad it will be your face to see mine last."

"As I saw Plutarch's." Hot tears welled in Lara's eyes. "Though it wasn't my face he saw at the end, but Hamm's and the lady Isabeau's."

"Plutarch?" Sophie's voice cracked. "Lady Isabeau?"

"He was the cook I traveled with until my discovery." Lara gave a sad smile. "He was kind to me, to Hamm. He told me tales of his life as a man-at-arms for Reginald and his wife, Eileen. Of their daughter Isabeau and Harald, how they'd married in secret, how he'd grieved when he returned to find her gone. Did you know this Harald?"

"I did," Sophie said after a long pause. "He was a man-at-arms under Orlando."

"Your second husband?"

"We were never actually married. Not by the church."

It seemed Lara wasn't the only keeping secrets. "You never told me that."

Sophie shrugged. "We lived as man and wife. We loved as man and wife."

And Sophie had lost him to war. As Lara would Talon.

"Oh Tante." She started shaking as if she'd woken from one of her dreams. "I see him fall. In my dreams, I see Talon pierced through with an arrow and fall off the Black into a pool of his own blood. And his eyes…" She shuddered and her teeth chattered. "Oh God. His eyes are as dulled and unseeing as Plutarch's were."

Sophie laid a gnarled hand over Lara's icy fingers. "So, you do love him?"

Lara shook her head as hot tears slid from her cheeks. "I can't."

"Yet you do."

"I did," Lara admitted. "Once. After the massacre at Roncesvalles."

Sophie gave Lara's hand a gentle squeeze. "It was inevitable. Everyone could see it but you two. Every person in the valley's been stepping around the chain pulling you two together since the day you met, getting tighter and tighter the more you both fought it." She eyed Lara, her expression serious. "Some people are meant to come together, whether for a moment, a day, a year, a lifetime. In the end, we can only love who and when we can."

Lara burst into sobs

"It's not that bad, is it?" Sophie asked. "Captain Guiscard is a good man, and a good lover, I'm guessing."

Lara nodded, then laughed and snorted through her tears. Not that she had anyone to compare his lovemaking with, but good didn't even begin to describe what she'd felt with him.

Sophie cackled. "That's what I thought."

"But, Tante, it was you who warned me to stay out of his bed. Who told me not to get my belly fat with his bastard."

"He would marry you."

"You've heard him." Lara sniffed. "He has no intention of marrying me or anyone. No intention of siring any brats. Besides, a man can't marry when he's dead."

Sophie said nothing. What was there to say?

"Tante?" Lara asked, her voice just above a whisper. "Was it worth it? Loving a man, only to lose him?"

Sophie gave a sad smile. "My husband and I were still getting to know each other as man and wife when he was taken from me. But Orlando I loved as fully as any woman ever loved a man, and he loved me. Though we only had five years together, I don't regret a single moment of them."

"Yet you grieve for him still, over twenty years later."

"I do. Though I thought I did a better job at hiding it."

"Would you do it again? Would you let yourself love Orlando knowing you'd be grieving him longer than you loved him?"

"I would," Sophie answered without hesitation. "I did. I knew he was a soldier, that soldiers die in battle in numbers that devastate entire provinces." She patted Lara's hand. "You're wrong about one very important thing though." She smiled and her lips trembled. "I haven't been grieving either of them longer than I loved them, for I love them still and will until my dying day."

***

Talon

Talon drank enough wine to keep his backside down on his seat in the common room after supper but not so much that his wits were dulled. He was spared having to interact with Nithard at least, who kept Charles in near constant conversation. Ravenna sat surprisingly quiet beside her father, listening to the king with the reverence of a nun in church. Her brother sat off in a corner, whispering back and forth with Fulrad, whose cousin, the king, had discharged him from the army and Talon's care.

"I go to my wife on the southern shore of the Garonne where she and our twin sons await me," Charles told the company. "The main army will winter in Auxerre, and since you're so comfortably garrisoned here at Crossroads Keep, Captain, you will stay and keep these borders secure until I muster the army, when you will help me secure the Saxon borders."

Not sure if he'd been given a reprieve or a lengthening of his sentence, Talon held his cup up. "I accept, my liege."

By the studied mask of indifference plastered on Nithard's face and the sneer on Ranulf's, it was easy to see they were less than pleased by the company's continued posting in the province. After lifting his cup to Nithard and then Ranulf, Talon drank deeply, then grinned and wiped his mouth with his sleeve before slamming his empty cup down.

Ranulf lifted his cup to Talon and didn't drink a drop: an insult not missed by many seated around the hearth fire, certainly not by Talon, who let the insult go, for now.

"See," he said to Charles, who had watched it all. "See how politic I can be when needed?"

"I do see, Captain." Charles steepled his fingers. "Very politic indeed."

"And now, my liege." Talon eased to his feet on unsteady legs. "I need to seek my bed, for my brain is fogged from too much drink and too little sleep."

"Go, find your bed, my friend." Charles waved him off. "Go dream of long-legged wildcats with pelts of fire and eyes of green and gold. Perhaps tonight's decisions will help bring her closer to you."

Talon was sure Charles meant well, giving him more time here, and he wanted that time. He wanted to make love to Lara again, to make her his. But would she let him? And if she did, what would become of her after he left? He stood at his full height and sucked in a deep breath to clear some of the drink from his mind. Once he was gone from here, there wouldn't be much he could do for Lara, but he could do something for her now.

"Before I retire for the night," he announced in a voice that commanded everyone's attention, "I have determined the *lidi*, Lara, has fulfilled her full wergeld. As of tomorrow, she will be a freewoman, beholden to none." The last he spoke directly to Nithard, then he turned to Charles. "As you have released your cousin from his military duty, I assume you will agree to this."

Charles didn't bat an eyelash. "The king declares it to be so."

Talon took the stairs to his chamber, all too aware that Lara wouldn't be there pretending to sleep, that if she didn't return sometime tonight, she'd likely never be in there again. He was losing her already, yet his loss was tempered by knowing he'd done what was right.

In his chamber, Talon stripped down to his breechcloth and plopped down on the bed. He closed his eyes with a bone-weary groan, expecting the sweet oblivion of sleep to overtake him, but a host of sights and sounds haunted him: his mother, her cheeks tear-streaked, her face ashen as she bade him good-bye; the copper scent of the blood that couldn't be staunched; his father's wracking sobs, his brothers', his own; the wails of the newborn babe whose birth had killed his mother. He lay in his bed praying never to hear Willem or Wyatt cry like that, that both Patience and her babe survived the grueling process of birth, that Lara wouldn't have to say good-bye to her friend so soon after Plutarch. He lay there in a half-drunken, half-dreaming stupor when he realized someone was knocking at his chamber's door. Once he'd rolled off the bed and found his feet, he opened the door, and a small, dark-headed woman darted beneath his arm into the room.

"Ravenna?"

"May I come in?"

Talon waved an arm toward where she already stood inside his bedchamber. "What do you want?"

She untied the sash to her robe and pushed it off her shoulders, letting it drop to the floor. Clad in the same sheer, one-shouldered sleeping gown she'd worn her last unannounced visit to his chamber, she sauntered over to the table and poured herself a cup of wine, smiling seductively as she ran a fingertip along the rim. "Your *lidi* is not here, nor will she be after tomorrow."

"What the king and I decided about Lara has nothing to do with you."

She dipped her finger in the wine and licked it off her fingertip. "What I meant is, you are not playing your game tonight. I thought you might like to play another?"

"With you?"

She offered a pretty pout and sidled up to him. More curious than aroused, Talon let her take him by the hand and lead him toward the bed. Wrapping her hands around his neck, she stood on her tiptoes and stretched up, her rouged lips puckered. Talon gripped her forearms to remove her hold from his neck.

"Ravenna, stop."

"But Talon…" She leaned into him, and he stepped back, taking her weight with him before bumping the back of his legs up against the bed.

The door burst open, and Lara blew in with Wolf. "Good news, Talon," she said. "Patience had a b—"

"A boy?" Ravenna still held tight to Talon's neck as Lara stilled. "How perfectly common."

Lara whirled around and ran out the door, Wolf on her heels.

"*Lara.*" Talon pushed Ravenna off, cursing. "Wait." He hurried out the door after her.

Fists clenched at her sides, Lara stopped at the top of the stairs as the loud chorus of a bawdy drinking song rose from the hall below.

"Listen to me," he said as she took in the sight of him clad only in his breechcloth. "She came to me unasked, as she did before. Nothing happened."

Lara snorted. "It didn't look like nothing."

"I swear. I was just curious what she would do. I wouldn't have let it go any further."

"It makes no difference to me." She shrugged but her eyes welled with tears.

"Then why are you about to cry?" He reached out to wipe the tear that slid down her cheek.

She slapped his hand away. "*Don't*," she hissed. "You don't ever get to touch me again. Go back to Ravenna. She'll give you whatever you want."

"*God's blood*, woman," Talon thundered, and the singing below stopped. "I don't want Ravenna. I want you."

"Then why play long enough to see what she'd do?" she cried.

"Ravenna has nothing to do with this, whatever *this* is between us," he snarled, and her eyes narrowed. "You came to me once. You loved me once." Her eyes widened. "Why won't you come to me again? You're playing me just as much."

"My resistance is different. I...can't."

"Can't?" He stepped up and took her by the arm as she tried to turn away. "Or won't? Tell me, Lara. Just tell me."

"Won't." She wrenched her arm from his grip and gave a sob. "I won't love you again only to lose you. I can't."

Talon shivered as if a ghost had walked through him. All the nights Lara had woken crying out his name, her body shaking and her eyes wide with fear. Fear for him. For Sophie and Wolf and Patience. Yet her fears for Patience mustn't have come to fruition, else she wouldn't have bounded into their chamber with such a lilt to her voice as she announced that Patience had given birth to a boy.

Her gaze slipped behind him, and he turned to find Ravenna slinking into the chamber she shared with her father and brother for the night.

"Will you return to our chamber now?" Talon said gently.

She glanced down the stairs where the bawdy singing had resumed, then strode past him back to their chamber. As Talon followed her in, she lay down on her cot, fully dressed, Wolf on the floor next to her and watching him with a chary eye. Talon sat on the edge of his bed as Lara tossed and turned on her cot. He could have told her of his and the king's declaring her a freewoman, but he didn't think that would help either of them get to sleep. He lay back and closed his eyes. If the nights past were any indication, he'd be holding her in his bed at some point in what was left of the night.

***

"*No*, oh God, no. *Sooophie.*"

Giving a frown, Talon rolled out of bed, gathered Lara in his arms, then carried her back to his bed. For a long while he sat cradling her and smoothing her sweaty curls from her forehead. "I've got you. You're safe."

"Talon." Her breath tickled his chest as she burrowed her nose into his neck.

"Aye, my rose. You had another dream."

"Sophie." She clung to Talon. "I dreamed of Sophie."

Talon rocked her in his arms and murmured soothing words into her hair until she stopped shaking. He pressed his lips to her forehead, and her body relaxed with one long, soughing sigh.

"Maybe if you told me what you saw this one last time. It might help."

She lifted her head and met his gaze. "One last time?"

"You march with the king when he leaves Crossroads Keep tomorrow."

She pushed away from him, a wary wildcat once more. "Why would I be leaving with the king tomorrow?"

Damn her hide, she thought he'd sold her wergeld to Charles.

"You'll ride out from Crossroads Keep alongside Charles as a freewoman who fulfilled her season of military service," he told her, and was instantly rewarded with her smile, a smile he could forgive anything. "I'll be your hated jailer no more, though neither will I be the one to hold you and comfort you when you wake crying out from your dreams."

Her smile turned bittersweet, then she leaned in and kissed his cheek.

"Thank you, truly, for almost everything." Her eyes crinkled up.

He took her hand in his and rubbed a thumb over the backs of her fingers. "I haven't given you even a hundredth of what I would have." His throat constricted with the depth of what he felt and wouldn't say. "I have, however, been able to give you the cloak of the king's protection, which will reach much farther than mine once I'm gone, most likely come winter." He gave her a purposely cocky grin. "Be sure to tell Sophie that, else she think me shirking my oath."

"Your oath to protect me?"

"And what a troublesome oath that turned out to be." His voice was stern, but he fought back a laugh.

As did Lara, then she turned serious. "Talon? How did I curse you?"

He laughed, short and harsh, then stood and went over to the cot before sitting down. He'd given up the bed up to Lara and Wolf for what was left of the night.

"You smiled my way, my beautiful, thorny rose. And then you bled me."

CHAPTER 16

Death

Lara

Sophie's hip was troubling her, so Lara put her to bed with extra blankets and a side table laden with hot tea and a slice of apple pie before she set off for market day. Pulling her mantle tighter around her shoulders in the early autumn chill of the morning, she shook the reins to Honey's harness and started the trek to the village square, her wagon full of cheeses and herbs and tinctures and soaps. Wolf loped alongside.

They passed Patience's house, where Willem was no doubt busy working on the many saddles the garrison's soldiers had ordered. He and his newly hired apprentice had been elbow-deep in newly tanned hide when Lara checked on Patience and the baby three days ago. Talon had shown up as well.

He'd brought a teething ring carved of linden and sanded as smooth as one of his ivory game pieces for the babe, and a horse in full armor for Wyatt. The boy had lit up at sight of it. Lara had watched as Talon held Wilric, not clumsy and afraid like so many men who weren't fathers, but close and tender, talking softly, smiling, then breathing in the scent of Wilric's downy head.

She tried not to dwell on the grin that he gave when he'd caught her watching him, or the fact that despite how comfortable he'd seemed with the babe, he'd sworn his intent to never sire a child loudly and publicly more than once. She blew her breath out and urged Honey on, thankful that her flux had come and gone in the past week, that she and Talon had both escaped a pregnancy.

Other than that day at Patience's house, she hadn't spoken to him since he released her from being lidi a nine days ago and had only seen him from a distance as he rode the Black on his rounds of the valley. As she pulled her wagon into the village square and set up her stall, she wondered if she'd see him today at the market. She'd made extra batches of sandalwood and rose soaps, just in case he did show and wanted to replenish his supply. As well as a last-of-the-harvest strawberry pie, which she kept hidden beneath the wagon seat with two apple pies.

Well into the afternoon, Lara had sold most of her goods and was considering leaving when she looked across the square. Phillipe and Anglbert walked to each side of Talon, herding him toward her stall like a recalcitrant bull into a field full of nettles. Bemused, she bit down on her grin as he stopped before her with his hands thrust deep into his pockets, despite Wolf's attempts to nose them out.

"Good day, Captain. Anglbert... Phillipe."

"It would've been a better day," Anglbert harumphed, "if a certain captain here hadn't dragged his feet so long and hard about coming in the first place." He looked over what was left of her goods. "You're out of pie."

He sounded so forlorn Lara couldn't help but play it out a moment, splaying her hands and shrugging her shoulders. Then she stepped over to the front of the wagon, reached under the bench seat, and pulled out two apple pies. She handed Anglbert and Phillipe a pie each, grinning as their noses were instantly in the cheesecloth wraps. Then she pulled the strawberry pie out and handed it to Talon. He reached for his purse, and Lara laid her hand over his. "My gifts to the three of you. Free of charge."

"Ahhh." Anglbert inhaled another whiff of his pie. "You're an angel, Lara. I always said she was an angel," he repeated to Talon and Phillipe, both of whom looked surprised at his declaration.

"She bakes like an angel." Phillipe pulled the cheesecloth away from his pie and scooped a fingerful of apple into his mouth. "Manna from heaven."

They all looked to Talon, who managed a terse, "Thank you."

"Don't mind him." Phillipe thumbed at the captain. "He's been a man of few words and numerous scowls lately."

"He's worse at night." Anglbert earned one of those scowls from Talon. "He drinks too much wine and bites your head off whilst playing Shah because the wrong person is sitting across the board from him. Perhaps you have a tincture or potion for what's ailing him?"

"I might," Lara said. Talon truly did look unwell. For such a normally robust man, his cheeks were hollowed and there were dark circles under his eyes, as if he hadn't been sleeping well, and he was a man who could normally sleep anywhere, anytime he had a mind to. "If I knew what ails him."

"There's the rub," Phillipe said as Talon glowered at him. "For he will not tell us, though I wager it's the curse."

"It's the curse all right," Anglbert said with a somber shake of his grayed head. "The wildcat eludes him still."

"Does she?" Lara feigned the ignorance that had blinded her for so long.

"I told him he must woo her first." Phillipe grinned. "Before he could ever hope to tame her."

Lara met Talon's brooding gaze. "I am sorry, Captain. I know of no potion for wooing wildcats." She turned from the disappointment in his eyes and pulled a vial of valerian root from her store. "But if you drink a tea of this root powder before bed, it will help you sleep. I warn you though, it's a bitter brew, you might want to sweeten it with honey."

"It can be no more bitter than what I swallow every night now," he said, holding her hand with the vial. "I've tasted the sweetest of honey and it is for want of more that I sicken and pine."

He pressed a kiss to her hand, then took the vial and turned on his heels before striding away as Lara stood dumbstruck. When at last she could think again, she turned to Anglbert and Phillipe, who watched her with amused grins. Giving them a scowl worthy of the captain's, she turned her back to them and loaded her cart for the return trip home.

She hadn't made it more than half a league from the village when Wolf stopped to sniff the air and stare at the road behind them. Giving a wag of his tail, he took off running toward Talon and his Black.

"Captain," she greeted him as he pulled the Black up beside her.

"Lara."

They rode on in silence, glancing back and forth at each other. Lara snorted. This was ridiculous. They'd shared the same bedchamber for a month, and the same tent for a month after that. She'd woken up from her nightmares cradled in his arms more times than she could count. They'd made love. Surely, they could find something to talk about. She glanced at the telltale bulge of the vial she'd given him in his tunic pocket.

"I hope the valerian helps you sleep," she said.

He patted his tunic pocket. "And you? Have you been sleeping well? Or do your dreams still wake you?"

"No." Lara gave a relieved sigh. "I've not had one since I returned to my home."

"Good. I'm glad to hear it."

"I, ah, I don't remember if I, ah, if I ever thanked you, for helping me when they, ah..." When she would awaken crying out and he would cradle her in his arms and soothe her, whispering sweet and low in her hair.

He gave a crooked grin. "You're welcome."

Lara cleared her throat and tried to think of something, anything else to talk about.

"Patience and Wilric are both doing well," she said, though they'd both seen them only three days ago. "If the babe's appetite is any indication, he'll be a strapping lad."

Talon shifted on his saddle and nodded. "It's a good thing Willem is getting so many orders for saddles then, with two growing boys to feed."

Lara tilted her head as if changing her view of him would explain this man who swore his disdain for children, yet made toys for Wyatt and melted at the sight of Wilric. Her musing led to other things that melted, like her insides as she took in his hands holding the Black's reins and remembered the feel of them on her skin.

If he'd been cursed by her, then she'd been cursed by him as well, for she couldn't look at his lips without tasting their bruising nectar, or at the broad expanse of his chest without feeling his muscled heat beneath her fingers, the narrowing of his hips without feeling them pressing against hers.

She gave Honey's harness a gentle shake. "Sophie's hip has been bothering her." Talon urged the Black into a trot as well. "I want to get home to her."

"How bad is it?" he said with genuine concern in his voice.

"It pains her enough she can't walk far on it for the first few days the cold sets in, until the teas and poultices start working. In truth, the pain's gotten worse and comes earlier each year. Last winter we moved her bed down next to the hearth fire and that seemed to help."

"Tree and I can move it down for you," he offered. "Anytime you wish before winter sets in."

Before the garrison left Crossroads Keep.

"Have you received orders to join the king?"

"No, not yet." His eyes pierced hers. "I don't expect them for another month or two."

Lara turned the wagon up the path to her house and pulled Honey to a stop.

The door stood wide open.

"Sophie?" Lara dismounted and went up to the house. An eerie silence greeted her, and with her heart pounding a little harder in her chest, she ran past Talon to the barn. Only Gaea and the goats grazed in the corral.

"Sophie." She bolted back out into the middle of the yard. *"Sophie."*

"Could she have gone somewhere?" Talon tied the Black to the post in the yard and joined her. "Maybe to tend a villager?"

"No, she couldn't walk any distance, and Gaea's still here." Lara tried to think, but all she saw was Sophie's face from her dreams, blanched and unseeing with water swirling around her. Lara's heart dropped to her feet. "The river," she whispered hoarsely. "She's in the water in my dreams."

She turned for the river and managed to take two steps before her legs gave out. Talon caught her before she hit the ground and propped his shoulder under her arm, holding her up as they walked to the dock, where they found Sophie's staff and the handle and shards of a broken water pitcher on the planks.

Lara turned her face into Talon's shoulder, her entire body shaking as the image of Sophie tangled amongst gnarled roots came to her from her dreams. "The old oak," she rasped. "She's in the old oak."

"Stay here. I'll go look."

"No." Lara lifted her head and squared her shoulders. "I need to be there for her."

On the river's bank, Sophie lay entwined in the roots of the old oak, her face as white as her hair, her eyes dulled, unseeing. A blood-leeched gash gaped above her left ear. Lara walked into the river without uttering a sound. She stood staring into Sophie's lifeless eyes. The woman who had been her mother, sister, teacher, and friend, and who had raised her and loved her for twenty-two years. Gone.

***

Talon

"Let me." Talon waded hip deep in the freezing water and carefully untangled Sophie's body from the roots that had kept her from floating farther downriver.

He carried her sodden body back to the house, Lara walking beside them as pale and silent as a ghost. After laying Sophie on the table, he brought the hearth fire back to life as Lara collected a washbasin and cloths, a pair of scissors, and a tub of oil that smelled of rosemary. Lara set them down beside Sophie and a shiver ran through her.

"You should change into dry clothes, before you catch your dea…" Talon trailed off. If Lara was aware of what he'd almost said, she didn't show it. He took her by both shoulders and gently led her to the loft's ladder, then stood by the fire, drying his own clothes until Lara came back down.

"Is there anything you need me to do?"

She shook her head, and Talon stood helpless to do more than rub Wolf's ears as Lara cut Sophie's sopping gown away and rubbed her body dry. She massaged the oil into the old healer's blue-tinged skin in an intimate dance that Talon felt privileged to witness, her hands saying their farewell to the woman who'd known her better than anybody, lingering lastly over the deep blue bruise on her temple that had been her death blow.

Sophie must have gone to fill the water pitcher, slipped on the wet pallet, hit her head, and fallen into the river. Whether she'd grasped the oaks roots to save herself from drowning or the oak caught her already dead, Talon didn't know. But he did know that knock to the head had killed her, and he was fairly certain she'd passed quickly and hopefully hadn't suffered much. It all seemed an ignoble end to Sophie the Sixth, who he'd always had a vague notion of going out fighting.

"Will you help me dress her?" Lara startled Talon. It was the first she'd spoken since finding Sophie.

They dressed her in a gray velveteen gown, and then Lara cut sprigs of rosemary from the garden before she sat in a rocking chair beside the hearth to weave the sprigs into a wreath without saying another word or shedding a single tear. When the wreath was finished, she stood over Sophie and ran a hand down the old healer's arm. With a heaving sigh, she drew Sophie's death shroud up over her and laid the wreath around her head. Standing there staring down at her shrouded body, Lara had gone to a place where Talon couldn't follow. A place he knew too well too young.

Talon pulled the rocker next to the table and sat Lara down on it, unable to do more than stay and watch over her until she came back.

He woke cold and bent and cramped in a chair, alone but for Sophie, who lay in state on the table. The front door was open, and he stepped out into the morning chill to find Lara standing in the middle of the yard, a woolen scarf around her shoulders, Wolf hugging her knee.

"Sunrise was always Sophie's favorite time of day," she said, her voice subdued as she gazed up into a brilliant amethyst sky with topaz clouds, a fitting tribute to Sophie the Sixth. "The dawning, she called it." She smiled, sad and bittersweet, her gaze never leaving the crystalline sky. "She should be buried beneath the old oak, facing east."

Talon hated leaving Lara, but the grievous news of Sophie's death and the business of burying her needed to be dealt with. Halfway out the door, he turned to ask Lara if she'd truly be all right, but she was already sitting in the rocker, her hand on the shroud over Sophie's arm, Wolf now lying on the floor beside her. He left them for what would be their last time alone together.

He entered the keep through the kitchens, where Berta sat at table with Anglbert eating a breakfast of cold ham and eggs, as close and cozy as an old married couple.

"One of the advantages to an old soldier's habit of rising at dawn," Anglbert said with a glint in his eye. Then he saw Talon. "Captain?"

He half stood as Talon pressed his lips tight. Talon looked to Berta. He'd searched for the right words to tell her that her lifelong friend was gone the entire ride to the keep. In the end, there was no kind way to tell her, so he simply said it. "Sophie's dead."

It took a moment for the terrible truth to sink in, and when it did, Berta's legs gave out. Anglbert caught her, and when she came to, it was his face, his eyes that reaffirmed the awful reality.

"I'm so very sorry." Talon laid a hand on her shaking shoulder as she sobbed into Anglbert's. He gave Anglbert's shoulder a squeeze as well. "I'll let the others know. See to your lady."

"No." Berta lifted her tear-streaked face. "I should go to Lara. There are preparations to make, funeral cakes to bake." She wiped her tears and smoothed her apron. "The Abbot Rogert needs to be sent for to perform the burial rites." She took in a shaky breath and let it out with a sigh. "He's at the Abbey St. Marie."

"Right." Anglbert gave her a kiss on her cheek. "I'll go for the abbot."

***

They buried Sophie under the oak at sunset with the Abbot Rogert presiding over the funeral rites and half the valley in attendance. Lara stood still and pale beside the abbot throughout the service, her gaze never leaving Sophie's grave until the last shovel full of dirt was patted down. Talon cupped her elbow and wrapped an arm around her waist, letting her lean on him as they walked back into the house. She sat in Sophie's rocker by the hearth and accepted the villagers', and several of his soldiers', teary condolences and heartfelt tributes, thanking them, comforting them with her soft smiles and words, performing her last duty to Sophie, as gracious as any queen. The abbot, who had spoken to Talon only to introduce himself when he'd first arrived, watched both Lara and Talon closely, and spoke privately with Berta in a far corner of the house for what looked to be a very serious conversation.

It was well into the night when Talon closed the door behind the last mourner, after assuring Berta he'd keep watch over Lara, who stood and rolled the rug back from the trapdoor that Talon had heard bump and squeak the day he'd talked to Sophie about his wildcat. She pulled the door open and stepped down onto a ladder, stopping when her head was level with Wolf's. She leaned her forehead into his, kissed him on the nose, and whispered something into the sad-eyed hound's ear. Lifting her head from Wolf's, she met Talon's worried frown with a tremulous smile, the first tear he'd seen her shed through it all slipping down her cheek. Then her face crumpled, and she went down the ladder and pulled the door shut.

Tired, lost in Lara's grief, he locked the house up, then pulled the rocker next to the trapdoor and took up his post. He and Wolf would keep guard as candlelight shone through cracks in the floor, Talon's ears attuned to Lara's pacing and weeping below.

The first gray streaks of dawn lit the sky when Talon realized it had grown quiet in the cellar. After slowly pulling the trapdoor open, he peered down into the cellar to find Lara sleeping on a pile of blankets in the middle of the planked floor. A hide-bound tome sat on a small table beside a guttering candle, and shelves on every wall were lined with bottles of tinctures and potions, wheels of cheeses, and baskets of roots and fungi. The tools of her and Sophie's trade.

He shut the trapdoor, spread out on the floor alongside it, and took the opportunity to snatch some sleep, only to be woken up a short time later by an insistent knocking at the door.

"Where is she?" Berta bustled past Talon as he opened the door. Anglbert, Phillipe, and Denys followed her in.

"Sleeping." Talon shook his head as Berta went to the ladder that led to the loft, then nodded toward the cellar door.

"Ah," Berta said. "How long?"

"She went down after everyone left last night. But she's only been sleeping since dawn broke."

"Poor lamb," Berta clucked. "She must be worn out." She looked around the house and set her hands on her hips. "I'll see to the house and the food." She nodded toward the table where Sophie had lain in state, now covered with gifts of breads and cakes and pies. "You men see to the livestock. Out, now." She shooed Talon, who was reluctant to leave his post, guarding Lara. "Out, I say, before you wake the poor dear with all your clomping about."

Talon shooed along with the others and Wolf, but while the three soldiers stood staring about the yard and stables, trying to figure out what needed doing where, Denys jumped right in.

"Here." He handed Anglbert and Phillipe an empty basket each. "The apples need gathering. Just the ones that've dropped. Don't pick any from the trees."

"Yes, sir." Phillipe saluted Denys, then elbowed Anglbert, who grumbled as they headed for the orchard.

Talon led Gaea and Honey out of their stalls into the little corral, where he spread hay for the horses and goats and watched Denys cajole a ruffled hen from her nest as he gathered eggs from their roost.

"How attached are you to being a stablehand at the keep?" he asked the lad.

"I like the work well enough," Denys told him. "And the pay's good. Better'n I'd earn anywhere else as I'll not work for the count."

Talon clapped a hand on his shoulder. "I may have a job for you, if you're interested."

***

Lara

Lara woke slowly to a dim light hovering over her. She focused her eyes on the square of light shining down through the open cellar door and sat up, her head pounding as she drained the pitcher of water on the stool next to her pile of blankets, her chest aching with a hole as big and empty as her stomach's. She had a foggy memory of Talon bringing the pitcher down and voices and movement in the house above, yet she had no recollection of time passing as she'd paced and wept and slept. She only knew it was night again from the low glow of candlelight above.

She used the chamber pot that had also been brought down at some point, then climbed the ladder and poked her head up out of the cellar. Talon slept on the floor next to the door, Wolf curled up beside him. She reached out to touch Talon's cheek, but reason and a grief so sharp it took the breath from her stayed her hand.

"No," she whispered to herself. "Don't."

Talon opened his eyes, his gaze level with hers. "Don't what?"

"Love you," she said, telling him what she'd foresworn not to. "Only to lose you."

Maybe it was true what the priests said: confession was good for the soul. Letting Talon see what was in her heart, seeing what she felt reflected in his eyes of honed steel, almost made the hurting worth it.

"I'm sorry," she meant to say, but only managed to mouth.

"Don't be." His voice was a low rumble. He ran his hand through her unruly hair, cupped the back of her head, then pressed his forehead to hers. "I understand. Better than most."

"I know you do." It was as Sophie had said: Lara was a healer, and this valley and its people were her home, her family, and they'd be needing her even more now that Sophie was gone. He was a warrior whose family of horse soldiers was as nomadic as he, whose home was whatever camp, battlefield, or garrison the king ordered them to, and who would be leaving the garrison of Crossroads Keep come winter, if not sooner.

After taking a deep breath in and blowing it out, she climbed up out of the cellar, squared her shoulders, and offered Talon her hand as he stood. "You are welcome in my home anytime, Captain Talon

Guiscard. You have been a good and true friend to me and Sophie, and I-I would miss your company. I have missed it."

"Yes." He took her hand in his and held it. "Sorry about that. I thought staying away would be easier, but, well…" He dropped her hand and rubbed the stubble of his chin with a shrug and a sheepish grin.

"Yes," Lara echoed, suddenly shy of him too. "Well." Her stomach growled so loud Wolf pricked his ears and cocked his head. Lara laughed, then she burst into tears before swiping them from her cheek to eye the table laden with food. A basket of fresh eggs and a loaf of sourdough bread caught her eye. "I'm starving. How do eggs scrambled with cheese and chives, plus bread fried in Sophie's prized bottle of olive oil all the way from Lombardi sound for breakfast?"

Talon grinned. "Like I'm going to weigh five hundred stone if this is how you feed your friends."

He not only stayed for breakfast but he stayed all day and night, never letting her out of his sight. He listened when she talked about something Sophie had said or done, and laughed softly with her over Sophie's witticisms. He held her when her grief washed over her with such force that her legs gave out and her whole body shook, and he'd whispered words of comfort as she sobbed into his shoulder. He was her protector, growling off anyone who tried to disturb her other than Berta and Patience, who sat with her while Talon settled Denys in the barn, where he was apparently taking up residence to work as her helper. After they left to prepare supper for the garrison, he sat with her until she must have fallen asleep in Sophie's rocker.

When she woke crying out Sophie's name in the pitch of night, he was there, pulling her from Sophie's rocker into his embrace and soothing her.

"Do you want to go up to your bed?" he asked when she stopped shaking and sniffing.

Lara rolled her head into his shoulder. "No. I can't sleep up there yet."

Lara sat back down on the rocker while Talon climbed the ladder to the bed loft and came back down with an armful of blankets, which he spread out on the floor. He took her by the hand and lay down beside her on the blankets, cocooning her with his big, warm body. Lara slept, dreamless for the first time in months.

***

The next morning, Patience showed up with Wyatt and Wilric, and Talon returned to the keep, leaving Lara to her friend's care. He rode back in the late afternoon and he and Lara enjoyed a light supper with Denys. After supper, Denys made his way to his new antechamber in the barn and Talon poured himself and Lara a cup of wine, which they sat sipping in peaceful silence, watching the sun set over the mountain's western peak.

"Will you stay with me again tonight?" she asked as they took their empty cups into the house.

"Of course."

He followed her up to the bed loft and spread out on a pile of blankets on the floor beside her bed, leaving Sophie's bed empty. Lara fell asleep to the sound of his steady breathing and woke up calling out his name.

"Tell me," Talon whispered as he cradled her in her bed. "Tell me what makes you cry out my name."

Lara burrowed her nose deeper into his neck. She'd told him her dream of the slaughter at Roncesvalles, and it had come to pass, just as she'd told Sophie she'd dreamed of pulling her death shroud over her face. She was afraid if she spoke aloud of seeing Talon fall in her dreams, it too would come to pass.

When she woke late the next morning, her bed linens still holding his scent, she stripped them and Sophie's and carried them down to the river to wash them, passing by Talon brushing Honey in the corral as Denys spread fresh hay.

Determined to keep herself so busy she wouldn't have time to mope and grieve over Sophie, Lara fed them all a breakfast of eggs, ham, and apples, and then she sent Talon off to take care of his own business, assuring him she'd be fine. She had Denys and Wolf and her animals and gardens, and she needed to restock her supplies of drying herbs and medicines.

Yet everywhere she looked, she saw Sophie. Every plant she touched, she felt Sophie's hands guiding hers, showing her how to pull weeds without disturbing a seedling's delicate roots, how to pick only the ripe berries, how to tie the sprigs of herbs up without bruising their tender leaves. Every gust of wind and soughing of leaves sounded like Sophie's voice in her ear, telling her she would get through this, that she was braver and stronger than she knew, that much depended on her.

She stood and straightened, squaring her shoulders as she surveyed the property where Sophie had raised her. Her home.

"I won't let you down, Tante," she said to the wind, the sky, the old oak. "I'll make you proud, I swear."

CHAPTER 17

Foretold

Lara

It was market day, half a month since Sophie had passed. Ten days since Lara had forbidden Talon from staying the night at her house, and ten nights straight of her waking from her dreams calling out his name.

He still came by her house daily and often rode with her as she made her rounds of the valley. It eased her heart and her grief to reminisce with the villagers about Sophie, and she was sent on her way with more food gifts than she could ever eat on her own, which Denys and Talon were both happy to help her consume. This morning, Talon had business at the garrison, so Lara set off on her own, her wagon laden with cheeses, herbs, soaps, tubs of liniments, and vials of love potion.

She'd sold all but two vials of love potion by noon when Ravenna sauntered over to her wagon, flanked by the steward Roumel's two daughters.

"Is that all you have?" Ravenna eyed the vials as the blonde-haired sisters preened and giggled.

"It is."

"I suppose they'll have to do." She set her coppers down on the wagon's tailboard, then handed a vial to each sister. "Happy hunting, ladies," she called out after them as they practically skipped off toward the square where musicians were setting up for the harvest dance. "I'm afraid they have their caps set on the captain," she told Lara with a false concern matched by her fake smile. "Since he's apparently finished with you, I admit I've encouraged them in their pursuit. I do hope you don't mind."

"Why should I mind?" Lara answered just as falsely. "The captain is free to do whatever he chooses, as am I."

"My brother will be so pleased to hear it," Ravenna said as she sauntered off to join the sisters.

Lara busied herself rearranging what goods she had left to sell, when the high-pitched squeals of the sisters rang over from across the square. Talon had arrived, along with Phillipe and several other soldiers. They tied their horses off at a post and surveyed the square, and though Lara didn't squeal out loud at his approach, she couldn't help but grin as he strode toward her wagon, ignoring the loud sighs and fluttering eyelashes of not only the steward's daughters, but several of the women selling their wares in the stalls he passed.

"I'd like to purchase a bar of soap." Talon stopped at her wagon and looked over her wares. "A very special bar infused with the attar of rose I understand can only be purchased from a beautiful but thorny west end witch. Would you happen to know where she might be?"

Lara's grin grew, and damned if she wasn't fluttering her eyelashes at Talon. "I might. Are you sure you can afford such a bar?"

Talon laughed lightly and jangled his purse, heavy with coin. "Why, I am such a wealthy man, I will buy two."

"A big spender, eh? That'll be two coppers a bar." She made a point of counting his coin before pocketing it and handed him two bars of her favorite rose soap. The soap he'd lathered her body with in the river on the march to Roncesvalles. Her cheeks heated at the memory of his big, strong fingers rubbing delicious circles into her back and other places. She coughed and busied herself with arranging the remaining bars.

"How goes the marketplace today?" he asked as he tucked the bars into his tunic pocket. "How many love potions have you sold?"

"Two dozen. The last two to the steward Roumel's daughters there." She indicated the dance floor, where the women stood watching them and whispering in each other's ears. "In anticipation of dancing with you."

"Me?"

You should go over there, talk with them, dance with them."

"What? Why?"

Why indeed? Because what she'd told Ravenna was true. He was free to live his own life and she, hers. Even if it meant letting her heart crack a little. Better that than have it broken into a thousand cutting shards when he rode out of her life forever.

"You don't have to watch over me all the time." She tried to reason with him, leaving her heart out of it. "I'll be fine."

He snorted. "Of course, you will. You get in and out of trouble as easily as a cat with nine lives."

Lara lifted her chin. "While I appreciate your sense of honor and duty, your oath was made to Sophie, and Sophie is..." She swallowed and swiped at the hot tears welling in her eyes. "I can look after myself, Captain. I release you from your oath."

He stood stiff and silent for a long moment, the muscle in the side of his jaw ticking. "If you think that's why I stay, then I may as well go."

Lara's heart thudded to her feet as he strode straight for the steward's daughters, who simpered and giggled at his approach, clutching their vials of love potion in their lily-white fists. Ravenna and Ranulf, who were sitting to the side of the dance floor with Lothair and Fulrad, who'd taken up residence at Oloron Manor after Charles cut him loose, watched with amused grins as the sisters practically swooned over Talon.

After giving the entire group her back, Lara packed up her wagon. The musicians started playing as she finished and hitched Gaea up to the wagon, and she couldn't help but take a peek before she left.

The sisters were draped all over Talon, hanging on to him as if they'd faint dead away without his big, strong arms holding them up. Phillipe and Dardinel joined the cozy trio, and soon the square filled with the sisters' high trills and the deeper, coarser laughter of the men, Talon's baritone booming out over the others.

Damn him for dancing with them. Double damn herself for suggesting it.

She'd freed him from being her protector as he'd freed her from being his lidi, because it was the right thing to do. Yet Lara felt neither noble nor right, only jealous and miserably wrong. She'd told him to go away, and he had, and he wouldn't be back because she'd insulted him, his friendship, his honor. She saw that as clearly as she saw him wrap an arm around each of the sisters and walk them over to the barrels of ale.

"Come on, Wolf," she said, climbing up onto the wagon's seat and clucking her tongue. "Gaea, let's go."

As the wagon plodded along the road to her house, Lara couldn't decide whether to continue home, pull her bedcovers over her head and cry her heart out, or turn back and tell Talon she'd been wrong to send him away from her, to invite him to her house for supper this night and every night he remained in Oloron. But what if he accepted? What if he came for supper and stayed for breakfast? Would she have the will to keep him from her bed? Would she even try?

If she didn't, and they became lovers again, just the thought of which made her body flush and an ache begin to throb between her legs, she feared Sophie's warnings would've been for naught, and she could still end up alone with his babe in her belly and lose him. She thought of how he fell in her dreams and laid a protective hand over her womb. She'd be a fool to make herself grieve him or leave her child a fatherless bastard.

No. It was better this way. Less grief. Fewer complications. For both of them. She gave Gaea's harness a shake, determined to continue down the road she had chosen, to move forward with her life, a life she chose of her own free will, a freedom she had fought hard to regain, when Wolf's low growl had her pulling up on the reins.

The hound stood in the middle of the road, staring back in the direction of the village, his growl growing louder as four horsemen rode toward them. For one brief, ecstatic moment, Lara thought Talon had left the sisters and followed her, but as they drew nearer, none of the horses were black and the tallest of the riders was too thick-set to be Talon.

"Lothair," she hissed. A chill ran through her as she recognized Fulrad astride his rangy bay.

She was out of the wagon and unbuckling Gaea's harness before conscious thought told her to, and on the mare's back as the riders broke into a gallop.

"Come, Wolf," she cried, urging Gaea into a run. After turning onto a game path, she pulled the mare up behind a thick patch of bramble a hundred paces in, hoping she'd panicked for nothing. Then the shouts of men and pounding of hooves came over her own panting. Her heart in her throat, she turned Gaea uphill and rode hard and fast. She was on her own. There was no Sophie protecting her from Nithard now, no Talon saving her from Lothair. She would have to get herself out of this mess, and her best, her only, hope was to outrun them and seek the safety of the Hollow.

***

Talon

Talon peeled the two simpering blonde sisters from his arms. Without Lara glaring at him from across the square for doing exactly as she told him to and dancing with them, there was no reason for him to put up with their high-pitched squeals and twitters. "Phillipe, Dardinel, I'm off for the keep."

"Off to Lara's you mean," Phillipe said, and Talon didn't bother to challenge his second's assumption.

He'd been keeping watch over her for three months now, and despite her protests and assurances that she could take care of herself, he knew he'd sleep better tonight if he made sure she got home safe and in one piece. He glanced around the gathering. Ranulf and Ravenna watched him from under the beech tree in the center of the square, but Lothair and Fulrad and two other men-at-arms were no longer with them. In fact, they were nowhere to be seen.

A niggling took hold in his belly and clawed its way up his spine as he set the Black to an easy gallop on the road west, keeping his eyes on the heavy tracks of four horses carrying riders overlaying those of a small wagon. A league from town, he spied a wagon sitting in the middle of the road. Lara's wagon. With no Lara, no Gaea or Wolf in sight, only Lara's boot prints next to Gaea's harness in the dirt.

He followed Wolf's and the mare's hoofprints, the latter set deeper now, as if carrying a rider, to a turn onto a game path that led into the wooded hillside. Heavier tracks of the four mounted horses joined them.

"Bloody hell, Lara, what trouble have you gotten into now?"

He looped back to her wagon and grabbed a stick. "Tracking the wildcat, T," he scrawled in the dirt beneath the wagon. Those who needed to would know what it meant.

***

Lara

Lara, Gaea, and Wolf stood panting at the edge of a meadow over three leagues up the mountain. The sun approached the western peak, and Lara figured if they made the meadow's far side before Lothair, Fulrad, and their other two riders chasing them caught up, they could disappear into the woods and make good time and distance in the dark of night. They were only half a day's ride from the Hollow, and the woods grew denser, the paths nothing more than game trails on the other side of this meadow. With the cover of night, she was fairly certain she could lose them by doubling back in circles and covering her tracks.

"Come on, girl." She patted Gaea's lathered neck. "One last run across the meadow, and then we'll disappear into the woods, and you can walk the rest of the way."

They reached halfway across the open meadow when the first arrow whizzed by Lara's head. She hunkered low over Gaea's neck, biting her lip to keep from crying out as another arrow barely missed Wolf. Glancing over her shoulder, she saw the riders advancing, two of them notching arrows to their bows.

An arrow whistled overhead and sunk into the earth in front of Gaea, who shied to the right. Lara clasped her thighs tighter around the mare's heaving belly and leaned them both to the left, the right, and the left again. Another screaming whistle, and Lara felt a searing pain as an arrow grazed her right shoulder. She cried out without meaning to and jubilant shouts came off the men. Another cry, loud, fierce, and fearsome, rent the air. Lara looked over her shoulder as the Black came crashing out of the woods to her back, Talon standing in his stirrups, holding his longsword high.

"Ride, Lara," he yelled as the men swung their horses around to meet him. "Ride."

"Get the witch," Lothair shouted, and Fulrad headed straight for her. "We'll take Guiscard."

Lara glanced at the woods she'd been riding for. She had a good chance of disappearing into them before Fulrad caught up to her, but she couldn't leave Talon to fight this battle alone. She wouldn't. Drawing her waist knife, she swung Gaea around and rode straight for Fulrad with a feral snarl.

Fulrad raised his short sword, and Lara grinned like a crazy woman, thinking it was a good thing she'd destroyed his knee, else he'd be wielding a longsword. Gripping her knife tight, she hunkered over Gaea's withers, intending to leap from the mare's back onto Fulrad and knock him off his horse—when Wolf surged ahead and grabbed Fulrad by the calf of his leg and pulled him off his saddle and onto the ground. Lara never slowed or looked back as the screams ended. She kept riding for Talon as Wolf finished what he'd started in the keep's stables.

She rode past one man lying on the ground, his arm severed from his shoulder, as another man, sword drawn, circled Talon. The arrow sticking out of Talon's thigh almost had her stilling. But then Lothair sat his horse twenty paces from the fight, setting an arrow to his bow, and Lara pressed Gaea forward, willing her breath into the exhausted mare as the Black charged the other horse chest first, sending it stumbling back. Talon stood in his stirrups, and holding his sword with both hands, clove the man's head from his shoulders.

Lothair let his arrow fly.

"*Talon.*"

Her warning was too late. The arrow hit Talon in the belly and jerked him back in his saddle. He grabbed at his side, and Lara's scream stuck in her throat as he slumped forward over the Black's neck, looked over at Lara, then slid sideways off his saddle and fell to the ground.

"*No,*" Lara cried as Lothair set another arrow to his bow. "Please God, no."

"Praying to God won't help." Lothair pointed an arrow at her. "Your man is dead, and soon you will be too."

"Then you had better shoot true, you spineless bastard." Lara hunkered down over Gaea's neck as they thundered toward him. "Because if you miss me, I will kill you."

Lara rode straight for him as Lothair took his time aiming, sure of himself, grinning with anticipation, but he hadn't anticipated Wolf, who was no more than ten paces from him when he saw the hound and shot, too quick and too wide. With no time to set another arrow, he jerked his horse's head around and made for the woods with Wolf snapping at his boots.

Once she'd jumped off Gaea, Lara ran to Talon and kneeled by his head. Blood pooled the ground from his wounds, and his eyes were half-open slits of gray. A keening moan rose from somewhere so deep inside Lara, she thought she'd never draw breath again as the nightmare plaguing her for months came to be.

"*No.* Not you. Please God, not you." She cradled Talon's head, rocking back and forth on her knees. "Please don't leave me. Please, please don't leave me. Not like this."

"Not a chance." His voice a rasp, his eyes fluttered open and focused on her. "I thought... I told you...you to ride."

"I thought they'd killed you."

Talon tried to smile but grimaced. "They damn near have."

"No." Lara had seen him fall. She'd seen him lying in a pool of his own blood, just as she'd seen him in her dreams. But unlike in her dreams, he was still alive. "They've not killed you yet, and will not. Not as long as I've anything to do with it."

"I'm all yours." Talon coughed and his eyes rolled back as his lids shuttered.

Lara sucked her breath in, held it, then let it out in a rush when his chest finally rose and fell, slow and shallow—but he was breathing. A loud whinny from the wood's edge sent her scrambling for Talon's longsword, and she stood with it gripped firmly in both hands as Lothair's riderless gray came crashing into the meadow, Wolf snapping at its hocks. Lara gave a short, sharp whistle, and Wolf came loping over, his tongue lolling out of his bloody muzzle. He sniffed at Talon, then looked up at Lara.

"Right," she said, looking around. The sun touched the mountain's western peak: it would be dark soon. "First things first."

After making sure Talon was still breathing, she approached the Black with her hand out and told him what she was doing as she stripped him of his saddle and blanket. She covered Talon with the blanket and searched his saddlebags, where his flint, an extra tunic, and a vial of love potion brushed her fingertips. Whether it was the vial Sophie had given him or one of the sister's, she neither knew nor cared.

Sending prayers out to her Tante, to God, to the setting sun and the rising moon, she cut and tore the tunic into strips and packed them around the shafts of both arrows. The bleeding from his thigh had slowed to a seep, but he still bled copiously around the arrow in his right side: dark blood, liver blood.

She stood and glanced around the meadow again. Four horses, including Fulrad's bay and Lothair's gray, gathered together near Gaea and the Black, forming their own little herd in the growing dark now their dead masters' bodies lay strewn across the meadow. She stripped the closest man's body of his tunic, waist knife, and short sword, then dragged him into the woods, where she gathered kindling and small logs, laid them in a pile next to Talon, and repeated her motions with the second man and then Fulrad, adding their tunics, short swords, and one longsword to her growing stockpile. She eyed the horses' gear and removed a skin of wine from a sorrel gelding's saddle.

She had a good fire going by the time the sky had turned from dusk to night, and a nice pile of tunics cut into strips and squares.

Pushing with all her might, she rolled Talon onto his left side, placing his saddle blanket over his chest and shoulders. She removed the bloody packing from around the arrows' entry points, took a big swig of the wine, then poured some over his wounds, worried that he hadn't so much as stirred during her ministrations. She laid her knife in the fire, grabbed the shaft of the arrow in his thigh with both hands, and started to pull. Talon shot his hand out and grabbed her wrist with a viselike grip. His eyes were open and staring at hers. Recognition filled them, and he loosened his grip.

"I have to pull the arrows out," she told him, her voice shaking almost as much as her hands. "Then I have to cauterize the wounds."

He dropped his grip from her wrist, licked his chapped lips, then nodded. "Do it."

Lara's lips felt as parched as Talon's looked as she pulled the vial of love potion from her pocket. "Here." She held the vial to his lips. "Drink this."

"Are you offering me a love potion?" His grin was even more lopsided than usual but ended with a grimace.

"Just drink it," she commanded, and he obeyed, drinking all but a last swallow.

"Now you," he said, raising Lara's brows. "You know it was meant for you, my beautiful, thorny wildcat."

He gave her another lopsided grin as she swallowed the last of the potion, then she wiped his brow and hers, flipped the blade in the fire, propped his calf up on the saddle, and used Fulrad's knife to cut a slit in his legging around the arrow.

"Ready?" she said. He grunted, and she gripped the shaft of the arrow with both hands and pulled with all her strength. Talon's body stiffened, and she thought his teeth might crack he clamped his jaw so tight. She continued to pull, slow and steady, until the arrow came out with a sucking sound. She gave the shaft and arrowhead a once-over to make sure it was intact, that no bits had broken off inside Talon, and then laid it on the ground, careful not to touch the arrow's head. Lothair was known to dip his in poisons or dung, bragging that if his arrows didn't kill a man right off, they would eventually from infection, a thing she wouldn't mention to Talon. Fresh blood flowed from the hole in his leg, and Lara let it. "You're lucky," she told Talon. "The arrow missed your bone and arteries."

"Somehow...I don't feel...so lucky." His face had gone from pale to ashen, and they hadn't even gotten to the worst of it.

Lara took another swig of wine and gave him one. Then she poured some wine over the open wound, flinching along with Talon as she did so.

"I am sorry for this," she said as she pulled the blade from the fire. Swiping the sweat from her brow, she pressed the glowing red tip to the hole in his thigh.

"Bloody hell." His entire body went rigid, then limp.

He'd passed out again, which was just as well as Lara had to repeat the process several times until the blood only seeped from the charred hole. Her eyes stung from the smoke, and she choked on the stench of burning flesh as she placed several squares of linen over the wound and wrapped two strips tight around his thigh, pulled the blanket up over his legs, then sat back and gathered her courage for what she had to do next.

She propped the saddle up against his shoulders, called Wolf over, and had him lie down over Talon's legs.

"Stay."

Wolf laid his head on his front paws, watching intently as Lara poured wine over the wound in Talon's side, then grabbed the shaft of the arrow and heaved. His body stiffened and jerked as she pulled the arrow out, but he never regained consciousness. Lara checked the shaft and arrowhead for any missing pieces and, not finding any, drank another swallow of wine and poured more over the hole in his side. She cauterized the wound with the blue-hot knife blade, his twitches and moans as comforting and concerning as the dark blood still seeping from the wound.

Rolling him back and forth, she managed to wrap strips of linen around his waist to keep the pads of linen she'd pressed to his wound in place and maintain pressure, breaking into a sweat with the effort. Both wounds were on his right side, so she kept him lying on his left. He'd bled too hard for too long: he couldn't afford to lose much more.

His skin was cold and clammy as Lara laid the horse blanket over him. She propped the Black's saddle up against his back and had Wolf lie next to his chest and belly, then she banked the fire and approached the horses. Fulrad's bay wouldn't let her near him, but the other three let her strip them of their gear, leaving their bridles and reins on them. She laid their saddle blankets over Talon and took stock, talking to the horses and Wolf and Talon. She'd known too many people returned from the hinterlands of death who'd spoken of hearing their loved ones' voices through the veil of consciousness. Voices they'd fought to stay connected with.

"We have a rope, a pair of leather gloves, three flints, another full skin of wine, five short swords, two longswords, and a bow and almost full quiver of arrows, along with three more saddles." She looked up the mountain's side. "We're halfway between Oloron and the Hollow, but if Lothair lives, he's between us and Oloron, and we can't chance running into him, even with you to fight him off, Wolf." She took a swig of wine from the half-empty skin. "We'll go to the Hollow. Hole up there, where I can tend to Talon in safety and peace." She sized up Talon, who weighed twice what she did and was in no condition to ride. The Black lowered his head to sniff and blow in Talon's hair, his reins dangling. Lara sat up straight. "If I could find two poles long and sturdy enough, I could use the rope and reins and make a litter to pull him up the mountain." She grinned at the horses. "Sound like a plan to you?"

The yips and snarls of wild animals from the woods told Lara the men's bodies had been found. It would be chancing attack by a predator if she went into the woods now. She'd wait until daylight to search for poles. In the meantime, she removed the reins from the Black and the other three horses, packed her meager supplies into the Black's saddlebags, and set the saddles several feet from Talon's back as a wind break.

She took a good draught of wine and dribbled a little onto Talon's lips, breathing a sigh of relief as he swallowed.

"Lie down, Wolf," she said, patting the ground in front of Talon, who instinctively sought the dog's heat.

Then she climbed under the blankets and curled herself around Talon's back, her nose burrowed into the nape of his neck.

She woke to a sky as gray as Talon's eyes staring listlessly into nothing, and she quickly laid her fingers on his neck, her heart stopping until she felt his pulse beneath her fingers, thin and weak, but there. She placed a hand on his brow and swore. "Damn you,

Lothair." A fever had taken hold of Talon during the night, and she had nothing to treat it with here. She had to get him to the Hollow.

She used the dead man's longsword to cut her poles, and had the leather strips lashed between them by early morn. Then she saddled the Black and hid the other saddles in the woods. She took a drink of wine, its warmth spreading through her limbs, and dosed Talon with as much, or as little, as he would swallow. Then she pulled him by one blanket onto the litter, covered him with the other, tied him down with what was left of the reins, and rigged the litter to the Black's saddle with the rope.

"Well then," she said to the horses jostling for position in their new herd. "We've got the better part of four leagues to go." She gazed down at Talon, His face was ashen but for his fever-flushed cheeks. "And the sooner we get there, the better." She gave the meadow one last look, making sure there was nothing left to tell of their presence.

"Let's hope if Wolf didn't kill Lothair outright, he at least bloodied him something fierce, causing him to run home to lick his wounds. And that his snake of a master will sit and wait to see what's become of us rather than come looking."

CHAPTER 18

The Hollow

Talon

The girl stood in the river. A young girl with side braids who smiled at Talon, warming him from the inside out. He tried to go to her, but a gripping pain in his side stopped him. His side and his leg were on fire, his head pounded, and his mouth tasted of dirt.

"Water."

Something cool and wet touched his mouth. He gaped like a baby bird, and a slaking ease slid down his throat as he swallowed.

"Sleep," a voice said.

A woman's amorphous face crowned with auburn curls floated above him. Eyes of green and gold peered down at him from where her long, willowy body sprawled out along the branch of an ancient oak. She stood, her naked body glistening wet, and gazed at him with a longing that made his gut grip and his manhood throb. He reached out for her, but she was gone, her voice of smoked honey laughing up at him from the river below as she was swept away. He dove into the freezing river and swam after her, stroking and kicking with all his might, struggling against the swirling water until his arms burned and his legs were as heavy as soggy logs. Still, he fought on. He had to get to her. To hold her safe in his arms. To tell her... something.

He gave one last heaving surge forward, and pain ripped through him. He cried out.

"Shush, love. It's all right. I've got you."

He was treading water in front of the oak, its gnarled roots holding her pale, listless body. Her waist-length hair swirled around her like dancing flames, then blanched to white, and her skin aged from smooth and fair to wrinkled and wizened. He reached out to touch her cheek, and her eyes flew open. Changeling eyes that seared his very soul.

"Lara?"

"Aye, love."

From close by, his mother sang lullabies. He ran down an empty hall searching for her, his footsteps echoing off the cold floors and stone walls. Walls without doors. Walls without end. He ran and ran, his footsteps echoing, his mother calling to him from beyond the cavernous maw.

"Mother," he cried out. "Mother. Don't go."

"Shush," a breath whispered. "I'm here."

"Sing?" he pleaded.

"Sleep," the voice sang.

***

Talon opened his eyes and tried to get his bearings. He lay beneath a ceiling of thatch over sturdy crossbeams of wood, a ceiling he'd never seen before. It wasn't unusual for him to wake in a strange place, but he'd always remembered how he'd gotten there. He tried to swallow. His tongue felt like it was three times its usual size and as dry as the Spanish plains. His head throbbed and his body was as weak and helpless as a swaddling babe's.

He turned his head to the side and a pull came from his neck to his shoulders. Lara slept in a chair beside the bed he lay in, her hair a wild tangle of auburn curls, her usually rosy cheeks wan and hollowed. She wore a linen nightshift and shawl of wool he didn't recall seeing before, nor did he recognize the small table next to her chair. He did recognize the waist belt and knife she wore and tried to think why she would be wearing them over her nightshift, then he remembered: chasing after her and fighting Lothair and the count's men; the arrows in his side and thigh, how Lara had pulled them out and cauterized his wounds. Then the searing pain, floating in and out of consciousness, floating in and out of strange dreams, vague images of sky and trees and horses swaying and bobbing above him, his body burning up with fever—then nothing.

His instincts told him she'd dragged him up the mountain to the place she and Sophie called the Hollow and that he'd have left his life's blood on that meadow were it not for her. Of course, it was because of her that his blood had been spilt there in the first place, but then that seemed to be his fate: to bleed for his thorny beauty.

He moved his left hand under the bedcovers and brushed the bandage wrapped around his waist and the one wrapping his thigh. He was naked except for his breechcloth. He tried to shift his body, and a ripping pain tore through his right side from his toes to his shoulder. He gritted his teeth so as not to cry out and wake Lara, taking slow, labored breaths in and out. The air smelled of rosemary and lavender, easing his chest and throat, and two cups and several tubs and vials sat on the little table by Lara.

He coughed, and his belly gripped. He shut his eyes with a grimace and opened them to Wolf's face in his, tongue lolling and tail wagging. He lifted a hand to pat the dog's head, causing his side to grip again, and dropped it.

"Welcome back." Lara smiled at him, the one true tonic that would cure him of any ill. Then her expression grew strained and somber. "I thought I'd lost you a few times there."

"Not a chance." He tried to smile, but his lips were dry and caught on his teeth. He swiped his only slightly damper tongue across them. "How long have I been out?"

She shifted in her chair and picked up one of the cups and held it to his mouth. "It's been three days since you took your wounds," she said as he sipped the cool, slaking water. "You've been wandering between this world and the next ever since."

Her voice caught, and the same fear he'd seen in her eyes when she'd woken from her dreams clouded them.

"Tell me, Lara. Tell me what you dreamt of me that night by the river, after we made love."

Color rose to her cheeks, then paled. "I saw you pierced by an arrow, slumped over the Black's neck," she said, her voice breaking. "Then you fell and lay in a pool of your own blood, your eyes dulled and unseeing." She held his gaze, and what Talon saw in hers pained him more than the prick in his side. "I thought I saw you die." Her voice was a raw whisper. "I couldn't bear to love you more, only to lose you."

Talon swallowed past the stone-size lump in his throat. "You should know by now I'm too stubborn to die simply because you've seen it in a dream."

Her eyes welled with tears and her body was trembling, much as Talon's had after a few especially harrowing battles.

"Come here." He patted the bed beside him, threw the covers aside, and shifted over to make room for her, wincing and grimacing as his leg throbbed and his side clenched. Lara was eyeing him closely, going nursemaid on him: the last thing he wanted her to do right now. "You won't hurt me." He reached for her hand with more difficulty than he let on and pulled her toward him. "I promise." Still she hesitated, and Talon put his bullheaded, stubborn pride that'd gotten him nothing but a cold, lonely bed aside. "Please, my rose. I've more need of you than all the medicines in this world or the next."

She smiled and swiped her tears away and climbed into the bed, one long, lovely leg at a time, stretching them out alongside his. She leaned her head on his shoulder, then ran her fingers back through his hair. He pressed a chaste kiss to her forehead and reached his good arm around her shoulders, coaxing her tighter into his chest, kissing her mop of curls.

"This is the only place I've ever felt completely safe." She nestled in closer.

"Are you referring to being in my arms or here in the Hollow?"

"Both." She gave a contented sigh.

A peace settled somewhere in Talon's chest. In his soul.

She craned her head and eyed him. "How'd you know this was the Hollow? I don't remember speaking of it to you. Or anybody, ever, other than Sophie."

"It was Sophie who first spoke of it. Your first morning as prisoner in my chamber, when you plotted to escape from the bathhouse. 'We have to get you to the Hollow,' were her very words, as I recall. I also recall her warning you to stay out of my bed." He gave her his best leer. "You listened to her about as well as you listened to me when I told you to ride."

"A good thing too," she said. "Else I'd be in this bed all alone and you'd be carrion for the vultures."

Talon tucked Lara closer and placed a kiss on top of her head. "I take it nobody else knows of this place?"

"It was a secret Sophie and I kept from all others. She said it must stay so, so that we'd have a haven to hide from the rest of the world if we needed."

"What of Lothair?"

"Wolf chased him off and came back with his horse and a bloody muzzle. I don't know if he lives or not. If he was able to make it back to the count or not. That's why I brought you here rather than try to get you back to the keep. I didn't want to chance running into him."

Talon nodded. "Smart thinking." If Lothair did make it back to Oloron, what story would he tell of their encounter? Would he admit Lara or Talon still lived, or declare them both dead? Talon needed to let his men know he was alive, but even he knew he was in no condition to ride yet. "We need to get a message to the keep. Preferably without letting the count know."

"How?"

"I'm not..." Wolf lumbered over and plopped down next to the bed and Talon and Lara looked to each other at the same moment. "Can he do it?"

"He's been here and back several times a year every four years of his life." Lara patted Wolf on the head as he rested his muzzle on the mattress. "Sophie was pretty sure he came up here looking for me when I was away with the army. I'm almost certain he'd go home if I sent him." She kissed Talon's cheek and slid out of the bed. "I have parchment and ink. We can write a message and tie it in a kerchief around his neck. Wolf knows Denys. He'll let him take the kerchief off, and Denys will figure out to take the message to Phillipe or Anglbert."

She gathered the parchment and ink and sat at the table that looked to be used for both preparing and eating meals at.

"What do you want it to say?" She held the quill tip over the bottle of ink.

"What phase is the moon in?"

"It's a new moon tonight."

Talon calculated the time he figured it would take his body to heal enough to travel and added several days for the purely selfish purpose of having Lara to himself. "Write, Eyes only. T injured. L safe. Watch Ms. Return and draw a waxing half-moon."

***

Lara

Lara stacked wood under the roasting pit outside of the cabin. After putting the pheasant she'd trapped and plucked on the spit, she started the cooking fire beneath it, grinning as the smoke wafted toward the open window of the cabin. The scent would eventually wake Talon, howling and ravenous from his afternoon nap. She picked up her basket and headed for the stream to gather greens for their supper, her own little herd of horses following, the Black leading, with the other three chargers and Gaea jostling in the middle, and Fulrad's bay, which Lara had taken to calling Shadow, trailing behind.

She'd been patiently gaining Shadow's trust, getting close enough to touch him one day, running her hands over him the next, and relieving him of his gear yesterday, leaving his bridle on when he spooked. Free of his cumbersome saddle, he'd perked up quite a bit, and it was his whiskers sniffing over her shoulder now as she picked handfuls of oily, pungent mint.

Lara patted the gelding's cheek and grinned as he blew into her hair. Standing slowly, she ran her hand up and down his neck, along the blaze on his nose, and under his soft, prickly muzzle. "How about I take that nasty bit out of your mouth?" she asked in a singsong voice. "Would you like that, Shadow?" Slowly, gently, singing nonsense, she pulled the bridle up over his ears and off his head, laughing as he practically spit the bit out. "I know. Who wants a piece of metal in their mouth day and night?" The horse gave a gentle nicker, the first such sound Lara had heard from him. "You poor soul, to have had such a cruel master." She rubbed both his cheeks and his nose over the indents left by the bridle. "You're free of him now. All you have to do here is laze about and graze to your heart's content. How's that sound to you?"

The horse bobbed his head and gave a loud whinny. Lara gathered the basket and bridle and set off for the cabin, laughing as Shadow kicked up his heels and cantered into the open yard between the barn and the cabin. She was still laughing at the gelding's antics when she saw Talon sitting on the bench on the front porch wearing nothing but his breeches with a blanket wrapped around his shoulders.

"What do you think you're doing out here half naked? It's too cold and you should be resting in a warm bed."

"I'm tired of lying about in bed," he grumbled, then gave her a crooked grin. "Unless you're in it with me."

"Aye, well." She set the basket down on the porch. "Someone has to feed us."

He grabbed a handful of her skirt, amazingly quick for a man so recently wounded. Lara tugged it away from him and Talon grimaced. She stopped tugging, and he grinned and pulled her in closer, knowing she wouldn't want to strain or tear his wounds open and using it against her every chance he got.

"Come here, my beautiful, thorny nursemaid." His voice was low and husky. "I've need of your medicine." He pulled her to him so she was straddling his lap, careful of his injured leg—then his mouth was on hers: hungry, feasting, his tongue tracing delicious circles around hers as his hands roamed the length of her back and cupped her backside. He trailed kisses along her jaw, down her neck, the hollow of her throat, and Lara figured it was a good time to remove herself from his lap while she could still think. He growled low, holding her tighter as she tried to push up off him. "Don't go, my wary wildcat."

"I don't want to reopen your wounds," she panted, slapping at his hands as they encircled her waist, impressed with the tenacity of their grip. Four days ago, he could barely hold his own cup; now he was grabbing her around the waist and holding tight. *Too tight*, her head told her. *Not tight enough,* her body countered. He shifted beneath her, maybe more to ease his growing hardness. "You heal too blessed fast." She jumped off his lap and smoothed her skirt.

He chuckled and stretched his legs out. "Unless you plan on keeping me sedated with your teas, I'm going to be all over you each and every chance I get." He gave her a lopsided grin. "I'm giving you fair warning, lady. Drug me, leave me, or make love to me, those are your choices."

"Fair warning, eh?" She tsked and sat on the bench beside him. His hand covered hers and she thrilled at his touch, at the heat and life in him.

"Aye." He lifted her hand and kissed her palm. "There's something else I must give you fair warning of," he said, his voice, his gaze, suddenly serious. "You know I'll leave Oloron come winter?"

Lara nodded.

"I can't promise you anything after that."

Lara shrugged. She knew soldiers didn't return to their sweethearts for many reasons. Death. Crippling injuries. A change of heart. And she knew how Talon felt about marriage. He'd made it clear on numerous occasions.

"Christ, Lara." He tapped the back of his head against the wall, the muscle on the side of his jaw ticking. "You do know what I'm asking of you?"

"To become what every other person in the valley's had me for months now. Your mistress."

"To the eyes of the world, yes. But to me…" His gaze bored into hers. "You are the one person I want and need more than any other in this world, or the next it turns out." He held both her hands in his. "Tell me, my prophetess. What will we be to each other?"."

Lara loved him, plain and simple. She hadn't meant to, and she'd certainly tried her hardest not to. Yet her head had given way to her body and her heart had followed. She was his, married or mistress. Sophie had been Orlando's mistress for five years, and swore she'd never regretted a moment of them. Five days, five months, or five years, Lara would take whatever time she could get with Talon, however she could. Plus, being considered a witch had its advantages. People might talk about her behind her back, but they weren't going to say anything to her face.

She stared into his somber gray eyes. "We shall be what we are, m'lord." He blinked once and let out a heavy sigh. "Lovers." He gave a slow smile. "As if I could refuse a man whose vows to me are fair warning and no promises."

Talon chuckled. "It must be that thorny, troublesome streak in you." He rubbed her fingers over his scarred palm, then pressed his lips to her hand, her wrist, slowly kissing his way up her arm.

Lara stood and pulled away. "I need to tend the pheasant. Though I'm not sure feeding you meat is the safest thing to do right now."

She'd just given the pheasant one last turn when Wolf, whom she'd sent off on his mission four days ago, came loping out of the hedges with a happy bark.

"Wolf." She laughed and petted him from head to tail as he wagged circles around her legs. Then she untied the kerchief from around his neck, unfolded it, and handed Talon the parchment from inside the pocket.

Talon read it out loud. "All good here. Tongues wagging. See you…" He held the message with a drawing of a waxing half-moon up to Lara.

CHAPTER 19

Idyll

Talon

The cure to his curse, Talon discovered, wasn't to tame the wildcat, but simply to take her as she was: wild and thorny and imperfectly perfect. A thing he found as easy as breathing in the quiet peace of the Hollow. As for the rest of the world, they'd deal with it when they returned to Oloron. For now, Talon was happy to be with Lara in their own little Eden that was the Hollow, a place he was exploring and learning more about each day while walking about with the help of a chestnut walking stick that had belonged to Sophie.

The cabin, Lara told him, had been built as a hunting lodge by Count Gerhard, Nithard's and Reginald's father. Neither of the brothers had been hunters, but Orlando, captain of Reginald's guard, had. He'd also been Sophie's lover, not, Lara admitted, her second husband. It was Orlando who'd first brought Sophie to the Hollow. They'd come for a time every summer for five summers, until Orlando died in battle and came home no more.

It was to the Hollow that Sophie took Lara as an infant, and where they'd stayed for the first year of Lara's life, from one autumn to the next. They'd spent a month here every autumn since, as well as an odd month each summer or spring, stocking and planting and tending the place until it was self-renewing.

The sturdy cabin, built of good timber to begin with, had been well maintained, making for a warm and comfortable home. The barn, built to stable the mounts of a full hunting party, were twice the size of the cabin, and almost as airtight, its meadow thick with good grass. Talon had never seen the Black so lazily content. Even Fulrad's bay, whom Lara called Shadow, was growing fatter and friendlier by the day.

An earthen aqueduct such as Talon had seen in old Roman towns moved water from a year-round stream to the orchard and the garden. There was a pond where Lara netted fish that she cooked with wild, bitter greens that grew along the pond's edges, and the orchard was ripe with apple, plum, peach, and pear trees, as well as a row of grapevines that separated the orchard from the vegetable garden full of yellow and green squashes, onions, garlic, and green-topped roots they'd been eating in delicious stews.

A hedge of rosemary and lavender bordered the garden on the other side, and vining mint and licorice root grew along the stream from which Lara made a sweet-tasting tea that calmed a person's head and belly. She'd taught Wolf to leave the covey of quail that lived in the meadow alone, guaranteeing them a steady supply of eggs, along with the squirrel, rabbit, or pheasant she trapped or Wolf caught.

Talon was sitting on the porch, shelling a boiled egg after his afternoon nap, when Lara came out of the woods beyond the meadow, carrying a basket full of something heavy by the way she was moving, Shadow on her heels. Wolf loped alongside them. Talon eased to his feet, intending to help her with the basket, but she pointed a finger at him.

"Sit."

Talon and Wolf both sat.

Lara laughed and set the basket down at Talon's feet. "There." She nodded at the basket full of pieces of ash, chestnut, and beech. "That should keep your backside down and your hands busy." She reached into her skirt pocket and pulled out Talon's carving knife.

"There are thirty-two pieces of wood here," she said, handing him the knife. "By the time you've carved them, I'll have the top of an old table from the barn dyed like a game board."

"You want me to carve pieces for a Shah game?"

She rubbed the dirt from her hands. "It'll give us something to do at night."

"I can think of plenty of things to do at night." Talon gave her a leer that brought a rosy pink to her cheeks. "But making a Shah game does sound intriguing. I've never carved so many figures at one time." He eyed the pieces of wood, sizing them up in his mind. "It'll take me two to three days at least."

Lara grinned, looking quite pleased with herself. "Good." She sauntered past him into the cabin, where pots and pans were shuffled around.

"What's for supper?" He picked a long piece of blonde ash from the basket and turned it about in his hand.

"Bee's knees and butterfly wings." That was her answer when she didn't yet know what she was going to cook and he was already pestering her about it.

"Yum, my favorite." He settled back on the bench, put his knife to the ash, and made his first cut, pleased with the color and grain. "Aye, this will do for my white queen."

He cut and carved and smoothed the piece until his queen was just as he wanted her, with a mop of short curls crowning her head and a body that flowed and curved with the natural grain of the ash. He stood, stretched, then hobbled into the cabin, where a bubbling cobbler sat on the kitchen table.

"What kind?" He went over and inhaled the delicious aroma.

"Blackberry. They grow wild upstream."

"Smells delicious."

"It's my favorite." She gave a sad smile. "Sophie would bake one every year for my birthday."

"When is your birthday?"

"October thirty-first."

"On All Hallows' Eve?"

"Aye."

Talon chuckled. "That explains a lot."

"Such as?" she said, brows raised and arms akimbo.

"Such as how you've managed to cast your spell over me, my lovely, lissome witch." He nibbled at her ear, and she gave him a playful slap. "And I'd have it no other way."

"You think me worth the price after all?"

"I always thought you worth the price." He offered his scarred palm, touched the scar above his eye, then laid his hand over his bandaged side. "And I've always paid it. Have I not?" She smiled in answer, and another part of their conversation her first day as his prisoner came to him. "How can you be certain of your exact birth date if you were left a swaddling babe at the abbey's gate?"

Lara stared at him for a lengthy moment. Then she took a deep breath, and her words came tumbling out. "I wasn't left at the abbey's gates. I was born here, on the thirty-first day of October in the year 755 with a full moon rising. My mother died that same night and is buried in an unmarked grave here in the Hollow."

When he could speak again, all Talon could say was, "Your mother?"

Lara nodded.

"Then you know who she was? Her family name?"

"No." Lara shook her head. "My mother swore Sophie to a secrecy she never broke, not even to me."

***

Lara

Lara set the newly finished game table next to the hearth, her fingertips stained a bluish purple from the berries she'd used to color the dark squares. She pulled the cabin's two chairs over and took one as Talon pulled the game pieces out of the basket and arranged them on the checkered board, putting the king of blonde ash and the queen with the crown of curls on his side, and the darker pieces on hers. She picked up a horse head of stained beech and ran her fingers up and down the proud arch of its neck, much as she had done her first night as prisoner in Talon's bedchamber at the keep only four months ago.

She gazed at him over the crude wooden board and pieces, so different from the glossy ivory and onyx pieces back at the keep, and thought of how different everything was now. She'd gone from freewoman to lidi to Hamm and back to freewoman, from hating Captain Guiscard, her captor, to loving Talon without really knowing when or how it happened, only that it had. She'd lived a lifetime in the past four months, and except for losing Sophie, she didn't regret a thing. Especially when he grinned at her like he was now.

"What?" she said.

"You look like a queen who just stole my king."

"I, ah…" She picked up her dark queen and ran her fingertip down the whorls of waist-length hair that blended into her robe. "I was thinking if you ever quit your wandering warrior ways, you'd make a good living as an artist."

Talon's grin grew. "I've been thinking the same thing. In fact, I had my eye on a tinker's wagon at the last market. Would've bought it too, if I hadn't had to go after a wildcat being chased by a pack of curs."

"Lucky for her you did, else it would've been her bones bleaching in the woods."

He clasped her hand with the queen and lifted it to his lips. "Lucky for me as well." He dropped his voice to a husky rumble. "Else who would I have to play with?"

Her entire body flushed at the tactile memory of where his hands and mouth had been playing last night. Then she remembered how he'd stiffened and grimaced when he'd twisted his side during their bed play, and thought it best they stick to playing Shah for now. She picked up a pawn and made her first move.

"Ah." Talon rubbed his hands together and bent over the board. "The game begins."

They played for two days and nights straight, stopping only to eat when they were hungry and to sleep when they were tired. It was the third morning when Lara woke to Talon roaming his touch the length of her body over her nightshift that she knew the distraction of the board game had run its course.

"Your wounds."

"Are healing well, thanks to my nursemaid."

"But…"

He cupped her backside and pressed her to the hard heat of him.

"You, Captain, are a rutting rogue."

His grin was pure male. "A rutting rogue in dire need," he rumbled. "A need only you can cure, my lovely nursemaid."

"Are you sure?" Lara weakened…wanted. "Your bandages were only removed yesterday."

"Does this feel sure enough?" He placed her hand over his full, hard erection beneath his breechcloth.

A melting warmth spread through Lara. "We'll need to be very careful."

"Ah, my beautiful, thorny, troublesome temptress. All you need do is say yes and I'll likely come undone."

His words filled her with a strange and wonderous power. "Yes," she murmured as she slowly straddled his hips. "Yes," she said, pulling her nightshift up over her head and tossing it onto the floor. "Yes," she growled, untying his breechcloth. He lifted his hips as she stripped it off him, her eyes growing wide as his unrestrained cock jumped free and kissed her flesh. "Yes," she purred, lowering herself over him, thrilling at the hot, hard heat of him nestled against her belly. "Yes." Her breath soughed into a low moan that reverberated to her core. "Yes."

"My sweet rose." Talon wrapped his hands in her hair and pulled her head down toward his, meeting her halfway, his mouth taking hers in a fevered kiss.

Delirious from his kiss, his hands on her breasts, his cock between her legs, Lara leaned back, breaking their kiss. Talon rose and suckled first one of her peaked nipples and then the other as she slowly rubbed herself against the ridge of his pinioned cock. He groaned and she froze. "Did I hurt you?"

"Hurt me?" He laughed, short and gruff. "No." Still his jaw clenched as he laid his head back down on the pillow.

"Are you sure?"

Eyes the brooding gray of a summer storm held hers. "Don't go nursemaid on me now, witch." His voice was low and rough. "I fear I'll go mad if I'm not inside you soon."

Lara pressed her palm to his chest. "I think your nursemaid can remedy that, Captain."

She lifted her hips, licking her lips and grinning as his cock followed. Just touching her aching flesh to the blunt, soft tip of his erection, she slowly lowered herself over him, thrilling at the feel of him as she took his throbbing cock deep inside of her one hot, hard inch at a time. She began to move in slow, rhythmic circles, gently at first, then faster and harder as he pressed his thumbs to her nubbin of flesh where every nerve in her body seemed to coalesce. She rocked back and forth, and he moved with her, grabbing her hips and pushing himself deeper and deeper into her body, into her very soul. Their fever grew in heat and need until it peaked and broke in a pitch of sensation, causing Lara to cry out Talon's name as she shuddered around him. He clamped her hips tighter and went rigid as he cried out her name in response, then he wrapped her in his arms and held her as she lay on his chest, skin to skin, heart to beating heart.

***

Talon

Talon was indeed a man undone. A man undone and remade each and every time Lara so much as smiled at him. For here in the Hollow, she'd shown him a new smile, a smile only for him: sweet and tender and lusty and knowing, a woman's smile full of the secrets she shared with him every time they made love.

Though they were seldom from each other's sides, Talon found he couldn't get enough of her. He couldn't look at her without wanting her, couldn't want her without touching her, kissing her, inhaling her, devouring her, and the happiest of surprises for him— she couldn't get enough of him either. She matched him smile for smile, kiss for kiss, thrust for thrust. Their wants had become their needs, and their needs in this peaceful, magical hollow were each other.

Lara's birthday was only two days away, and their planned departure the day after, which cast an ever-growing shadow over their dwindling days here. A shadow Talon contemplated as he sat on the bench, watching Lara cross the yard with her basket full of greens and her parade of hound and horses.

"Good morning, sleepyhead," she said, greeting him with a smile that warmed him even more than the late morning sun peeking out from behind the clouds. She set the basket down and gave him a kiss he prolonged by twining his fingers through her chin-length curls. When he let go, she swayed on her feet, her gaze unfocused. Talon wagged his brows and nodded toward the cabin door and the bed inside. "Later." Lara offered a promising grin. "I want to show you something."

"Tired of playing with me already?" he groused.

"Aye. I'm on to bigger and better things."

"Well, I don't know about bigger."

"Nor better," she said, laughing. Then she grew serious. "I want to take you to visit my mother's grave."

Talon stood. "I was wondering if you were ever going to take me there."

Lara took a deep breath in and blew it out. "My mother giving birth to me here, being buried here, was the one thing Sophie made me swear to never tell anyone, ever."

"If you'd rather not—"

"No. I want you to know."

She led him across the meadow, into the woods, to a small, ferned glen where vining red roses heavy with the last of the year's blooms climbed over a bier of stacked stones. Lara cut a blood-red bud from the vine and held it out to Talon.

"Sophie planted the roses on my eighth birthday. We stopped here on our way home the summer we traveled north to the Neustria Sea."

Talon reached for the rose and stopped, his hand hanging mid-air as Lara stood smiling at him with the same openness and light a young girl had once bestowed upon him. He took the rose and held it to his nose, breathing in the spicy sweet scent of it, of Lara.

"That summer you traveled north with Sophie," he said. "Did you go to a riding tournament in a town by the sea?"

Lara tilted her head and looked at Talon as if she'd never really seen him before. A slow dawning of recognition lit her hazel eyes and she smiled, as bright and warm as the sun shining down on him.

"There was a rider on a fire red stallion, the youngest there." Her voice shook. "He rode under the name—"

"Vagus. The Wanderer."

Lara stood wide-eyed and speechless.

"There was a young girl there," he continued, "with freckles across her nose and cheeks and her red hair in side braids. She watched every match he rode in, her smile his reward whenever he looked her way, though she wouldn't come close enough to speak with him."

Lara blinked and licked her lips. "She was so shy of him. He was as a god to her, racing the very wind itself and flying through the heavens on his fiery steed." She smiled as if to herself. "He won every match that day, and the right to choose the Queen of the

Field." She met and held Talon's gaze. "He chose her, an eight-year-old girl, above all the other women vying for his crown of flowers."

"And in turn, she plucked a single red rose from the crown—" Talon twirled the rose bud in his fingers. "—and offered it back to him with a smile so pure and sweet, he's carried it in his heart ever since."

Lara smiled up at him beneath lowered lashes. "The crown lies in a chest at the foot of her bed to this day."

"The rose lays dried and wrapped in my chest next to the carving of a beautiful, thorny, woodland witch I met in a river the first day of summer. The same troublesome wildcat who ransacked my chest her first night of captivity in my chamber."

Lara's smile turned cheeky. "As any prisoner with a lick of sense would've."

Talon took her hand in his and raised it to his lips. "You were never just any prisoner. In truth, I've been prisoner to your smile these fourteen years past." He lowered their hands but kept hold of hers. "Where did you go that day after the tournament? I looked everywhere for you."

"After you crowned me, Sophie said it was time to leave. That we had seen what we had come to see."

"What was it you had seen?"

Lara shook her head. "I never knew, and Sophie never said. But that was her way about many things." Her eyes welled. "I wish she was here so we could ask her." A single tear ran down her cheek. "I wish she was still here."

Talon pulled her to him and held her close. "Know what I think?" he whispered in her ear. She rolled her forehead against his chest. "I think Sophie the Sixth cursed me then and there with your smile. Cursed me to search far and wide until I found it, found you, again."

Lara lifted her gaze to Talon's. "The night Patience gave birth to Wilric, Sophie asked me if I loved you. I told her I didn't want to, that I'd tried so hard not to." She smiled, sad and wistful. "I told her I'd loved you once, that night at the river. That I was scared to let myself love you again, only to lose you." Her smile brightened and her eyes shone green as emeralds. "I'm not afraid anymore, Talon."

Talon swallowed, hard. He cupped her chin, unsure if he wanted her to say the exact words or not. Afraid of what it would mean if she did. Of how she'd expect him to answer. He'd wanted her from the first moment he'd laid eyes on her standing him off in the river with nothing more than two knives and a dog. Which was, he'd only now discovered, actually the second time he'd laid eyes on her. He'd held the memory of her as a young girl, smiling at him as if he were a god, close all these years. He'd recognized something in her even then and felt more for her now than he'd felt for any woman ever. But he was a king's soldier, destined to leave her before the first snows fell.

"Lara..." He tried to tell her with his eyes what he couldn't with his words.

She lifted her chin and bestowed a smile on him that clove his heart in two. "No promises, I know."

CHAPTER 20

The Leaving

Talon

Wolf between them and the line of dead soldiers' horses behind them, they crossed the river Talon had chased Lara through a little over four months ago under the light of the waxing half-moon. The freezing water plastered against Talon's leggings, and Lara's gown was soaked up to her knees. Talon let out three short, sharp whistles as they approached the back gate, and was quickly answered by the same. The gate opened as they dismounted, and Phillipe and Oswald stepped through.

"It's good to see you," Phillipe said, clasping Talon's arm. He grinned at Lara. "And right on time."

Phillipe gave Lara a long, too long, hug, as Talon clasped Oswald's hand in greeting, and only let go when Talon rapped him on his shoulder. Talon held his arm out and Lara hunkered into his side.

"Ha," Phillipe crowed. "You two have won me eighteen pieces of silver."

Talon rubbed up and down Lara's arm. "What was the wager?"

"Day of return and together." Phillipe rubbed his palms together. "Which is why your second is standing out here freezing his *beallucas* off."

Lara looked up at Talon, who explained. "To collect your winnings, you must not only pick the correct date and time, but also stand guard the time you pick for someone's return."

Her eyes widened, and she fixed a baleful glare on Phillipe. "You bet on us?"

"We did," he said, not at all chastened. "And I won."

"Then I hope you have to stand guard the entire night through, at the very least."

"Oho, Talon," Phillipe chortled. "The wildcat still has her sharp points. You've not tamed her yet."

"I gave up trying." Talon grinned. "I find I prefer her sharp points to the dulled edges of others." A violent shiver racked Lara's body, and Talon hugged her closer to his side and motioned to Phillipe and Oswald. "We'll talk as we walk. My lady needs dry clothes, a warm meal, and a hot bath."

They handed the horses over to the hands who came out of the stables rubbing their sleep-filled eyes.

"It was Lothair, two other of Ranulf's men, and Fulrad," Talon told the men as they headed for the hall. "They chased Lara halfway up the mountain before we all caught up with her." He rubbed his side, where his newly formed scar still pulled tight. "I took two of them before that bastard Lothair shot me through the side and leg. Wolf chased him off into the woods. He finished off Fulrad too, didn't you, old man?" he said to the hound, whose tail was wagging as they neared the kitchens.

"Lothair showed up three days after you two disappeared," Phillipe said. "Half-starved and a leg and arm torn up pretty bad."

"He healed up yet?" Not that it mattered to Talon. Healed or not, he intended to kill the brute.

"He didn't stick around long enough to tell," Phillipe answered.

"What do you mean?"

"Lothair, Ranulf, Nithard, Ravenna, they've all left Oloron. Packed up their wagons and took off the day after Wolf showed up.

We told no one of the messages he carried. I guess the sight of Wolf here was enough to send them scurrying."

Talon growled low. "Damned cowardly curs. Still, can't say I'm surprised. Any idea where they went or for how long?"

"No. If any of their people know, they're not talking."

Talon unclamped his jaw. "Any other news of note?"

Phillipe glanced uneasily at Lara. "Our orders came two days ago. We're to join Charles in Worms by the end of the month."

***

Lara

Lara woke alone and late by the daylight filtering in through the shuttered window. She yawned and stretched, then burrowed her nose into Talon's pillow, breathing in the scent of him, her body warming at the memory of Talon rousing her when he'd come to bed late last night, at how they'd finally made the bed theirs. With a languid sigh, she sat up and gazed over at her cot, still in its corner, then she was off the bed and grabbing for the chamber pot, losing what little she had left of her supper into it. She was still hunched over it when a quick knock at the door announced Berta's bustling entry.

"Good morning, dearie," her cheery voice rang out and around Lara's swimming head. "I've brought you bread and sweet butter, pork sausage and boiled eggs, and a pot of— Oh, oh my." She laid a motherly hand on Lara's back as the thought of sausage and eggs had her dry-heaving over the chamber pot. "Oh dear."

"It's nothing." Lara wiped her mouth with the washrag Berta handed her.

"Nothing?" Berta tsked, staring hard at Lara's naked breasts, which had grown heavy and tender over the past few days.

"I'm fine." Lara grabbed her nightshift from the foot of the bed where Talon had tossed it last night and pulled it on. She stood and the room swayed, so she sat back down. "It was a long ride yesterday," she said, swiping beads of sweat from her cheeks. "I'm just overtired, is all."

"I'm sure you are." Berta tore off a piece of bread and held it out to Lara. "Eat this. It'll settle your belly."

The thought of food still made Lara queasy, but she took a bite to appease Berta, and then another, and another, her belly growling for more. Berta handed her a cup of warm, mulled cider and removed the trencher of sausage and eggs from Lara's sight.

"Thank you," Lara said after she'd finished off the thick slice of bread and a pear. "I feel much better now."

"Good." Berta continued to watch as Lara splashed water on her face from the washbasin and doffed her nightshift.

"Do you know where Talon...where the captain is?" Lara asked as she donned one of her old under tunics and gowns from the chest beside her cot.

"Aye, dearie. He and Phillipe and a few of the other men rode over to Oloron Manor with a missive meant to reach the count and his son, wherever they are. What it says, I'm sure you have as good an idea as I."

Lara didn't know the exact words of the missive, but she knew the general gist of it would be to leave her in peace and good health or suffer the consequences at the end of Talon's sword.

"I don't know where you two were all this time." Berta set the trencher of sausage and eggs down for Wolf, who gobbled it up. "Wherever it was, I swear the captain's gained a stone or two around his middle."

"I discovered he likes berry cobbler," Lara said with a grin that had Berta muttering as she fussed around the chamber, though she was head cook and there were chambermaids to do the tidying.

"Gone the better half of a month, don't let anybody know if they're dead or alive, and he's got holes in his side and leg, and she's talking berry cobbler. She's yours all right, Sophie the Sixth. And just as mysterious as you ever were about taking off for a time and showing back up all fat and fine."

Lara heard every word, as she was meant to. Berta had always taken it as a personal insult that Sophie'd never told her best friend about the Hollow, even though Sophie had explained many times that it was for Berta's safety as much as theirs. A plan Lara meant to stick to.

"I'm off to my place, to check on Denys and the house," she told Berta. "I'll stop at Patience's too. I'll be back in time to help with supper."

"There's no need for you to help in the kitchens," Berta said. "You're not the captain's *lidi* anymore, you're…"

Lara waited as Berta searched for the words to describe Lara's presence in the keep now. In the captain's bed.

"The captain's lady."

Lara gave Berta a kiss on her cheek, thankful for her kindness. Not everyone in the valley would be so kind. She told herself it didn't matter what others called her. She'd been called names her whole life by those people. Bastard. Witch. Whore. She squared her shoulders and lifted her chin as she entered the stables. Let them. She knew who and what she was, and so did those who truly cared about her. Those names had never stopped the people of the valley from seeking her out as a healer, and she didn't think they would now. Of course, she could mitigate any consequences by refusing to stay at the keep and returning to live in her own house, but her time with Talon was limited, and she didn't want to miss any of it. Especially not to mean-spirited gossip. If her reputation was tarnished by her living openly as Talon's mistress, well, it'd never been shiny in the first place.

She'd rather have Talon while she could.

Shadow put up such a fuss when she started to ride Gaea out of the stables, she let him out of his stall to follow her home, where Denys had taken such good care of the property and the livestock, all she had to do was walk around outside and admire the shape of things.

Lara pushed open the door to the house and walked in. Denys had stayed in the antechamber built in the barn for him and had only gone into the house when necessary. As she stood in the middle of the common room, she understood why. A strange, uneasy quiet thickened the air. A quiet that no longer held Sophie's presence.

She turned to walk right back out of the house when Patience burst in, Wilric squirming in her arms.

"The captain said you'd be here." Patience hugged Lara until Wilric let out a howl at being squashed between them.

"I see his lungs have grown apace with his cheeks." Lara admired Wilric's round face.

"The captain said almost the same thing this morning when he stopped by on his way to Oloron Manor." Patience tucked Wilric into his sling and searched Lara's face. "We were all so worried about you. Phillipe said the captain had gone after you, that as long as you two were together you'd be fine. But you were gone for so long, and now you're back, alive and well and in one piece."

"It wasn't for lack of them trying to kill us." Unsteady on her feet, Lara plopped down on one of the chairs at the table. The table where Sophie had lain in state. She took a shaky breath and promptly burst into tears. "I'm sorry. I, I don't know what's happening with me." Her breakfast threatened to come up, and she swallowed hard and managed to keep it down, barely. "I threw up this morning in front of your mother, and I've been so tired the past few days. I must be coming down with something."

"Aye," Patience said. "Unless I miss my guess, it's called pregnancy."

Lara's belly lurched.

"Are your breasts swollen and sore?" Patience asked.

Lara nodded dumbly. She'd thought them tender from her and Talon's play, which had only advanced to intercourse seven days ago. Still, she'd tended other women who swore they became pregnant one night and threw up the very next morning.

"When was your last menstrual flow?"

Lara tried to think. It had been before market day, before the Hollow, over a month ago now. She looked at Patience, who stood rocking Wilric with a sympathetic smile.

"Since you didn't know yet, I take it the captain doesn't either."

"No."

"When are you going to tell him?"

"I'm not." Lara decided that then and there.

"He's a good man, Lara. He'll do right by you and the babe. I know it."

"What you don't know and I do is that's the last thing he wants: to be tied down with a wife and child."

"But—"

"His orders have come. He and his company are to join the king in Worms by month's end, and I cannot, I will not send him off to war worrying about me and the babe. He may not want a wife or child, but he will worry about us, because he's a good and honorable man, and I love him too much to have him thinking of me and the babe, to be worrying about one or both of us dying during childbirth, as his mother did, when he should be worrying about some Saxon trying to split his skull open with an axe." She shook her head and squared her shoulders. "As selfish as this sounds, as selfish as it is, if he does come back, I want him to come back to me, to come back for me, because he wants to, not because he's tied and bound to me by an oath he's spoken before God to give our child a name."

"Are you sure?" Patience asked. "Pregnancy can make a woman do and say some crazy things, your speech just now being a good example."

"Yes, I'm sure." Saying it, Lara felt a peace settle in her chest, though her belly still roiled. She saw Patience's pruned face and made one of her own. "And no, I won't be changing my mind about it."

"But raising a child on your own?"

"Married or not, I'd be raising this child on my own until he came back." She closed her eyes against the unbidden image of Talon lying pale as death in a pool of his own blood in the meadow. "If he comes back."

"Still, if you were married before he left, your child wouldn't be born a—"

"Bastard?"

Patience had the good grace to blush.

"I may have been born a bastard," Lara said, "but I had Sophie. I was raised with love, and so will my child."

"Of course, it will." Patience offered a kind smile. "And when the captain returns from the wars in Saxony and marries you, your child will know its father's love as well."

"If he doesn't strangle me for not telling him first."

***

Lara was putting a berry pie into the oven when Talon, Phillipe, Tree, and Dardinel rode in. Wolf loped over to greet Talon as he handed a stablehand the Black's reins, and Berta, who'd been watching Lara like a hawk since she'd returned from her house that afternoon, glanced meaningfully at Lara's belly as Talon started toward the kitchens.

Lara sighed and wiped her floury hands on her apron. She'd bet every piece of coin she'd made selling her pies to pay off her XXX ergild, coins Talon had never asked for, that Berta had come to the same conclusion about her condition as Patience had. What she wouldn't bet a single coin on was how long her condition would remain secret.

She'd left her house not long after Patience's visit, leaving the property and livestock in Denys's capable hands. She'd left Gaea there in her home barn with Honey, and ridden Shadow bareback to the keep rather than walk. She knew it was normal to feel tired during the first few months of a pregnancy, but knowing it and feeling like you could fall asleep standing on your feet was another thing entirely. Still, she wasn't ready to add fuel to Berta's fire of conjecture, so she'd gone to the kitchens and pared berries and rolled out dough enough for four pies, her thank you for the troop's sincere welcome backs. And the way they all acted as if her staying here at the keep and sleeping in the captain's chamber were nothing unusual.

Which had her wondering if it weren't. If he'd had mistresses live with him before. He'd told her he needed her up at the Hollow, that he wanted her more than he'd ever wanted any woman, but he'd never told her he loved her, not even after she'd confessed her love to him. She more than understood his need for freedom, and she refused to trap him with her love or their child. She'd meant what she told Patience. If he came back, she wanted him to come back because he wanted to, to her, for her.

Wolf nosed her leg, and she glanced from him to Talon as he strode past the table where three more pies sat, ready to be baked, the muscle along the side of his jaw ticking.

"I instructed Berta you weren't to serve in the kitchens anymore," he said.

"I know, she told me as much. I wanted to bake pies for you and the men." His brows quirked. "Free of charge."

He chuckled as he leaned in close and ran a hand down her back. "I liked it better when you baked pies just for me," he whispered hotly.

Lara slapped at his hand on her backside. "I'm sure you did, you greedy man."

"Greedy for you, my sweet." He nibbled her neck, raising goose bumps on her arms.

"Greedy for my cooking," she chided, shrugging his nipping lips off her neck.

"I am." He bumped her backside with his pelvis. "Both in bed and out."

Heat flushed from Lara's core to her cheeks, then her uncertain belly threatened to revolt. Clamping a hand over her mouth, she held her other up to Talon, motioning for him to stay where he was, and bolted for the stables, Wolf on her heels. She glanced back over her shoulder at Talon standing where she'd left him, gape-jawed and head cocked, then she disappeared into the dusky coolness of the stables and made her way to Shadow's stall. She leaned against the wall as a wave of nausea overtook her, then left her midday meal on the straw-strewn floor, rolled her forehead against the wall, and swiped her mouth with her sleeve.

"When are you going to tell him?"

She swung her head around and leaned against the wall until Phillipe stopped swimming before her. Then she shuffled straw over the puddle of her vomit with the toe of her boot.

"I'm not." She fixed him with a jaundiced eye. "And neither are you, or Berta, or Patience, or anybody else who knows. Who else knows?"

"Berta told Anglbert her suspicions, and he told me."

"Swear to me you won't tell anyone else, that they won't tell anyone else, especially Talon."

"Why not Talon?" Phillipe asked. "I assume he's the father."

Lara raised a chary brow. "Of course he is."

"Then why not tell him? He has a right to know."

Lara shook her head, adamant. "You know him as well as I do," she said, her cheeks flushing hot as he glanced down at her rumbling belly with raised brows. "What do you think he'd do if he knew?"

"Marry you. Give your child a name."

"And when he leaves for Worms, for Saxony? When he's on a battlefield and should be worrying about himself, his men?"

"He'd be worrying about you and the babe. About you both surviving childbirth."

"Exactly," she said, assuaged by the fact that his best and longest-standing friend knew this about him as well. "I want him to come back to me, alive and in one piece. You understand now, don't you, why he mustn't know. Not until he comes back and finds me and his child alive and waiting for him."

"I understand. But I don't agree. Neither will Talon."

Lara took a deep breath in and let it out slowly. "You let me worry about that."

"I don't know." Phillipe shook his head. "If he ever finds out I knew and didn't tell him, there'll be hell to pay."

"Please, Phillipe. I need you to do this for me. Promise me."

He laid a hand on her shoulder, giving it a brotherly squeeze. "All right. I promise."

"What's this?" Talon's voice boomed from the stable's door. He strode over to them and glared at Phillipe. "Still trying to steal my woman from me?"

"Damn." Phillipe winked at Lara before turning to face Talon. "You caught me red-handed." He held his hands palms out. "Alas, as always, she will not have me. It seems her heart is set on a certain arrogant ass."

"Aye." Talon laid a possessive arm around Lara's shoulder and pulled her into his side. "An arrogant ass who bleeds for her."

He leaned in to kiss her, and Lara turned her face so his kiss landed on her hair rather than her mouth, which surely reeked of vomit. His arm stiffened around her. "What were you two talking about?"

Phillipe shrugged. "Nothing in particular," he said before sauntering away.

"It looked a serious conversation for nothing," Talon rumbled, shooting daggers into Phillipe's back.

Lara tried to shrug as nonchalantly as Phillipe had. "We, ah, I ah, made him promise me something."

"What?"

"To bring you back to me alive and in one piece."

His arm relaxed around her. "Is that so? Afraid I'll find some big-bosomed Saxon wench to warm my bed?"

Lara stepped out of his embrace and glared at him. "More afraid you'll smash your thick skull against some big-chested Saxon's axe."

***

Talon

Talon lay with Lara, her head nestled into his shoulder as he watched the inexorable gray of dawn creep its way into their chamber. He heard movement in the hall below and closed his eyes with a heavy sigh. Their time together was coming to an end.

He buried his nose into her chin-length curls and breathed in the spicy sweet scent of her rose soap. She stirred, and Talon slipped his arm from under her head and kissed her cheek, as cool and soft as a petal. His smile was bittersweet as she burrowed her nose into his pillow and then he slowly slipped out of the bed she'd been openly sharing with him since they'd returned from the Hollow.

Her nightshift lay at the foot of the bed where he'd tossed it after stripping it off her and making love to her last night. They'd been saying their long good-byes every time they made love, every time they kissed or held hands or even met each other's gazes across the yard or the hall, but last night had been different. Last night their lovemaking had been almost desperate, as hard and hot and fast at first as it had been slow and soft and tender before they'd drifted off to sleep in each other's embrace in the dark before dawn. A desperate tenderness that swelled in his chest and constricted his throat now.

He sat on the bed beside her and brushed a lock of hair from her cheek, memorizing the line of her chin, the fullness of her lips, her pert nose, sooty lashes, and the high arc of her auburn brows. He swiped at the hot tears welling in his eyes and grit his jaw. Riding away from Lara would be the hardest thing he'd ever done, next to burying his mother, but he was damned if he was going to cry, even if it felt as if his heart was being ripped from his chest. Besides, Lara had made him promise not to shed a single tear as they said their farewells in front of his men, or she would cry too.

She'd cried lying in his arms several nights ago when she'd thought him asleep, softly, silently, her shaking shoulders and smothered sniffles giving her away. And he'd noticed her red-rimmed eyes and peaked cheeks more than once when he'd shown up at her property unexpectedly. The open, carefree lover he'd known at the Hollow had disappeared, and his old friend, the wary wildcat, had returned. Still, he'd take his wary wildcat over the hole in his chest that'd grown every day, every moment his departure neared.

A departure he could no longer delay.

"Lara, my love," he whispered into her ear. "Time to wake up."

Hazel eyes blinked open and met his. She smiled up at him, as bright and warm as the summer sun shining down on him, then her eyes clouded over, and her smile dimmed.

"Time to say good-bye," she whispered hoarsely.

"Aye, love."

She tilted her head at his endearment and wrapped her hands around his neck, pulling him down and kissing him with such sweet passion that Talon was hard-pressed to keep his promise not to cry. He scooped her up in his arms and reveled in the sensuous warmth of her body as she slid her bare legs down the length of his and stood skin to skin in his embrace.

"God's blood, Lara," he rasped. "How am I to let you go?"

"It's you who are going," she said, her voice as strained as his.

He tucked her head beneath his chin and nodded. "So it is." He held her close, her full breasts pressed against his chest, his ever-eager cock growing hard against the soft swell of her belly. "So I must," he rumbled, and stepped away from her. Away from the greatest pleasure he'd ever known. He coughed and cleared his throat, his mind. "We should get dressed and go down to breakfast."

"As you say, m'lord," she said with a dainty dip of her knee.

"Ha," Talon barked with laughter. "It's a little late to be playing the good *lidi*, my lady."

She gave him a saucy shrug, and Talon grinned as she turned her shapely backside to him, greedily watching as she donned her under shift and long tunic of mossy green. He dressed himself by rote, never taking his eyes from her as she splashed water on her face and combed out her wild mass of curls. Talon sat on the edge of their bed and pulled his boots on as Lara opened the chest by her cot and reached in for something.

She walked over to him and held out her hand. A braid of auburn hair tied off with green ribbons at both ends dangled between her fingers. "I want you to have this. To keep it, and me, close to your heart."

Talon took the braid and tucked it into the inside pocket of his jerkin. He coughed to clear the lump from his throat. "Neither it nor you shall ever be far from my heart, lady." He patted his jerkin over the pocket. "It will now and forever be my talisman."

Long, doleful faces met them as they took their seats at the table, and poor Berta was red-eyed and sniffing as she and Enid and Marta served the company their last meal at the keep for what would likely be a very long time. For some of them, forever.

Lara picked at her feast of eggs, sausage, and flat cakes with cream and the last of the autumn's blackberries, pushing more food around her trencher than she actually ate, reminding Talon of their supper at Count Nithard's house the night of Mallus. The night he'd been saddled with a troublesome *lidi*, who'd turned out to be the best thing that had ever happened to him.

He forced himself to eat the entirety of the overflowing trencher Berta set down in front of him, not because he had any real appetite, but because he didn't want to insult Berta, and he knew he'd need a full belly for the road ahead.

When they were finished and the entire troop had thanked Berta and the others for the months of delicious meals, Anglbert disappeared into the kitchens with Berta. Talon led Lara back to their chamber, where they gathered her sack of belongings. His had already been taken down and packed onto the roan and the sorrel.

He carried her belongings to where the troop's mounts and pack horses stood at the ready outside the stables, tied the sack to Shadow's saddle, and helped Lara up onto the gelding's back. He gave her booted ankle a gentle squeeze, much as he'd done the day she'd raced off to help birth Wilric, then he swung up onto the Black's saddle, took one last, long look around the keep's courtyard, and gave the order to ride out.

Lara rode beside him as they made their way east, her jaw tight, her gaze fixed forward. Too soon, they were at the cart path to her property, where they stopped and she sat astride Shadow as his men rode past, each of them saying their good-byes to her. Phillipe was the last to say his farewells, and the only one forward enough to brave Talon's scowl as he leaned over and gave Lara a long hug, whispering into her ear. Talon shifted on his saddle as Lara teared up and nodded. He knew how she felt about him, she'd shown him with her words and actions daily, and that she considered Phillipe a good friend. She'd never purposely done anything to rile his jealousy, other than let him think Ranulf had been her lover, and yet...

"Leave off, Lieutenant." His grumble grew to a low growl as Phillipe let go only to plant a kiss on Lara's cheek and grin at Talon. "I'll catch up with the company after I've said my good-byes."

"Aye, Captain." Phillipe gave Talon a cocky salute, Lara one last, serious look, then he turned his mount's head east and rode off with the rest of the troop.

Lara met Talon's gaze, her own veiled, and turned Shadow toward her house, Wolf loping ahead and Talon trailing behind. Denys came out of the barn as they rode into the yard and took Shadow's reins as Lara dismounted. Talon dismounted from the Black and offered his hand to Denys.

"Thank you," Talon told the lad, who'd agreed to stay on and help Lara with the livestock and the property for the price of his room and board and the chance to become her aide and apprentice in the healing arts. "I feel better knowing you'll be here."

"Thank you, Captain. For giving me this chance. I won't let you down."

Talon clasped the lad's shoulder, which had grown thicker with the steady work and meals here. "I know you won't."

Denys led Shadow off to the barn and Talon turned to Lara, who stood with tears in her eyes, chin up and trembling. He laid an arm around her shoulder and tucked her close as he walked her into the house. As soon as the door shut behind them, he enveloped her in his embrace and buried his nose into her hair, breathing in the spicy sweet scent of rose soap and earthy woman. Of her.

"I love you, Lara," he whispered roughly. "I have since the first moment you smiled at me fourteen years ago." She lifted her head and met his gaze, hazel eyes swimming with tears. "I've wanted you as a man wants a woman from the moment I saw you standing bare-legged in the river, your damp clothes clinging to your lovely body, and I've only wanted you more, loved you more, every moment since." He cupped her chin and lifted it up, running his thumb along her smiling lips, wet with her tears. "I will come back to you, my rose. I swear it."

CHAPTER 21

Battles

Talon

"Why so dour, Captain? 'Tis the eve of Christ's Mass. You should be celebrating."

Talon looked up from his fifth cup of wine. Gertruda, a striking brunette with perceptive brown eyes wearing a low-cut gown of red velvet, sat down on the couch in the king's salon beside him. A few years older than Talon and the widow of a general he'd served under in Lombardy, she was a favorite of the queen's court. She and Talon had celebrated Christ's Mass together at court two years ago, and by the look in her eyes and her suggestive smile, she was inviting him to join her again.

"Sorry, Gertruda." Talon sloshed his wine around his half-empty cup and took another swig. "Not in the mood."

Gertruda rose her slim brows high on her powdered forehead. She laid a pale hand on his sleeve and ran her long, tapered fingernails from his elbow to his wrist and back again. "I can change your mood," she purred. "You know I can."

Talon brushed her hand off. "I doubt it."

Gertruda eyed him with something akin to amusement. "Who's the lucky lady?"

Talon drained the last of his wine. "Who's what?"

"Who's the woman that causes you to stew in your cups and glower at any other female who dares come within ten feet of your scowling visage?"

"What makes you think it's a woman?" He sat back and crossed his arms across his chest. "Maybe my favorite horse died."

She laughed lightly. "Does this horse have red hair and hazel eyes, whose braid you carry in your pocket?"

Talon pressed his hand to his breast pocket, where Lara's parting gift to him nestled over his heart. "How'd you know about..." Lara's name stuck in his throat.

Gertruda smiled, not unkindly. Talon followed her gaze to where the queen sat surrounded by a gaggle of women watching him and cackling among themselves.

"The king told the queen about a certain cook's lad who was a girl. A young woman who had so blinded the stout-hearted Captain Guiscard that no other woman need even try to catch his steely eye."

"Ah." Talon cocked a brow at the queen and her clutch of hens, many of whom had approached him at one time or another since his arrival in Worms. Gertruda had simply been the most recent and forthcoming.

"A handsome, virile man in love with another woman," she said with a slow, sensuous shrug of her exposed shoulders, "is a challenge to some women."

"I'm sure he is," Phillipe, who'd been drinking with the king and several other men across the room only moments before, said from behind the couch. "But his one wildcat of a woman would happily claw the eyes out of any other woman brazen enough to go after her man."

"I see." Gertruda rose with a polite smile. "Thank you, for the warning."

Phillipe nodded as she walked away, heading straight for the queen, no doubt to impart her new bit of gossip.

"Keeping your promise to Lara?" Talon said as Phillipe took the now empty seat beside him.

"What promise would that be?"

"No need to play dumb with me. She told me of the oath she made you swear to her."

Phillipe's guileless, well-practiced smile dropped. "She told you?"

"Of course, she did. Do you really think she'd keep such a thing from me?"

"No wonder you've been such a dour, grumpy bastard," Phillipe said. "Brooding on her and the babe as you have been."

"Babe?" Talon opened his mouth to say, though he wasn't sure any sound actually came out. "What babe?"

Phillipe's jaw dropped. "You said you knew. You said she told you."

"About your promise to watch my back. To make sure I made it back to her in one piece."

"So you didn't know?"

"That she carries my child?" Talon pinned him with an accusatory glare. "Do you really think I'd have left her to bring my child into this world unmarried and alone?"

"No." Phillipe shook his head. "I didn't, I don't, and I told her as much."

"Then why?" Talon wanted nothing more at that moment than to throttle his best friend. "Why didn't you tell me? Why didn't she?"

"She didn't want to worry you." Phillipe took a swig of his drink. "She wanted you concentrating on keeping your own hide intact, not fretting about her or the babe." He threw his hands up, palms out. "Her words, not mine. I swear on my mother's grave." He paled. "Oh, Christ. I'm sorry. Bad choice of words."

"Bad choices all around." Talon stood and glared around the spinning room until he spied the door and made for it on legs that felt as if they'd been cut off at the knees.

***

"This month is almost at an end," Phillipe said as Talon turned his back to him and picked up the Black's hoof to look at the same shoe he'd already inspected. "How much longer do you plan on not speaking to me?"

"Yes." Talon set the Black's hoof down and eyeballed Phillipe. "Likely, awhile."

Phillipe laid a hand on Talon's shoulder. Talon shrugged it off.

"I'm sorry I didn't tell you sooner, on my own," Phillipe said. "But in my defense, it wasn't my idea to keep her pregnancy a secret from you. It was hers. You know how convincing she can be."

"Hardheaded stubborn's more like it," Talon growled.

"And as smart as she is stubborn," Phillipe said.

Talon snorted.

"Right too, as it turns out."

Talon scowled. "How so?"

"You've done nothing but fret and brood and snap and snarl at anyone foolhardy enough to approach you since I gave her secret away, driving yourself crazy worrying about her and the babe. Driving the rest of us crazy and walking on eggshells around you."

"She still should've told me."

"What would you have done differently if she had, other than worry sooner?"

"I would've married her. Given our child my name."

"So, marry her when we get back. People have short memories for these sorts of transgressions, especially when they're righted. Sometimes later rather than sooner, but righted nonetheless."

"What if we don't get back?" Talon spoke his greatest fear out loud. "How would I right that?"

"You wouldn't." His words twisted in Talon's gut. "But she would live knowing you loved her, that your child was conceived of that love, and God help any fool who'd dare call her child a bastard and expect to come out of it unscathed."

Talon stared down at his scarred palm and clenched his fist. "I should be there with her, taking care of her and our unborn babe, not halfway across Gaul, sitting on my ass waiting to go chase Saxons through frozen marshlands."

Phillipe let out a wry chuckle. "I've good news, then." He pulled a parchment out of his tunic pocket and handed it to Talon. "We march in a month's time."

"Good." Talon patted the Black's flank, anxious to shake the rust off the both of them. "The sooner we get to it, the sooner we get back, the sooner I can claim my prize." He grinned for the first time in over a month, thinking back on a certain conversation between himself and Lara. "An old jest," he explained to Phillipe. He glanced at his scarred palm. "And well worth the price."

"What price?" Phillipe asked. "For what prize?"

"My blood and my sword for Crossroads Keep," Talon told him. "I've decided on it as the land Charles promised me, once this campaign is over."

"It is a nice piece of land," Phillipe said.

"It is."

"With a well-built, comfortable manor house and a stable to rival the kings."

"It has."

"What do you plan to do on your nice land in your comfortable house?"

"Raise fat babies and sleek foals."

"Need a partner? For the foals, I mean."

Talon considered it. "The more mares bought and covered—"

"—the more foals to sell," Phillipe finished.

Talon offered Phillipe his hand, and they shook on it.

"Odds are Anglbert will want in on it too," Phillipe said. "The old miser has more coin saved than the pope and hasn't quit bemoaning the lack of Berta's cooking since we rode out of Oloron."

"Well then." Talon shut the gate to the Black's stall shut. "Let's go find Anglbert and Charles and stake my claim."

***

Lara

By February, Lara's belly had stopped sending back half of what she ate, and by March she was eating twice what she normally would. By April her belly was noticeably rounded and the acrobat in her womb was turning somersaults on a daily basis, and by May, she had no more material in the seams of her gowns left to let out and had added side-panels of linen from Sophie's old gowns to make room for her growing belly.

It was the last market day of May, and she set her wagon up alongside Willem and Patience's, laying out her baskets of herbs and dried flowers, wheels of cheeses, bars of soaps, and vials of tinctures, including a dozen of Sophie's love potions.

"Spring is always a good time to sell love potions," she said as Patience eyed the distinctive vials renown in four provinces. She laid a hand over her taut belly and grinned as the babe moved under her palm. "Hopefully, I'll sell enough of them to buy a bolt of fine linen from the tinker to start making some baby gowns with. I've already made two dozen absorbing cloths from what's left of Sofie's gowns."

Patience nodded her approval. "You'll need at least six infant gowns," she said. "One to wear, a clean one to change into, and four drying on the line at all times."

"Lovely."

Patience was still laughing as a group of village women walked by and waved, their baskets swinging. Patience and Lara waved back. Though most of the people had responded to Lara's pregnancy as a natural matter, there were some who turned their noses up at her and whispered behind their hands. Not that Lara had expected any different.

"How many vials did you sell Marta?" Patience asked as Marta and Denys strolled past, arm in arm, gazing at each other as if they were the only two people in the square.

"None." Lara gave an indulgent smile to the young lovers. "She didn't need any. They figured it out all by themselves."

"Aye, once Marta realized the captain was taken by you, which, by the way, she figured out much quicker than you did."

"Everybody figured us out quicker than I did," Lara said with a rueful grin. Ravenna sashayed toward them across the square, her arms linked with the steward Roumel's daughters. The same two who'd thought to snare Talon with the vials of potion Ravenna had bought for them. "Well," she added with some satisfaction, "not everybody."

Count Nithard and Ravenna had returned to Oloron Manor right after the new year, without Ranulf or Lothair, neither of whom had shown their faces in the valley since the attack on Lara and Talon. Lara had caught glimpses of Ravenna and the count as she made her healer's rounds of the villages and toths, but today was the first time Ravenna had come within fifty paces of her, walking over to Lara's wagon and staring at her belly.

"So," Ravenna said with a snide smile. "It's true. The *lidi* is with child. How common."

Patience gasped and then hissed through her teeth, but Lara smiled.

"I might have taken offense as you intended, except I know you speak from jealousy." She rubbed her hand over her round belly, remembering the feel of Talon's hands on her skin. "I can't say I blame you. The captain truly is a man to be jealous over."

"Bah," Ravenna huffed. "You're nothing more than a cheap camp follower whose soldier is off to get himself another whore before getting himself killed on some battlefield."

Lara's breath caught, and it was Patience who answered Ravenna's taunt.

"You may be jealous of the captain's attentions," she said, "but you so do not know him."

"All I need to know is he left her pregnant with his bastard." Ravenna sniffed and wrinkled her nose. "My father will be so pleased to learn the rumors are true. The witch is breeding." She gave a toss of her long black hair and turned on her heels. "Come, ladies. We've seen all we needed to."

Lara let her breath out in a low hiss. "Talon was right to name them a pack of curs."

"Aye. What a bitch."

Lara laughed and gave Patience a hug.

"Hey now." Willem walked up to them with Wilric in his arms and Wyatt by his side. "Trying to steal my wife, are you?"

Lara gave Patience a wink. "I might be. I could use a good wife."

"Speaking of wives." Patience indicated Denys and Marta as the couple headed toward them. "When is that lad going to turn man and make a wife of her?"

"He says not until he can buy a patch of land and build her a proper house on it," Lara said.

"They'll have to move from here then." Willem spoke out loud what they all knew but were reluctant to say. "No one but Nithard has land enough to sell here, and he won't sell. He'd rather starve out the few of us who do own land here, so he can have it all."

"He can try," Lara said fiercely. "He will fail."

"Have you seen this?" Patience asked hopefully.

"No. But I feel it." Before Lara could say more, Denys and Marta approached them.

"There's to be musicians and a dance tonight," Denys told Lara as Marta eyed her with anticipation. "Will you stay?"

"I plan to be sitting by a fire with my feet up by nightfall," she told the crestfallen couple. "But that doesn't mean you have to leave, Denys. Stay, enjoy the dance with Marta."

"Are you sure? The captain told me to watch over you."

"I'll be fine for one night, Denys."

The lad glanced from Lara's reassuring smile to Marta's pleading one. "If you're quite sure?"

"Go." Lara waved them off. "Have fun. Stay as late as you like." She grinned as they skipped away hand in hand.

"I don't think Denys is going to get his land and house before his marriage," Patience said as the young couple stopped to kiss. "He keeps that up, and Marta's going to be as full of child as you next spring."

***

Lara

Lara trudged up the mountainside, her feet sore and her belly heavy with child. She made her way through a thicket of brambles into the glen where her mother was buried. A doe-eyed woman with curls of gold stood beside the rose-covered byre with a swaddled babe in her arms.

"Who are you?" Lara asked.

"I was Isabeau." The woman's voice sounded as sweet and trilling as a lark's. She held the babe out to Lara and laid it in Lara's arms. Lara gazed down at the head of soft auburn curls and wide gray eyes staring back up at her. "She is Isabeau."

Lara looked from the babe to the woman, whose hair grew white and her skin wrinkled. She was no longer staring into the woman's eyes, but into Sophie's.

"Run," Sophie said, her breath turning to smoke. "Now."

Lara woke with a start to Wolf's bark. Glancing wildly around the dark, she recognized her bedchamber, blew a shaky breath out, and ran a hand back through her sweat-dampened hair. From below, Wolf's barking became louder and more insistent. Lara slipped out of bed and crept over to the window facing the river and peeled a corner of the oiled skin back. Three men sat on horses, one holding a burning torch.

"That's her hellhound barking inside," one of the men said. "It's never far from the witch's side. Light your arrows. The count wants her dead."

Lara clasped her hand over her mouth to keep from screaming. They meant to burn her alive in her home. She crawled on her hands and knees and peeked out the window facing the road, where two other men waited on horses with lit arrows. If she tried to run, she had no doubt they'd spit her and roast her over the coals.

She threw her cloak on over her nightshift and grabbed her boots and one of the gowns she'd altered, then scrambled down the ladder as the first arrow hit the thatch roof with a thunk and a hiss. Then another. And another.

"Come, Wolf." The smell of burning thatch filled the air, so she pulled the trapdoor open and pushed the shaking hound down into the cellar, then dropped her clothes and boots down after him.

She grabbed the pot of water hanging on the spit over the hearth and took it into the cellar, then climbed back up, closed the trapdoor, and poured the bucket of dish water over it. Glancing around the room, she swiped the carving of the elephant Talon had made her off the mantel, climbed down the ladder, and pulled the dripping wet door shut. She lit a candle and cut one of the blankets in the cellar into strips that she dipped into the pot of water and stuffed into the cracks around the door, then she huddled with a trembling Wolf in the far corner of the cellar under another blanket.

The smoke soon became thick and choking, burning her throat and eyes. She dipped the corners of the blanket into the pot of water and held the wet ends over her face and Wolf's, concentrating on slowing her shallow breaths as the roar of the fire drowned out everything but the beat of her galloping heart.

***

Talon

The army left Worms the first of March and marched east until they met up with the Saxon bands raiding across the Rhine. It took them a half a month to beat the Saxons back across the river, and the entire, miserably wet and bloody month of May chasing down and skirmishing with those still scattered and hiding in the hinterlands before their leader surrendered to Charles. By late June, the king and the bulk of his army were back in Worms, where Charles gave Talon the deed to Crossroads Keep along with three hundred acres of field and pastureland. His troop of twenty had lost three men in battle, and of the remaining soldiers, five decided to join Talon and start new lives in Oloron, four rode for other homes, and eight joined another company.

It was decided that Anglbert, Dardinel, and tree would return to Oloron first. Anglbert, to prepare for the others' eventual arrival, hire workers, and set Lara up as mistress of the keep while enjoying Berta's cooking and other attributes; Tree to be Lara's and the babe's personal guard, and Dardinel, son of a farmer, to oversee the tilling and planting of fields and fencing of pastureland. Talon would ride for Frisia with Phillipe and Oswald to buy a string of broodmares with their collective coin, coin that Charles had added generously to as a wedding present for Talon and Lara, and first choice at buying any foals Talon was willing to sell.

They left for Frisia the middle of July, nine months since Lara had first lain with Talon at the Hollow, which meant their babe was due to be born any time now. He told himself Lara was strong of both mind and body, a healer surrounded by women like Berta and Enid and Patience, who'd borne their share of children. She'd be fine. The babe would be fine. He told himself this day in and day out, his constant, silent prayer, which let him do what he should, which was ride north, away from his lady and his child, so he could return ready to make a life with and for them. A long, prosperous, happy life.

He intended to marry Lara as soon as he returned to Oloron. If she would have him.

He'd wronged her by not marrying her after the Hollow, by not telling her he loved her until the day he rode away. Her smile when he'd finally admitted it out loud had kept him warm during the long, interminable days and nights he spent slogging through the swamps of Saxony. The light in her eyes kept him determined and hopeful he'd return to her a whole man.

Ready to be a husband and father.

To spend the rest of his life with her.

Talon rode hard for that life, making Frisia by August and returning to the northern border of Gaul by September with two dozen broodmares in tow. They stopped in Tours for the Fall Festival, where they were joined by a miller, a blacksmith, and a tailor all looking for a new place to settle and ply their trades. And where Talon won an emerald ring in an all-night game of Shah from the Bishop of Tours, and bought a bolt of forest green silk and a baby blanket of finely woven indigo wool, his gifts for Lara and their baby, and himself. The closer they got to Oloron, the more his daydreams were of Lara in a sleek-fitting, low-cut gown of the slinky silk, her hazel eyes smiling at him as green and bright as the emerald on her ring finger.

He'd gained company in his lovesickness. The miller, Arnulf, a stout, watchful man, had a daughter, Doralice, a brown-haired, doe-eyed waif who left Phillipe moon-eyed and tongue-tied in her presence. Talon and Oswald suffered no such afflictions and teased Phillipe mercilessly, until it was hard to say who blushed more at sight of the other, Phillipe or Doralice. Arnulf, watching it all, kept his daughter close and his axe closer.

When they finally rode into the valley of Oloron in early October, the trees were in their full autumnal show of reds and golds and greens, the colors of Lara's flaming hair and changeling eyes. Eyes that would either blaze with golden embers of ire when she first saw him again or grow soft and mossy green.

They rode past Oloron Manor, which looked to be inhabited again by the servants bustling around the courtyard, who stopped to stare at their passing. There were no obvious signs as to who was in residence, something Anglbert would surely know. As they rode past the village, the few people milling about watched them with the same slack-jawed stares, as did the field workers they passed farther down the road. A niggling began to stir in Talon's gut. Something was amiss.

"I'm off," he told Phillipe. "I'll go by Lara's house first, then meet you at the keep."

There was nobody outside of Willem and Patience's house when he rode by, though he did notice the new addition to Willem's workshop. He urged the Black into a gallop, slowing only when they turned onto the path to Lara's property. His gut tightened in anticipation as they cleared the windbreak of chestnut trees, then twisted into a strangling knot at the sight of the gutted, burnt-out ruin that had been her house.

The world swimming around him, Talon noted that the barn was still standing, and Honey and Gaea were in the paddock with several goats and chickens. He dismounted, the ground shifting under his feet, and ran into the barn, where he checked the little room that had been Denys's sleeping quarters and saw a man's leggings and tunic hanging on the wall peg. He made a quick round of the rest of the barn but saw no signs of Lara. He told himself she'd probably moved into the keep by now, that he'd find her and his babe there, safe and sound under Anglbert's care, but his feet took him to the old oak, where two new graves lay alongside Sophie's.

There were no markers or headstones on the new graves, and by the grass growing over them, they'd been there since at least early summer.

Talon's chest seized as he dropped to his knees and his mouth worked wordlessly. One of the graves was of a size for an adult, but the second one was smaller, large enough for an infant in a coffin. Like his mother's and the babe's whose birth had ripped her apart and killed her.

A keening moan rose up from his belly and rent his chest. "*No*," he railed, cursing God and the heavens. "You cannot have her, damn you. She is mine. My curse. My rose. My love. My life." He buried his face in his hands. "I should have come straight home to you. I should never have left you. Damn me. Damn Charles and his cursed wars. Damn this world for ever letting you leave it. Leave me. Oh God, Lara, how could you find me again, how could you love me, let me love you, only to leave me forever?"

Because death was forever, this much Talon knew. He knew the hollow emptiness of wanting someone and never being able to hold them again, of missing them and never being able to see them or hear them, except for dreams and memories. Lara was gone. Gone from this world, from him, and with her, their child, of whom he only had dreams and no memories.

"Oh God. How am I to live without you?" He threw his head back and gazed up into the heavens, finding not the slightest peace knowing she resided there. "What manner of god are you to torture a man so? To bring me to her, only to take her away? Why? When you know I have more need of her than you?"

He collapsed onto the cool earth of her grave and wept as he hadn't since he was a boy and his mother had died. He wept and cried and sobbed and cursed until his body was as void of tears as his soul was of feeling, then he rolled over and lay between the graves, staring up into the vast and endless emptiness stretching out before him.

"Captain?"

He blinked his swollen eyelids and focused on the voice floating above him. "Denys?" he croaked.

"Aye."

Talon stared up into a face much the same, yet much changed from the lad he'd last seen. "What happened here?" he asked, his voice as raw as the gaping maw in his chest. "Where is my lady? My child?"

Denys shrugged and shook his head and his mouth curled into a strange smile. "I don't know. But they're not buried here."

"They're not?"

"No, sir."

Talon's heart went from stone cold and still to beating triple time. "Then who is?"

"Goats."

CHAPTER 22

Isabeau Juditha

Lara

Sleep. Lara wanted sleep, needed sleep, craved sleep, but with Isabeau howling to nurse, the goats needing to be milked, and the last of the squash needing to be harvested, she wasn't going to get it any time soon. Yawning and leaning her head back against the headboard, she put her daughter to breast and gave a weary sigh as the babe suckled with vigor. At least one of them was thriving. With every pennyweight of flesh Isabeau gained, it seemed Lara lost two. Her gowns, let out for pregnancy, now hung on her like sackcloth, but she had neither the time nor the energy to take them in. There were more important things to tend to, such as keeping the Hollow producing and her child fed and clean and clothed. A never-ending cycle of gardening, cooking, and nursing and changing cloths, a basket of which awaited her now.

She let herself doze while Isabeau nursed, then set the babe in a front sling, slung her bow and quiver of arrows across her back, picked up the basket of washed laundry to be hung to dry, and opened the cabin door.

"Come on, Wolf."

The hound loped after her, free of the limp that had plagued him for a month after the fire. The pads of his feet had been blistered when they'd climbed out of the smoky cellar and run across the smoldering ruins of the house, despite Lara having wrapped them in strips of wet cloth. The soles of her boots had been singed as well when she'd kicked white-hot embers down into the cellar, making sure it burned.

With their sore feet and her belly heavy with child, it had taken them three days to reach the Hollow, a journey that would normally take a day on horseback. But Lara had left all three horses in the stables and had only taken her best two milking goats with her, leaving the paddock gate open so Denys would think they'd wandered off. She'd made sure to leave no signs she'd survived, not even a message scrawled in the dirt floor of the barn for Denys, whom she'd been teaching to read. It was vital that Nithard think her dead.

She set the bow and quiver against the drying line post, settled Isabeau into her own basket with a blanket tucked around her, and began to hang the laundry, Wolf on guard beside the babe's basket. She was hanging the last of Isabeau's changing cloths when Wolf's ears stiffened, and the jay that had been scolding them nonstop went quiet. She picked up her bow, slung the quiver over her shoulder, pulled an arrow, and notched it to the bow's string.

"What is it, Wolf?" she whispered as the dog stood at full alert, his ears cocked toward the high brush along the stream's edge, a low growl rumbling from his chest.

There was movement along the edge of the brush, movement that took the shape of a man, thick-set and crouching low as he crept toward the yard. She set her sights on the man's head, which was covered by a cap and his face with a full, dark beard. She lowered her aim to the man's chest and let it fly. The man dropped.

"God's blood, woman," a familiar voice yelled as she set a second arrow to her bow. "You've shot at me."

"Talon?"

"Who else bleeds for you on sight, you troublesome wench?"

Lara threw down her bow and quiver and ran straight for him as he stood to his full height and stepped out from behind the brush.

"Talon." She threw herself into his arms. "It's you. It's really you." She leaned back to see the tear in the upper sleeve of his jerkin. "Your arm."

He laughed it off. "It's only a scratch from a wildcat."

"You were sneaking up on me."

"I wasn't sure of who or what I'd find here." He pressed her close. Lara burrowed her nose into his neck and inhaled the scent of leather, horse, and *him*. He ran his hand back through her shoulder-length hair and held her face in his hands. "Thank God, I've found you alive and well," he rasped. "And our babe?"

Of course, he knew. He'd have ridden through the valley, where any number of people would have told him of her pregnancy. "Our daughter is alive and well." She lifted her chin toward the yard, where Wolf stood guarding the babe's basket, wagging his entire body, waiting for the okay to come greet Talon.

He slapped his thigh, and the hound came bounding over, leaning up against Talon's legs, whining and wagging his tail as Talon rubbed his ears and patted his rump. "Thank you for watching over my wildcat and her kitten, old man." Talon gave the dog a good-natured thumping along his ribs.

He straightened and wrapped his arm around Lara's shoulder. "Introduce me to our daughter."

Lara wrapped both arms around his waist as they walked toward the basket.

"Denys told me what happened," he said. "The fire, the shod hoofprints around what was left of the house: the fact that two of your best milking goats were missing. It was the missing goats that gave him the idea for the graves to make people think you dead and buried."

"Graves?"

He stopped and held her tighter to him. "I thought you dead," he whispered fiercely. "I lay on what was meant to be your grave, thinking you gone from me forever." He pressed his lips to her hair until his ragged breath eased. Then he loosened his hold, stepped back from her, reached into his tunic pocket, and held out a ring of gold encircling an emerald the size of a hummingbird's egg. "Marry me, Lara? Be my wife?"

Lara opened her mouth to say yes, to shout it to the heavens, then clamped her mouth shut. "When did you acquire this ring?"

He cocked his head. "September. I played the Bishop of Tours for it in a game of Shah. I put up my best new broodmare in the wager."

Lara chuffed. "At least I know my worth."

"Your worth?" He cocked his head the other way and the muscle in the side of his jaw started to twitch. "What are you talking about?"

"When did you find out about the babe?"

"At Christmas. Phillipe let it slip."

"I see."

"I don't." He stood at his full height and squared his shoulders. "Nor do I see why you didn't tell me you were pregnant with my child before I left."

"Because," she snapped, suddenly ridiculously close to tears, "I didn't want you worrying about me or the babe while you were gone. I wanted you to come back to me for me, not out of any sense of obligation."

His steel-gray gaze pierced hers, and the scar across his right cheek shone white. "My child is my blood, not some obligation.

"And you, you beautiful, thorny, troublesome, maddening wildcat of a witch, are the love of my life."

"I am?"

He snorted. "Which is why I asked for and was given Crossroads Keep and three hundred acres of pastureland for my service, from which I've been released."

"You did?"

He nodded curtly. "After which I sent Anglbert and a few others to the keep to watch over you and my claim whilst I rode north to Frisia, where I bought two dozen broodmares for the Black to cover so I could breed horses and secure us a good and prosperous life in the valley, thinking you loved me as I loved you."

Lara sucked a shaky breath in and burst into tears. "I do love you, you arrogant ass." She threw her arms around his neck.

"Enough to marry me?"

Lara sniffed. "Enough to marry you and drive you mad for the rest of your days."

He bumped his pelvis against hers. "And nights?" he rumbled.

"Oh yes."

He kissed her, long and hard and demanding, and Lara gave him all that was left of her, panting and falling into his solid chest as he broke the kiss. "Can I meet our daughter now?" he whispered in her ear.

Lara took him by the hand and led him to the basket where their daughter stared up at Talon with wide gray eyes.

"Talon Guiscard." Lara lifted the babe out of the basket and placed her in Talon's arms. "Meet Isabeau Juditha Guiscard."

He pushed the swaddling blanket back from her head and grinned at her soft cap of red curls for a long moment before he lifted his gaze to Lara's. "Isabeau Juditha?"

"She's named after her grandmothers."

"You said you didn't know who your mother was. That Sophie never told you."

"She didn't. Not while she lived. They came to me in a dream the night of the fire. My mother told me the babe was to be Isabeau, as she was before her, then Sophie told me to run. They saved our lives."

***

Talon

Talon's empty belly growled as he returned to the cabin from the stream where he'd bathed. He hadn't eaten at the keep yesterday, insulting Berta no end. But he'd been in such a hurry to get to the Hollow, and hopefully, Lara, that he'd only stopped there long enough to speak with Anglbert and Phillipe and to saddle the roan and fill the sorrel's packs with bread, cheese, sausage, wine, and a sack each of flour and oats. He'd left the Black at the keep to stud, whispering in the stallion's ear that he'd be well pleased with two dozen black foals come next summer, and then he was off and a third of the way to the Hollow before it became too dark to ride. He'd built no fire, just chewed his hardtack and slept a bit, waking in the dark and back on the trail as dawn broke, never stopping until he hit the ground as Lara's arrow grazed his arm.

He entered the cabin and stopped still, his breath sucking in at the sight of Lara's pear-shaped buttocks as she bent over, dipping a sponge in the rinsing bucket, then squeezing the water out and down the long, lean length of her leg to her foot. He let his breath out in a great rush, sounding, and feeling, like he'd been gut-punched. Lara straightened and turned, showing him the full roundness of her milk-heavy breasts.

"You are a sight for sore eyes, lady." He closed the distance between them slowly, taking in the thatch of auburn curls at her sex, the mouthwatering curves of her hips, the nip of her already slender waist. Then he noticed how pronounced her hip bones were, how her belly, always taut, sunk in, and how sharply her collarbones jutted out. He looked long and hard at her face, at the dark shadows beneath her too-large eyes, the deep hollows of her cheeks. "You haven't been eating?"

"I have. It's just, I'd rather sleep than eat given the chance, and I've only so many chances in a day."

She sighed and leaned into his chest. The feel of her skin against his was the succor he'd been riding back to since the moment he'd ridden away from her. He nibbled her neck and ran his hand down her back, feeling her prominent spine. His daughter lay naked on the bed, enjoying the warmth of the fire after her bath, staring up at her pudgy fingers and kicking her legs, which had three rolls of plump flesh along each thigh.

"Your daughter would rather eat, from the looks of her," he said.

Lara nodded and yawned into his shoulder. "The little leech never sleeps for any length of time."

Talon chuckled. "My mother complained the same of me as a babe." He gave Lara a hearty kiss that promised more later. Right now, they both needed to eat. "I've cheese, bread, sausage, and wine from Berta." He went to his pack and emptied it. "What shall we devour first?"

Their bellies sated, Talon stretched out on the bed beside Lara and watched in fascination as she nursed their daughter, whose perfectly formed little hands and feet turned circles apace with her suckling until both slowed and eventually stopped. After lifting the babe to her shoulder, Lara patted her on the back until she let out a loud burp.

"She'll sleep now," Lara said, stifling a yawn as she laid the babe down between them. Talon offered his shoulder, pressing a kiss on Lara's forehead as she snuggled into him. Isabeau whimpered and Lara drew the babe into her arms. "Shush, baby," she murmured. "Your papa's here. We can both sleep. We're safe."

Talon tucked them closer. Lara had told him the men who'd tried to burn her alive had done so on Nithard's orders, that she'd run, or limped, up to the Hollow without letting anyone know she was still alive. Then she'd lived here, pregnant and alone but for Wolf and then their infant daughter, in constant fear and constantly on guard since. No wonder she was exhausted and worn out. He vowed to deal with Nithard once they returned to the keep and fell asleep curled around his sleeping woman and child, planning retribution.

He woke to a small foot kicking him in his belly and gray eyes studying his.

"Sizing up the interloper, are you?" Isabeau kicked and gurgled with glee as her foot connected with his belly again. He grasped her pudgy foot, and she kicked harder, squirming and grinning at him. "You are your mother's daughter, aren't you, you troublesome little sprite." She kicked and cooed and seemed to be waiting for him to answer. "Come on then." He scooped her up as Lara stirred. "Your mama needs her sleep."

He checked her changing cloth as he'd seen Lara do. Happy to find it still clean and dry, he wrapped her in a blanket and walked outside into the crisp fall night with Wolf at their heels. The moon was a night away from full and cast a bright light down on them as they took their first walk alone together.

Isabeau's eyes shone as bright as the stars and her toothless smile smote him as surely as Lara's ever had. "Aye, you are your mother's daughter. You have her sweet smile, auburn curls, and big cat eyes, eyes I'd have wagered would be a mossy hazel, whose dove gray make your papa's breeches burst with pride." He nuzzled his daughter's petal-soft cheek and his heart melted at her coos of delight. "Isabeau Juditha Guiscard, my little dove."

They walked, talked, and stared at the stars and each other until the moon was high overhead and the chill of night began to seep through Talon's tunic. "We'd better get you back inside before you take a chill," he told his daughter. "Then I'd really be in trouble."

Lara still slept soundly, and Talon banked the fire and sat by it with Isabeau's back propped up against his legs, making faces and noises at each other until the babe began to alternately fuss or fight her closing lids. Talon laid her in the bed beside Lara and the babe rooted at her mother's breast. Lara groaned and her eyes fluttered open. She slipped the sleeve of her nightshift off her shoulder and put the babe to her breast, nodding off as the babe suckled until she too fell asleep. Stripping his clothes off and slipping under the covers with them, Talon closed his eyes.

***

Lara

Lara twitched her nose at the savory aroma of roasting meat, and she opened her eyes to daylight streaming into the cabin through the open door. The deep timbre of a man's voice and an infant's cooing floated in from outside, and Lara's heart stopped for one horrible moment as she glanced down at the empty space in the bed beside her where her daughter usually slept. Then the man chuckled, and she recognized Talon's deep, throaty laughter. She tumbled out of the bed and stumbled out the door to find two pairs of gray eyes smiling at her.

"Talon?" She still wasn't completely certain he was standing there holding their daughter in one arm while turning a pheasant on the spit over the fire with the other and that she wasn't dreaming it.

"Aye, love. None other." He peered hard into her face. "You should sit before you fall down."

Lara plopped onto the bench as Wolf left Talon's side to sit beside her, still trying to fit the sight of a cooing Isabeau in Talon's arms in her muddled mind. Yesterday, she'd woken to yet another day of endless chores, little sleep, and a voracious daughter. Today, she'd slept in until after noon and awakened to a meal being cooked and her daughter taken care of. Feeling her empty breasts, she had a vague recollection of the babe nursing in bed and Talon's voice urging her to stay and rest.

"How long did I sleep?" she asked, stifling a yawn.

"The night and half a day through. During which time we've been getting acquainted, haven't we, Miss Issy?" He juggled the babe, who gurgled and kicked him in the belly with as big a grin on her toothless face as was on her father's. "She kicks like a mule, our daughter." Talon grabbed her foot and shook it gently. "I pity the lads she kicks in the shins for getting too fresh."

Lara leaned back, still a little disoriented, and took in the horses grazing alongside the goats, whose udders looked to have been milked. "You've been busy."

"That we have," Talon said. "Wolf caught us the bird while Issy taught me to milk a goat and how to change her changing cloth, which is quite disgusting by the way."

Lara laughed at his screwed-up nose, the first time she'd laughed out loud in a long time. She felt the grit in her unkempt hair and smoothed the milk-stained front of her tunic. "Do I have time to bathe in the river before supper?"

Talon grinned. "You, we, have all the time we want."

Lara returned from the river in a clean tunic and skirt, feeling more refreshed than she had in months. And hungry. They feasted on the pheasant and a bowl of freshly picked greens along with what was left of the bread and cheese from Berta until they were both groaning with full bellies. After supper, Lara nursed Isabeau, and woke up some time later to Talon curled around both of them. With a contented sigh, she gave herself up to blessed sleep.

When next she woke, the sun was high in the noon sky and her breasts were only slightly full. She dressed and went outside to find Isabeau sleeping in her basket on the porch while Talon chopped firewood, shirtless.

"You let me sleep in again." She admired the play of his muscles as he swung the axe down and split a log.

"You needed it. The way our little leech of a daughter nurses, it's not surprising you're so thin and worn out."

Tears sprang to Lara's eyes. "Is that why you haven't done more than kiss me since you've been here? Why you don't want me now? Because you think me too haggard and skinny?"

Talon buried the axe in the log and walked over to Lara. He ran his hand back through her hair and cupped her chin, the scent of his sweat stirring urges that had laid dormant in her for months now.

"I think you worn out and half-starved from lack of sleep and proper food." His voice, his gaze, were both gentle. "I think you've given everything of yourself to keep this demanding child of ours alive and thriving. I've only been tending her for two days, without having carried her in my womb for nine months prior, or nursing her from my own body these three and a half months past, and I'm near worn out. I think you deserve all the rest and nourishment and time you need to recover enough so that I can show you how much I want you, you beautiful, nurturing woman. And the fact that you've come so easily to tears tells me you're not there yet." He tilted her chin up and placed a tender kiss on her lips. "I've waited eleven months for you, I can wait a few more days."

***

Lara laid a sleeping Isabeau on the bed and cocooned her in the soft woolen blanket Talon bought for her in Tours. She turned to Talon with a hungry smile, though they'd just finished feasting on venison steaks from the buck he'd shot two days ago. The day after he'd told her he could wait until she was rested up enough for him.

As grateful and thankful and somehow not at all surprised that he'd dove right in to taking care of Isabeau and the livestock and property while she rested, she was even more eager to resume relations with him. She was ready to be Lara and Talon again, not just mama and papa to Isabeau. By the gleam in Talon's eyes, he was ready too.

She pulled off her tunic, dipped a cloth in the warm water left in the basin from Isabeau's bath, and washed any trace of her daughter's nursing from her breasts under Talon's intent gaze.

"I have something for you," he said.

Lara dropped her gaze to his breeches. "Yes. You surely do."

He chuckled. "I have something else I want to give you first." He went to his pack and pulled out a parcel wrapped in green linen. "I was waiting for the, ah, right moment to do so."

Lara unwrapped a folded length of iridescent green cloth that slipped lightly through her fingers. She rubbed her cheek against the sleek softness. "Is it silk?"

Talon grinned. "It is. I saw it in the marketplace at Tours and thought of you."

"Oh Talon. I love it." Lara let the silk unfurl over her arm. "It's so light and sheer." She pulled it up over her shoulder and the silk fluttered in the fire's light. "It's like having wings of gossamer."

"It's to make you a gown of gossamer." He hooked a finger between her shoulder and the silk, then ran his knuckle along her skin. "I've dreamed of you wearing such a gown for so many nights now."

He unfolded the cloth and wrapped it over both her shoulders, groaning as it fell over her breasts. Lara's nipples pebbled at the featherlight touch of the silk and went rock hard as Talon ran the callus of his thumb over one, his groan deepening.

Lara leaned into his touch until he cupped her breast. "I've missed this, missed you." She sighed. "So much."

"I know, love." He pressed her to him and took her mouth with his. "Me too."

The next thing Lara knew, they were stripping each other's remaining clothes off and tossing them to the floor. Lara took in the sight of Talon's naked body greedily, the sight of his broad shoulders tapering down to his trim waist ridged with muscles and the dark trail of hair leading to his half-hard cock stoking the ache growing between her legs. She reached out and touched the telltale weal of a newly healed scar that slashed across his right hip.

"It looks worse than it was," Talon told her. "Nor was the king's healer half as comely as my west-end witch."

She ran her finger along the scar. "Are there any more scars newly added to your collection?"

He shook his head and laid his hand over hers. "None any worse than the nick from your arrow."

Lara touched the light scab that had already formed over the scratch on his arm. "I am sorry I shot at you."

"It's of no matter."

He pulled her down onto the bearskin rug, where they lay on their sides whispering soft words of love while rediscovering each other's bodies. Talon straddled her and probed between her thighs with the blunt head of his cock until the ache between Lara's legs became a throbbing need. Her breath caught as he slowly buried himself inside her, filling that need. She let her breath out in a low moan as her intimate muscles tightened around him.

"I'm sorry, my love," he whispered, his voice low and rough. "You feel so good, and it's been so long, I fear I can't hold back."

"Then don't," she whispered back fiercely. "I won't break."

But she did. She broke atop the peak of their passion, shattering into a thousand shards of light and flame and raw nerves, then melting back into her boneless, weightless self, held together by his body wrapped around hers.

***

Talon

Talon threw the outside bolt to the door, then mounted the sorrel's bare back and nodded to Lara, who sat in the roan's saddle with Isabeau snug in her sling. "Let's go home."

Home. The first one he could call his in years.

He turned the sorrel's head southeast, with Lara following and Wolf herding the two milk goats. He'd been at the Hollow for twelve days, and he'd savored every moment of them with Lara and Isabeau, but it was time to return to Crossroads Keep, to assume their new lives as lord and lady of the keep with their daughter. A life he'd left his old one as a soldier for without regret. A life he looked forward to.

He also looked forward to dealing with Nithard. Lara told him what she'd heard the men say before they'd torched her house, that they'd been ordered by Nithard to burn her alive, and though they had no other proof, her word was enough for Talon. Plus, if Lara's dream had been true, and they always were one way or another, then she was Nithard's illegitimate niece. Both situations which Talon intended to confront as soon as they returned to Oloron.

But before he dealt with Nithard or the keep or anything else, he intended to marry Lara.

They made the Abbey St. Marie at nightfall, where the Abbot Rogert took one look at Lara and the babe and fell to his knees.

"Thank God." He raised his hands to the sky. "Thank Mary, Mother of Jesus, you survived. Mother and child survived."

Lara pushed the blanket back from the babe's head as the abbot stood. "Abbot Rogert," she said, "meet Isabeau Juditha."

"To be christened Isabeau Juditha Guiscard," Talon added. "Right after you marry her mother and father."

The abbot placed his hand over the crown of the babe's head and smiled down at her as she blinked up at him. "Isabeau," he murmured. "Welcome home."

The reverence of his voice, his manner, stood Talon at attention. "You knew," he said. "You knew Lara was Isabeau's daughter."

The abbot dipped his head with a beatific smile.

"How long?"

"Since the day Sophie brought her down from the mountains as a one-year-old child and had me write her name and birth beneath the recording of her parents' marriage, which I officiated at in this very church."

CHAPTER 23

Count and Countess of Oloron

Talon

Talon woke without the familiar jab of his daughter's foot in his belly, filling him with a strange mix of elation she'd finally slept the night through in her crib, yet also fear that she'd slept in her parents' bed for the last time. Of course, his fear likely had to do with Lara waking up in the middle of the night, crying out Isabeau's name and reaching for their daughter between them, panicking when Isabeau wasn't there. Talon had showed her Isabeau sleeping peacefully in her crib, then he'd held Lara and whispered soothing endearments into her hair until she'd calmed and fell back to sleep, as he had so many nights a lifetime ago.

Today was the summer solstice, two years to the day since Lara had stood him off in the river with Wolf. Two years since he'd chased the thorny wildcat down and kept her captive in his chamber. Two years since she'd captured his heart and soul, and eight months since they'd married and become the Count and Countess of Oloron.

The Abbot Rogert had returned to Crossroads Keep with them after marrying them and christening Isabeau, bringing with him the abbey's book of records, which proved Lara the legitimate daughter of Isabeau Midered and Harald Rousell, and rightful heir to Oloron Manor. Nithard and Ravenna had fled the province the day after Talon had ridden in and discovered the two new graves under the oak, leaving no other Midereds in the province to contest Lara's inheritance.

The people of the valley had welcomed their new count and countess with great cheer and hope. Both of which Talon and Lara were determined to deliver on. Their first act had been to declare Crossroads Keep their home, for neither of them wished to live in Oloron Manor, which would remain the county seat and where Talon held Mallus the first Saturday of every month. The very first Mallus he'd presided over, with Lara at his side, they'd pledged a living wage for the field workers and promised that no person would go hungry through no fault of their own.

Phillipe stayed at the keep as the captain of Talon's personal guard, which consisted of Oswald, Tree, and Dardinel. With Oloron Manor to maintain as well, they installed Anglbert and Berta as stewards, where they would live until Isabeau was of age to claim her birthright. Though they lost Berta as head cook for the keep, Enid gratefully took over the position with Marta as her helper.

Marta and Denys lived in the new house built over Sophie's old house, a gift from Talon for Denys's ploy with the goats, which had, no doubt, kept Nithard from searching for Lara after he'd burned her out. For her part, Lara had deeded the land and Shadow over to them and continued to teach Denys the healing arts as they tended the valley's people together.

Twenty of the brood mares' bellies were thickening with foals, the orchards were ripe with summer fruit, and the fields green with grains to be harvested come the fall. The miller who'd come to the valley with them from Tours was so busy, he'd hired three new helpers, and kept his axe sharpened and on his shoulder every time Phillipe came around his daughter.

All in all, Talon and Lara's first eight months as count and countess had gone well, though Talon wasn't sure he'd ever get used to the title. Thankfully, his men still called him Captain, and Isabeau had called him Papa for the first time seven days ago. Mama and Woof, it seemed, had a new word a day, and she'd even taken her first shaky steps on her own before plopping down on her backside with a grin to match her proud parents'. And last night she'd slept the entire night in her crib. A crib she still slept soundly in.

"Wake up, wife," he whispered into Lara's ear. "Wake up and kiss your husband before he has to leave you for the day."

She buried her face deeper into his pillow and he took a strand of auburn hair and gently pulled it down to the lower edge of her shoulder blade.

"Are you measuring my hair again?" The pillow muffled her sleep-softened voice.

"Aye, wife." He kissed her cheek, flushed from sleep. "I am."

She rolled over and gave him a sly grin. "I'm thinking of cutting it again." She ran a hand back through the tangled mass. "It's so much easier short. You men don't know how good you have it."

"I know exactly how good I have it," Talon told her. "And I don't want to lose a single inch of it."

"No?" Her sly grin turned impish.

"No." Talon pushed a curl back behind her ear, trailing his finger along her jaw and cupping her chin. "Not one inch."

She sat up and leaned back against the headboard, exposing her bare breasts. "I suppose a wife should obey her husband about such things." Her grin was anything but servile.

"I do remember hearing something about that whilst kneeling before the abbot." He rubbed his short beard. "Besides, if you cut your hair, I can stop cutting my beard."

"Oh no." Lara shook her head and her curls bounced over her breasts. "No husband of mine is going to let some scraggly, nasty beast grow from his chin." She raised an eyebrow and leveled her gaze as Talon lifted his from her breasts. "You are my husband, are you not?"

"Aye, wife." He sighed. "I have been these eight long months passed." She narrowed her eyes. "Eight glorious months?" he said with a grin calculated to make her laugh, but she gasped and clutched at the empty space between them where their daughter had been every other morning of their life as lord and lady of the keep.

"Isabeau."

"Shhh." Talon put a finger to his lips and nodded toward the crib. "She's sleeping safely."

"Oh." Lara grabbed her chest as she laid eyes on her daughter. "Oh thank God."

"What did you see in your dream last night?"

"She was gone," she rasped. "In my dream, Issy was gone. She was just… gone."

Talon rubbed up and down her arm. "It was most likely your body reacting to her absence from our bed," he soothed. "This is a good thing. We may get to have our bed back to ourselves for entire nights at a time."

"It was rather pleasant to sleep the night through without your greedy little monkey waking me to nurse."

"Well." Talon feasted his eyes on Lara's full breasts. "I can't say as I blame her for that."

He gave her a lusty grin, remembering the short time they'd shared a bed before he'd left for Saxony, before Isabeau's birth, when they would spend the mornings wrapped up in each other. He leaned in and gave her a kiss, sweet and tender as those lazy mornings had been at first, then growing with need and intensity as something else grew.

"See," he whispered hoarsely, wrapping her touch around his erection. "See how proud I am to be your husband?"

She laughed, low and throaty. "Would that all husbands were so proud." She squeezed, then kept her movement slow and sure.

He pushed his cock in rhythm, groaning with anticipation, when a knock came at the door.

"*What?*" he snarled.

"Dawn's breaking, Captain," Phillipe called.

"I'm up."

Lara covered her laugh with the hand that had been stroking his cock a moment before.

"Sorry." Talon could have sworn he heard Phillipe chuckling. "Your orders."

"I'll be down shortly."

"Aye, Captain."

"Captain," Talon grumbled as he rose from the bed and pulled his tunic on. "Would that I were still only a captain. Then I wouldn't be leaving my comely wife's bed to sit through a day's worth of complaints."

"Says the captain who swore to follow his king's laws to the letter," Lara reminded him. "And the king's laws say that the count of a province must rule over Mallus. And so, you will leave your wife's bed to go do your duty, sir Count."

"So I will." Talon pulled his breeches on over his disappointed cock, then glanced at Isabeau asleep in her crib. "Unless you wish me to stay?"

Lara followed his gaze. "No. I'm sure you're right. My dream was me reacting to her absence from our bed. It's the first time she hasn't slept part of the night beside me since her birth." She gave Talon a tremulous smile that told him she too had mixed emotions over this milestone. "Besides." Her smile brightened. "What would you do all day at Marta's with a gaggle of women and babies? Even Denys is fleeing with Willem and Wyatt to Tent Town for the day."

"Maybe we'll ride with them into town then." Talon strapped on his belt. "Willem may know something of this tinker's complaint against the silversmith in Tent Town. I'm to hear their case today."

Tent Town was the name given the field outside of Oloron Manor where the tents of traders and tinkers and tradesmen had sprung up as word of the new count and countess had spread through the lands of western Gaul. They'd come looking for a chance at fair work and trade and had brought with them new commerce as well as new problems.

Lara rose up onto her knees and smoothed his jerkin. "I know you prefer to be prepared for your battles, Captain. As I know you do just as well when meeting them head on. I have faith you'll figure it out and deal with them fairly, though I will say I've heard the silversmith called an honest tradesman by more than one person in the valley."

Between her smile and how the bed linens pooled at her knees, Talon was sorely tempted to make Phillipe and the others wait. After all, being count had its advantages. Mallus couldn't start without him. He started to unbuckle his belt when Isabeau let out a lusty cry, letting the world know she was awake and ready to start her day.

"Damn." He planted a kiss on Lara's lips. "Until tonight, wife. I promised Anglbert that the men and I would stay for supper after Mallus. I think he misses our company, though he'd never admit it."

Lara smiled as Isabeau started to fuss. "Until tonight, husband."

Talon gave Wolf a hearty thump on the chest. "Keep a watch out, old man. I've got to go be politic."

***

Lara

Lara sat at the table along with Berta, Enid, Patience, and Doralice under the shade of the old oak and handed Marta the package wrapped in linen, grinning in anticipation as Marta unwrapped her present.

"Oh Lara." Marta rubbed her fingertips over the star of green silk sewn onto a square of white velveteen, then laid it over her belly, six months swollen with child. She and Denys had been married on Christmas Eve at the keep, and she'd become pregnant almost the same night. "It's so beautiful. Is it silk?"

"It is. Talon bought it in Tours."

"I can't accept it, then." Marta laid the square back on the table, its top covered in squares of linens, wools, and stuffing for the quilt making.

"Yes, you can. I have plenty more."

"You do?" Patience said. "I've never seen you in a gown made of this."

"Nor will you," Lara said meaningfully. The green silk had been made into a low-cut, body-skimming nightgown that she wore only for Talon.

"Do tell." Patience hid her grin behind her drink of cold cider. "We are all friends here."

Lara glanced at Doralice, whose cheeks were flushing pink. "But not all are married."

All attention turned to Doralice, who flushed bright red.

"What's taking that man so long?" Berta sorted through the squares of cloth as birds sang from the oak's branches above them. "According to Anglbert, Phillipe's been smitten from the moment he laid his pretty blue eyes on Doralice."

"Oh he's smitten, sure," Lara said. "He's just reluctant to admit it. Still, when he does, and he will—" She smiled kindly at poor Doralice, who was obviously as smitten as Phillipe but too shy to do anything about it. "—he'll have been worth waiting for."

Doralice sat pink-cheeked and tongue-tied, and Lara reminded herself that she was still young, only seventeen, and had been raised by her widowed father since she was six years old. Lara had been twenty-two when she met Talon, an old maid by most standards, and she'd had Sophie to guide her. She gazed at the grassy mound that was her Tante's final resting place and gave silent thanks to her, for her. It was Sophie who'd kept Lara's true lineage a secret. Sophie who'd kept Nithard at bay with her curse.

Lara looked around Marta's outdoor table at her dear friends, old and new, at Issy playing in the grass with Wilric, at the new house built over the ruins of her and Sophie's old house: a testament to the tenacious strength of the women enjoying the day and each other's company. And the Midereds' deceit and spite. She pressed her lips tight, refusing to think any more today of Nithard or Ranulf or Ravenna. Or the steward Roumel and his two blonde daughters who'd stayed in the valley after the Midereds had left, and who'd been nosing around her and Patience a month ago market day when they'd bought the tinker out of his bolts and scraps of cloth for the quilt making today.

"Mark my words," Berta told Doralice. "You'll not have to wait much longer for your man to get down on bended knee." She winked at Lara. "I'm sure the countess would be happy to supply you with a vial or two of Sophie's love potion."

"Love potion?" Doralice set her doe eyes wide.

"It's responsible for two score or more marriages in over four provinces," Berta said. "Including Patience and Willem's, and Enid and her husband's."

Doralice looked to Patience, who grinned. "It only took Willem ten and four days after I gave him the potion to propose."

"How long?" Doralice's eyes grew even wider.

Patience laughed. "I knew he was mad for me, and I let him know I was mad for him by offering him the love potion."

"Which is the true secret to the potion," Lara told Doralice. "I'll make up a batch and give you a vial. Phillipe will know what it is and what it means, and we'll be having a wedding at the keep before the summer is out and sewing a quilt for your firstborn this time next year."

Red crept across Doralice's cheeks and down her neck, and Lara thought it a good thing Phillipe was a kind man with enough experience to make their wedding night special.

"Mama." Isabeau toddled toward Lara, a dandelion in full bloom clutched in her little hand. "Mama, ook." She scrunched up her face and blew with all her might at the feathery seed ball and missed.

"Here, Issy." Wilric, almost a year older, took the dandelion stem in his pudgy hand. "Yike dis."

He held the stalk still, making sure Isabeau watched as he blew. Next to their mamas and papas, they were each other's favorite people in the world: a preference so obvious that Willem had been teasing Talon about his daughter's dowry since Wilric first laid eyes on Isabeau. Issy clapped as the dandelion puff blew into a hundred floating pods, and Wilric beamed and marched around in circles with the bare stalk brandished high. The women all laughed and clapped their approval, when Wolf, who was lying in the cool grass next to Sophie's grave, lifted his head and cocked his ears toward the river.

He stood, sniffing the air, and Lara went to stand beside him, shading her eyes with her hand to gaze across the water at the far shore where shadows and light moved amidst the trees. The hairs on the back of her neck rose as Wolf's bristled.

"What is it, Wolf?" she asked. The women at the table had fallen quiet too, so she glanced over at the bench outside the barn where Tree had been sitting while whittling away at a piece of wood. He had stood and was surveying the river's edge.

"Ladies." Lara kept her voice calm and serious. "Take the children into the house." She pulled her waist knife and gripped it tight.

An arrow whistled and struck Wolf in the haunch with a sickening thunk.

"*Run*," she yelled over her shoulder as she dropped to the ground beside Wolf, who snarled and chewed at the shaft sticking out of his thigh, a shaft with a cresting and fletching that she'd seen sticking out of hundreds of dead men and horses at Roncesvalles Pass. "Take the children and flee. Now."

Tree came running toward her and Wolf, but arrows struck him down in his chest, arm, and leg. Loathe to leave Wolf, Lara broke off the shaft in his leg close to his wound so he couldn't do as much damage to himself and stood to go to Tree.

Before she'd gotten three strides, a volley of arrows pinned her to her spot, followed by a second volley pinning the women and children scrambling away from the table. Doralice held Isabeau, who started crying, and Berta shielded a still-seated Marta. Patience had a hold of Wilric, and Enid glanced wildly about at the palisade of arrows circling them.

"Stay where you are," a man called out from the river, his voice heavily accented, "and you will not be harmed."

Lara nodded to the other women, sheathed her knife, then held her hands up. Six men dressed in plain brown breeches and tunics with arrows notched to their bows, all aimed at the women, crossed the river. Tree lay unmoving as Wolf pulled himself up and limped over to stand next to Lara, a low growl rumbling in his throat.

As the men made the near shore, Wolf's growl grew louder. One of the men lowered his arrow's point at the hound's chest.

"*No.*" Lara dropped to her knees and wrapped her arms around Wolf's neck. "You don't need to shoot him. He'll not attack if I tell him to stay."

The man pointing the arrow at Wolf looked to a swarthy man with shoulder-length brown hair and a trim beard, waiting, it seemed, for his decision.

"I swear to you," Lara said directly to the man she guessed to be their leader. "The dog will do what I say."

The man nodded.

"Down, Wolf." She helped him lie down on his good side, then kissed his nose and laid her hand on his head. "Stay." She stood to face the raiders as they stopped no more than three paces from her.

"*Otsoa,*" one of the men muttered. The Basque word for wolf.

"*Bat da txakurra,*" the leader snapped. *It's a dog.*

Lara stared blankly at the men, pretending not to understand a word of what they'd said. Though she was nowhere near fluent in the Basque language, she'd grown up on the border knowing a little and had learned more from Talon. He'd also taught her the value of letting your captive, or captor, think you ignorant of their language until it was to your advantage not to.

"Your knives," the leader, who obviously spoke and understood the Frank language, said, holding his hand out. Lara handed him her waist knife. "Leg knife too."

How would he know she wore a dagger tied to her thigh?

"Leg knife, now."

Lara lifted her skirt and handed the blade to him. He motioned with it toward the other women and children, who were being herded together by the other four raiders. Reinforcing her stay command to Wolf with a hand signal, Lara joined the other women and took a hiccupping Isabeau in her arms. "What now?" she asked the leader.

"Now, we tie you together, take you with us."

"To where?"

"You find out when we there," he said as two of his men poked and prodded the women into a straight line and a third man started tying their hands to a line of rope.

"Is it a long journey?" she asked, switching Isabeau to her hip.

"Long enough."

Lara indicated the heavily pregnant Marta, who stood crying into her grandmother's shoulder. "She is too far along with child. She won't survive a journey of any length, and the babe won't survive if born this early."

The leader had a quick conversation with the slightly older man who'd threatened to shoot Wolf and who seemed to be his second. She heard the words "baby" and "die" and "slow down" and "move fast."

"She can stay," the leader told Lara. The older man went to Marta and started to pull her away from Berta, who went red-faced and mother hen, screeching and slapping at the man's hands.

"Berta," Lara called out over the din. "Berta, stop. They're letting Marta stay here. She'll be safe here." *Until our men find her. Then she'll be able to tell them what happened.*

"Baina, Inigo," one of the other men said. "Ranulf…" The only other words Lara recognized were "all" and "women."

"*Ez keskatu.*" *Don't worry*, the leader, Inigo, answered. "*Lortuko du haren sariak preziatua.*" *He'll get his precious prizes.*

Forewarned by the Basques speaking Ranulf's name, Lara was prepared when they crossed the river into the woods where a hooded man waited with horses enough for each man and woman, plus a spare, no doubt meant for Marta.

"Hello, cousin," she said to the hooded man, whose slight frame and slender fingers gave him away. "When do we meet up with my uncle?"

Ranulf whipped the hood from his head as Inigo and his second exchanged glances. "What makes you think you or your brat are going a single step farther?"

Lara tilted her head, absorbing the fact that he didn't seem surprised at her calling him cousin. She smiled, slow and smug, baiting him. She wanted to see who was in charge, and prayed it was the Basque, Inigo, who'd shown mercy to Marta and her unborn child. Ranulf would have killed them both rather than leave them behind.

"I know if it were up to you, I'd already have an arrow through my heart," she said. "Your father must have other plans for me, or he figures this time it will work only if he kills me himself, since you've failed twice before."

"Shut up, witch," Ranulf hissed.

"*Sorgina*," one of the Basques muttered. *Witch.*

He and two other men crossed themselves and stepped back from her. Talon had told her what he knew of the Basques during their march up the Pyrenees to join Charles, and one of those things was that they were a very superstitious people. A fact she intended to use against her captors in any way she could.

"*Bai*," she said with her fiercest smile. "*Sorgina.*"

Ranulf spit onto the ground, the men muttered and crossed themselves again, and Inigo spoke to a fourth man, who untied Lara's hands and indicated that she should mount a horse another man held next to her. They did this with each woman in turn, tied the horses to another line, and rode west up the mountain's side with one rider taking point, Inigo, his second, and Ranulf riding behind the point man, followed by the line of women, and brought up the rear by the other three Basques.

They rode from noon until dusk, and only stopped then because Berta fainted and fell off her horse. Holding Isabeau tight, Lara jumped off her mount and kneeled at Berta's head. She let Isabeau loose to walk around while she lifted Berta's lids to see her eyes rolled back in her head.

"Water," she called out as Inigo and his second were making their way to her and Berta. "She needs water."

Wilric started crying that he needed to go pee, and Doralice slid off her horse and hit the ground in a pile of skirts and tears.

"Everybody, dismount," Inigo ordered. "Stretch legs, drink water, relieve selves."

He handed Lara a water skin, and she dripped some onto the hem of her skirt and wiped Berta's flushed and sweaty face with it. Berta's eyes fluttered open.

"It's me, Berta. You fell off your horse." Lara held the water skin to Berta's parched lips. "Take a sip. Slowly, slowly, you don't want to make yourself sick drinking too much too fast."

When Berta was able, Lara and Inigo helped her back onto her feet, then Enid escorted her mother behind some bushes to relieve herself.

"Thank you," Lara told Inigo as Patience and Doralice walked in slow circles, whispering to each other and loosening stiff joints while Isabeau and Wilric chased each other in a wider circle around them. "They aren't used to such journeys."

"You are, I think."

Lara nodded. "I've been chased up this very mountain by my uncle's men before. Yet I've always been the one to make it back down alive and whole," she added for good measure. "You do know my husband will come for his wife and child," she said with a smile meant to unnerve him, but he only bowed his head, as if offering his condolences.

"Your uncle," he said, "counts on it."

***

Talon

Talon took his seat as count of the province in the center of the long table, with Anglbert to his right and Phillipe to his left. The day had been long but productive, and he was ready to relax and enjoy a meal with his friends and comrades before riding back to the keep, where Lara would likely be sleeping by the time he returned. He grinned, anticipating waking her and making sweet love to her in their bed, as long as Isabeau was still in her crib. If she wasn't, there was always the pile of pelts.

"You did well today, Talon," Anglbert said as the kitchen maids set trays of summer fruit and cheeses on the table. "You were very politic and count-like in settling the dispute between the tinker and the silversmith, along with the other twenty-odd arguments and complaints brought to you." Anglbert grinned. "Now, if only you could settle our friend Phillipe here as well."

"What, pray tell, do I need settled?" Phillipe speared a strawberry and bit it off his fork.

"Your love life," Anglbert said, causing Phillipe to choke on the berry. "Or rather your lack of." He took no mercy on the sputtering Phillipe. "I swear, lad, you're acting as dense as our friend Talon here did."

Phillipe swallowed, coughed, then turned to Talon, his eyes begging for mercy. Talon pressed his lips together and shook his head. He'd show Phillipe as much mercy as Phillipe had shown him. "Do you love the girl?" he asked.

"Lo-love?" Phillipe stammered. "I-ah-uh."

Talon almost felt sorry for Phillipe as he cast his glances about the table and realized all eyes and ears were on him. Almost. "It's a simple enough question. Do you love Doralice: yes or no?"

Phillipe opened his mouth, clamped it shut, and nodded.

"Then do yourself a favor, go to her house this very night and get down on bended knee and ask her to marry you."

Phillipe tried to reply but failed.

Talon clapped his hand on Phillipe's shoulder and held his gaze. "I thought my lady, my love, gone. I lay on her grave and thought her lost to me forever, and the only thing I regretted was each and every moment we'd been apart."

"You're right," Phillipe said at last. He ran a finger around the neck of his tunic. "It's just, the thought of marriage, it's like a noose tightening around my neck."

"Aye, friend," Talon said with a wry smile hard earned. "And so it is. A silken noose tighter and stronger than any rope, but soft and giving too. You must trust your wife will not pull too tight or sever the tie, but keep it bound with love and tenderness, and honor and loyalty."

"You think she will have me?" Phillipe said with such a pathetic edge to his voice that every man at the table burst out laughing.

"Good God," Talon asked the table at large. "Was I this bad?"

"Worse," Anglbert chortled. "Kept brooding about, snapping our heads off, and falling off your horse." He turned to Phillipe. "Of course she'll have you. Though her father may not give his consent as easily."

"Aye," Oswald added ominously. "He'll not want to be giving his only child in marriage to just any man."

"Especially one with a reputation as a ladies' man," Dardinel piled on.

"True." Talon eyed Phillipe sternly. "Fathers can be overly protective of their daughters."

"And the miller carries a really big axe," Willem, who'd accepted an invitation to supper, said with a laugh as Wyatt sat grinning beside him, happy to be included in the men's company.

"Thanks." Phillipe winced. "You've all been so…helpful."

"We do what we can." Anglbert chuckled.

Phillipe cleared his throat and straightened his shoulders. "I guess I'll be buying that piece of land from you sooner rather than later," he told Talon.

Talon offered his hand and Phillipe shook on it. "We'll talk price tomorrow."

"There goes that fine broodmare you've been bragging on," Anglbert said.

"And your first ten foals," Talon teased as Phillipe swallowed hard and tried even harder to act as if the cost would be nothing to him, while all around the table his friends spouted more and more ridiculous terms.

Dardinel was up to three broodmares, twenty foals, a hundred gold solidi, and Phillipe's firstborn child when Denys burst into the hall, panting, his face ashen.

"They've been taken." He gasped as he laid an arrow down on the table before Talon. "Lara and Isabeau, Patience and Wilric, Berta, Enid, Doralice. They've all been taken."

"Basques," Anglbert growled down at the arrow as Talon stood and gripped the table's edge, the room spinning around him.

"Damned slavers." Phillipe stood with his hand on his knife's hilt. "They will get no gold or silver for our women and children, only blood."

The scraping of chairs and angry voices barely matched the roaring of Talon's blood in his ears. He glanced around the table. The men stood there watching him, waiting for him to give them their orders, to tell them how to bring their women and children home, how to save his wife and child from a band of ruthless slavers.

"Did anyone see anything?" he asked Denys.

"Marta did." Concern laced his eyes at how he must have hated leaving his wife after this. "Lara convinced the leader she was too pregnant to survive a journey of any distance. They left her gagged and bound in a chair under the old oak."

"Tree?"

"Had three arrows sticking out of him, which he wouldn't let me remove before I came to you. Wolf has an arrow in his leg too."

Talon nodded, grateful no one had died. Yet. "Did either of them say how many men there were?"

"Tree counted six."

"Did they put them on horses or march them out on foot?"

"Tied them to a line and marched them."

Talon looked to Anglbert. "They'd want to be moving fast."

"Which means there were men nearby with horses," Anglbert said. "Maybe more waiting at a camp."

"Twenty should give us an edge in numbers," Phillipe said.

Talon addressed the room. "I need twenty men who can ride hard and fight harder."

Every man there stepped forward, including Willem, who was no soldier used to days in the saddle, no warrior used to wielding a sword. But he was a man who loved his wife and child, and he had the right to fight for them.

"We meet at black of dawn," Talon told them. Night had already fallen, and by the time Talon gathered enough men and supplies, it would be midnight. "We'll leave from Denys and Marta's place; their tracks will be freshest from there. I want every man to carry three days' supplies and a second saddle horse. They've got almost a day's ride ahead of us, fresh horses may give us an edge there."

"Aye, that and trying to keep Berta astride a horse." The lightness of Anglbert's words belied the hard glint of his eyes. "That should slow them down a bit."

"The Basques take women to sell." Phillipe spoke what every man there feared. "They've got to know we'll be coming hard and fast on their tail. They won't have time to—"

"Phillipe's right," Oswald seconded. "They're slavers: they won't want to be dealing with women who are injured in any way. They'll want their coin from them, not their blood, or other things."

Talon grunted. They were right. The women would be worth more unharmed. And if they were wrong, he hoped Lara would submit to her captors, that she wouldn't fight or give them a reason to hurt her or Isabeau, knowing full well she'd fight them tooth and nail.

CHAPTER 24

Numbers

Lara

They rode into a camp after dark where two more Basques and a big, dark-haired man stood as they reined their mounts in. Lothair. Lara held a sleeping Isabeau closer to her chest as the flap to the single tent set up flew open and Nithard stepped out. His black eyes met hers, then his gaze dropped to Isabeau.

"Good evening, Uncle," Lara said, taking any bit of advantage she could from him. "I'm sure you're anxious to meet your grandniece, Isabeau Juditha Rousell Guiscard. She's named after her grandmothers and grandfather." Lara shifted Isabeau in her arms so that her face was in profile. "I never knew my mother. Do you think my daughter resembles her, of whom you were said to be so fond?"

Nithard stood staring at Isabeau as if seeing a ghost, his thin lips moving wordlessly.

"I say the brat will make a pretty little whore." Ranulf sidled his horse up alongside Lara's and grabbed her by the hair, pulling her head back. "You're mine now, bitch," he hissed. "And your little witch's spawn is my father's to do with as he will."

He let go of her hair as abruptly as he'd grabbed it, and Lara had to hold on to her saddle horn with her free hand to keep from falling off her horse while holding Isabeau tight with the other. Isabeau woke up whimpering, which turned into full-blown wailing as she squirmed to break free of Lara's hold. Her body shaking uncontrollably, Lara slid down from her mount and held a squalling Isabeau tight as they made their way over to the camp's fire, where the Basques were directing the women to sit. She sat down on a log before her legs gave out.

"Be careful of the fire, Issy," she told her daughter as she and Wilric toddled around. "Hot."

"Hot, Issy, hot," Wilric repeated, and Isabeau giggled.

"They'll be fine." Patience scooted closer to Lara. "Now they're together."

Lara held shaking hands out to the fires heat, though the night air was warm. She watched Issy and Wilric picking up twigs and showing them to each other, and then she met the worried gazes of Berta, Enid, and Doralice. "We'll be fine too," she told them. "We've simply got to stick together and give these Basques no reason for violence." She thought of Talon's fury once he found out what happened to them and grinned. "We'll leave that to our men."

"I pity the man whose head meets up with Anglbert's mace," Berta said. "Or your father's axe," she said to Doralice, who didn't look convinced.

"Think of Phillipe," Lara told her. "Of the man he is. Know that he'll come for you and won't stop until he finds you. And when he does, I for one would not want to be at the end of his sword's point."

"Nor I." A small smile played at the corners of Doralice's mouth.

Lara glanced around. Nithard, Ranulf, Lothair, and Inigo stood deep in conversation, leaving the women under the guard of two Basques who hadn't shown any indication of understanding their language while the others took care of the horses. She motioned for the women to lean in closer. "The Basques know our men are coming," she said in a low voice. "Their leader, the one called Inigo, told me this. He said Nithard was counting on it. We're the bait in their trap. We need to leave a warning for our men."

"How?" Patience asked.

"I don't know, yet," Lara said. The men's conversation broke up, and Nithard returned to his tent with Ranulf and Lothair while Inigo spoke with the older Basque. "Keep an eye on Issy?" she asked Patience. "I'm going to go see what I can find out."

The two men stopped talking as she approached, and the older man stepped back, eyeing her.

"Sir," she addressed Inigo. "May I speak with you?"

"Yes."

"Your name is Inigo?"

He nodded.

"My name is Lara. Countess of Oloron."

"I know who each of you are."

Lara darted a look at Nithard's tent. "Of course you do." She lengthened her spine. "What do you plan to do with us?"

Inigo nodded at the women huddled by the fire. "They be sold at slave market in Pamplona. You and you daughter be given to the Frank and his son. What they do with you?" He shrugged, and Lara would have sworn she saw a flash of sympathy in his brown eyes.

She thought of Ranulf's threat but refused to dwell on it. If she let her fear of ever being under Ranulf's control overtake her, she'd be useless.

"You and your men would do better leaving us here when you break camp tomorrow," she told Inigo. "Dead men cannot collect coin for women they don't have. My husband—"

"Was a butcher of Pamplona," Inigo spat.

"Yes, he was at Pamplona," Lara admitted, sure that Nithard and Ranulf had told the Basques this and many other things about Captain Talon Guiscard. "He was at Roncesvalles as well. Yet it's Pamplona that haunts him and gives him nightmares still. To war against women and children, he said, was wrong."

Inigo chuffed. "Yet war he did. Committing murder and rape to women and children, to my people, for his king."

"No. He didn't. He kept his troop, the very same men who will be coming after us, with him, outside the city's gates once the raping and pillaging started."

"So you say."

"So I say. I, who survived Roncesvalles as well." She saw the quick rise of his brows. "I marched with my husband. I was at Roncesvalles, and yet I live. I've been chased up this mountain before by Lothair and three other men sent by my uncle to kill me, and yet here I am."

"As is Lothair."

"Aye." Lara allowed herself a quick smile of satisfaction. "Minus a bite or two of flesh taken by my wolf, in whom you put an arrow."

"*Otsoa?*" the older man said. He made a slashing motion along his left forearm. "*Otsoa ziztada Lothair?*" *Wolf bite Lothair?*

Inigo gave a curt nod and the man crossed himself.

"When I was six months pregnant," Lara made a rounding motion over her belly and pointed at Isabeau, "Nithard had several of his men try to burn me and my unborn child alive in my house. And yet, here we are. We have taken our rightful places as heirs of Oloron, and Nithard and his pack of curs have made a mercenary deal with you to—"

"With my uncle," Inigo said quickly. "Deal is with my uncle."

"What do you and your uncle get out of this deal, besides women and children to sell?"

Inigo held her gaze for a long moment before answering her. "A wagon of Fank steel."

"Weapons?" Lara's head spun. Nithard would've had to have been buying or stealing weapons for months to have a wagon full. "How long has your uncle been making deals with Nithard?"

"They first come to our village one year ago October, when Lothair's arm still injured. They come and go since, live under my uncle's protection when in our village. Ravenna there now. Frank weapons will bring us much protection against our enemies."

"And us women and children will bring you much coin?"

Inigo dipped his head to her. "You go sit, eat. Tomorrow come early, last long."

***

"Mama?"

"Shush, baby." Lara held a fingertip to her lips and finished scratching Nithard's name in the dirt at her feet with a twig. "Mama's drawing a secret."

Isabeau squatted down and mimicked her mother's finger to her lips as Lara scratched the word *trap* in Latin below Nithard's name, along with the initials R and L. She glanced over her shoulder at the guard standing watch with his back to the women as they relieved themselves behind a hedge of bushes, then tore a piece of her skirt's hem and hung it on a low branch of the bush she squatted behind. Then she stood and made a noisy show of trudging over to their horses with Patience and Doralice.

Poor Berta stood rooted, looking forlornly at her mount. Lara gave her a leg up and reminded her to tuck her skirts under her legs to avoid chafing. She handed Wilric up to Patience, who tucked her skirts under her and around her son as she'd seen Lara do with Isabeau, then gave her friend's leg a grateful squeeze for her steady calmness. Patience was no more used to a full day's riding than the other women, yet she'd uttered no more than a stiff groan when lying down to sleep on the hard ground last night and mounting her horse this morning.

Lara lifted Issy up onto her mount's saddle, then swung her leg up and settled in behind her. She was tying Issy in with her skirts when she caught Inigo's second, Ortzi, walking the edge of the camp, straight for the bush her blue strip of hem dangled from.

"Hold on, Monkey," she whispered into Isabeau's ear, tightening her one-armed hold on her. "Mama's going to make horsey dance."

She kicked the horse hard in the sides and pulled up on the reins at the same time, causing the cob to rear up. She faked a scream and hoped her daughter's squeal of glee was taken as fright as she let the horse take a few stunted jumps forward before reining it in. She didn't have to fake panting from the effort or the wild look in her eyes as she searched for Ortzi, who stopped his searching and stood with his back to the bush, crossing himself.

"Did you see that bee?" she said, every eye on her. "It flew right at the horse's face."

***

Talon

Fifty men rode out with Talon at first light, half of them field workers riding their cart horses and armed with everything from pitchforks and wooden staffs to old family swords that had lain in chests for a generation or more. The other half consisted of Talon and his men-at-arms, six of Nithard's previous guard who'd chosen to stay in Oloron when he'd left and had sworn fealty to Talon, the keep's stable hands, and various villagers and tradesmen. Denys stayed to tend to Tree and Wolf and his pregnant wife, and had given Shadow to Willem to ride, as Willem's horse was more used to pulling carts than riding into battle.

Touched and proud as he was by the show of men, Talon let it be known he'd be moving fast and hard and would wait for no one. By the time they reached the remains of the Basque camp mid-morning, only twenty-three were still with him, including Willem, Arnulf, the miller, and the silversmith whose grievance against the tailor Talon had presided over and ruled in favor of yesterday at Mallus. Rilke was his name, a sturdy man of middle age who rode a gray as sturdy as he, with his cart horse as a second, who wore a jerkin of lacquered leather with a silver hilted longsword slung across his back.

"I haven't always been a silversmith," Rilke told Talon as they looked over the campsite. "I rode under Carloman's banner until his death."

"And now?" Talon asked. It was well known there'd been bad blood between Charles and his brother, and the rumor that Charles had poisoned Carloman to gain sole control of the kingdom had run rife.

"Now I ride for the Count and Countess of Oloron. For a chance at a fair life in a fair province."

"It's a good thing I ruled in your favor, then." Talon clapped Rilke on the shoulder. "An experienced sword arm is always good to have on your side."

"It is yours, my liege," Rilke vowed. "Yours and your fair lady's."

Talon ground his teeth and kicked at the cold embers of the fire the Basques had made no attempt to bury, just as they'd made no attempt to hide their trail.

"They mean to outrun us," he said to no one in particular.

"Aye." Anglbert pulled on his beard as he came over from making his own rounds. "Which is good for us, bad for them. Nobody's ever outrun us before, and that's without women and children slowing them down."

"True." Talon's gut knotted at the sight of women's and children's footprints ringing the fire pit.

"They had a tent over here," Phillipe called out from the opposite edge of the small clearing.

"Why would raiders set up a tent?" Talon ran a hand through his sweaty hair. "Unless someone of importance travels with them, a Suleiman perhaps, bent on revenge for Pamplona?"

"Was not Roncesvalles vengeance enough?" Anglbert grumbled.

"Against our soldiers, surely," Talon thought aloud. "But what of their women and children? Why else would they have taken ours and nobody else's? Why didn't they take anything else? No horses, no food stores. Why raid a small place like Denys's and not the keep? They obviously knew we were away for the day."

"How did they know where our women and children would be and when?" Anglbert frowned. "That's what I'd like to know."

"A spy?" Talon rubbed his jaw. "It would be easy enough to hide out in Tent Town."

"Captain." Oswald stood by a hedge of bushes along the clearing's edge. "Over here."

Talon walked over and stopped at a bush Oswald pointed down at. A bush that had a scrap of blue cloth tied to a low branch.

Scratched into the dirt beneath it were the words Nithard, trap, R and L, written in Latin.

***

Lara

Lara sat cross-legged on the ground beside Patience, whose head bobbed and nodded as she fought the sleep the other women and children had long given in to. At last, the scout rode in and reported to Inigo and Ortzi, who woke Nithard, Ranulf, and Lothair.

Trying to act more interested in the fire than their conversation, Lara shifted closer and held her hands out to it.

"They're half a day's ride behind us," Inigo translated what the scout said for Nithard. "Twenty at least, maybe two, three more."

"Twenty fighting men, knowing Guiscard," Nithard said.

Inigo said something to the scout, who nodded and answered. "All armed, two horses each," Inigo translated.

"That's just like the bastard," Ranulf spat. "How do we keep ahead of them, dragging along women and children who can barely hang on to their mounts?"

"We ride early, ride long, don't stop," Inigo told him. "We need keep ahead one day more, then we let catch up."

"And spring our trap." Nithard looked as smug and pleased as a weasel that'd just spied a fat, lazy vole.

Ranulf kicked at the dirt. "There are only six men waiting at the pass. That doesn't give us any advantage in numbers."

Lara recalled Phillipe's warning about numbers not counting for everything to Ranulf when he'd demanded to beat her after Hamm's unveiling, and the corners of her lips twitched up.

"Our advantage be position and surprise," Inigo said. "This Guiscard expect us keep running, not be waiting to ambush."

"I do like that advantage," Ranulf said with anticipation.

Lara ground her teeth so hard her jaw clenched up. She rubbed it, working the ache out, and realized the men had stopped talking and were watching her. Ortzi crossed himself and even Inigo took a step back, his dark eyes watching her keen as a hawk's. Ranulf glared at her and a chill ran down her spine at the possibility of ever being at his mercy. She glared back. She'd die by her own hand before she succumbed to him. Nithard was staring at her with something between hatred and terror, and Lara saw exactly what it was Sophie had given her as a weapon against him.

"You'll need more than an ill-conceived ambush to kill my husband or me, or our daughter," she said to Nithard, who startled when he realized she was speaking to him. She smiled. "I've seen you die, Uncle, in my dreams. Would you like me to tell you how?"

Ranulf spat, Lothair snarled and muttered a curse, but Nithard remained silent as he stood staring at her, his face pale in the fire's light. Smiling as if she really had seen him die in her dreams and liked what she'd seen, Lara turned her back on them and lay down beside her daughter.

***

Talon

"Captain." Dardinel pointed to the ground behind a hedge of bramble, a grin on his face. "She's left you another one."

Talon squatted down and lifted an upside-down bird's nest. Beneath the nest sat two rocks, and between the two rocks were two stems of yarrow with their white flowered tops pointing west, straight up the mountainside. He stared down at them, trying to think of what little he knew of yarrow plants, to what purpose Lara would have placed them where and how she did. An image of her picking some to use for medicines when they'd ridden through Roncesvalles Pass on their way to join up with Charles came to him, and he stood and rubbed the back of his neck. "This is why I love my wife."

"So she can leave mysterious clues to help you chase her up and down mountains how many times now?" Phillipe said.

"Exactly." Talon motioned for his men to circle around. "If I'm reading these clues right, they're planning to ambush us in a pass two days from now. Now we know when, the question is where and how." He looked to Anglbert. "What do we have in numbers?"

"Twenty-three here now. At last count, twenty-seven trailing behind."

"And them?"

"Nine riding with the women. But at the pass, waiting?" Anglbert adjusted his mace over his shoulder. "I'd guess four to six more. They wouldn't have left more waiting than they used to take our people. They'd know they'd need numbers in case we did catch up with them."

Talon looked to Willem, who'd been born and raised in Oloron. "Any idea where this pass is?"

"No. I've never been west of the valley."

"I know these hills," Rilke, the silversmith, spoke up. "I've been trading up and down them the last five years."

"Trading?" Talon said. "With Basques?"

"With some Basques, yes. With these Basques, I don't know. I do know a pass two days' ride from here."

Talon looked to Phillipe and posed his silent question. After a moment's thought, Phillipe nodded. He looked to Anglbert, who stared hard at the silversmith before giving Talon a nod as well. Talon eyed Rilke. The silversmith stood tall and square shouldered at his perusal. He suspected Nithard had planted a spy in the valley, though he had no idea who. He'd heard no harm of Rilke before or since Mallus, and something in the man's steady gaze told Talon he could trust him. And yet.

"Before you answer me, Rilke, think hard on what I say." Talon lifted his chin toward Willem. "This man stands to lose his wife, his son, his wife's sister, and their mother." He jutted his jaw toward Anglbert. "This man his wife, or as good as." He looked to Phillipe. "This man was a step away from going down on bended knee to his intended." Talon drew himself up and watched Rilke's gaze follow him. "Nithard and his Basque cohorts have taken my wife and child." He swallowed his gall. "Lie to me now, and your life is forfeit."

"I've had the honor of meeting your ladies, sir Count." Rilke never let his gaze waver from Talon's. "The countess ordered a present for you from my wares, for the one-year anniversary of your marriage. Your lady wife is as gracious as she is beautiful, and your daughter a sprite's version of her mother."

"Then you know," Talon said, his voice catching. "You know I can't lose them."

Rilke nodded.

"You're sure of this pass?"

"I am."

Talon made his decision. "What's the terrain like between here and the pass?"

"Straight up. Not too rocky. Trees thin out the higher you get."

Talon gazed up the mountain's side. "Can we ride around them, get ahead of them in two days' time?"

Rilke rubbed his stubbled jaw. "We'd have to double our pace and hope they don't do the same."

"They won't. They don't want to lose us. They keep their pace to ours." Talon glanced down the mountain to the cloud of dust from the valley's men still plodding on behind them. He took the measure of the men there with him. Oswald was the closest to his size, but he didn't want to be missing his bow or his sword arm when the fighting came. The Black would likely let Anglbert ride him, but Talon knew better than to ask him to stay behind when Berta was one of the captives. Plus, he was still deadly with that mace of his. He looked to Dardinel. "Can you ride the Black?"

"Captain?"

"I need someone to ride the Black, wearing my armor and leading the farmers behind us as if he were me, and the farmers, armed warriors."

Dardinel glanced down the mountain and then back to Talon, his disappointment showing.

"I'd rather you were riding with us as well," Talon told him. "You're a good man in a fight, but we need to give them something to watch and worry about while we swing around them."

Understanding dawned in Dardinel's eyes. "Aye, Cap—"

"No." Willem stepped up. "I should stay behind and pretend to be you. I'll only slow you down and be of little use in a fight. I can be of more use this way, and you'll have one more sword arm to save my wife and child."

Though Willem was no horseman, the Black knew him well enough. It could work. "Can you ride the Black?"

"I've got an apple in my saddlebag to bribe him with. You can tie me onto his back if that's what it takes." Willem glanced over at Shadow, one of the few horses ever who hadn't taken to Talon. "What about you, will Shadow let you ride him?"

Talon cocked his head at the rangy bay. "Got any more apples?"

CHAPTER 25

Ambushed

Lara

Isabeau was getting harder to keep confined to a horse's back all day and a circle's worth of ground at night. She'd made a break for it every time they stopped, and though she didn't get far on her toddler's legs, she put up a loud fuss every time Lara caught her.

"Like mother like daughter." Inigo chuckled as they stopped for the night and dismounted. Issy had already made her run for freedom as soon as her feet hit ground.

"Do you have children?" Lara grabbed her daughter and held her and her squirms tight.

"Three," Inigo said, handing his horses reins to one of his men. "Two boys, one girl."

Lara jostled Isabeau on her hip. "What would you do if someone abducted them, intending to sell them into slavery?" She glanced meaningfully at Nithard and Ranulf, who'd dismounted and were stretching out their backs as one of the Basques took care of their horses. "Or worse?"

"I do anything, everything, to get them back," Inigo said. "To kill *sasikumeak* who took them."

"My husband will do no less." Lara let go of Issy's hand so she could join Patience and Wilric, who were heading for some bushes.

"I sure he try." Inigo had something akin to sympathy in his eyes. "Does not change anything. Deal was made. I not go against my uncle's word."

"Nithard won't live long enough to know if the deal was kept or not," she bluffed. "I've seen this in my dreams."

"You say this to Nithard before." The sympathy in his eyes changed to wariness. "Nithard believe you. Why?"

"Because my dreams always come true. One way or another."

He eyed her for a long, serious moment then eventually spoke. "Feed you child while men making camp."

Lara did as he suggested. She was still nursing Isabeau a few times a day, and it helped calm Issy down, though it also inevitably drew many of the men as close as they dared to watch, craning their necks for a glimpse of Lara's breasts. Ranulf and Lothair practically drooled when they were watching, and Nithard watched Isabeau rather than Lara, which made Lara more uncomfortable than the other men's leering gazes.

While the Basque cook started the pot of beans over the fire, she finished nursing Issy and sat with the other women, watching Issy and Wilric play as Orttzi and Lothair rode in.

"They're a little more than half a day behind us," Lothair reported as he joined Inigo by the fire. "They slowed down a bit, waiting for ten more men to show up."

"Just like soldier of Gaul," Inigo said. "Thinking numbers win him battle."

"Does Guiscard still lead them?" Nithard asked as he went over.

"Aye," Lothair said. "Saw him with my own eyes: his helmet, his armor, riding his black."

"What will that matter?" Ranulf poked at the fire. "They've given us a greater lead to the pass, where we will pick them off one by one."

He smiled at Lara as he counted off, and she closed her eyes against his vitriol and prayed Talon had found her messages, especially the last one. It was unlike him to slow his chase for numbers, but Lothair had seen them, had recognized Talon's horse and armor.

Opening her eyes, she caught Lothair's glare.

"What are you looking at, witch?"

Lara smiled. "I was thinking of the last time my husband chased you up this mountain, and the chunk of flesh you left in Wolf's mouth running back down it."

"So what? Your husband's too slow to catch us and your dog's dead. And I'm the one's going to finish you off once me lord here—" He jabbed a finger toward Ranulf. "—is done with you."

Lara widened her smile. "Wolf isn't dead."

"What?" Lothair bellowed at Ranulf. "You promised me that damned hellhound would die."

Ranulf shrugged. "I told them to kill it. They chose to wound it."

"Why would they do that?"

"Because," Lara said, holding her hands out to the fire, "even a Basque knows better than to kill a witch or its familiar. Something neither you, nor your young Master Snake here, have yet to learn." She shifted her gaze to Nithard. "Isn't that right, Uncle?"

Nithard startled and looked from Lara to Lothair.

"I'll tell you what I have learnt," Lothair said with a sneer. "I've learnt that a witch dies as easily as any wench. Your old Sophie the Sixth—" He made a hatching motion and grinned. "—her head split open as easily as an overripe melon."

Lara went stone cold, then white hot. She pointed directly at Lothair's heart. "You, Lothair, are a dead man." Then she turned to Nithard, who blanched. "And you, Uncle, Sophie's curse will come to fruition soon."

"What curse?" Inigo asked.

Lara smiled as Nithard stared off into the night at something no one else could see. "He will die choking on Frank silver."

***

Lara gave Berta a leg up onto her mount and knew the poor woman wasn't acting when she let out a loud groan of pain.

"Remember," Lara whispered as she placed the reins in Berta's chafed, swollen hands. "As soon as you see my signal."

The women had discussed trying to escape last night after Lothair and Ortzi's report. With the path narrowing the higher they climbed, the Basques had removed their horses' tie line, and Lara had wanted all the women to break away at the same time, to ride in separate directions and make the Basques split up to chase them. But Patience had pointed out that none of them save Lara could ride well enough to make it any distance, so it was decided that Berta would act as a diversion while Lara and Isabeau made a run for their men.

Lara gathered Isabeau and mounted their horse, tucking her skirts under her legs and tying the hems extra tight around her daughter. She glanced around the breaking camp. The men were all busy saddling their horses, no one was watching her.

"Hold tight, Monkey," she whispered in her daughter's ear. "We're going to ride horsey really, really fast."

She nodded to Berta, who let out an ear-piercing shriek and threw herself off her horse. Lara whirled her mount's head around and broke for the trees.

"Get her," Ranulf screeched. "Get that witch and her spawn."

More yelling and whinnying followed Lara as she guided her horse through the trees to the path they'd ridden up. Her mount was just working into a gallop when Lothair and his gray jumped in front of them. She tried to turn her horse into the woods, but Lothair bellowed and it spooked and reared. It was all Lara could do to hold on to Isabeau and keep them from being thrown. She was barely hanging on when Lothair grabbed the reins from her. Lara started to throw a leg over her horse's neck when Lothair grasped her by the hair and jerked her head back so hard her neck cracked. With a strangled cry, she held one hand up in surrender, the other clasping Issy tight.

"Now that's a good little witch," Lothair said as they were surrounded by chattering Basques and a purple-faced Ranulf.

"Tether the bitch." Lothair looped a noose around her neck as Ranulf sidled his horse next to Lara's and ripped Isabeau from her grip.

"*No.*" Lara's scream strangled as Lothair pulled her noose tight. She tore at the rope, and Lothair pulled her hands from her throat and tied them.

Isabeau screamed and kicked with all her might against Ranulf's hold as he tried to wrestle her onto his horse, in front of him.

"You cursed little witch's spawn." He yelped as her foot struck him in the groin, and he shook her and slapped her across the face.

"*Stop it,*" Lara yelled hoarsely as her daughter wailed. "Leave her alone." She glared at Ranulf. "If you must beat something, beat me. It's my flesh you've always wanted."

"There be no beating of flesh until deal is done," Inigo, who'd shown up at some point, commanded. He held his hands out toward Isabeau. "Give me child," he told Ranulf. "I have children. I know what to do."

Ranulf hesitated, and Isabeau gave him another kick to his gut. "Here." He shoved the howling child into Inigo's arms. "Take her. For now."

***

Talon

Talon took the point position on a log behind a thick bramble where a wide, shallow river snaked down and into an open meadow, giving him and the ten men with him an unfettered view of where the murderous bastard Nithard and his Basque slavers would have to cross to get to the pass a league farther up the mountainside.

Anglbert took the woods closest to the other shore with the other ten men, which made twenty-two archers between them, every one of them a swordsman as well. The Basques were to be the bowmen's first targets. Talon's was Nithard and Phillipe's was Ranulf, Oswald would take Lothair.

"Here." Phillipe handed Talon a strip of jerky.

Talon had no appetite, but he took it because he knew he needed the energy for the fight to come, and it kept him busy chewing something besides the inside of his cheek.

"I saw you speaking with Arnulf before we left him with the horses," Talon said. "What about?"

"He told me come what may, he would be proud to call me son from this day on."

Talon coughed and rubbed at an invisible gnat in his eye. "Congratulations."

A short, quick whistle had them crouching low and notching arrows to their bows. Where the path opened onto the meadow, Talon counted two Basques before Nithard and Ranulf rode out, followed by the line of women with four Basques riding along either side of them, one of them next to Lara, who was last in the line and had a rope around her neck and wrists. "Bloody hell."

Lothair rode out behind her, and two more Basques brought up the rear. Wilric rode with Patience, but Talon didn't see Isabeau with Lara or any of the other women. He sucked his breath in as he made sure she wasn't with Nithard or Ranulf, then let it out in a slow hiss as the Basque alongside Lara shifted something from one shoulder to the next. His daughter and her head of red curls settled into the man's neck.

"Nobody shoots the Basque with Isabeau," he told Phillipe. "Spread the word."

He lifted his arrow to aim at Nithard, but Lara jerked her head back and tugged at the rope around her neck. Behind her, Lothair raised his fist and gave the rope another jerk.

"Plan just changed," he said. "I'm going for Lothair first. We'll deal with Nithard and the Basque with Isabeau later."

"Should I tell Oswald?" Phillipe asked.

"No. I want that bastard Lothair dead."

He waited what felt like an eternity until the first Basque urged his horse into the river to cross it and another eternity until all the horses were in or near the water, then he gave three short, sharp whistles.

Lara snapped her head up again and thrust her bound hands between her neck and the noose. Talon let his arrow fly, growling with satisfaction as a second arrow pierced Lothair's chest a handsbreadth from his. Lothair fell from his horse, yanking Lara backward and sending her tumbling off her horse, into the river.

"*Lara.*"

***

Lara

Lara had just enough time to gulp air into her lungs before she was pulled backward off her horse. She heard her name a moment before she hit the water and went under, jolting as her back landed on the stony bottom. But she managed to keep her head from knocking against the rocks and twisted away from her horse's hooves and scrambled to get her arms and legs underneath her, scraping them on rocks as she managed to push herself up onto her hands and knees when a pair of hands whose touch she'd know anywhere grabbed her at the waist and stood her up, coughing and sputtering.

"Talon."

"Aye, you troublesome wench."

He yanked her to him, and Lara buried her nose into his neck, breathing in the masculine scent of man, horse, and sweat, then reared her head back. "Isabeau?"

Talon nodded to the three men held captive on their horses: Nithard, Ortzi, who had an arrow sticking out of his thigh, and Inigo, who held Isabeau in his arms. Lara blew out a breath of relief, and Talon pulled the noose from her neck and cut her wrist ties. All around them, her Basque captors lay dead or dying, as well as Lothair with two arrows in his chest. She glanced upriver to where Ranulf's body lay on the riverbank with three arrows in it.

Talon pulled her into his shoulder and walked over to where Nithard, Inigo, and Ortzi sat on their horses, marked by Frank arrows. Anglbert and Phillipe helped the other women dismount as Talon stood next to Inigo's horse and held his arms out.

"A wise choice," he told the Basque as he handed Isabeau over.

Lara broke into gasping sobs as Talon kissed his daughter's head and then offered her over. She held Isabeau tight, her tears falling on her daughter's head. Talon pulled his longsword.

"For keeping my daughter safe," he told Inigo, "your deaths will be swift and far kinder than you deserve for the rest of it."

Inigo nodded and looked to Lara. "Forgive us," he said. "Pray for my family, pray they not suffer for what I do."

He and Ortzi dismounted and stood with their heads high, waiting for their deaths.

As Talon drew back his sword, Lara laid her hand on his forearm.

"No more." She met his gaze. "No more killing, no more death, please, Talon. Let these two men live. Let them go home to their families."

"They would have sold you into slavery or worse," he ground out, the scar across his cheek gone white.

"But they didn't." Lara laid her open palm over the scar on his cheek. "They protected me and Issy from the others."

"They did a piss-poor job of it," he growled, touching the raw weal on her neck from Lothair's rope.

"Please. Let them go. Let them return to their home, to their families in Pamplona, and us to Oloron with ours."

"They are from Pamplona?"

Lara nodded. "Let this be the end to the bloodshed."

The muscle on the side of his jaw twitched, then Talon motioned for his men to lower their arrows. "Go," he told Inigo. "Take your dead and don't ever cross this pass again." He looked to Nithard, who still sat astride his horse, staring at his dead son's body, mumbling about being cursed by Sophie the Sixth.

"You. *Nithard*," Talon said, louder, sharper. Nithard looked at him with the hollow eyes of a man not all there. "You will be given the same mercy you gave my daughter's namesake, left to wander the wilderness unarmed and alone." He looked to Inigo. "You are not to aid him."

"I rather kill him myself," Inigo swore. He dipped his head to Lara. "Countess, for my life, my family, I thank you."

"You should have listened to me," she said. "I warned you."

Inigo dipped his head to her. "You did." Ortzi said something to Inigo that made him smile. "He say I should have listen to him, let witch go first night. He want you know it was him who only wound you wolf."

Lara grinned. "Tell him that's why he still lives."

Inigo crossed himself before he told Ortzi and Ortzi crossed himself after.

Lara set Isabeau down as Wilric came running over toward them and turned into her husband's shoulder. "Let's go home."

"*No.*" Nithard kicked his horse forward, clutching the reins with one hand and his dagger in the other. "Isabeau is mine." He rode straight for her and Wilric. "She is *mine.*"

Talon pushed Lara behind him and leapt, grabbing Nithard by the tunic and yanking him off his horse. Nithard landed on his knees with a shriek and then screamed, high and thin, as Talon thrust his sword up Nithard's throat and out his mouth, the silver blade dripping red.

***

Talon mounted the Black and pressed his lips into the tangle of Lara's curls as she settled back into his chest, holding their daughter in her lap. They'd met back up with Willem and the farmers masquerading as soldiers after sorting out the dead and sending the

Basques on their way, and though they had enough horses for Lara to ride her own, it would be a while, a long while, before Talon let her out of his reach again.

Willem was astride Shadow with Wilric in front of him after helping Patience and Enid mount their new horses, courtesy of the Basques, and Anglbert was helping Berta mount hers. Phillipe stood kissing Doralice next to their mounts with the miller grinning nearby, and his comrades cheering loudly.

"There will be another wedding at the keep before the summer is out," Talon told Lara.

"Aye, and another quilt making come spring."

"You know," he whispered in ear. "We could veer off on our way back and stay a while at the Hollow, just you, me, and Issy."

"We could. Or we could go home, tend to Wolf and Tree and Marta until her baby comes, maybe spend my birthday at the Hollow this fall."

"Maybe make a baby there." He nuzzled her neck. "We made such a wonderous child there the first time, I think we should make all our babies there."

Lara craned her neck to face him. "What happened to Captain Talon Guiscard, the fierce warrior who swore he'd never marry, never sire children?"

"He became enthralled with an auburn-haired, hazel-eyed witch when he tried to pluck a red rose from her curls," he confessed. "I am ever cursed to want you, to bleed for you, my thorny beauty."

Lara gave his arm a playful pinch. "You didn't bleed so much as a drop this time."

"Nay," he whispered hoarsely. "My heart bled out a thousand times a day these past four days, knowing I let Sophie down, failing my oath to protect you, thinking I might never hold you or Issy again."

"You never once let Sophie, me, Issy, or anyone in Oloron down," she told him. "You are a good and honorable man and I love you."

He kissed her, sweet and tender. "God's blood, I love you, Lara. I have since you first smiled at me as a girl in side braids. I'll never stop until the breath leaves my body."

Lara smiled. "That, my love, is how you tame a wildcat."

ABOUT THE AUTHOR

Michele James lives in a southern California beach town with her understanding husband, two lazy house cats, and two crazy cattle dogs. She is the proud mother of an adult son and daughter, and is Oma to the world's most adorable grandson.

A mostly retired veterinarian technician, she enjoys reading everything from cereal boxes to serious tomes, watching movies without commercials, cooking, gardening, walks on the beach (especially in winter), and practicing yoga.

CONNECT WITH MICHELE:
website: michelejamesauthor.com
instagram: @michelejamesauthor
facebook: /michelejamesauthor
pinterest: /michelejamesauthor
goodreads: /19960951.Michele_James

www.BOROUGHSPUBLISHINGGROUP.com

If you enjoyed this book, please write a review. Our authors appreciate the feedback, and it helps future readers find books they love. We welcome your comments and invite you to send them to info@boroughspublishinggroup.com.

Follow us on TikTok and Instagram, and be sure to sign up for our newsletter for surprises and new releases from your favorite authors.

Are you an aspiring writer? Check out www.boroughspublishinggroup.com/submit and see if we can help you make your dreams come true.

Love podcasts? Enjoy ours at www.boroughspublishinggroup.com/podcast.